SON OF THE ALPHA

THE ALPHA KING'S BREEDER
BOOK NINE

BELLA MOONDRAGON

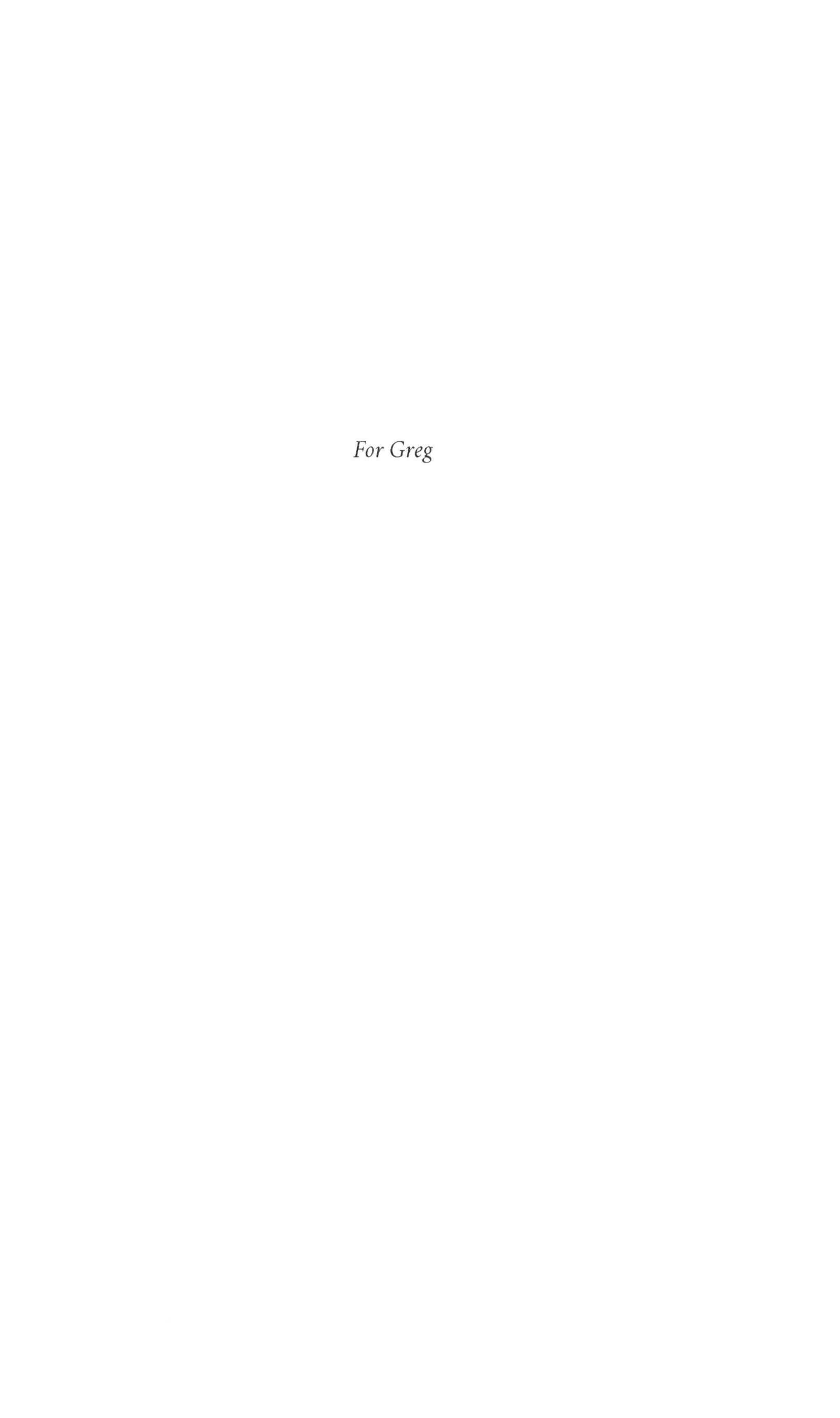

For Greg

CONTENTS

1

——————

THE COLD, HARD TRUTH

It's warmer down here under the grow lights. Electricity hums through the air as I move from plant to plant, pruning, plucking, and watering. Outside the frosty windows, the Neutral Zone is every shade of silver in the unforgiving cold.

Someone passes bundled against the frigid, windy air. Their red hat disappears into a rush of snow being swept by the wind down the street.

I shiver despite the slight warmth in the air.

I've been cold for weeks. Cold, hungry, and stressed beyond belief.

The baby swaddled in a sling across my chest wriggles before falling back asleep, his cheek pressed against my breast.

I move to the utility sink in the storage room and wrench on the pump, but the water doesn't start. The pipes are frozen solid.

"Shit," I whisper, closing my eyes and trying to swallow past the lump in my throat.

Mr. Foxglove, my landlord, was supposed to be here this morning to fix the heat to the building. My one room apartment upstairs has been freezing cold since Tuesday last week, the day after my son was born. I've resorted to turning the oven on and letting it run empty to heat the space. Empty, because I have no money for food. Every single cent I have to my name is going toward my rent, which has doubled every month since the snow started to fall.

"I'm sorry," I croak, tearfully, to my thirty, wilting plants. No water for them today again. My precious blooms of begonia and lily tremble in answer. My orchids are fried. I can't bring those back from the dead, even if the water returns.

It wasn't supposed to be like this. A year ago, I rented this space and the apartment upstairs. I painted the walls and the exterior door my favorite color–pink. The most magnetic fuchsia the world has ever seen.

I got a contract to provide the florals for some of the balls at the summer mating festival. People came in droves to buy bouquets for their newly found mates in the weeks that followed.

But then the rebel threat brought Crescent Falls into war.

People stopped buying flowers.

The royal family stopped throwing balls and parties, as did the Alphas of the dozen or so packs that surrounded the city.

And Mr. Foxglove started raising my rent.

I sink onto the rickety stool behind the counter and stare out at the wind whipping the snow against the window.

The baby stirs again, letting out a frustrated grunt. I reach for my shirt, pulling it away enough to free my breast so he can nurse and wince, my eyes watering, at the sharp pain of it.

I'm so hungry. I'm so, so cold. The patchwork coat I've been stuffing with fluff from my mattress upstairs barely shields me from the cold, but it's all I have.

I've sold everything. Every piece of furniture, every item of clothing, just to have a roof over my head.

All because I had a dream… and then got pregnant.

And the kingdom went to war.

And no one cares about flowers in the winter.

I bite back a sob and gently bounce the baby, trying to get him to settle. I know he's hungry too. My milk is barely there, probably because I don't eat very often.

The exterior door wrenches open sending a burst of freezing cold air into the shop.

"You said you'd be here this morning," I say, trying my best not to send the words off my tongue in the snarl my landlord deserves.

Mr. Foxglove—a man of maybe fifty with black hair and devilishly green eyes—smirks at me, taking his time shutting the door. The cold air funnels around the room, ruffling the leaves of my already frail plants and blossoms. "You're not my only tenant."

"The heat has been out for over a week. Ms. Elosie upstairs has been burning newspaper in her wood stove to try to keep warm." I clutch my baby tighter against my chest to fight the chill now creeping into my bones. "We're freezing here. The pipes are frozen, and we have no water—"

"Well, if that's the case, I doubt I'll be able to get anything fixed today." He checks his filthy nails, smiling at me. "At least it's somewhat warm in here, right? With all the lights you have burning up your utility bill."

The baby makes a grunting noise before he starts to whine.

Foxglove rolls his eyes, leaning his hip on the counter. "I'm not here to fix shit, Ms. Greenly. You owe me rent for this month."

"I'm not paying you a single cent until the building has working heat and water!"

"Then get out," he smiles, teeth flashing.

I look at the window again, at the raging wind storm outside. He's still giving me a cool smile when I meet his gaze once more.

"Where," he says slowly, tapping a finger on the counter, "is my money, Sarah?"

I reach into the pocket of my coat with trembling fingers and clutch the wad of cash resting there. I slam it onto the counter.

He picks it up, weighing it in his hands before counting. "Great start, but you're short by at least half."

"Wh-what?" I stammer? "No, it's all there—"

"Nope. You're short. If you want heat and water, you'd better come up with the rest by tomorrow–"

"You've tripled my rent over the last three months!" My voice edges on despair. That's all the money I have. It should have been more than enough. I should have a few dollars left over for food, but now…

He pockets the money and leans down so one of his elbows rests on the counter. He reaches for me, twisting a lock of my ashy blonde hair around his hairy, ring-laden pinky finger. "My offer still stands, you know. You want water, heat, and a roof over your head? It would only take a few minutes flat on your back to make that happen–"

I pull myself away and step back until I hit the wall, nostrils flaring with hatred and disgust as I fight to catch my breath.

He clicks his tongue and shrugs. "Well, in that case, pay the fuck up, or you and your bastard will be out on the street come sunset tomorrow. Mark my words."

He turns on his heel and leaves the shop, not bothering to close the door behind him.

Tears burn down my cheeks as I rush after him, shoving the door closed against the howling, bitter wind. My son wails in his sling as cold bits through my coat.

I lock the door and draw the blinds, whispering reassurances to the screaming baby before going through the side door leading to the stairwell. It's dark, empty, and lifeless.

The dark steps blend with the peeling gray paint as I hurry up to my apartment holding back a torrent of tears.

I knock on my elderly neighbor's door and yank it open, glancing inside. Ms. Eloise is curled up in a blanket on her bed like usual, her wood stove barely puffing enough heat into the room to keep frost from coating the windows.

I watch her chest rise and fall then slowly edge out of the room and turn toward my own door.

My apartment is a stark contrast to the bright florals of my shop below. The walls are gray with patches of wood and stone showing beneath the peeling paint and fraying drywall. The floor is old, faded wood that leaves splinters that bite into my feet if I ever walk barefoot.

A twin mattress rests on the floor. I sold the bed frame a few weeks ago. No art hangs on my walls any longer, only a few faded photos from a time in my life that feels like a lifetime ago.

I close the door behind me and rub my cold hands together before moving to the oven and turning it on. It'll take a few minutes for the room to heat up, so I shrug off my coat and take my baby from his sling, and curl into a ball around him in bed while he nurses.

Silent tears fall down my cheeks and seep into the mattress as I stare at the pictures on the walls.

Me, only ten or so months ago, dressed to the nines in the center of a gaggle of young women my age. Me, a year ago, posing outside the pink door to my shop downstairs, beaming with pride.

Pictures of me with friends whose faces have blurred with time. Friends I shared apartments with, drank with, and gossiped about everything from boys to music to the royal family the tabloids always love to gossip about.

I cup my son's head and close my eyes.

None of those friends have been around for months. Once I began to show… once I stopped going to the bars and clubs with them or out to brunch…

Everyone simply vanished.

But one face remains in the sea of lost memories.

Hadley comes through the door without needing a key. The lock has been broken for weeks.

Her dark brown curly hair pokes out beneath a pale blue hat, and the tip of her nose is bright red.

I rise up on an elbow, taking my coat and the raggedy quilt I found in the trash with me. "What are you doing here?"

"Goddess, Sarah, it's freezing in here!" Her smile fades as she looks around. Her hazel eyes meet mine again, giving me that same pained look she always gives me. "I brought food."

"You shouldn't have. You'll get in so much trouble for being out–"

"My brother can kiss my ass." She tries to smile, but it falls flat. I sense the nerves in each word as she edges toward the row of countertops that act as my kitchen. She sets a paper bag of groceries on the counter, pulling out a carton of milk and a bag of oats. Butter, salt, six eggs…

"I got you some vitamins. My–my friend said these are the good ones." She sets them down on the counter before turning around, but my heart is aching.

"Does he know you're here?" I ask, sitting up and fixing my shirt. The baby is fast asleep beside me, his tiny fists under his chin.

Hadley shakes her head. "I can't stay long. I have a shift at the bar, and you know how my brother gets about me being outside of our territory." She looks around, her eyes glistening in the darkness. "I'm trying to get you out of here, okay?"

"I never asked–"

"You can't stay here, Sarah!"

"My shop," I tell her, fear and heartache twisting its way through my heart like a heated blade. "I can't just leave everything I've worked for behind." I flash her my best "I got this, seriously," smile even though inside, I'm falling to pieces.

"Did you get the contract with the royal family? The upcoming ball?" Her eyes are full of so much hope.

I shake my head.

Providing the flowers for Queen Madeline's upcoming party would have made it possible to get out of this hellhole. Now, I'm in too deep. I'm out of money. Foxglove has me backed into a corner, and I have a baby to think about.

But I'm packless. Hadley is my only support, and her brother has her under lock and key.

I can't pull her into my drama, anyway. I can't even think about it.

It's better for everyone that I remain alone.

She shakes a smaller paper bag. "I got you a burger and fries," she says softly.

But a distant, rhythmic thudding echoes up the stairwell.

"I think that might have been the shop," I say, peeling myself out of bed carefully so as not to disturb the baby.

"I'll stay with him," Hadley says as I open the door and look down the stairs into the growing dark.

Another knock, but not from the private residents entrance that faces the alley.

A few seconds later, I'm standing in my shop squinting through the frosty windows at the wind-blown street.

A man walks away, his hands tucked in his pockets and his head bent against the wind.

2

ENDLESS MISSION

Cosette screams into the foyer, her apron knotted so tightly in her hands that her slim fingers are white. Her light brown hair is flaked with silver, and her dark brown eyes glow like embers in the chandelier light as they narrow into a glare.

I shut the front door to my manor firmly behind me, ignoring the incessant screech of the wind howling outside, and eye my housekeeper–my life manager, honestly–as she huffs a breath and glowers at me.

"Am I past curfew?"

"Alpha Sydney, I thought you were dead!"

"It's just a blizzard." I shrug out of my coat as Dalia–the only other person I employ at my house–comes up behind me to take it, gathering my coat, gloves, and hat in her tiny hands. I give the mousy, red-haired maid a gracious, silent smile before turning back to Cosette with a frown.

"Don't look at me like that, Your Grace." She plants her hands on her hips and looks up at me as I approach her. "It's below zero out there and blowing like hell has frozen over."

"You're just upset I'm late for dinner."

"Late for dinner *again*," she huffs, following me with her eyes as I step past her and start hiking up the stairs.

"Put it in the fridge for me, Cosette. I have plans tonight." Plans to work. Plans to sit in my office going over dead-end leads, again, into the mysterious circumstances surrounding Sasha of Eastonia.

"You're going to work yourself to death!"

Her mumbled reply falls on deaf ears as I deftly unbutton the starched white dress shirt I've been stuck in all day. I walk down the main hall on the second floor of the manor–a stately home where, a long time ago now, my father was almost born.

My grandparents came here to seek refuge after returning from Maatua to rival Alphas trying to take over our castle and my father's throne.

Over forty years later, it's my home now. It's been renovated to my tastes with modern, sleek finishes and dark hardwood floors, and the surrounding ten or so miles all falls within my territory.

I open the door to my bedroom and close it with my foot, stripping out of my shirt and pants. The second I toss my phone across the room, where it lands with a soft thud on my bed, it starts to vibrate.

Ryan's name lights up across the screen with a rather unflattering picture of him posing drunk against one of the marble statues in my mom's rose garden during one of her parties last spring.

I close my eyes, sigh, and try to gather myself before answering. "What?"

"Oh, fuck off. I guarantee I had a worse day than you, prick," he jests, then groans as if stretching out. "What are you doing?"

"Just getting home–"

"What were you up to in the NZ tonight? You were so close to my territory and didn't even stop to say hi to your own twin."

I pull a sweatshirt from my dresser. "Are you still tracking my location?"

"You keep your location services turned on on your phone," he chuckles. "Sometimes I like watching you bop around town."

"Is there a reason you're calling?"

"I don't know what things are looking like in your neck of the woods, but the bar is still open in Silverhide if you want to come out for a drink. You can crash here, if you want."

It's a tempting offer. I put my phone on speaker as I pull my sweatshirt over my head and fish for a pair of jeans. "I can be there in half an hour."

"You didn't answer my question–" I hang up the phone, button my jeans, and run my fingers through my hair, ruffling it free of its usual swept back style. My reflection in the mirror over my dresser catches me off guard. The dark circles under my eyes. The pinched expression. The ruddy cheeks nearly blistered from the cold.

No one should be out in this storm tonight, but there I was, walking through the Neutral Zone, heading right toward that flower shop I can't get out of my head.

I think about her all the time–Sarah. I don't know her last name. The last time I saw her was two months ago.

I don't know what drove me to go there tonight. I've been trying to come up with reasons to go talk to her again. But I'm not like Ryan. I can't walk into a room and schmooze my way into any crowd. I need a reason to talk to her. I need this feeling to make sense.

I tried to ignore it, and thankfully, it was a busy enough winter that the last two months flew by in a blur of running my engineering company and investigating any leads on Sasha, Gabriel's cousin.

The most wanted woman in the Allied Kingdoms.

I lay down on my bed for a moment and stare up at the ceiling while the wind whips snow against the second story windows to my right.

In my defense, I did knock on Sarah's door. I wasn't surprised to see her shop wasn't open tonight. Everyone is hunkered down, riding out the blizzard.

Not me. I was out like a fucking idiot unable to stop myself from just… laying eyes on her again.

Something about her nags at me like nothing else I've ever experienced before.

Huffing out a breath, I roll off the bed, grab my phone, and go downstairs.

"Seriously?" Cosette follows me down the hallway leading to the garage. "Alpha Sydney, I insist–"

"Take the night off, Cosette." I halt with my hand on the doorknob and lean down to give her a kiss on the cheek.

Her face burns red as I slip into the garage. She murmurs some prayer to the Goddess ripe with curse words before stomping off, her heels clacking on the floorboards.

I grab the keys to my truck and give myself another second to back out.

Ryan's going to want to know why I went to the NZ.

Maybe it'll be good for me to talk to someone about that *why*, even if I don't want to think about the conflicting feelings roiling in my gut.

I remind myself of the promise I made to myself all those months ago in Eastonia, when Evander nearly died in Kenna's arms, as I climb into my truck.

"I DON'T THINK this winter could get any longer," Ryan says over the rim of his beer as he scans the rustic bar around us. Everything is dark wood and country style music; a sharp contrast to the more modern, sleek bars and clubs in the city center.

Ryan's pack is incredibly old school. Blue collar, homestyle, and more in tune with their wolfish abilities.

He takes another drag from his pint and leans back.

I tap my glass. I've been sitting here for twenty minutes, and we've barely said a word to each other.

"It's a shame we weren't able to vacation in Maatua this Solstice," he says absently, his eyes meeting mine. They're identical to mine, but other than our height, that's about all we have in common.

"Mom said Misty is still mad at them for sending her away," I reply.

"She likes her school out there, though. She gets to lay out on a beach and watch surfers all day."

I roll my eyes to the ceiling. While I agree that Maatua is the best place for our baby sister right now, given the circumstances, Misty has always balked when it comes to listening to anyone other than the little devil on her shoulder. Our mom has commented on how Misty takes after our grandma in looks, but her personality?

Misty and Kenna might have been mixed up somewhere in the heavens and given to the wrong parents because Misty is the reincarnation of Aunt Ella in personality.

Maybe worse than Ella, honestly.

"I didn't bring you here to talk about Misty." Ryan shifts his weight on the barstool. It creaks under his weight. "You've been weirder than usual."

I give him a look. "Uh, thanks?"

He waves a hand in dismissal. "Look, I'm worried about you, all right? I get that things fucking sucked in Eastonia last summer. Shit, I saw the aftermath myself when I brought some of my own warriors over to help with rebuilding villages of those packs the rebels took out in the Roguelands. But it's been over six months. You've been gallivanting around Crescent Falls since you came home looking for that Sasha girl with no end in sight."

"I haven't been *gallivanting*," I say through gritted teeth. "It's a mission–"

"Yet you have no backup, no team in place to run leads. You're doing this all yourself while our dad, uncle, and aunt go back to business as usual. What gives?"

"I'm not sure what you want me to say–"

"Then consider this an intervention." He knits his fingers together on the table between us in a way that immediately reminds me of our father. "You gotta stop looking for her, man. She's long gone. This is a waste of time. When was the last time you went out and had any fun? Hell, when did you last shift?"

"Order up!" A sing-song female voice drifts through the air in our direction.

Ryan straightens and plasters a soft smile on his face as a young woman with a mop of curly brown hair skips up to our table and places two fresh pints of cheap beer between us. The yellow ribbon holding her hair away from her face trembles as her eyes slide to Ryan's, and her "customer-service" smile turns into something so bright it could light up the room.

"Thanks, Hadley." Ryan reaches into his pocket and pulls out a twenty-dollar bill. He slips it into her hand… and maybe I'm imagining it, but his touch lingers for a second too long.

Hadley's cheeks go a rosy pink before she bites her lip, grins, and hops away.

"That can't be James's little sister." I breath, arching my brow at Ryan.

"She's not so little anymore," he replies steadily, but his eyes are downcast on his beer.

Hadley has to be twenty by now, at least.

"She started classes at Crescent Falls University this fall for teaching," Ryan says without prompting, turning his frosted glass in a circle. "I offered to pay for it, you know, as Alphas should do for members of their packs, but my Beta forbade it." He clicks his tongue and eyes me.

James, his Beta, is an asshole. I get why they're friends, sure. Ryan and James go way back to when we were all in warrior training together as teenagers. Both love to fight, workout, and watch sports, but Ryan doesn't have the mean streak James possesses.

I'll never understand why Ryan chose Asher to be his Beta.

I technically don't have a Beta, at least not for another year, when Asher turns twenty-one and can step into his Goddess-destined role. He's the son of my father's Beta, Cassian, and his mate Hannah. Right now, he's in training to take over the role, and I keep him busy enough tending to minor pack issues.

"That shouldn't have been James's decision," I argue, but Ryan shakes his head.

"I've learned not to get between those siblings. They're all they have, you know. No parents. Immigrants, the like."

I chew the inside of my lower lip. James and Hadley were born in Eastonia and came here as children with their family. I don't know the details of how they ended up orphans.

I've never asked, but I don't get the opportunity to pry, because Ryan says, "Do you still look for that woman you had a one-night-stand with last summer?"

"No." The word slips out so rapidly I wonder if I've said anything at all.

"Maybe you should," he says, shrugging. "You haven't been with anyone since then."

"That's my business, Ryan."

"I am worried about you, Syd." His gaze is honed on mine and serious, not a single glimmer of jest in those stormy blue eyes. "After what happened–"

My phone rings at the perfect moment. Sighing with relief, I pull it out of my pocket.

"It's Mom. I should get going, anyway. Thanks for the beer." I rise and leave my untouched pint behind, answering the phone on my way out the door.

"Hey, Mom–"

"Oh, Sydney. I need your help. Can you come over first thing in the morning?"

She sounds stressed. "Is everything okay?"

3

A REASON

THE BOTANICAL GARDEN is a thirty minute drive from the city and even longer from the castle. Juxtaposed against a sea of silver trees, the glass domed building sticks out as a bright pop of color against ribbons of pure white snow.

I pull my truck to a stop, checking my watch.

Someone opens the front door to the building and steps out, bundled against the biting sub-zero temperature in a pale purple sweater and gray leggings.

Mom's wine-red hair is pulled in a bun piled on the top of her head. She waves at me, motioning for me to hurry the hell up.

"You said you'd be here at eight!" she says by way of greeting as I hike up the snow-covered steps.

"It's 8:15," I reply as she motions me inside, pulling the heavy glass doors closed behind her.

My thick coat and hat are suddenly suffocating inside the humid warmth of the building, but I don't bother taking them off. Whatever she needed me to come here for at the crack of dawn, I'm sure I'll hear all about it in a matter of seconds, and then I can go back to my usual day as planned.

We pass through an entry room before reaching the center of the indoor garden. It's beautiful. I've always loved coming here, especially during events and parties. I look up that ceiling, past the thick foliage, and notice the white lights strung back and forth from one end of the dome to the other.

But… that's about it.

I look down at my mom who's frowning and tapping her foot. She looks completely out of sorts as she runs a hand over her make-up free face and looks up at me through her fingers.

"Don't you have a party here in three days?"

"Yes, and that's why I called you."

I glance around at the undecorated tables and general lack of color, save for the green of the plants at the center of the wide, open space and the snow clinging to the glass panes on the ceiling. "I'm an engineer, not a decorator–"

"I'm not asking you to help me decorate," she replies with a shake of her head. "My usual florist backed out at the last minute. I'm honestly not surprised. I've had to twist her arm the last few times I've hired her to get her to do anything on time." She huffs, still tapping her foot on the shimmering silver tiles. "This place was supposed to look like a beacon of summer. I don't know what I'm going to do."

"I have some flowers in my atrium," I tell her. My atrium flares to life in my mind. It's similar to this place but on a smaller scale. I don't pride myself on being able to make things grow, however.

But Mom shakes her head. "I need a professional. Someone who can design arrangements, and fast. I needed this whole place swimming in color. I figured, since your father has had you canvasing every inch of our kingdom, you'd know someone. A few other florists sent bids to me about the Solstice Ball a few weeks ago, but I can't find the paperwork and I'm running out of time–"

"I know someone," I say without meaning to speak.

She turns to me, hope welling in her eyes. "Someone who can do this in three days?"

"You just need a few vases filled, right?"

She smacks my arm. "Sydney, seriously–"

"I'll see what I can do, okay?"

"I can ask Ryan, too. He has more than enough time on his hands–"

"I got it." I squeeze her arm and practically sprint out of the room.

My heart hammers in my chest as I slide into my truck and punch the gas, skidding in a circle to get back on the narrow highway leading into Crescent City.

It's a clear, sunny day, which means it's even colder than yesterday. My truck groans as I kick up the heat, fighting the steadily dropping temperature. I can't remember a colder winter.

But I don't even try. Not when I have a reason to go talk to Sarah now. A real reason, not that I just couldn't get her out of my head and didn't do anything about it for two months, until it was far too late.

But when I pull my truck into the NZ, my confidence wavers.

She was pregnant last time I saw her. She might have had her baby already.

That baby's father could be back and…

I can't think like this. I don't have feelings for Sarah. She's just… she's intriguing, and maybe actually seeing her again, talking to her, and working with her in a more intimate sense while we help keep my mom's head glued on will clear my head.

The idea of Sarah has been my only distraction from finding the missing Eastonian girl. That, and the fragmented memory of the woman from the ball.

I get out of my truck and tuck my hands in the pockets of my coat to try to keep my fingers from freezing solid as I walk down the main street of the NZ, which is a network of commercial buildings, houses, apartments, shops, bars, and the like.

But the NZ fades into a colorless wasteland a few blocks away from where I parked my truck at the gate to Silverhide.

Windows are boarded against the cold. A few wolves trot by, their eyes scanning mine as they scurry to the other side of the street.

I pass the coffee shop I visited two months ago and find the windows boarded and a "for rent" sign hanging on the door, faded from exposure to the sun and cold.

And across the street, the pink door to Sarah's shop isn't nearly as vibrant as I remember it.

I was just here last night, but seeing this place in the daylight sends a ripple of shock and unease coursing through my body.

Snow is piled in front of the door from last night's storm, and the curtains in the front window are drawn.

I furrow my brow as I cross the street and walk up to the shop, rapping on the door. My knocks echo down the street into the vacuum of silence brought on by the frigid air.

I look up to the second story. More boarded windows.

She didn't answer the door last night either…. Is she no longer here?

My stomach drops with disappointment, but then a waft of cigarette smoke clouds my senses.

"This must be why she doesn't have my rent this month," a male voice clucks somewhere behind me. "Never answering her door for customers."

I slowly turn. An older man with thick, dark facial hair dotted with crumbs from his last meal raises a brow at me.

"You own this building?"

He nods. "Rupert Foxglove." He waves at himself before taking a pull of his cigarette once more. "Can I help you?"

"I'm looking for the owner of this shop–"

"Doubt you'll find her."

Something in his voice has adrenaline prickling over my skin like little needles. "Why is that?"

He chuckles darkly, stubbing out his cigarette under a polished, rather expensive looking boot. "Look, it's not my problem that these tenants of mine can't keep up with their rent. Times are tough after that little skirmish over in Eastonia."

I narrow my eyes at him. "Again, I'm looking for Sarah–"

"And I knew she wouldn't be able to keep up with her business after that hussy got knocked up during the Mating festival last summer. I knew she was a whore. I should have seen this coming–"

I step toward him, and he retreats, taken off guard. "What did you just say?"

"Sarah Greenly," he repeats, smirking up at me. "That little whore can't pay her rent, blames it on the baby. Says she can't keep her shop open in these conditions." He waves toward the building. "I thought keeping the heat off would teach that little slut a lesson."

My hands curl into fists. "You turned the heat to the building off?"

"Two weeks ago," he says with a shrug, pulling another cigarette out of his pocket. "The pipes froze, you know, and caused some damage. Now she can't water her precious flowers, and I can't make the needed repairs because, well, she needed to learn a valuable lesson."

I grab his coat, lifting him a few inches off the ground. He squeaks in surprise, writhing like the snake I know he is under his fancy, designer clothing. "How much is her rent?"

The number he tells me is so astounding I nearly drop him in the street.

But what he says next has me spiraling.

"You know how these broads are," he says as I lower him to the ground. He lights his cigarette, totally unfazed. "I offered her an out, you know. All she'd need to do to get a discount on her rent would be to get on her knees. It'd be easy now without that disgusting stomach in her way–"

I grip his throat, pick him up, and toss him across the street so hard he shifts out of pure surprise. He yelps, tangled in his now shredded clothes he probably bought by siphoning money off Sarah.

His eyes gleam in the sunlight as he looks in my direction.

For a moment, I wonder if he's going to make a move.

But the rat of a man takes off at a full sprint down the street, disappearing from sight.

Fury rips through me. The transformation signal ripples like an electric current through my body, turning my fingers into talons.

They fade back into fingers, and I slowly turn back to the building and pound on the shop door until it nearly comes off its hinges.

No answer.

I rush around the side of the building and yank on the private entrance that I hope leads somewhere, anywhere, that she might be, and I'm met with a poorly maintained staircase cast in near total darkness.

It's freezing here. Each breath I take burns down my throat. The air smells like smoke as I walk upstairs.

Two doors greet me. One of them is open already, but the room is empty. It's a studio apartment in horrible shape. A wood stove sends laces of dark, acrid smoke through the air, but the room is empty. The bed is neatly made.

A creaking sound and muffled sob catches my attention. I turn around, eyeing the door just across the hallway.

The scent of honeysuckle clouds my senses, igniting some long forgotten memory that rushes back in severely fragmented pieces I can't possibly put together.

But I edge toward the door, furious and honestly petrified that I'm about to walk in to find Sarah and her baby frozen to death.

I grab the doorknob and shove my way inside. The lock comes off completely, bouncing to a stop on filthy, frozen floorboards.

She whirls, dressed in a huge coat and hand-knit hat.

Her violet eyes are exactly how I remember them.

"Alpha Sydney?" she breaths in disbelief, her cheeks wet with tears.

4

YOU'RE NOT TAKING MY BABY

SARAH

I'M HALLUCINATING.

I have to be because Alpha Sydney of the Shadowcrest pack is standing in my doorway looking like he's ready to rip someone in half.

He's handsome. Too beautiful to be real. His face has been carved from the purest marble by craftsmen who spent their entire lives dedicated to their art. Soft, slightly curly dark brown hair glints with copper as he takes a single step into my apartment.

A jawline that could cut glass. A strong, stately nose. High cheekbones.

But the one thing about him that haunts my dreams are those dark blue eyes that feel like I'm looking into a pool full of pure magic when I meet his gaze. Such a dark shade of navy that they edge on a stormy, blue-gray.

And right now, those eyes are scanning my face with such fervor I feel my cheeks going crimson.

My lips part to ask him why he's here, but his eyes lift to scan the room beyond where I stand frozen in the center of my apartment.

My baby wriggles in his sling. Sydney's eyes dart to my chest where the baby is cloistered away from the biting cold.

"Where are your boots?" His voice–deep and dripping with venom–laces through the air and settles deep in my chest.

I glance toward the kitchenette where the oven is making creaking noises as it blares whatever heat it can muster into the room. My worn, sorry excuse for winter boots lay haphazardly on top of each other on the floor next to the refrigerator.

My toes curl in the thick wool socks I found in Ms. Eloise's apartment this morning.

He slowly looks from my boots back to me. "How old is the baby?"

"A-A week," I stutter. "Eight days, actually, I–"

He stalks across the room to the single crumpled paper bag leftover from when Hadley dropped off groceries last night. He violently shakes it back in shape and begins to move around the room, tossing whatever he can get his hands on inside it.

"What are you doing?" I rush out, clutching the baby against my chest. He squirms, letting out an annoyed squawk.

"Put your boots on," he says so steadily I wonder if I'm dreaming. His voice betrays the look on his face. Sheer, unadulterated fury blurs the sharp planes of his mouth and brow.

"Why–"

He pauses at the pictures on the wall behind me. My heart stops, my lungs ceasing their gentle rise and fall.

"When is your neighbor expected back?" he asks as he picks the faded Polaroids off the wall after a few seconds of inspection. He doesn't even look at most of them. I watch the picture of Hadley and I smiling deliriously into the lens after a concert last summer fall into the bag.

"She's not," I manage to reply. My chest is impossibly tight. I can't swallow, especially when he turns his head over so slightly to look at me over his shoulder.

"Why?"

"She died last night. I found her this morning." I'm shaking now–from the cold or the sheer shock of what the last few hours have been like.

I was sure I was going to die last night. I spent the entire night curled up in front of the oven with the baby covered in blankets, praying to the Goddess to keep us safe until morning.

It was so horrifically cold.

It's a miracle we're both still alive.

But Ms. Eloise didn't make it. I found her in her bed, cold to the touch, clutching a picture of her mate and her adult son, whom she lost during the war twenty-two years ago.

A rogue tear slides down my face. Alpha Sydney watches it glide over the hollow of my cheek and along my jaw before something snaps behind his eyes and they go nearly black.

"Boots, now."

"But–"

"Do I need to carry you both out of here?" His icy tone makes the air between us feel tropical.

I gape up at him as he crosses the room, closing the distance between us. He arches a brow, fixing me with a look that I'm sure makes grown men cower.

He will, I realize, carry me out of here if I don't do what he says.

"My b-boots," I mumble, tearing my gaze from his, and walk on trembling legs to where I left them after watching the group of men who own a dry cleaning business down the street carry Eloise's body away less than an hour ago.

I protectively clutch the baby to my chest as I slip my freezing feet into my boots. I can feel Alpha Sydney watching me closely.

When I fumble with the laces, tears starting to trickle down my cheeks, he lets out a long sigh and is suddenly kneeling before me, his head bent to the task at hand.

The Alpha of Shadowcrest tightens up my boots, his fingers moving with practiced grace.

I've never felt so small as he ties them.

Without a word, he takes me by the shoulder and hurries me out of the apartment.

I should ask why he's doing this. I should be asking him why he's here, carrying a single paper bag full of my things and guiding me up a windblown street, but I'm exhausted and heartbroken.

I'm so tired. I'm so cold. My plants and my shop barely register in my mind as he cuts a sharp corner and lights flash up ahead against the hazy golden glow of the sun.

A black truck with tinted windows roars to life before we've even crossed the street.

He opens the passenger door and tosses the bag holding everything I have left to my name at my feet after helping me inside.

Hot air rolls over my face for the first time in weeks.

I gasp out my breath at the sensation, my eyes watering from the shock of it.

Somewhere in the hazy distance, he closes the door and walks around the front of the truck, but I feel like I'm floating. I can't focus on anything other than how good it feels to be warm.

My numb body prickles back to life, but by the time I hurtle back to reality, Alpha Sydney is in the driver's seat and tearing through the winding, snow-drenched streets leading out of the NZ.

It dawns on me that I might be in serious trouble.

I failed to report a death this morning to the proper authorities. I didn't know what to do, honestly. I'd been so shocked and distraught to find Eloise dead that I rang the first number I could think of–the shop down the block from me–where I knew someone would be up and working.

I don't know where they took her body.

I click on my seat belt, wishing I had a car seat for my son, but I don't. "I didn't know what to do with her," I whisper, unable to look at him. "I didn't call–I wasn't sure who to call about her when I found her–"

He pulls his phone from his jacket pocket and dials a number without looking down at his screen, then presses it to his ear.

I purse my lips and jostle the baby, who's now fully awake and likely very confused about what's happening.

"I need backup in the NZ."

I glance at him as I unzip my coat just enough to reach inside and pull up my shirt so the baby can nurse. He roots around, latching onto my skin instead.

I wince and hiss out my breath.

Alpha Sydney glances in my direction.

I look out the window, grimacing, while fishing around under my coat to try to help the poor baby find what he needs.

"How many warriors can you get on the street today?" Alpha Sydney asks whoever he's speaking to.

I wish I could hear the conversation taking place on the other end. I'm waiting for him to say he has me, the woman who probably killed her elderly neighbor in cold blood to steal her socks, and is taking me to whatever prison awaits me now, but he says, "I'll meet you there in an hour."

He slides his phone back in his pocket and rolls to a stop at a stoplight.

The only sound is the gentle hum of the engine.

I fight the urge to turn his radio on just to cut through the deafening silence.

He probably wouldn't like that.

He exhales deeply, his eyes locked on the stoplight.

The second it turns green, we're speeding toward the blur of glowing lights roughly a mile away.

I know where we are because I used to come to the mall here often. I'd drink coffee and walk for hours with Hadley, looking at shoes we couldn't afford and trying on dresses for whatever party or concert we were going to that night. We'd throw coins in the fountain at its center, wishing for silly things like to find our fated mates and for our future wolf forms to have a particular colored coat.

That feels like a different life.

He drives past the mall and pulls into the parking lot of a shopping center, throws the truck in park, and gets out without a word.

I reach for the door handle, but the truck locks up tight.

I whirl to look out the driver side window as he hurries away, his head bent against a gust of wind carrying a sheet of snow in his direction.

This is a strange situation. I'm sitting in the Alpha of Shadowcrest's truck in a parking lot. He's supposed to be driving me to whatever prison cell awaits me, but he's shopping instead.

I try the door handle. I flip a few switches in his spaceship of a truck but can't figure out how to unlock it from the inside.

I press a button on the center console and music bursts from the speakers so loud I scream in surprise, which in turns sets off the baby.

His startled wail echoes through the truck. I'm sure I'm not imagining the windshield rattling as I hurry out of my coat and make quick work of getting him to latch to my other breast.

He's incredibly angry, however. He thrashes, turning purple with rage. I slap my hand against the counsel, shutting off the music, but I hit something else that causes the car alarm to blare incessantly.

"No, no, no!" I press every button I see while the baby screams for someone, anyone, to take him away from this nightmare he's living.

When I somehow turn the wonderfully heated air to something so frigid I could have sworn he had his AC unit crafted on the peak of Crescent Fall's highest, snow-covered mountain, it's just the cherry on top.

I burst into tears, and my baby screams for mercy at the very moment the car alarm suddenly switches off, and Alpha Sydney reappears.

He opens his truck door and looks at the two of us. I'm sure it's a sight to behold. I'm sweating from stress, disheveled, with tears running down my face, and my son is the color of an eggplant.

He reaches into the truck and turns the heat back on, his eyes locked on mine, and shuts the door again.

"Shhh, shhh," I whimper, trying to get the baby to settle.

Sydney opens the back door on the driver's side and starts throwing plastic bags into the truck without ceremony. I wonder if dropping in on me got in the way of his usual Tuesday morning grocery run.

But then I hear a click, and the sound of tape tearing, and then the truck jostles a bit.

I turn to look over my shoulder and see Alpha Sydney, the prince and heir of the Crescent Falls, installing a car seat in the back of his truck.

"What are you doing?"

"Will you bring the baby around so we can get going? It's freezing out here."

My heart skips a beat then starts thundering in my chest. "I–If you're going to take my baby–"

"I'm not taking your baby," he says calmly, his voice losing its earlier ice. "It's just a bumpy, uphill ride to my territory, and the roads are awful this time of year. It's not safe to have him in your lap."

"O-Okay," I breathe. I feel like I'm in flight or fight mode. My mind is a blur as I step out of the truck with the baby in my arms and hurry to Sydney's side.

He glances down at me, seeing me without the giant coat for the first time.

A thin, burgundy sweater and black sweatpants clutches my chilled body. My hair is in two long, messy braids that dust over the small of my back. Milk has leaked through my shirt, and I'm sure my face is blotchy from crying.

I'm a mess, not that it matters. I'm about to go on trial for murder, most likely.

He reaches for the baby, and I jolt back.

"I'm not taking the baby away from you," he says, raising his hands in surrender. "But you're shivering. Let me put the baby in the car seat so you can go sit back down where it's warm."

He towers over me by at least a foot, if not more. I have to tilt my chin to look up into his eyes.

I can't do more than nod. This has to be a dream. Or a nightmare. Or I am actually dead, and none of this is happening.

Alpha Sydney takes my son out of my arms and gently sets the screaming baby in the brand new, state of the art car seat I'm sure cost him a small fortune.

"It's all right," he coaxes, adjusting the straps with practiced skill before clipping him in. "You're fine, little–"

Alpha Sydney looks at me expectantly.

"He's a boy," I say, my teeth chattering, and I'm not sure it's totally because of the cold.

"Little man," he continues, a ghost of a smile tugging on his lips, revealing a dimple in his right cheek.

My stomach goes hollow at the sight of that smile. My chest aches as his large hands tuck my son in tight.

"Get in the truck, Sarah," he says in a near whisper.

I obey because what else am I supposed to do right now?

But that's when I notice it. The bags of things he bought in the store. Diapers, wipes, bottles. Baby soap. Baby clothes. Blankets and swaddles.

"Where are you taking us?" I ask, meeting his stormy blue eyes.

"Somewhere safe."

5

HIS PRISONER

WE PASS the main gates to the Shadowcrest territory. They fall away behind us, cloaked in frost covered vines.

It's been a silent drive. Silent—and I'm terribly sick to my stomach. Alpha Sydney was right about the uphill drive being bumpy and dangerous, but his pack lives in one of the more remote territories surrounding Crescent City.

A stone wall runs alongside the truck as he continues driving uphill, turning with great effort around a sharp bend in the hillside. My view from the window gives way to a small, bustling city below, the roof tiles mingling with thick, snow covered trees, and in the distance?

The castle of Crescent Falls rises like a beacon overlooking a sprawling metropolis.

He turns onto a side road, and eventually, we meet a private gate that swings open for him automatically. No guards linger around the entrance to what I assume is a private driveway. A dense forest hugs the road on either side, not a building in sight.

I sit up a little straighter as the trees suddenly drop away, revealing a sweeping view below.

"All of that is Shadowcrest," he says over the hum of the engine. His tone is even, impossible to decipher. He's tense, that's clear. Angry over something, which is why I haven't pestered him with questions... yet.

A few narrow streets wind through the woods below us as he drives along a cliff edge. Beyond the guard rail, I see a few larger buildings–a school, perhaps, judging by the enormous playground, and a library. Townhomes hug the town center where people and wolves are nothing but little dots that move back and forth between stores and cafes.

Houses sprinkle the forest beyond. Some are larger than others, with lawns and parks between them.

It looks nothing like the choked, colorless streets of the NZ.

It's beautiful here.

It feels... safe. Secure. A hidden treasure in a city where over a dozen packs bleed into one.

My gaze is still on the town below when Alpha Sydney presses the garage door opener on his sun vizor.

I nearly snap my neck to look through the windshield, and then I find it impossible to breathe.

A three story stone manor rises in front of us. The front yard is completely cloaked in snow and swirling ice fog that coats every tree in shimmering crystals that gleam in the sun. Smoke rises from four chimneys that tower above the dark tiles of the roof.

Pale blue shutters bring a pop of color to the manor, which has to be ancient.

I've never seen anything like it.

I gape out my window as he pulls around the house toward an attached garage, which is obviously an addition.

"Who lives here?" I can't completely lose my mind now and get comfortable, despite the warmth and promise of safety for me and my son, who's fast asleep in his new car seat. I could be walking into a room full of Alphas waiting to fight over whose pack gets to be the one to judge my fate.

This could be nothing more than a meeting house. A pack house, which would be even worse, but there's so few of those left in Crescent Falls.

He pulls into the garage and shuts off the truck, the garage door rolling closed behind us.

Silence chokes the air between us. He grips the wheel, his eyes on the nondescript door I assume leads into the manor.

I sense tension. Serious tension. I stare at him, watching his eyes. Watching how the fluorescent overhead lights shining through the windshield give me a little glimpse behind those pools of blue.

He's trying to decide something right now. I just don't know what.

He gets out of the truck and walks around it to open my door.

He extends his hand to me, and I take it without thought, but when I try to step out of the truck, I'm stuck.

He leans over me and unbuckles my seatbelt, his shoulder brushing my chest.

He smells like…

"Alpha Sydney? What is–" A sharp, female voice rings through the air at the same moment I step out of the truck.

A middle-aged woman darkens the doorway, looking more than confused.

Her eyes are just as cutting as her tone, but when they rake over me, they soften.

"Your Grace?" she says slowly, hurrying down a short flight of steps.

"Cosette, get a guest room set up. The yellow room," Sydney says, shutting the passenger side door. "She needs a hot meal and a bath."

"Yes, of course, but–"

"I need Dalia to help with the baby."

"The what?" Cosette is suddenly beside me, taking me by the hand.

With a grunt, Sydney lifts the entire car seat out of the truck and walks in our direction.

Cosette looks at me. I look at her, hoping she can see the silent pleas behind my eyes.

Why am I here? What does he want with me? What have I done?

Her grip on my hand tightens as Alpha Sydney walks past us. My baby is still fast asleep, his cheeks a ruddy pink and smooshed against the car seat straps.

He looks peaceful for the first time in his young life, and the sight of it rips me to my core.

Cosette watches Alpha Sydney disappear into the house before slowly turning back to me. Her eyes are deep brown fanned by golden stripes. She caresses my cheek, her thumb sliding down the bridge of my nose, and pauses at the kink from an old, poorly mended break.

"Is that your baby?"

"Yes."

She smiles tightly, her eyes searching mine. For what, I don't know, but she nods to herself and guides me into the house.

The gray walls and polished concrete of the garage give way to sprays of color. Warm reds. Deep purples. Dark hardwood floors and matching paneling. Art hangs in sleek frames throughout the foyer, and thick curtains are drawn against the bitter cold and blinding sun.

But it's warm here. So, so warm. The walls don't drip with condensation, and it smells fresh, like clean laundry, instead of mildew and smoke.

When we reach the foyer, where Alpha Sydney stands with the car seat, his eyes scanning mine… I burst into tears, unable to hold them back.

"Get her upstairs, now," he says sharply, and Cosette hurries me through the foyer.

"But, wait–my–" I reach for Alpha Sydney, for the car seat.

"He's fine, honey," Cosette says, gripping my wrist.

What can I possibly do? I can't fight her and run back to my son. I can't force the Alpha to let him go.

I'm weak right now. My mind is a tangled mess of emotion. I'm barely healed from giving birth, and I haven't eaten a real, hot meal in weeks.

Maybe months.

My body revolts against my mind, and I relax, letting Cosette guide me up the grand staircase. My worn boots leave a trail of damp on the crimson carpet runner covering what looks like pure black marble.

I keep my eyes on my boots until Cosette turns us into a room on the second floor.

The yellow room. It's aptly named. Sprays of muted yellow wallpaper hug each wall. A four poster bed bigger than my apartment invites me in.

"I'll have some flowers brought up to warm the place up a bit," Cosette says absently as she lets go of my wrist and disappears into an ensuite bathroom.

The sound of water running shocks my system. More tears flow freely down my cheeks. A chill–not one brought on by the cold, finally–licks up my spine.

Cosette peaks around the doorframe, steam wrapping around her ankles as she wipes her hands on her apron. "Ready? I'm sure this will feel great. I keep Alpha Sydney's cabinets well stocked with the best oils and shampoos the kingdom has to offer."

She's obviously trying to tempt me into following her into the bathroom. As someone who can readily admit to loving stuff, I'm considering it.

But I glance toward the door we just came through.

"The baby is perfectly safe with His Grace," she says softly. "I promise."

I nod, swallowing past the tightness in my throat, and follow her into the bathroom.

I've lost all feeling of self-consciousness after having a baby. I don't squirm or flinch when Cosette peels my sweater from my skin and tosses it outside of the bathroom. But I know she's looking me over with a critic's eye as I take off the rest of my clothes and lower myself into the bath, wincing at the hot temperature.

But it's divine. Fragrant water laps over every inch of my body, and I melt into it, choking back a grateful sob.

"How old is your baby?" she asks, kneeling beside the claw-foot tub to unbraid my hair.

"A week."

She stands still for a moment before starting up again. She runs a comb through my hair, gently working through each knot. "How are you feeling?"

Awful. Terrified.

"I'm all right."

"He's a beautiful baby," she says before pouring hot water over my head. I tilt my face to the ceiling on instinct, closing my eyes as she rubs shampoo over each strand. I hear her murmur, "Poor thing," and I know she's not talking about him.

She's talking about me.

My heart quakes. No one has taken care of me like this in a very long time, and I've forgotten how to convey my thanks.

She says nothing further. I'm sure she has questions. I have them too, but the water and her touch has me calming to the point I'm nearly falling asleep.

But soon I'm standing in a fluffy robe in the center of the guest room, my hair wrapped in a towel, watching Cosette flutter around gathering something for me to wear.

"We don't have women's clothing lying around," she says with some annoyance.

For whatever reason, this eases some of the anxiety clouding my senses. It sounds like Sydney lives here alone.

Cosette obviously runs the house.

A young woman appears in the doorway just as Cosette walks toward me with a pair of soft, cotton pajamas that probably belong to Alpha Sydney.

The woman's bright red hair catches the sunlight coming through the windows. She's pretty. She must be young. No more than eighteen.

"Oh, good. Dalia, I need you to call that boutique in town and have them send some clothing up to us. Shirts, pants, underthings–" She waves a hand to the ceiling. "Practically everything Sarah will need."

I wonder how she knows my name. I must have told her while I was slowly falling asleep in the bath.

I wonder what else I told her as Dahlia nods along to Cosette's requests.

But my chest is in knots.

"Where is my baby?" I ask, turning to Dalia.

"He's asleep." She points to a door on the opposite side of the room to the ensuite. "Just through there."

"Alpha Sydney has a nursery?" I ask before I can stop myself.

It would make sense. He knew what to buy and how to install a car seat. He has some skill in the art of holding newborns.

My stomach sinks.

"Oh, no," Cosette says in a pinched voice. "But his last maid had a few young children who came here while she worked, so we have what we need, for now."

I nod, but my head is spinning.

"Where–Where is Alpha Sydney? I need to talk to him."

Both women look at me. I wait for their soft, concerned expressions to shift to something cold and disgusted because I'm a prisoner, right? He must think I killed Ms. Eloise. He must have seen the conditions I was living in and decided I was an unfit mother, and is going to have my son taken from me.

I square my shoulders in preparation for my fate.

"He went back into Crescent City to track down that shameful slumlord who allowed you and an infant to live in squalor and cold," Cosette says hotly, her cheeks flaming with fury. "Don't worry yourself, honey. You're safe. That man can't hurt you again. He'll be caught and tried for murder for the death of your poor elderly neighbor. Now, let's get you dressed and go downstairs to have something hot to eat. It's been so long since I've had someone to cook a real meal for." She smiles wistfully. "What would you like? Chicken pot pie? Roast beef? Stew?"

My mouth pops open in shock.

6

<hr>

WARMTH AND REST

SARAH

I CAN'T REMEMBER the last time I felt full.

I look down at the plate in front of me, which Cosette is piling with food for a third time. A piece of lusciously dark chocolate cake stares up at me while she arranges a scoop of vanilla ice cream next to it.

Everything is homemade.

Everything is delicious and filling.

I take a bite and close my eyes, fighting the urge to moan.

Cosette clucks in approval, and as I finish off the cake and ice cream, I wonder what she's going to bring me next. I couldn't possibly eat another bite, but after weeks of the occasional bowl of oatmeal and scrambled eggs, I'll keep eating her food if she wants me to.

But she brings me a cup of tea spiked with warm milk and so much sugar it makes my teeth tingle as I take a sip. She sits across from me at the snug kitchen table, stirring her own cup as her dark eyes look over me critically.

"Are you feeling better?" she asks lightly, her spoon clinking against her cup.

My mouth feels odd. There's a slight metallic taste I can't place.

"I am," I reply, leaning back. The kitchen is softly lit with warm, light wood finishes and white marble countertops. It's comforting here, and I'm at ease in the soft glow of the lights and Cosette's company. I can tell this is her domain. It smells like her–like the homemade bread she bakes throughout the day and the teas and spices she has on hand.

She sips her tea, testing the flavor, before adding another heaping spoonful of sugar.

I can't help but glance at the darkened doorway leading into the formal dining room, which in turn leads to a sitting room, then the foyer. For whatever reason, I imagined an Alpha, let alone the prince of Crescent Falls, would live somewhere more opulent. I've been here since this morning and haven't come across a single golden sconce or bust carved in Sydney's likeness.

This is a home, not a palace.

But I remind myself for the thousandth time that I can't let myself get comfortable.

I sit up a little straighter. Cosette notices my sudden change in demeanor and lifts a brow. "Are you waiting for me to tell you that you're going to be cuffed and hauled away? Well, you're not."

"I don't understand why I'm here in Alpha Sydney's house, though," I reply, curling my hands around the warm cup of tea. I take another sip, and the inside of my mouth tingles again.

Cosette sighs heavily and gives me a motherly smile. "You're here because Alpha Sydney wouldn't have ever left you and your son in the conditions you were trapped in."

"It doesn't seem right," I retort, my cheeks flushing as a warm sensation prickles through my body.

Cosette makes a mean cup of tea.

I finish it off while she watches me drain the very last sip, looking pleased.

"He's not like most Alphas, I can admit that," she says, stirring the sugar into her cup in lazy circles. "He's young, you know. He'll be twenty-two this spring."

I nod along to her words. She pours me a second cup of tea heavy on the milk and sugar, which I greedily accept.

She continues, "You'd think an Alpha so young would be off partying and chasing women or getting in fights with other packs for no reason, but Alpha Sydney is different. He's the quiet type. He likes order, yes, but he's kind and protective over his pack."

"Why are you telling me this?"

"Because I want you to know, before you make up some delusion in your head about him and his intentions, that he's a kind, brave, and selfless man. He brought you here because you were in danger and has tasked me to see to your care until you're well enough to leave. You and your son."

I take a drink. This cup doesn't have the same kick that the last one did, but I'm feeling lighter than air and rather sleepy when I drain it.

Silence cloaks the room, only adding to the fatigue now creeping into every joint and muscle.

"Can I ask you about your son?"

I glance up at Cosette as she gathers the tea service off the table and turns toward the large, porcelain sink.

"You want to know why I'm alone–"

"No, honey. That's your business to tell. What kind of baby is he? Does he sleep well, nurse well?"

"Nursing–it hurts. I was told it would get better but…" I trail off as tears suddenly sting my eyes. All I've had the past few weeks has been Hadley, who knows nothing about pregnancy and babies. The midwives at the clinic in the NZ tried to help me, but I was in so much pain and so disoriented after my son came into the world that I forgot practically everything they told me about his care, and mine.

Then I was on my own, in a freezing cold apartment, with no money and no one around to give me the support I probably should have had.

"I was going to give him up," I say before I can stop myself.

Cosette turns off the sink and sighs but doesn't turn back to me.

Feeling like I have to explain myself now, I continue, "I had a family picked out and everything, but then the attacks here and in Eastonia happened and I...." I've been alone for so long. My friends faded away once it became obvious I was pregnant. I couldn't–wouldn't–tell them who the father was because it didn't matter.

I knew, from the moment I sank to my knees in the bathroom gripping the positive pregnancy test, that I was doing this on my own.

"I couldn't do it," I whisper, roughly wiping a tear from my cheek. "It was so selfish of me. I wasn't ready for a baby. I thought I was. My business boomed all summer. I had money saved up. I started looking for a bigger apartment, a bigger space for my shop, but then winter came, and everything changed. By then, I was so pregnant. I was sick all the time, and Mr. Foxglove was squeezing me for more and more money. He threatened to kick Eloise out of her apartment because she couldn't pay, so I paid her rent too and..." I hang my head in my hands, choking back a sob.

Cosette lays a hand on my back–calming and gentle. It's the kind of touch I'm not familiar with, a touch that brings torrent of faded memories of a time when I was loved rushing back to the surface of my mind.

"I lost my mate during the war twenty-two years ago," she says softly, her touch sweeping over my shoulder as she sits down beside me.

I peek at her through my fingers to find her smiling, but her eyes are wan and damp with unshed tears. "I was twenty-three and had recently found him. He was the son of a seamstress, and both of his parents had passed. He ran her shop, and I'd come looking for work. And there he was, my mate. It was love at first sight in so many ways."

Her eyes crease with pleasure as she tells me how they married soon after and ran the shop together.

"It was the most blissful five years of my life," she admits, her eyes shining with those memories, "but then the attacks began. When Alpha King Isaac called on his kingdom to fight, my mate... he was ready to protect our home and me." Her hand slides absently to her belly and her smile fades.

"He left for training camp while I stayed behind sewing uniforms and armor for the army. I found out I was pregnant shortly after he left. I didn't want to tell him through a letter. He promised he'd come back, and I believed him. I decided to keep the pregnancy a secret so I could surprise him when he came through the door again."

My heart quakes as I watch despair and grief fill her eyes. "But the only man who darkened my doorway in the weeks that followed was a commander who'd come to tell me my mate had died at war."

So, Cosette was alone. In the years following the war, a great rebuilding effort took place in Crescent Falls. Things like fine clothing were shoved to the side so packs could be rebuilt, new territories opened to replace fallen packs and their Alphas, and her business suffered to the point she shuttered the shop that held so many memories.

"I started working in the house of Beta Cassian and his mate, Hannah," she says with a smile, dabbing at her tears. "Such kind people. My daughter ran wild on their property until she was old enough for school, and the royal family paid for her tuition for a boarding school nearby. She recently graduated from Wellington University and is going to be a physician." Pride shines from her eyes, bright enough to light up the room. "Her father would have been so proud. But I nearly gave her up, too."

"You did?"

Cosette nods, closing her hands around mine on the table between us. "I was young and scared. I had no money, no family. I felt like I was doing her a disservice by keeping her. I was so grief-stricken in those early years of her life. I often wondered if she would have been better off without me... but she was the only part of her father I had left, so I hung on."

Her fingers stroke mine in a comforting touch. But I'm starting to tremble, full of guilt and stress.

"You're going to be fine," she tells me steadily, smiling.

"You don't know that," I argue in a near whisper. "I've lost every-thing. I can't support him without my shop."

"You have support now. Here—with us! Don't you see?" She waves a hand toward the ceiling. "Dalia is one of eight siblings if you can believe it. The oldest, too. She loves babies and will make the best mother one day, but she's eighteen and far too young to find her mate yet, so for now, this is a dream for her. Let her dote on—" she pauses, arching a brow at me. "What is your son's name?"

"He doesn't have a name," I tell her, realizing how ridiculous it sounds.

"Well, it's very hard to name babies. There is no rush on that. Anyway," she smiles, patting my hands. "Let us help you. I under-stand it's difficult to let go of the reins and accept the support you need, but you just had the baby and have been a practical popsicle for the past week. Take this time to rest. Everything else will work itself out."

She's right. I do need this time to rest and heal. I've been in pain for the past week. I've been hungry, tired, and cold. I haven't had a chance to heal from the birth that took place just over a week ago.

"Come now, let's get you to bed. I'll have a nurse from Shadow-crest come here tomorrow morning to help you get the hang of nurs-ing, all right?"

All I can do is nod as she guides me through the quiet, dark house. It's after sunset. Snow falls in dizzying spirals through the windows as we walk upstairs and down the hallway to my guest room.

Dalia slips out of one of the doors, nodding without saying a word as she closes the door gently and walks past us.

I haven't heard her speak a word yet, but her quiet demeanor adds another layer of comfort I hadn't realized I'd needed.

Neither of these women have pried. Sure, Cosette asked about the baby, but that came after making sure I was clean, comfortable, and fed to the point of bursting.

The borrowed pajamas drag on the floor as Cosette coaxes me into bed, tucking me in like I'm nothing more than a child.

I half expect her to give me a little kiss on the forehead and read me a bedtime story, but she turns off the lamp beside the bed and leaves the room without so much as saying goodnight.

I slip into sleep so quickly it catches me off guard. My body goes numb, my legs suddenly so heavy I couldn't get out of bed if I tried.

But I wake hours later to voices outside my door.

I might be dreaming because it's Alpha Sydney's voice I hear–calm, steady, but stern all the same.

"The baby is in good health and sleeping," Cosette whispers. "You don't need to worry about that, Your Grace. She was able to pump a few ounces of milk. It was enough for the night. Dalia and I are taking shifts."

"Good. I don't want her disturbed until morning."

"I did what you asked me to do," Cosette says after a breath, lowering her voice to the point I have to strain to hear. "Your grandmother's tears made her tired, but I didn't notice any dramatic effects. Whatever plagues her is internal, in her head. I'm sure this is all very traumatic."

"Did she tell you anything about the boy's father?"

"Of course, not. I didn't even ask."

"You should have–"

"Ask her yourself in the morning if you're so curious," Cosette snaps, which causes me to sit up a little, my head spinning from exhaustion as I ride on the edge of sleep. "She's alone from what I understand. No family nearby. Also, she hasn't come into her wolf powers yet, Alpha."

"You're sure?"

"Positively sure. She's young. Twenty, maybe. I'm sure with a few days of rest and not being hounded by the same kind of incessant questions you're asking me, she'll be willing to open up a bit."

"I'm not hounding you, Cosette."

"You're exceedingly worked up, Alpha Sydney." There's a slight sly edge to her voice. "Is there something you'd like to tell me about this woman?"

"Goodnight, Cosette," he says gruffly.

I'm asleep again before his footsteps stop sounding in the hallway.

7

BOTANIST TO BREEDER

THE SUN HASN'T RISEN yet when a peel of anguished cries thunders down the hallway. Brie's image flashes in my mind–Brie being held to that altar while Gabriel taunts me, taunts her–and I'm out of bed in a second.

My heart hammers against my ribs to the point I find it hard to fill my lungs with air. The entire room spins, and I can barely get my bearings.

But then I remember where I am. The deep navy wallpaper and dark wood crown molding comes into view as gray, early morning sunlight ghosts through the silken curtains.

I slowly sit on the edge of my bed and lower my face into my hands.

It was just a dream. Another nightmare. Everything is fine. Brie is safe with her parents in Veiled Valley. Everyone is safe and secure.

Another faint cry sounds from down the hallway, and I'm up again, sprinting through the near silent second floor toward the source of the sound.

My mind revolts against my body. I can't slow down. My heart thunders in my chest as I yank open the door to the small sitting room connected to Sarah's bedroom expecting to find her dead on the ground, her neck slit from cheek to cheek, and Gabriel holding her son in the air by his ankles but…

"Get out!" she shrieks, trying to cover her exposed breasts.

I close my eyes and turn for the door, mumbling an incoherent apology at the very moment I run directly into the doorframe.

"Fuck!" I hiss, rubbing the bridge of my nose as I step to the side and try to edge out of the room.

"Alpha–wait," Sarah whispers, sucking in a breath. It's obvious I startled the hell out of her when I barged in here without so much as knocking. "I didn't mean to yell at you, I'm sorry–"

"Don't apologize," I rush out, not risking a glance at her over my shoulder in the event she's still exposed from the waist up. "I shouldn't have–"

"It's all right, it's your house. I'm sure his crying woke you–"

"I was awake–"

"I'll try to keep him settled so he doesn't bother–"

"Neither of you are bothering–"

"I don't think he's used to being so warm," she says loudly, drowning out my rushed reply. We've been talking over each other, trying to explain both of our actions.

I slowly turn to look at her. Her cheeks go pink as she cradles the baby like a football, her other hand resting on her chest, where the fluffy, baby blue blanket I picked up at the store yesterday covers her breasts.

"He's been cold since he came into this world. This must be a shock for him." She gently bounces him, her violet eyes locked on mine in the darkness.

I've never seen anyone with eyes like hers before. Right now, they're pale lavender. When I found her in her apartment yesterday morning, her eyes had burned like polished amethyst, a much darker, richer shade.

I thought about those eyes all day yesterday while I roamed the NZ with Ryan looking for her landlord to no avail.

I spent the entire evening at my father's castle grilling the Alpha of Crescent City, Magnus, about his lack of control of the mile-long piece of territory that technically falls under his jurisdiction.

Then I came home and immediately went to bed, sleeping for the first time in what feels like years.

"Are you okay?" Sarah asks.

I blink, hurtling back to reality. "I am. I didn't mean to barge in here like that and startle you. I thought something was wrong."

"You're not used to babies crying," she says absently, adjusting the blanket.

I turn away again, my hand gripping the still open door, as she adjusts the now sleeping baby in her lap and makes quick work of slipping her arms into what I believe might be one of the fancy pajama shirts Cosette got me for Solstice a few weeks ago.

I chew my lower lip for a moment before turning back to her. "I'm just not used to having guests in my home. That's all."

She nods, her eyes downcast on the baby.

I haven't heard her say his name yet.

I should leave. I should give her some space. I should go find Cosette and ask her again how yesterday went, prying every detail out of her until I get the full picture.

But I stay, my feet locked in place.

"Do you have family you can call?" I ask.

She shakes her head, rocking the baby. "I don't."

Curiosity gets the best of me as I gently close the door and step with silent feet to the ottoman across from her. "What pack were you born into?"

Her eyes meet mine as I sit. "I'm not sure. My parents never aligned themselves with a pack, from what I know about them."

"Then you were born in the NZ?"

"No, I wasn't." She keeps her eyes on me as I rest my elbows on my knees, sitting only a few feet away from her.

Still, from this distance, her scent briefly clouds my senses. She smells like lavender soap, which is likely Cosette's doing. A vanilla and bourbon hair oil has been laced throughout her long, stick-straight blonde hair. But there's something else behind all of that, past the scent of milk and baby-powder.

I can't describe it, but it's something familiar.

"How did you end up alone?"

She looks back down at the baby and runs her knuckle over the curve of his cheek. "I grew up out east, on a rural farm. It was a group home," she tells me, refusing to meet my gaze. "That's where I learned my trade. I'm good with plants. As a teenager, I came here to Crescent City to attend school and studied botany." She smiles wistfully like some memory now takes up space in her eyes, but blinks, and the vision clears, leaving what I can only describe as tattered remains behind. "I never finished school. I worked at one of the greenhouses in the city and saved up until I could start my own shop, but I… I chose the wrong place, apparently."

She meets my eyes again, searching.

"Did Cosette explain that you're not in trouble for anything?"

She swallows hard, glancing at her son. "Yes, she… she did."

I nod, watching the torrent of emotions play over her stunning face.

She is the most beautiful woman I've ever seen. I remember feeling exactly like this the first time I saw her when I came to her shop a few months ago. There's an exotic air about her, something both new and ancient, like she was crafted by some long lost god or goddess.

Even in the dim light, she shines. I wonder if she's aware of it.

I look away from her, staring out the window instead. The sun is still barely above the horizon, but it's cloudy, and snow falls in gentle, silver sheets. "There's a cottage in Shadowcrest that's being prepared for you. It should be ready by tomorrow."

"What? But I'm not–I'm not part of your pack."

"That doesn't matter. You have nowhere to go, and you have an infant with you. I can't allow you to return to the NZ."

"My shop is there–"

"My warriors cleared it out yesterday."

When I meet her eyes again, her cheeks are a deep crimson. She looks at me with uncertainty, maybe even skepticism. "Why?"

"Because you're alone, penniless, and my morals won't allow me to just toss you back out in the street."

"We're not your responsibility," she argues, clutching her son to her chest.

"I'm an Alpha," I tell her.

"You're not *my* Alpha," she retorts with a shocking amount of attitude.

I raise my brows at her.

"I mean," she corrects, clearing her throat and mumbling something under her breath before continuing, "I'm not part of your pack. You don't need to rescue me. I appreciate this, though." She waves a hand around the room. "But we'll be fine."

"Where exactly are you planning to go, Sarah?"

"Anywhere, I guess." She adjusts her weight in the rocking chair. "Somewhere I can work, for one. I don't need your charity, Alpha Sydney. I don't like feeling useless–"

"You are not useless," I tell her, holding her gaze for a few seconds longer than I need to, but something in her tone sets me off. It sounds like she's been told that before, that she's useless, and it makes me want to find whoever said that to her and rake them over the coals.

"You don't know me at all–"

"You're going to stay in Shadowcrest," I cut in with finality. "And if having a job would make you feel better about it, it's your lucky day. I have a job for you."

She narrows her eyes, and I realize she isn't weak, submissive, or docile at all. The memory of meeting her for the first time months ago flutters back to me, reminding me our exchange had been cordial, but I was her customer.

Not her captor, which she obviously thinks I am right now.

I don't know her well enough to realize I've made a mistake by telling her what she's going to do.

Sarah does not like being out of control, apparently.

And it shows in her next words to me.

"And what is that?" she asks, tilting her chin. "Are you going to keep me as a breeder?"

I glare at her. "What gives you the impression I'm interested in you like that?"

She glares right back at me.

"Plus," I continue, waving my hand in her direction, "You've been recently… bred. If I were to have a breeder, I'd choose someone able to do so immediately."

Her scowl sets alight a fire in my chest I've never experienced before. I fight against the sensation of my lips trying to pull into a smile.

Apparently, a little food, warmth, and rest is enough for the real Sarah to come back to life, and I really enjoy her, but I'm not sure letting her know that is going to help my case right now.

How does one help someone who doesn't want it?

"I am going to make sure you and your son are secure within my pack. You'll have your own home. You'll have access to everything my pack has to offer. Schooling for the baby when he comes of age, health care–"

"At what cost?"

"Helping my mother with her upcoming party."

She stares at me in shock then goes entirely pink in the cheeks. "You're joking."

"I'm serious. She needs a florist to help her finish preparations for the party taking place at the botanical gardens this weekend. You're a florist–"

"A botanist–"

"A botanist," I correct, cutting her off. "Therefore you're perfect."

"What's the catch?"

"Why would you think there's a catch?"

"I just don't believe any Alpha would be so willing to step in and help a stranger, let alone a packless one. I have nothing to offer you, Alpha Sydney–"

"Sydney is fine," I tell her.

Her eyes fade from pale lavender to polished amethyst. I make note of the change, still wondering if I'm imagining it.

"So you're giving me a job working for the *queen* in exchange for a *house*?"

"In exchange for joining my pack."

Sarah stares at me, her mouth slightly parted. The corners of her lips turn up at the edges like she's about to smile and thank me, telling me I'm the best Alpha in the entire world, and whatnot.

But she lets out a cackling laugh instead.

"What's so funny?" I hiss as she chuckles, tears in her eyes.

"What do you take me for?" she asks, patting her son on the back.

"Do you not trust me?"

"I don't know you," she replies in a near whisper as the baby starts to wake up. "I can't just say yes and hope that your word is good. I have him to think about!"

"Exactly," I grind out. "I don't understand your confusion–"

"I'm not confused. I just don't–" her expression twists, her eyes growing darker than before, if that's even possible. "I just want us to be safe, that's all."

"What can I do to make you believe that you are?" I hold her gaze, my chest going impossibly tight. Sarah's brow pinches as she looks down at her son.

The baby is nearly bald save for a light dusting of dark brown hair on the top of his head. I haven't seen him with his eyes open yet, not that it matters. They'd still be the inky-dark, colorless spheres most newborns have.

But I see Sarah in a different light all of the sudden. Streams of dried tears shine like threads of silver in the soft daylight starting to filter through the curtains.

She's right. I don't know her. I don't know why she ended up alone, if that was something she decided or if she was abandoned, but her distrust is clear.

I am just another man trying to cage her in.

"What you accomplished," I begin, and her eyes slowly raise to meet mine, "with your business… it's phenomenal. You're very talented, and yesterday morning I came to find you to ask for your help with my mom's party. When I found you in that apartment I…."

I wanted to tear the place to shreds. I wanted to hang Mr. Foxglove from the exposed rafters and let him freeze to death for putting her and her baby in that position.

"I couldn't leave you behind. But I can't let you go back for obvious reasons." I motion toward her son, and finally, Sarah shoulders slump, and she exhales deeply.

"I'll repay you."

"No," I say, standing. "There's nothing you need to repay me for."

She watches me walk toward the door.

"Will you come down to breakfast?" I ask, but she shakes her head. "I'll have it sent up, then."

"I was thinking of naming him Callum," she says abruptly, and I stop in my tracks.

For whatever reason–like I'm guided by some unseen force–I say, "That's a nice name, but I like the name Blake, better. I always imagined I'd name a future son Blake." And then I leave the room.

8

ANOTHER PINK DOOR

SARAH

IN THE END, it isn't the Alpha of Shadowcrest darkening my doorway with breakfast.

Cosette comes into the sitting room, beaming, her arms full of clothes in colorful fabrics. Within a few minutes, I'm dressed in a perfectly tailored pair of comfortable khaki trousers and a shirt made of light pink cotton, and I'm sitting at the kitchen table, surrounded by an endless amount of food once again.

Cosette rambles about the clothing she ordered yesterday that some poor seamstress in Shadowcrest likely worked on all night to have ready so soon. When she offers me coffee, I shake my head, and she's delighted when I ask for a cup of tea like she made for me last night.

Dalia sits in a sunny, frost covered window with my son in her arms, letting him curl his tiny fingers around her impossibly small pinky.

I remind myself how young Dalia is despite her expertise in

newborns and allow myself to scarf down as much breakfast as I can possibly handle.

I'm not going to deny myself nourishment. Who knows? Tomorrow Alpha Sydney could come in here and show me his true colors and kick me out onto the street. I've learned that everything comes at a cost. This food, these clothes, a warm bed… he has to want something.

There has to be a reason he's taken so much of an interest in someone like me.

I'm on my second plate of breakfast when a woman hurries into the kitchen dressed in a puffy blue coat that covers her down to her trim ankles.

Beautiful and spry, she introduces herself as Evelyn, a skilled healer, with a spirited shake of the hand while Cosette tries to get her to accept a cup of coffee, not that this woman needs it. She looks like the kind of person who wakes up every morning with a smile on their face and has never seen a rainy day.

She's the nurse, I learn, and soon my shirt is completely unbuttoned, my breasts are exposed, and Dalia, Cosette, and the nurse are teaching me how to nurse the baby.

I'm not used to this. Even back when I had a gaggle of girlfriends to paint the town with, I was always the outlier. The quiet one, the reserved one, the one who pinched pennies and stayed away from the handsome men who always tried to pepper us with attention.

I never had this. People who cared. People who cared what I ate that day, whether I slept well, and what vitamins I was taking regularly. Hadley was the only one who could help me, and I did my best to push her away because of the trouble she could get in with her brother.

I try to keep track of the conversation between Cosette and the nurse as she packs her things. All the while, Blake is nursing happily, painlessly and I'm…

Blake.

I just called him Blake. In my head, I guess, but still. That's the first time I've allowed myself to stake some kind of claim to him, to let myself fall into the delusion that I can do this on my own.

Dalia gently takes him out of my arms and cradles him with so much love and tenderness I almost burst into tears.

My heart is in my throat as I button up my shirt and scan the room, scan the faces of the two women who treat me like a person.

Two women who see me and care for me.

I shouldn't have this.

I know better than to get too close.

"Are you up for a walk?"

I leap out of my seat and whirl to the doorway leading into the dining room. I've been so locked in my own head that I hadn't noticed Dalia is gone with the baby, and Cosette has also left the room, clearing the plates and pouring me a third cup of tea on her way out.

"Me?"

Alpha Sydney looks around, his hands tucked in the pockets of a very casual pair of jeans. He's wearing a bright red winter coat that makes the blue in his eyes and the faint streams of copper in his slightly unruly hair pop.

"Yeah," he replies, shrugging. "How are you feeling? It's warm today."

I look out the window at the snow, which is still falling in spirals, but he's right. It's not nearly as cold as last week. A bit of sun peaks through the clouds in the distance, casting everything in a soft gray glow.

"On a walk?"

"You've never been to Shadowcrest."

"How do you know?" I say, then bite my tongue.

His mouth quirks into a ghost of what I can only describe as a boyish smile. "I would have remembered seeing you here."

I watch his throat bob as he smiles, as if he's nervous. As if, which I'm probably imagining, he's wondering if what he just said sounded too forward.

I can't explain this blossom of warmth in my chest, but it's definitely there.

"I guess I could go for a walk."

"Great." He checks his watch. "Cosette said she ordered you new clothes. You should have leggings and sweaters upstairs now."

I nod, watching him turn on his heel and disappear into the dining room.

I wait a few minutes, then tear through the house, praying I don't run into him again. I don't know why. Maybe it's because seeing him makes my heart rate skyrocket and my mind feel all fuzzy.

I need to keep my head on straight, but the Alpha of Shadowcrest is apparently making it his mission to befriend me, and I don't know how to feel about that.

"Don't get too close," a female voice echoes in my mind. *"It's dangerous."*

"Yeah, yeah," I murmur, banishing my own internal dialogue as I close myself in my room and flip the light switch.

I hear a soft lullaby coming from behind the door leading to the sitting room. It must be Dalia, her voice lifted in the gentlest of sons as she rocks Blake to sleep.

I take a few deep breaths and go through the new clothes Cosette laid out on the bed, finding a pair of gray leggings lined with something so soft I could swear it's cashmere. I pull a comfy red sweater over my head and whirl to the mirror above the vanity, braiding my hair.

But I can't find the coat or hat I arrived in yesterday.

When I reach the foyer, wearing nothing but heavy socks, the leggings, and the sweater, Alpha Sydney is waiting for me.

"I can't go," I tell him, coming to a stop on the bottom step.

"Why not?" He steps toward me, a hint of concern edging his tone.

"Cosette must have thrown out my coat and boots… and my hat. I made it myself."

"I know," he says with a bit of a chuckle that makes my cheek blaze with sudden heat. "Not that it was a bad hat, by any means."

"It was terrible," I say, and now his cheeks are going pink and I'm… smiling.

I banish the smile as quickly as it comes.

He clears his throat, glancing at me as I take the final step into the foyer and rest my heels on the ornate rug warming the room. "Cosette did throw your coat out, I guarantee it. I'm sure she has one on order for you. She has a particular taste when it comes to dressing us for the weather, I'm afraid." He points to the red jacket he's wearing. "But I have a coat you can borrow. I did get new boots for you this morning."

"Oh, thanks," I mumble, choking a bit on the words out of sheer surprise. Why? Why buy me new boots?

The question lingers in my head as I follow him to the garage. Sure enough, a pair of black snow boots sit in a box on the steps.

He walks toward a rack of clothing on the far wall, moving through several coats and parkas. I eye him as I slip into the boots. A perfect fit, of course. Everything here has been too perfect for words. I'm starting to think I'm going to wake up any minute now and find that this was all a dream.

I pinch myself just in case before he turns with a coat draped over his arm. "It's going to be too big on you."

"I wore your pajamas to bed last night," I tell him.

"Again, I'm not used to having guests. Especially not female ones."

I arch a brow as he helps me into the jacket. "I find that hard to believe. Aren't you Crescent Fall's most eligible bachelor? You probably have women falling all over you everywhere you go."

He steps away, handing me a basic gray knit hat that I promptly pull on.

"You're thinking of my brother Ryan." He holds a side door open for me. "If anything, I've been called the stuck up, lonely heir that resides in a castle as far away from Crescent Falls as he can get."

"Are you a stuck up, lonely heir?"

He smiles softly, leading me around the side of the garage toward the driveway, but we don't stop there. A small trail leads into the woods–a wolf trail. Narrow and well packed, like he uses it often.

"It depends on who you ask. The tabloids like to think so."

He walks in front of me, and I take a moment to glance back at the house as it falls away from view.

"I don't think you're stuck up," I offer, turning back to look ahead, where the forest thickens as it heads downhill. In fact, I'm following him down a network of zig zags, the town below slowly coming back into view.

He looks at me over his shoulder skeptically, saying, "This morning you seemed dead set on chewing my head off. What changed?"

"I was just hungry," I murmur, but my mouth pulls into a smile as his eyes dance with something light and teasing.

"I'll remember not to bother you until you've had something to eat, then."

Again, that warmth spreads through my chest despite the chill.

We walk for a few minutes in companionable silence, and eventually, the trail evens out again. Soon, we reach a well paved road. I can see what I assume is downtown Shadowcrest from here. Steam rises above the terracotta colored roofs in little puffs, mingling with the falling snow.

He turns away from downtown and walks across the street to another set of trails, these ones wider and coated in gravel.

"Why do you live so far away from the city center?"

"I prefer it out here. It's quiet."

"Won't you have to return to the castle one day, to rule?"

"A few decades from now, I suppose."

We turn to the left, passing a few stately cottages. A man waves at us, leaning on a snow shovel. Sydney waves back as we pass the man's front steps.

I can tell Sydney doesn't want to talk about it and find that odd. He's old enough to be thinking about being mated and settling down, popping out a few heirs.

But his short, rather curt response to my question sends a prickle of unease down my spine.

I open my mouth to press him further anyway, but he comes to a stop.

I nearly run into his back as my boots slide over a patch of ice.

I grab his jacket for support, yelping in surprise as my feet slide out from under me. He grabs me around the waist and hoists me upright.

"Thank you–"

My mouth drops open. That warmth in my chest erupts, sending a shockwave through every fiber of my being.

A stone cottage rises before us, small and cozy, its front steps recently shoved free of snow and windows glistening in the faint sunlight.

It has a pink front door. The same color as the one at my shop.

"That paint is still wet," Sydney says, his arm wrapped protectively around my waist.

"Who lives here?" It's a stupid question that I already know the answer to. But I can't fathom a world like this one, a world where someone, somewhere, notices something as small and insignificant as my favorite color.

"You and the baby."

"Blake," I tell him, looking up into his eyes.

For a moment, I swear time stands still.

I tear myself from his arms, my cheeks going bright red.

"Blake," I repeat, nodding to myself while Sydney scans my face. "You were right. Blake is his name."

9

———

I KNEW HER

THE INSIDE of the cottage smells strongly of paint. I watch Sarah move through the first two rooms anyway, keeping out of her way and staying in the snug hallway right off the front door where a small kitchen sits on one side and the living room on the other. Sarah moves lightly from room to room, opening doors and closing them again.

Her face is unreadable, blank, and those eyes are a stunning pale lavender, which is my only hint that she's happy.

I watch her closely, unable to stop myself from noticing the way her fingertips graze over the worn, faded wallpaper in the bathroom at the very end of the hall, like she's marking each swipe of color and texture with her touch.

I might have overstepped. Her expression cracks, her eyes going dark and watery, and she looks over her shoulder at me.

"Are you sure about this?" She tucks her hands in the pockets of her jacket, my jacket, which brushes her ankles and hangs off her slim shoulders.

"I am."

"Why?"

That word holds so much weight. I have the opportunity to really lay it on thick, telling her she deserves a roof over her head, heat, and opportunities.

But I say, "Why not?"

She holds my gaze for several seconds, searching my face. "You're a strange man, Alpha Sydney."

"Just Sydney," I reply, clearing my threat.

But she's smiling softly as she turns off the bathroom light and steps down the hallway, her boots squeaking on the freshly waxed floorboards.

"Sydney." She stops roughly three feet away in a shadow that turns her eyes to polished, gleaming gems. Again, I'm wondering if I'm seeing things as her eyes shift to a dark shade of lavender. "This must be some party if you're giving me a house for helping you out."

"All of my mom's parties are rather grandiose," I admit with a shrug. "She likes to entertain."

"I've never even seen the queen in person." She grips the archway leading into the snug kitchen and peeks into it, her long, blonde braid falling over her shoulder.

Her hair is like white silk. I fight the urge to touch it, to confirm how smooth it would feel between my fingers, as she turns back to me.

"Does your mom have a lot of friends?"

"She does, actually. She doesn't keep a typical court, though, and this party is mostly just to break up the long winter." That's what she told me, at least. "With everything that went on in Eastonia over the summer, I imagine this has more to do with getting my dad out of his office and socializing with old friends than anything else."

"That's kind of her."

I nod, and the air between us feels suddenly tense and somewhat stale.

I brought her here for more than one reason. Sure, I wanted to show her the cottage in an attempt to get her to stay here in Shadowcrest, but she mentioned something earlier this morning that stuck with me.

"My mom was alone too," I tell her, leaning on the wall and crossing my arms over my chest. "She… well, it's not talked about much. I think the official story told to the public was that my parents met at the ball held for his twenty-first birthday, which is partly true."

"What's the real story then?" She leans on the archway in a totally casual stance, her ankles crossed and hands tucked in the pockets of her enormous coat.

"They lost track of one another. A few years later, my dad was looking for a wife, someone to put on the throne so he could go off to war without a civil war breaking out amongst the Alphas in Crescent Falls. She was… essentially forced into the role."

"By your dad?" She looks shocked and slightly appalled.

I shake my head. "Not… not *totally*. It's not as bad as it sounds."

"Is that what you're trying to do to me?" she asks lightly, giving me an arch of her brow. She isn't wearing a lick of makeup, but her cheeks are rosy, which lights up her entire face. "Hold me captive and make me your Luna out of convenience?"

"You caught me."

She rolls her eyes to the ceiling and huffs a laugh, but my heart is racing.

That isn't what I'm doing.

Just a few months ago I was dead set on growing old and decrepit with no heirs, dying alone. Mateless. Passing on the title of Alpha King to whatever kids Ryan manages to raise as long as they aren't half-feral.

Nothing has changed.

I refuse to let anything change.

My tone darkens as I say, "My mom was sold to breeder traders and taken over the border of Celestoria to Crescent Falls. She had no one. Her real parents and adoptive parents were dead. Her step-mother sold her for the equivalent of a few bottles of wine and some meat. That's what she believed she was worth. But she trusted my father, an Alpha, to make sure she was taken care of."

Sarah stares at me, swallowing hard. I watch the narrow column of her throat bob, which sends my body into a sudden frenzy I'm not sure I can tamp down.

"I just want you to trust me. I understand why you don't, but I'm not like your landlord. I'm not like half of the Alphas in Crescent Falls who would present this offer with fine print that makes it impossible for you to leave if you're not happy here. I just need to know that you're safe, and selfishly–"

Selfishly, I wanted to see her again.

"Selfishly what?" she asks, tilting her head a bit.

"Selfishly I like being a hero sometimes."

She rolls her eyes again, and there's that smile that I think might be my undoing. For a single fraction of a second, I get a flash of memory that temporarily paralyzes me. That smile. That same unbothered, utterly happy smile as I press my mystery woman against a wall in Ryan's house, leaning in to kiss her again.

I slept last night for the first time in days. I usually dream about her and have flashes of memory throughout the day, but since finding Sarah?

Nothing.

A sudden throbbing sensation in my left temple erupts. Nothing more than a headache, probably brought on by three cups of coffee and no breakfast this morning.

"Are you okay?"

"I'm fine," I reply, rubbing my head for a moment. "Just a headache."

"Cosette probably has a tea for that."

"Oh, she does. I'm sure she has it waiting for me back at the house." I glance around at the empty space. "It's not a great time of year to paint, but I'm hoping it's dry enough to start moving furniture inside tomorrow, or the next day–"

"Don't you want to make sure I can actually deliver before giving me a house, Sydney?"

"I'm not worried about that at all." My head really starts to hurt. I turn toward the door, yanking it open. Snow has already started to cover the front porch again. "We should get back."

She brushes past me while I hold open the door for her, but she looks over her shoulder at me, her brow knitted in concern. "You don't look well."

"I get migraines from time to time. It's nothing."

"Do your grandma's tears work on them like they worked on me last night?"

I pause on the bottom step, looking down at her. "You heard that?"

She purses her lips, nodding.

"I–I should have told you. Cosette didn't like the idea of drugging you but–"

"I needed it. Thank you."

I roll my lower lip between my teeth as I search her face. I can't tell if she's actually thanking me or not. She has a sarcastic edge to her voice sometimes, which I don't have much experience with outside of talking to Ryan.

There are only a few people in this world that aren't intimidated by me.

Apparently, Sarah is one of them.

"Can I ask you something?"

"What?" She turns so we can walk side by side as I step off the porch.

I need something to distract me from the throbbing ache traveling through the left side of my skull.

"You mentioned you grew up in a group home. Which one?"

"It wasn't in Crescent Falls," she says after a brief pause. "I don't think it had a name at all."

We cross the road back to the trail leading to the manor.

"Where was it if it wasn't in Crescent Falls?"

"Is this something you really want to know?"

"I'm looking for someone."

I stop walking and turn to her. The air around us is silent and still as snow falls in giant heaps that quickly covers our shoulders. There's a fresh bite in the wind as the clouds darken, another storm rolling in overhead.

But I can feel a sudden tension between us as I look down at her. Her eyes fade to amethyst in the shadow of the clouds.

"Did you live with someone named Sasha? She would have been roughly your age, I assume."

"Why are you looking for her?"

"Did you know her?"

She looks at my chest, her gaze absent as if searching internally for any recognition.

It's useless, I already know it. I've canvassed every square inch of this kingdom, turning every stone.

"I knew someone named Sasha. Briefly."

"Briefly?"

She nods, her expression twisting slightly as she meets my eyes. "You're right. I think she was my age. But…" she trails off, turning to look at the forest hugging us from either side. "I was ten when I came to live with Mr. and Mrs. Havisfield. I was shy and didn't talk to anyone for a long time, so I didn't know her well."

"Do you know what happened to her? Where is she now? I need to talk to her."

"You can't," she says sadly, kicking snow with the toe of her boot. "She died a few months after I arrived. She was very sick, from what we were told."

I draw in a breath and let it out slowly, looking over the top of her head at the snow-covered forest. "You're sure she's dead?"

"I was there when she was buried."

I don't know Sasha's last name. It was one detail Atticus didn't give us. It's likely, based on what we know about Gabriel's coven, that a young female child wasn't allowed to take his last name despite her parentage, and instead, absorbed something along the lines of "of Draven."

Sarah tells me, as we walk back to the manor, where to find the group home, and I realize there was one stone I left unturned. It's an area where I didn't think to look.

I'm not sure it even matters now if Sasha's dead.

I wonder if Gabriel knows. Sasha was supposed to be immensely powerful. He's been hunting her for at least a decade. He'll be looking even harder now that his coven has been disbanded, and he's on the run.

But if she's dead, he's likely been running into the same dead ends I have in his hunt for her.

"Oh, Goddess above, thank goodness you're back. I was just about to send the warriors looking for you," Cosette says from the side door as we approach the garage, rubbing her arms against the cold. "Don't you ever acknowledge the mind-link?" I don't admit that I hadn't noticed her trying to reach me. "There's another huge storm rolling in tonight, You're Grace. I'm sure we're going to lose power any minute now."

"Show Sarah the atrium, please," I say with some effort. My head feels like it's about to explode, and my vision is starting to blur at the edges in my left eye. "I'm going to–make a few phone calls."

I step past Sarah and brush past Cosette on my way into the house.

Behind me, I hear Sarah say, "He told me he had a headache but I'm worried. He doesn't look good."

"He's had them since he came back from Eastonia. It's just stress. It's nothing to worry yourself over. I'll have Dalia bring him some tea. Come, Blake has missed you."

I don't register my movements in the house, but I'm suddenly in the dark recesses of my room, falling flat on my back in bed, still wearing my coat and boots. The ceiling spins and cracks, and somewhere in the distance, I can feel the fire of Kenna's powers as she rips apart the guards who had me and Evander in silver chains.

Gabriel's laugh cuts through the pain exploding in my skull. I shove the memories away, pulling my phone out of my pocket with a trembling hand.

Ryan answers on the first ring, like usual.

"Are you up for a road trip tomorrow?"

ROYAL SECRETS

SARAH

THE ATRIUM IS on the smaller side, built onto the far back side of Sydney's manor. Snow glides off the domed glass ceiling, falling in giant piles along the exterior glass walls.

Beyond the glass, the world is cast in silver as the clouds choke the sun and cloak Shadowcrest in darkness.

Cosette was right about a storm coming. Wind rattles the walls of the atrium as I walk through the maze of plants planted directly into the ground, where a stone path gives way to patches of raw dirt and soil. Blake is fast asleep in a sling against my chest, my shirt clutched in his tiny fist.

"Does Sydney take care of these plants?" I ask, running my fingers over massive leaves belonging to tropical plants that definitely wouldn't survive, even in this humid, deliciously hot atrium, without delicate care.

"Oh, Goddess no," Cosette snorts, shaking her head. We meet up again, having taken different paths to the center of the room, where there is a wide, open space dotted with chairs and a bistro table.

"Dalia and I like to come here to have our afternoon tea. We do the best we can with the plants, but as you can see–" she points to some rough looking foliage, overgrown and starting to brown in spots, "We're housekeepers, and plants don't need housekeepers, do they?"

I gently sway on instinct, patting Blake's back. "No," I smile. "They don't."

Cosette gives me a playful roll of her eyes and motions to the ground we're standing on. "I had Queen Madeline's head housekeeper send over her requests for the floral arrangements. I figured this would be a good place for you to work. Plenty of space."

I nod along as Cosette, who has been walking around with a tidy clipboard during our tour of the atrium, begins to give me the rundown about what the queen wants for her fancy party.

It's all doable. Bouquets and centerpieces. A few large, potted arrangements for the entrance of the building. Some floral streamers that will need to stretch from one side of the room to the other.

But I glance at the sad group of pots and buckets full of my severely neglected flowers Sydney brought over from my shop and sigh. I don't have enough for this.

Cosette, who might be a mind reader, gently taps a pen against her clipboard.

I turn back to her, arching a brow.

"I compiled a list of the nearest greenhouses and asked about their inventory, so all you need to do is tell me what kind of flowers you need, and they'll be delivered as soon as possible."

We both glance at the windows hugging the room, where the wind is howling in great, white and silver funnels outside.

"Most likely in the morning, when the storm passes."

That will give me a single day and night to finish everything before the party.

I don't really have a choice, do I?

"That's fine," I tell her, but my heart lurches at the idea of doing this much in that small amount of time. During the festival this summer, I'd been contracted to help decorate a few of the smaller balls, but I was one of what felt like many other florists who all worked as a team.

This, I'm doing completely on my own.

And I have to absolutely *crush* it.

My brain starts whirling–a flash of color and texture. I imagine the arrangements as if they're right in front of me. I mentally conjure up the botanical garden, which I've only been to a few times, as I start designing the layout in my head and where I'll put my art when it's complete.

All the while, Cosette watches me in silence, ready and waiting to start taking notes with her pen.

Within twenty minutes, Cosette has a list of the flowers I need, and I have a rough idea of what I'm going to do. She sits me down at the bistro table with some blank paper and a few pencils, then takes Blake on another walk around the atrium while I sketch all of the images that have filled my mind.

The darkness outside swells to the point it's impossible to see beyond the spray of snow illuminated by the soft glow of the indoor lights.

But the gears grinding away in my mind start to slow as I finish the last group of sketches and lean back.

Cosette is sitting in a lounge chair nearby with Blake lying between her thighs as she plays with his hands. She eyes me, a soft smile brushing over her lips. "Finished?"

"For now." I set my pencil down and roll my neck. Without this project to work on, my thoughts rush back to this morning, to the cottage, to Sydney's questions about my past, and then to Sydney himself.

"Sydney healed my finger once, when we first met." I look down at the finger in question, which I'd sliced open with sheers. "Why can't he heal his headaches?"

Cosette lifts her brows and looks down at Blake, who's awake and wriggling in her lap. "That's a good question. I've been wondering about that myself."

"Does this happen often?"

She tilts her head from side to side like she's digging back in her memories for an answer. "Not often, no. It started this fall when he returned from Eastonia. He was so tired when he came home, he barely left his room. But then I found out what he was doing in there, and I think these migraines have something to do with the fact he doesn't sleep, rarely eats, and has been nose deep in the kingdom's archives looking for the poor missing girl from Eastonia for months with no respite." She clicks her tongue, her eyes downcast on the baby.

I straighten up a bit, noticing the sharply edged concern lacing her words. "Why is it so important that he finds her? I thought he was some kind of civil engineer, not a... private investigator?"

She waves a hand in dismissal. "I have no idea. The royal family is very private, Sarah. This is some kind of mission that was given to him by his father and his uncle, the King of Eastonia."

I nod. Sure, there were reports about the battles in Eastonia and the attack on their capital city, Moonrise, but no details trickled all the way to Crescent Falls.

Life went on as normal here.

But life didn't return to normal for Sydney when he came home.

I slouch in my seat as the memory of him tearing into the sitting room early this morning comes flooding back to the forefront of my mind. I'd screamed at him before seeing the fear in his eyes.

That fear didn't lessen until he'd had a chance to actually look at me—at us. Me and Blake, and saw that we were okay.

"What happened to Sydney in Eastonia?" I ask Cosette, but she shakes her head.

"Sydney is quiet and private, remember? I might know every other aspect of his day-to-day life, but this is one thing he keeps to himself. I have no idea why he needs to find this person so badly, but it takes up every waking second of his day."

"Sasha," I say, the name rolling off my tongue in a familiar lilt.

"Yes, Sasha. I doubt she's a real person. You'd think after months of this, he would have found her by now. If she even exists, she's probably some kind of criminal, I'm guessing, hiding out like those rebels from last summer."

"Sure, that's likely it."

"Speaking of his royal highness," Cosette says with some effort. "I should go check on him. Plus, this little prince is getting rather hungry." Cosette swoops Blake into her arms and carries him over to me.

Sure enough, Blake starts rooting around, making little grunting noises when I can't get my shirt unbuttoned fast enough.

"Any requests for dinner? I need to start on that, as well," Cosette asks from the doorway.

I turn in my chair. "No, thank you, but... do you have a phone I can borrow for a minute?"

Cosette grips the doorframe, furrowing her brow. "Do you not have a cellphone?"

My cheeks go pink. "I–I sold it a few weeks ago." I don't tell her I needed food more than a phone, but she knows.

Her expression softens. "Yes, of course. My office is off the kitchen. You're welcome to use the landline there anytime."

"Thanks, Cosette."

She nods and smiles before dipping out of sight.

I remain in the atrium for another twenty minutes while nursing Blake and watching the storm tear through Shadowcrest.

When Blake falls asleep again, I make my way to Cosette's office, which is in a snug, cozy room off a hallway near the kitchen. This area of the manor is old and mostly unrenovated, with stone walls and ancient stone tiles.

But Cosette's pale pink office is a warm, welcoming space. A fire roars in a hearth likely as old as the manor itself as I sit down behind her desk and grab the phone sitting neatly in one corner. I dial the only number I know by heart and wrap the spiral cord around my fingers as it rings and rings.

"Hello?"

"Hadley, I–"

"Gotcha! You've reached Hadley. Leave me a message, and I'll call you right back, most likely! Bye!"

I growl into the phone as the line beeps, then murmur, "Hadley, you bitch. I told you to change your voicemail greeting months ago. You need to call me back on this number as soon as you can, okay? You'll never believe what happened." The line beeps again, cutting me off.

I hang up and close my eyes, my heart rate spiking. Blake nestles his face into my neck, sighing deeply as he sleeps.

Hadley probably thinks we're dead. I didn't even have a chance to leave a note telling her where we went, and I've been here for two days now.

I leave Cosette's office a few moments later and go upstairs to put Blake down in his crib.

But when I leave the cozy sitting room and step back into the hallway, I turn to the far side of the wing I'm in instead of the grand staircase leading down to the foyer and the kitchen where the smell of dinner is wafting toward me, beckoning.

I don't know where Sydney's bedroom is, but it has to be on this level, right?

I know Dahlia and Cosette have rooms on the third floor.

The second floor is so formal. It makes sense he'd have a place here, somewhere.

I shouldn't be worrying about him right now. He's a grown ass man. An Alpha. Migraines don't kill people, do they?

But it's been hours since we got back to the manor, and I haven't heard his voice or seen a glimpse of him since then.

I edge through the dark hallway, turning a sharp corner that opens up to a common area lined with bookshelves that touch the ceiling. It's a library, obviously, small and narrow, but the hallway opens up again on the far end through an archway leading into pitch black nothingness.

A trio of doors greet me in the silent dark. I open one, finding an office. A computer screen sets the back wall aglow in dim blue light, but no one is inside.

I close the door and move to the second one, but the soft cry of a baby cuts through the silence.

My hand hovers over the doorknob anyway. I feel in my heart that this door leads to where Sydney is stuck in his own head, in pain, in the dark… alone.

Don't get too close. You know it's dangerous. Everything you touch is at risk.

I yank my hand back and turn away from the door, shoving my hands in my pockets, and go to fetch my son from his crib.

11

TEMPLE BY THE SEA

It's 4:00 AM when I finally roll off my bed, wondering where the hell I am and how I lost an entire day. My body feels light as air as I walk downstairs in the dark in search of a drink of water, maybe even a cup of coffee, and find that I'm not alone.

Cosette sits at the kitchen table–an informal setting with four chairs–and looks up at me as I shield my eyes from the sudden onslaught of light.

"You survived," she smirks, straightening up and shifting her weight to face me.

"You should have woken me up yesterday afternoon," I grumble, leaning against the kitchen island. I run my hand over my face, pinching the bridge of my nose as my body slowly comes back to reality.

"I wouldn't dream of it," she says, clicking her tongue. "There's a bag of potato chips and some fresh coffee waiting for you."

"Salt and caffeine," I hum to myself, rubbing my eyes.

"The best cure for migraines. Or for hangovers." She eyes me with a slight grin on her face.

"I'm not hungover." I walk across the kitchen under the glow of Cosette's soft overhead lighting. She hates what she calls "big lights," and my home is, therefore, full of lamps and candles.

I'm thankful for the dimness as I pour myself a cup of coffee and grab the bag of potato chips off the counter.

But then I hear a soft coo.

I glance at Cosette over my shoulder. "I was wondering why you were up at this hour."

Cosette adjusts the baby's weight against her shoulder while he tries to lift his neck, fails, and squishes his face into the side of her neck instead. "Dalia's visiting her parents this weekend in Winding Gorge. She just left for the train station."

I sit across from Cosette and… Blake.

I feel a bit of pride at the fact my suggestion was the name Sarah went with, but I hide the color rising in my cheeks by lifting my mug and drinking deeply. The caffeine blooms through my veins, shedding the lingering ache in my skull. "That's right. Her younger sister is getting married."

"So young, too," Cosette says with a frown. "Seventeen. Can you imagine?"

"We should send flowers, nonetheless."

"I already have. Funeral flowers."

"Cosette," I laugh, unable to help it. Cosette looks smug, but tired, as she gently strokes Blake's back. He's rather wiggling this morning, however. "Let me hold him."

She narrows her eyes at me. "You've been blacked out for almost a full day–"

"I'm fine, and you look like you could use a cup of the coffee you just made."

Cosette relents and places Blake in my arms before striding across the kitchen, talking about how long Sarah spent in the atrium yesterday, what they had for dinner, and how Sarah sat in the formal living room downstairs for hours with Blake, cozied up in front of a roaring fire, before she finally went to bed around midnight.

But my focus is on Blake. I haven't seen him this close before. I did lift him out of Sarah's arms and stick him in his car seat, but other than that, I've kept my distance.

He's warm and solid in my arms but feels impossibly small. Fragile. Breakable.

I have a sudden flash of memory, thinking of when I literally threw my young cousin–Brie–through the air like she was nothing more than a football in hopes Kenna would catch her, and instinctively tighten my grip on the baby in my arms.

He looks like Sarah… I think. He's only ten days old or so, but the shape of his eyes is remarkably like hers, not that I've been looking at them closely or anything.

His hair is slowly turning from dark brown to something paler, more red, but it's probably just the amber-hued glow in the room all around us.

He wraps his tiny hand around my thumb and briefly opens his eyes–still the color of all wolf shifter newborns. I hope, deep down, he has his mother's eyes.

Because they're the most incredible thing I've ever seen before.

"Sarah's flowers will be here by 7:00 AM," Cosette says somewhere behind me over the sound of a knife she's sharpening.

I finish my coffee, forgoing the chips. I feel fine. I feel about as good as I think I can feel as I slowly stand up with Blake in my arms.

"Where do you think you're going?" Cosette asks as I start to walk out of the kitchen. "I'm just about to start breakfast!"

"He's falling asleep. I'm going to put him to bed, and then I have to meet Ryan in Silverhide. I won't be home until later this evening."

Cosette frowns at me and sets the knife down on the cutting board. She jabs a finger at the baby swing I hadn't noticed in the corner of the room. "Do not walk up those marble stairs in the dark with that precious angel in your arms, Alpha Sydney. You look like death."

"It's always a pleasure talking with you, Cosette," I grumble, resigned to following her orders.

She's the real Alpha here, at least in my house.

Blake pouts as I clip him into the swing. He's rather cute, I have to admit.

∿

Ryan yawns from the passenger seat of my truck. I glance at him, catching a glimpse of the windblown, gray landscape beyond his window. We've been driving for four hours, covering so much ground that our father's territory is coming to an end right before my eyes.

Shifting would have been nice, especially after spending an entire day in bed, but this journey was far too long to do on foot.

The rocky landscape fades in a rush of thick fog that turns the dreary morning into something out of a creepy nightmare.

But then lights come into view.

Ryan straightens up as I drive my truck along a bumpy, ill maintained dock and right onto the back of the ferry.

"Where exactly are you taking me?"

"I told you it would be a long trip," I sigh, blinking a few times to adjust to the sudden rush of fluorescent lights. A few other trucks are in front of us, parking in the snug lower portion of the boat. Box trucks, mostly, running supplies to the network of rural islands off the western coast of Crescent Falls.

Ryan gets out of the truck with a groan. I follow him upstairs to the deck where we drink coffee and watch the fog roll out to sea. It's still morning, close to 10:00 AM, but the sun has barely risen over the watery horizon when the ferry makes its first stop.

Ryan crosses his arms as he looks over the railing, watching the trucks disembark.

"This is about Sasha, isn't it?"

I nod. I'm thankful Ryan rarely asks questions about my motives for anything. He's always along for the ride.

We pass another island, then another, everything a wash of gray and white against a bitter winter wind. Most of these islands only have a single pack calling them home.

Finally, we depart the ferry and drive out onto a flat, slightly hilly island with white-washed homes dotted over a three mile or so area.

There's a single roughly paved street leading through the center of the townsite, but the only thing open is a bar.

Even the clinic, in the same dreary row as a feed warehouse and small grocery store, is closed, shuttered against the winter wind.

"Lively place," Ryan says, tucking his hands in the pockets of his jacket.

Two wolves ghost past us, their gray coats blending into the fog.

But the eerie silence cracks as we reach the bar.

I duck inside, finding myself cloistered in pale wood paneling and the scent of beer and fish on the grill behind the shabby front counter.

A few men sit near the bar or around high top tables. A trio of wolves accepts brown paper bags of what must be an early lunch from the bartender before brushing past us. Everyone looks at me and Ryan. Everyone is dressed in rainwear, thick sweaters, and waiters.

This place–Mononoke Island–has only one trade.

Fish.

Which is why I find it hard to believe a couple lives here and runs a group home for young children.

I doubt there's even a school in this pack.

"Long way from the city, boys," the bartender says as Ryan leans against the bar. "What can I do you for?"

"Too early for a pint?" Ryan asks me, arching a brow.

I give him a dismissive look and turn back to the bartender. "I'm looking for a property nearby. I need to speak to the owners." I give the bartender the details Sarah told me–how the house was two stories high and painted white with yellow shutters. How there were two large barns with horses, cows, pigs, and sheep. How the couple that ran the group home grew pumpkins, etc.

The bartender nods, leaning an elbow on the bar. "Aye, well, you'll be looking for the Havisfield property, then."

"How do we get there?"

"It's about a mile from here on the far side of the island. You'll be wasting a trip, though."

"Why's that?" Ryan asks, cracking open a peanut shell and popping the contents into his mouth.

"The Havisfields died a few years back. The missus went first then Rodney. Poor old bastard. They're buried at the temple up the road. The properties' been empty for some time now, five years or so."

Ryan gives me a look, cocking his head toward the door. "Do you have archives in your temple?" he asks the bartender.

"'Course. Every birth and death is accounted for, though we see more of the latter. Not many kids in these parts anymore."

I rap my knuckles on the bar in thanks and follow Ryan outside.

"So, there's no chance your missing girl is here, then, huh?"

"She'll be here," I tell him, and we make a quick walk through the only street in town which leads directly to a derelict temple of the Goddess.

A cemetery sits below the fog as I push open the wrought iron front gate and step through it.

Ryan makes a choked noise in his throat as he trips over a low-lying headstone. "I can't see anything."

I squint up at the sky before we walk up the temple steps. It's dark, cloudy. Another unforgiving winter day.

But I feel like I'm running out of time with this mission. Every day that passes is another day that Gabriel is on the run and another day he's free and able to hurt my family, and Sasha, if she's still alive.

Part of me doesn't want to believe she's dead, but as I look up at the mural of the Moon Goddess–painted in her wolf form, with her beasts on either side–I think maybe it's best she's gone. Sure, the last six months of my life would have been wasted on finding her.

But she would have been tortured by Gabriel if he'd found her first.

And she would have been a prisoner of the allied kingdoms if I'd found her instead.

Ryan looks around as I walk up to the altar where a huge leather-bound book sits on its surface. Inside, written on paper yellowed with age, hundreds of names are scribbled spanning back nearly a thousand years.

It takes us several minutes to find Mr. and Mrs. Havisfield. Both passed away within the last five years. But neither had children.

"Look," Ryan says, pointing to the top of the page. I scan up, and my breath catches in my throat.

Sasha.

The entry doesn't have a lot of information, not even a last name. Only that she died on May 10th the year she turned ten years old.

I look at Ryan. He blows out his breath and steps back, taking a picture of the faded ink. "Can your *captive* confirm this is the same Sasha you're looking for?"

I frown at Ryan. I've told him very little about my situation at home, and I don't plan on telling him much else. Hell, he doesn't even know Sarah's name.

"I plan to formally interview her, get the details I need to take this evidence in front of the commanders and make it official." I take a picture of the book as well.

But when we turn toward the door, the sun is peeking through the clouds, and the fog is receding back into the hills.

I have to be sure. A name in a book doesn't mean much without physical evidence.

And I find it twenty minutes later beneath a gnarled tree. The flat, wide rock is overgrown with dead, frozen grass, but her name is etched into its surface.

Sasha was just a child. She came here, hidden by her own father, to keep her safe and even then...

Ryan stoops, picking something out of the grass. He hands it to me, and I turn it over in the palm of my hand.

It's a necklace. A tiny moonstone rests in the center of a bronze full moon no bigger than the tip of my thumb.

And on the back, the letter S is inscribed beside the letter *G*.

I feel sick to my stomach as I slide the necklace into the chest pocket of my coat.

This is confirmation enough.

Mission completed.

Ryan's phone rings. He blows out his breath and lets it go to voicemail.

"Who was that?"

"Hadley, again. She's worried about a shop owner in the NZ that she's friends with. Hasn't seen her in days, and James won't let her go look for her, for obvious reasons. Some woman named Sarah. I said I'd go out on patrol for a while after I got home from this."

I turn to my brother. "Hadley is friends with *Sarah?*"

12

———

SOMETHING FAMILIAR

Sarah

I FEEL alive again for the first time in... well, I don't know how long. My fingers are stained with juices from the stems and petals of the hundreds, if not thousands, of blooms I've been working with all morning, and the air is heavily scented; reminiscent of a fine, hot, summer day.

I'm nearly done with the centerpieces. I doubt I'll be allowed to actually go to the event to set up, so I've been arranging them in large glass vases myself while Cosette takes stock of every finished piece so far.

Blake lays in the middle of the madness on a blanket, squirming, and lifting his little fists in the air. We've been taking turns all day with him, and it's probably a good thing he doesn't do much but eat, sleep, and need his diaper changed right now.

I've never been this busy before, but the deadline is tomorrow morning. I can't stop for a break even if I wanted to.

Tomorrow night, the queen of *freaking* Crescent Falls will be holding her fancy party surrounded by my art.

My stomach pitches at the thought.

"I'm going to put Blake to bed now so I can start on dinner. I'm famished, which means you have to be absolutely starving." Cosette picks Blake up and pats him on the back, glancing around the room. "You really have a magic touch with these flowers. They were barely in bloom this morning."

"Don't jinx me, Cosette," I laugh, trimming the thorns from a rose stem before placing it in a vase. "I still have hours left to go before I'm done."

"Well, I'll come fetch you in an hour or so when dinner's ready. You're going to eat at the kitchen table, Sarah. Not on your knees in the dirt." She motions to the mess all around me but smiles nonetheless.

I watch her walk away with a grin on my face and shake my head as I bend back to my task.

It feels great to have busy hands. My mind is quiet and peaceful from hours of pruning and plucking.

But one glance at the tall glass windows has me thinking about Sydney.

I haven't seen him since yesterday morning when we got back from our walk into Shadowcrest. Cosette said she saw him very early this morning, and he was going somewhere with his brother on official business....

My shoulders go rigid with sudden tension at the thought of what that business might be, but I already have a hunch.

I told him about growing up on the island off the coast of Crescent Falls. I gave him the names of the couple that ran the group home.

I told him Sasha, the girl he's looking for, is dead.

And it's the truth.

I swallow hard and start gathering the loose stems and leaves I've pruned off a dozen buckets of roses for the past hour and try to stand. My knees pop, and my muscles cry out in protest after being in a kneeling position for so long.

I look around at the mess of flowers laid out all around the atrium.

I'm halfway done, I think. Tomorrow morning, all these flowers will be loaded into two box trucks and driven to the botanical gardens all the way across the city, and that's that.

I try not to think about what might happen when this is all said and done. I need to focus on this one job, this one step forward for Blake and me.

I'm still not sure we can stay, honestly.

It would be so much easier to remain a rogue, able to up and leave whenever we need to.

But I have no money, no plan, and no one to run to if anything goes wrong.

I'm about to kneel again after drinking a huge glass of water when a scream echoes through the atrium behind me. The glass falls from my hand and shatters at my feet as I whirl toward the source of the sound .

Sydney eyes me with concern as he walks forward, gently pushing me out of the way so he can clean up the glass. I have a split second to react before a dark haired woman is bounding toward me, her eyes wide and full of shock.

I lock my arms around Hadley and squeeze, getting a hint of her strawberry shampoo as her curls brush across my cheek.

"I thought you were dead!" she cries out, pushing me away to look me in the eyes.

"She would have been had Sydney not gotten there in time," Alpha Ryan, the other prince of Crescent Falls, says from the doorway leading into the atrium. He has to duck just like Sydney does to step into the room.

I'm not sure how to act in the presence of royals. I don't think I've ever bowed my head to Sydney, or lowered my gaze to the floor in submission.

But Ryan isn't even looking at me as he enters the room. He watches Hadley turn back to him, and his expression softens with something like immense relief. "I told you she was fine," he says softly.

"You've been here this whole time?" Hadley asks, turning back to me.

"It's a long story," I begin to say, but I glance at Ryan and he's…
Looking right at me.

He cocks a brow, his eyes going wide momentarily.

My chest goes impossibly tight as I watch his expression shift. My heart beats out of my chest as unease prickles over my skin and then…

His brow furrows, and he shakes his head, looking over to Sydney as he rubs his left temple and stoops to help him pick up the glass.

I feel like I can't breathe for a moment.

"You okay?" Hadley asks, laying a hand on my arm.

"I'm fine. I tried to call you, you know. Your phone was off."

"I know… James took it when he found out I'd been sneaking into the NZ."

I search my friend's face. I've never liked her brother, James, although I've never met him. He's fiercely protective of Hadley to the point that he's controlling.

"But Alpha Ryan said he'd help me find you, and he did!" She beams at Ryan, who looks over his shoulder at her with a faint smile.

I can almost taste the tension in the air as Sydney straightens up holding a small cardboard box full of glass shards.

He takes a moment to look at me, scanning my face, before saying to Hadley, "I have a meeting with your Alpha. We'll be back in a few minutes."

Hadley nods, and we watch them walk out of the room.

Finally, I feel like I can breathe again. Adrenaline courses through my veins as I fill my lungs, pushing past the tingling sensation lacing over my fingers.

I sink into a chair at the bistro table and stuff my hands between my thighs, feeling suddenly cold.

"What's the matter? Aren't you happy to see me?" Hadley jokes, but she notices the pained look in my eyes. She sinks to her knees beside me, laying a hand over my knee. "I think you should tell me everything. Start from the beginning. How did you get tangled up with the Alpha of Shadowcrest?"

"It's a long story, Hads."

Sydney

"WHAT ARE you going to do about your Beta, Ryan?" I ask as I sit behind my desk. Ryan perches on the corner, crossing his arms over his chest as he looks down at the folder I'm opening. His navy blue sweatshirt tugs his frame as he flexes, then relaxes, and blows out his breath.

"Hadley is his business. I don't feel it's fair that he forces her to remain in Silverhide day in and day out, but I understand where he's coming from to an extent. I mean, look at what our parents did to Misty. She's still in Maatua."

"What extent is that?" I look down at the file I keep on Gabriel. Everything I know about the man and the history of his coven is laid out before me, only worth two pieces of printer paper.

"James and Hadley came here from Eastonia, for one. It was just them after their parents died. He went to warrior training, and Hadley was put in a boarding house for teenagers in Crescent City. She explained that's how she knows Sarah... who, by the way, is super familiar."

"Do you know her somehow?" I ask absently as I jot down notes from our journey in preparation to take what I found to the commanders.

"Did we meet her at one of the balls last summer? I could've sworn we did."

"We?" I look up at him.

"Yeah... that ball we took Kenna to, the one where–" he cuts himself off with a sharp laugh. "Wait, is she the–"

"No, she's not. And no, I didn't meet her at a ball during the festival this summer. I met her this fall, at her shop."

"Huh," Ryan says, rolling his lip between his teeth. "Maybe I'm thinking of someone else. Those eyes, though. Weird, right? I feel like I've seen them before."

I go back to the folder and scratch a few more notes about the temple archives and the necklace I found then close it just in time for Cosette's voice to ring inside my head, alerting me that dinner is ready.

"Are you staying for dinner?" I ask.

"Nah, I need to get Hadley back before her shift."

"She's welcome to come back anytime she wants to visit Sarah. I think it would be good for Sarah to have a friend here."

"She's staying, then?" Ryan gives me a look. I know that look. It's easy to remain quiet and reclusive around our extended family, but Ryan is my twin. Nothing gets past him.

"She's staying in Shadowcrest, at least. I have her set up with a cottage in town and have a job lined up for her within my company once the snow melts."

"What? Planting flowers around your territory?" He smirks, his eyes gleaming with mischief. "Planting flowers around your house? While you sit on the deck and drink lemonade, watching her–"

"Designing and maintaining our parks, yes. I had twenty new babies born in the pack, and several new members marrying this year alone. We're building a new neighborhood of family homes and a second elementary school that should be completed in the next two years or so, and Sarah will be kept busy making sure my territory remains pristine, natural."

"You're really thinking long-term here, aren't you?"

"My pack–"

"Not about your pack." He leans forward, smirking. "Sarah, huh?"

"Sarah was in a horrific situation, and I'm doing what any Alpha would do–"

"You're doing what you and I would do, not just any Alpha," he corrects, easing off my desk and checking his watch. "You're absolutely sure she isn't your mystery woman from the ball?"

"Is she?" I ask him sarcastically, standing as he walks toward the door. "You're the one who introduced us that night."

"I honestly don't remember," Ryan says, but his tone drops. "It's weird, isn't it? How I don't remember a Goddess-damned thing from that night before the rebels attacked?"

I nod, but Ryan just shakes his head and gives me a teasing smile. "I guess we were drinking more than we thought that night, huh? See you at the party tomorrow."

I give him a nod in farewell and watch him close my office door.

Several minutes later, I'm sitting at the kitchen table with Cosette and Sarah who are talking about the flowers and the work Sarah still needs to do tonight. I look at the baby swing, at Blake, who is content being rocked back and forth as he watches the table with a sleepy look on his face.

"I have so much work to do," Sarah says briskly, standing up with her plate to take it to the sink.

"I'll get Blake down for bed, don't you worry." Cosette rises as well. Neither of them have said a word to me all evening. In fact, Sarah seemed dead set on not even looking in my direction.

"There should be some extra milk in the fridge," Sarah huffs then tears from the room without even speaking to me, like I'm not even here.

Cosette, too, clears the table and the plate of food I'm not even done with without saying anything and scoops Blake into her arms, disappearing into the depths of the house.

Normally I'm the one too busy to pay any mind to what's going on around me.

I leave the table and go to the atrium where Sarah is on her knees finishing the centerpieces.

"Do you need any help?" I ask.

Her shoulders go rigid. She doesn't turn around as she says, "No, I have it handled. Thank you."

"Are you sure? I can–"

"It's all right, Alpha Sydney. This is my job, remember?"

Her tone is like ice, and it catches me off guard.

"Goodnight, then," I reply curtly, stepping back out of the room. I close the glass doors behind me and watch her work for a moment, and Ryan's words are an echo in my mind.

Sarah has secrets. Everyone does, so it's nothing I should be too worried about. But her face when she saw Hadley running toward her today wasn't the surprised elation I'd been expecting.

She looked… worried. Upset, even.

Nothing feels right when I fall into bed.

I don't sleep. I can't. I roll the necklace I found today in my palm over and over again until it warms.

13

LIKE A PRINCESS

SARAH

I WAKE up in my bed to bright, unforgiving winter sunlight shooting directly into my retinas. I wince, covering my eyes with my forearm.

I have very vague memories of getting back to my bedroom in Sydney's house. I remember being lifted and carried but thought maybe I was dreaming. I'm sure I dreamt it, actually, because it was the man of the house himself who lovingly carried me to bed after I'd fallen asleep face down in the center of the atrium, surrounded by potting soil and discarded flower stems.

I can still smell him, though. That rich, forest scent laced with musk and sandalwood.

It wasn't a dream.

I blink rapidly to adjust my eyes to the blinding sunlight and squint at the clock on the bedside table.

My scream echoes through the room as I leap out of bed and fall onto the ground, my ankle caught in the bedsheet.

I'm still in my clothes from yesterday. Dirt smudges the sheets as I yank the fabric away in an absolute panic and run toward the door.

It's 11:00 AM. I should have been downstairs working, making sure everything is absolutely flawless.

I stop dead in my tracks when I hear an engine roar to life and whirl to the windows overlooking the driveway, finding it impossible to swallow.

"No, no, no!" I run to the window, frantic, and watch as the two box trucks full of my flowers drive away.

I wasn't ready. I didn't mean to fall asleep. Everything needed to be perfect. I needed to make sure every petal and stem was in the right place before the trucks left this morning but now….

Tears well in my eyes as my hands start to shake, but then the door opens wide.

"Good morning–"

"It's 11:00!" I shout, whirling toward the door, but then I freeze.

Sydney is standing in the doorway holding Blake. My son is looking right at me, content in Sydney's arms.

"What did you do?" I whisper, my hands curling into fists. "I needed to finish–"

"I found you in that atrium at five this morning, Sarah. I brought you to bed. Everything looked great–"

"I wasn't done. Everything needs to p-perfect." I can't calm myself down. My whole body tenses as Sydney steps into the room looking concerned. He skillfully adjusts Blake in his arms, resting him against his shoulder.

"It was perfect. I assure you. I already sent pictures to my mom and she's–"

I cover my face with my hands to hide the flood of crimson creeping over my cheeks.

"Sarah," Sydney coaxes, closer than before. "Everything is fine. Everything is perfect. I… we're both truly in awe, my mom and I, of what you were able to accomplish in so little time."

He steps closer. I feel him hesitate before gently laying a hand on my shoulder.

I peek up at him through my fingers, noticing how Blake is trying to gnaw on his shoulder, banging his head as he roots around.

Sydney's touch is… grounding. An instant, calming sensation that blurs and dismantles the spiral of anxiety threatening to pull me under and drown me.

"Where's Cosette?" I ask, lowering my hands.

Sydney doesn't back away as he replies, "She's very busy this morning. She insisted on making your dress for tonight, but I just cooked a quick breakfast downstairs for you. I fed Blake earlier but he's hungry again–"

I ignore everything else he just said and ask, "My what?"

"Your gown for the party tonight."

I blink, absently reaching for Blake, who squawks in protest before calming into my touch and familiar scent. "Why would I need a gown?"

"You're going to the party, of course," Sydney laughs, retreating a step.

I turn from him, unbuttoning my filthy shirt and realizing how much of a mess I am for the first time this morning. I desperately need a shower, but Blake is clawing my chest with his little nails in desperation to nurse.

I don't turn back to Sydney, who has retreated to the door at this point, as I help Blake latch.

I'm not sure I understand. "So I can make sure all the arrangements are in place?"

"No, you're going as my–my guest. My mom wants to meet you."

My heart falls into my stomach as I look at him over my shoulder. Me? Meet the queen? "I'm not sure," I tell him.

Sydney faces the door, his hands tucked in the pockets of a casual pair of jeans. He's wearing a dark blue sweater nearly the same shade as his eyes. He glances at me, his cheeks going ruddy.

He's trying to give me as much privacy as he can allow right now without leaving the room while Blake nurses.

I wonder why he's still here, but then he says, "Was something wrong yesterday?"

Great. He caught that. He noticed I'd been avoiding him at all costs after seeing his brother and Hadley.

"No. Well… maybe. Yes."

He arches a brow.

Blake sighs deeply and promptly falls asleep still latched. I release him with a wince and adjust my shirt before turning to fully face Sydney. "I hate that Hadley is roped into this. Her brother…"

"Is an asshole, I know," Sydney says with a soft, confirming smile. "Ryan has his hands tied in that department, I'm afraid. James is his Beta."

"I don't want her to get in trouble because of me."

"I understand. I should have told you they were coming. Hadley didn't give Ryan much of a choice when she found out where you were."

I nod, but my stomach is in knots.

"You don't like people getting too close to you, do you?" he asks, and the question hits me right in the heart.

"I'm used to being alone in the world. It's not easy for me to trust others."

"I understand," he says, and that's it. No further prying needed on his part.

I'm surprised by that, honestly. Would I have told him the truth about where my anxiety and difficulty trusting others comes from anyway?

Probably not.

Definitely not.

He tilts his head toward Blake. "Can I take him so you can shower and eat?"

I nod and surprise myself by doing so. He comes forward again, closing the distance between us, and takes Blake in his strong arms. The sight of them together, and that slight smile on Sydney's face as he looks down at my son, does something to my body, to my heart, that I quickly banish.

We're safe here. Blake is safe here. That's all that matters. The warmth in my heart that threatens to spill throughout my chest and force my guard down doesn't matter.

"I'll just be in my office with him," Sydney says, smiling.

"Are you sure? He can be wiggly and fussy–"

"It's nice having him around," Sydney shrugs, and with that, he leaves, closing the door behind him.

I stand there for a moment, dumbfounded, then walk into the ensuite like a ghost and take a shower. My mind is totally blank, and it's likely that I'm in shock. My body still feels all tingling from what I was sure was about to be a panic attack before Sydney touched me.

I rinse soil from my hair and scrub my fingers until the stains from the rose petals are gone.

When I step out of the bathroom a half hour later, wrapped in a towel, Cosette is bustling into the room wheeling a cart full of makeup and hair supplies.

"Oh, good, you're awake," she huffs, her face slightly red from excretion.

"What's all that?" I ask nervously.

She beams at me with mischief lighting behind her eyes.

"You're wasting your time," I tell her, wincing as she sets another tight curl with a roller. "My hair won't hold a curl."

"You act like I haven't seen all of those pictures of you and your girlfriends that Alpha Sydney saved from your apartment," she chides, spraying my head liberally with hairspray.

I cough, and she swats my shoulder. "You're too beautiful to not be dressing up and showing yourself off still."

"I had a baby a couple of weeks ago," I remind her, and that sinking feeling sets in again.

I've always had curves, but I never considered myself a total bombshell. Now, I'm softer all over, rounder, and nothing fits right– especially around my breasts.

I'm not sure how Cosette means to stuff me in whatever gown she made for me today, but I'm truly along for the ride as she fixes my hair and starts doing my makeup.

It does feel good to do this–getting ready. Having my nails

scrubbed, clipped, and filed until they're gleaming with a pleasant "ballerina pink" polish is nice. But as the day drags on, and the clouds start to darken the sky, I start to feel nervous.

"Is there a reason why Sydney wants me to go with him other than that his mother wants to meet me?"

"She'll love you," Cosette says, a bit dreamily. "I'm so thrilled."

"Cosette," I urge, closing my eyes as she brushes blush over my cheeks and the tip of my nose.

Cosette just shrugs her slim shoulder and clicks her tongue. "I'm sure our Alpha is just as nervous as you are."

I narrow my eyes at her. "It's not like I'm going as his date."

"Sure, darling," she smiles, stepping back to admire her work. She checks the slim watch on her dainty wrist and yelps, setting the makeup in her hands down on the vanity. "We need to get you dressed right this instant. I'm sure Alpha Sydney is already waiting for you downstairs."

I reach for the breast pump, which I'm not a huge fan of, and get to work while Cosette rushes out of the room to fetch the dress I haven't seen yet.

Blake is asleep in the room next door. I'm thankful he sleeps so well and long here and that he'll have Cosette with him tonight, but I haven't been away from him yet, and the idea of going across town for an evening makes my chest go tight with worry.

When Cosette returns with a dress bag and a pair of strappy, dainty lavender heels in her hands, some of that worry dissolves.

Cosette loves us. Both of us. She'd never let anything happen to Blake.

I stand and let Cosette flutter around me, helping me into a silk slip that sits at my waist. It's the only underwear I'm being given, apparently, as I cover my breasts with my hands.

"Oh, please," she says, waving a hand at me.

"I don't need a bra with it?"

"Women would fight tooth and claw for breasts like yours, Sarah. You should enjoy them while they last."

I frown at her, but that frown turns into a perfect O as she pulls the most beautiful gown I've ever seen in my life out of the dress bag.

The lavender shade of silk is a perfect match to my eyes.

I'm speechless as Cosette helps me into the dress, zipping it up for me. The back of the dress is low, nearly to my waist, and the fabric of the skirt is ruched around my waist and belly, and falls to the floor in rippling, glimmering purple silk. I adjust the thin spaghetti straps and stare at my reflection in the full length mirror as Cosette makes small adjustments to the fit.

"There's padding in the bodice in case you leak milk," Cosette says as she runs a sewing needle through one of the straps to reinforce the hold. "You'll need me to help you out of this when you get home tonight, though. Don't worry, I'll be awake."

She motions for me to sit down which is honestly a little difficult. The dress is tight, fitting every curve like a glove tailored to fit every inch of my curves.

I watch Cosette take the rollers out of my hair, twirling each curl around her finger before letting them flow down my back, then sweeps my hair into a classy updo that makes me look...

"Like a princess," she whispers, smiling over the top of my head at my reflection.

I try to swallow but find it impossible.

This dress—this entire look—seems almost too much for being a guest of the Alpha, a guest who's just there because I did the flowers.

"All right, we're done," Cosette murmurs, spraying me with perfume, then she quickly ushers me out of the bedroom, telling me that everything is fine, and Blake has enough milk, and she'll call Sydney if there're any problems.

But my head is spinning so much as I round the corner to the staircase landing overlooking the foyer.

Time slows to a crawl when I spot Sydney in a beautifully fitted black-on-black tuxedo, his unruly hair swept back away from his shaven face.

His eyes go wide, and his mouth pops open in disbelief as I wobble on the top step.

He doesn't even try to hide his expression.

He thinks I'm stunning, and that realization works its way through every fiber of my being and sets fire to the feelings I've been trying to keep locked away–forgotten.

Cosette looks between us, smug, as we reach the foyer.

"No rush coming home tonight," she grins, giving Sydney a look, then disappears around a corner.

14

IN THE AIR TONIGHT

Sydney holds open the garage door for me, silently, and I step inside. He turns on a light switch. Light spills over the large space. Stupid, menial things I shouldn't be paying attention to come into focus.

I'm counting each breath I take and each movement he makes in the short amount of time we've been together tonight. I make note of the way his freshly polished, fancy shoes sound on the concrete floor, the way his watch catches the fluorescent light overhead as he reaches for a large garment bag laying over the washer and dryer, and how his eyes light up again as he glances at me before opening it.

That roaring in my ears has to be my heartbeat; otherwise, Sydney has some serious issues with the furnace on the far side of the room.

He turns toward me, discarding the garment bag back onto the washing machine, and holds open the most luxurious fur coat I've ever seen in my entire life.

My mouth goes dry as I scan the pure white fur and creamy silk interior.

"Is that for me?"

"I was actually planning on wearing it," he says, smirking. "You can borrow a coat if you need one, though."

Don't laugh, Sarah. Don't even smile at him and his teasing....

The corners of my mouth twitch into a smile despite my best efforts to look neutral, maybe even bored.

Sydney shakes his head, smiling just as much as I am, "Come on. Try it on. If you hate it, you don't have to wear it."

"When you said Cosette was ordering me a coat, this isn't what I had in mind."

"That's because Cosette had nothing to do with this. I just spent the last two hours tracking this down and had to buy it off some wealthy Alpha's wife," he tells me, helping me into the sleeves. "I literally stopped her in the street."

It's heavy and deliciously warm. I hug myself, trying not to whimper at how wonderful it feels.

"You're joking," I say, twirling. "What kind of fur is it?"

He brushes past me to open the passenger side door of his truck for me. "Let's just say you shouldn't make an enemy out of the Alpha of Thornbrook."

I can't tell if he's joking or not, but it doesn't matter. Whatever curt or equally teasing reply I had in mind vanishes the moment he shuts my door and climbs in the driver's seat, and then we're off, the lights of the house falling behind us in a dizzying onslaught of snow.

Music plays softly on the radio, but the drive is mostly silent. Sydney makes a few comments when we pass through certain pack territories, describing the Alphas who rule there, and some quiet memories of what this place used to look like when he was a child.

Crescent Falls has grown so much in the last two decades, but especially the past ten years. Crescent City has boomed, and now the capital of the kingdom is a sprawling metropolis that stretches as far as the eye can see.

But the city fades into the distance as we start driving back uphill, and soon the botanical garden comes into view.

Traffic slows to a crawl, but my heart starts to race again.

"You okay?"

"Honestly," I whisper over the music, swallowing hard. "Why didn't you take someone more… I don't know, royal?"

Sydney taps his fingers on the steering wheel, staring ahead at the tail lights turning the falling snow a soft pinkish-red. "Like who?"

I think of the daughters of the Alphas around Crescent Falls who are essentially celebrities; princesses in their own right. Beautiful, talented, well-educated and filthy, filthy rich.

I have nothing to my name. Absolutely nothing.

"Like Mirabella Ashcroft," I say, glancing at him.

"The daughter of the Alpha of Crescent City?" Sydney asks, lifting a brow. "Have you ever met her?"

"No, of course not!"

"You wouldn't like her if you did," he laughs.

"I bet she likes you, though." I shift in my seat to face him. "That's all the tabloids talk about. Which Alpha's daughter is the heir of Crescent Falls going to choose as his bride? Which one is his mate?"

"Because my mate can't be someone common," he adds with a wry smile that I match. "The Goddess would never allow it."

"Never," I agree, a bit tartly, but we're smiling at each other again, and I feel my cheeks growing warm, which has nothing to do with the fur coat.

Once again, Sydney abruptly ends the line of conversation. He's rather good at that.

It's something we have in common.

In a matter of moments, he pulls the truck up to the steps of the botanical garden, where a valet rushes out to greet us. He opens the door, and I slowly get out of the truck.

"Ready?" Sydney asks, looping his arm around mine. I tell myself he did so to help steady me on the icy steps, but his proximity is overwhelming to every sense as I lean into his touch and let him guide me into the party.

The first thing I notice is the music. It's lively and more hip to the times than I'd imagined. This isn't some snotty, upper-echelon party where everyone is drinking champagne.

I watch a woman pass with a fruity cocktail and start to wonder if I'm wrong about the royal family as Sydney helps me out of my coat.

Then, I see the flowers.

"I told you everything was perfect," he says, leaning down to brush the words over the edge of my ear.

He's right. It is perfect. The staff who picked up the flowers this morning followed the written directions and blueprint I'd meticulously crafted and given to Cosette for safe keeping.

My heart's in my throat as Sydney guides me deeper into the party. People stop to greet him, some bowing and giving him a generous amount of space, while others seem to know him better, clapping him on the shoulder and occasionally pulling him in for a hug.

He introduces me, telling everyone I was the one who did the flowers, and I'm sure my cheeks are the same deep shade of red as my lipstick by the time we've walked around nearly the entire garden.

But then I see her. The queen. And my heart nearly stops.

Queen Madeline is beautiful. That's well known, of course. The whole kingdom loves her, practically worships the ground she walks on, and I understand why as she beelines for us.

Her wine-red hair is loose and falling over her shoulders in a perfect blow-out, and her stormy blue eyes–the same shape and shade as Sydney's–are bright and excited as she takes Sydney's hands and kisses him sloppily on the cheek.

He goes bright pink.

"Syd, I didn't think you'd make it. They're shutting down roads in Crescent City already. Apparently, it's getting really bad out there." She motions toward the snow piling on the glass dome all around us. "But I'm happy you're here. Ryan is, too, and he brought a *date.*"

"Who?" Sydney asks, looking skeptical.

"Annabell *something*, I can never remember," she says with a wave of her hand. "I guess she's the daughter of the Beta of... Goddess, I can't even remember her pack."

Her eyes suddenly slide to mine.

I fight to swallow, unsure what to do.

I try to curtsey but the dress is far too tight.

"Oh, my Goddess, you must be Sarah!"

I've barely risen to my full height before I'm squished against the queen's chest in a tight embrace.

"Mom, please," Sydney says shortly.

"You did such a fabulous job. I've been at a loss for words all day. I thought–" She pulls away, holding me at arm's length. "I thought you'd throw a few centerpieces together and call it a day, but this is seriously something else. You are so talented!"

"Th-Thank you, Your Highness."

The queen of Crescent Falls is touching me, looking into my eyes, with the biggest smile I've ever seen on anyone's face.

Because of *me*.

Suddenly, Sydney takes me by the elbow and says, "I'm going to get her something to drink."

"Of course." Queen Madeline beams at us both, but I notice the slightest arch of her brow as she looks at Sydney for just a moment longer than I expect. I can't decipher the look she's giving him, but he's giving her a hard look right back, shaking his head ever so slightly.

Mind-link. That's what they're doing.

Before I can blink, he whirls me around and herds me toward the bar on the far side of the room.

"Are you okay? Your eyes practically rolled back in your head back there. I thought you were going to faint," he growls, leaning down to brush the words over my cheek.

The motion sends a ripple of desire down my spine that makes me squeak in surprise. I shove it away, feeling suddenly too hot and cold all at once.

Someone bumps into me. Sydney places a hand on the small of my back to steady me, glaring at the drunken man wobbling away from us.

"What do you want to drink?"

"Water," I tell him, my mouth dry for a multitude of reasons. What the hell is wrong with me right now?

He orders me a water and himself a glass of the finest scotch before quickly guiding me into a quiet corner of the garden where a small waterfall trickles into a pond full of fish.

The thrum of the music is only a slight vibration from here, but I can see the partygoers, and I can see groups pointing and discussing the arrangements I worked so tirelessly on.

I sip my water and feel like I'm being watched.

I glance at Sydney, finding that he is the culprit.

"What?" I ask, narrowing my eyes at him.

"Nothing. Just admiring."

I blush, and he smiles, but then chuckles, sipping from his drink.

"Why don't you go *admire* some of the women desperate for your attention. I can see people staring at you from here."

"I'd rather stand here with you in the quiet."

"What's the point in that, Sydney? I'm not here as your date. You should be out there meeting someone to make your Luna one day. That's what you were talking to your mom about, weren't you? She was probably wondering why you were dragging me around when–"

"She told me I should ask you to dance tonight and not waste the opportunity to find a little bit of happiness for myself."

His voice is so level, so void of emotion.

I look up at him, seeing the darkness behind his eyes as he scans the crowd, that pinched expression he always hides with a charming smile.

I tell myself I shouldn't care. I've promised myself, actually, that I'd keep this man at a distance. He's out of my league. He's kind, generous, and sweet and I'm…

Lonely.

So is he.

But for the first time in months–maybe even years–I don't feel so alone while in his company.

"You're shy," I tell him. His gaze slides back to mine. "That's your problem, isn't it? It takes a lot for you to actually go and talk to someone."

"You're right."

"What if I helped you–"

"Helped me what?" he turns to me with an expectant expression that immediately makes me square my shoulders. "Are you going to drag me out there and introduce me to women you don't even know and force me to dance with them? Goddess, my mother is going to *love* you."

"That's not–first of all," I say, shoving a finger into the center of his chest. "You're an Alpha, Sydney. You live in that big house all alone, and poor Cosette is desperate for you to find your mate, marry, and give her some babies to look after. What is she going to do when Blake and I go to live in that cottage, huh?"

"I can't live my life just to make Cosette happy."

"Then live your life to make yourself happy."

"I have no interest in marrying or having children," he says sternly. It's a tone I haven't heard from him before.

I drop my hand, taking a step away from him, but he grabs my wrist, holding me in place.

"I won't find my mate," he continues, his eyes lighting on mine with such intensity it's making my knees slightly weak. "So none of that matters. As for my titles, I have it all planned out already. Ryan will find his mate, I'm sure. He'll have as many children as he possibly can, and one of my nephews will be the Alpha of Shadowcrest, then the Alpha King one day."

"But why not…. You might find your mate one day and then–"

"I won't," he says again, and I realize with startling clarity that it's not because he's confident he's never going to find his mate but because he doesn't want to.

"Why?"

He's still touching me. His thumb absently slides up and down my wrist, over my pulse. His eyes are downcast, and for a moment, I think he's looking at my breasts but… no. He looks up at me as my heart begins to race, thundering against my ribs. He can sense it.

"I've seen the cruelty in the world, the danger my family is in every waking moment because of our powers, and I can't–" He bares his teeth, and I realize how close we are to each other. He runs his tongue along his lower lip. "I refuse to put my mate in danger, so I refuse to find her."

I hold his gaze. I'm sure he expects me to say something like, "That's stupid." Or, "What a waste."

But I say, "I understand completely."

Just then, the music softens, and whatever haze we've been sucked into snaps.

But he doesn't back away. He simply knits his fingers in mine and leans in to say, "We have to dance, at least once, otherwise it will have been a waste of a dress."

15

WRECKED

Sydney

I don't miss the fact I just told Sarah something no one knows. Not even Kenna. Not even Ryan or Evander.

It doesn't matter. At least, I tell myself that. I'm not going to ruin her night by dragging her down into the depths of my own despair over my choices, which I've practically written in blood and all but pledged to the Goddess.

I can't deny how good it feels to have Sarah in my arms, though. She holds my hand as I softly spin us around the garden with the other couples. We're probably the youngest pair on the dance floor. I spot my dad talking with a group of other Alphas. I don't think he's even noticed I'm here, but that's probably for the best.

All we've had to talk about lately is business. Ever since Uncle Ryatt had to close the borders between the two kingdoms, there's been nothing but stress weighing down my dad's shoulders.

I catch a glimpse of Ryan from across the crowd though. He's talking with our mom, and they both look at me and Sarah, mom's eyes as bright as the moon.

Damnit.

She's waving us over.

"We're being summoned," I say to Sarah, but I look down and notice the radiate smile on her face as I take her through a final twirl.

She looks absolutely stunning. I can't put into words what seeing her for the first time tonight felt like, but it damn near took my breath away.

The more time I spend with her, the more difficult it's becoming to ignore the fact that I do find her…. *Attractive* isn't even the right word for it. She's everything. Everything I think about. Everything I try not to think about when I close my eyes.

I also notice Sarah's hesitation as I lead her up to Ryan and my mom. Ryan arches his brow at me, smirking around the rim of his glass of scotch, but Mom only has eyes for Sarah.

"Everyone is asking me about you, Sarah," she says, taking my date's hands. "You might be the busiest florist in the kingdom once this is all said and done. Do you have room in your schedule–"

"It's a party, Mom. You already said no talking business," Ryan cuts it.

Mom glares at him but softens her expression as she looks back at Sarah. "He's right. I'll call on you sometime this week, okay? I'd love to chat one on one. Sydney had such wonderful things to say about you."

"Oh." Sarah squeaks. Ryan and I exchange a glance, but I shrug off his attempt to mind-link, probably to ask me if I've seen what Sarah is wearing and how I landed someone like her.

"We actually need to be going," I tell them, laying my hand flat on Sarah's lower back. "It's getting late."

"Late?" Mom asks, looking at each of us in shock. "It's not even ten, Sydney. What's the hurry?"

"Sarah's son is home with Cosette," I tell her, since Sarah seems too nervous to say anything to my mother, which I understand, I continue, "He doesn't like taking a bottle."

Mom's mouth drops open. Sarah winces. Ryan lifts a brow at me, once again trying to cut through the barriers I've built around the mind-link to keep him out when I need to.

"You have a baby?" Mom asks Sarah, looking her up and down.

"Yes. He's only a few weeks old–"

"And you've had her on her feet, dancing? Let alone doing all of this?" Mom waves a hand around the party, at the flowers covering practically every surface. "Sydney!"

"Why are you mad at me?" I laugh, but mom has already swooped in on Sarah, taking her hands again and mumbling apologies for my behavior, like I kidnapped her or something and forced her to do this.

Sarah gives me a smirk.

I didn't kidnap her. I saved her life.

I cross my arms over my chest while Sarah absolutely melts into my mom's attention, but I clear my throat, tapping my watch. "Sarah, we do need to leave."

"I know." She smiles at my mom. "The honor is mine, truly."

"When you've rested and are ready to work again, please let me know. I'd love to talk to you about the spring festival this year."

"I'll see you tomorrow," Ryan says to me before he starts to turn away.

"What's tomorrow?"

"Aren't you going to see Dad and take all your evidence about Sasha's death to him and his commanders?"

Sarah looks between us, a flash of concern behind her eyes, which fade to a deep amethyst at the mention of *Sasha*. I can't imagine what it would have been like for Sarah having witnessed the burial of someone so young, someone her age.

"Right." I nod to Ryan. "Tomorrow."

I quickly usher Sarah out of the room, grabbing her coat and helping her into the sleeves before waiting for the valet.

She says nothing as we wait, but she's toying with her nails and watching the snow fall in thick sheets.

Other people are leaving early as well. The weather is getting bad, and several Alphas and Betas drove sportscars to this event, of course, to show off their wealth and status like absolute idiots.

The valet pulls my truck around, and within a few seconds we're driving down the winding road leading away from the botanical garden and the forest that hugs it.

"I'm sorry we brought up Sasha in front of you."

"It's fine," Sarah replies, her eyes on the windshield. "I didn't really know her, remember?"

"But you were there when she was buried. That must have been a shock to you, being a child and all."

"Yeah," she says after a moment. "Why do you need to confirm her death with your dad?"

I tilt my head from side to side as I debate telling her the truth. It's a confidential mission, but who would Sarah tell? Hadley?

"Her cousin is a wanted fugitive from Eastonia, and we believe he's looking for her."

"So you were looking for her to keep her safe from him?"

"Partly," I admit. "She's said to have powers beyond explanation, which is why he wants her. He needs her for something. It was my job to find her and turn her into the Allied Kingdoms. It's likely Alpha King Ryatt would have had her imprisoned until they could prove she wasn't a threat and use her as bait to draw Gabriel out of hiding."

Sarah's silence is deafening. I glance at her, noticing the way her eyes are fixed on nothing and everything all at once as she looks out the window.

"It's boring, I know. I won't drag you down with it any further."

"I'm just tired," she says with a soft smile. "I did have fun tonight, you know."

"I had fun too–"

An engine behind us roars, and suddenly a sports car dashes around us, scraping the passenger side. I lose control, my truck tires sliding sideways as the truck hits a guardrail and bounces back into the middle of the street.

"Hold on," I say as calmly as possible as I try to regain control, but the road is slick, and the embankments on either side of the narrow highway leading into Crescent City are thick with snow.

In a split second, we're totally backward, spinning in a circle before the truck comes to a rough, jolting stop with the front wheels lodged in the embankment.

I immediately reach for Sarah. "Are you all right?"

"I'm fine," she replies breathlessly, her eyes a bit glassy. "Are we stuck?"

I look out the windshield, where the snow is so deep it covers part of the hood with ease. "We're very, very stuck."

We sit there for a moment in silence. My mind reels over what to do. I could mind-link with my parents and have them send a warrior down to pick us up, but the road conditions are awful, and I'm sure anyone else coming down the roadway is facing similar issues getting back to the city.

I look at Sarah. She looks at me. "You can't shift yet."

She shakes her head.

"It's a good thing you have that coat," I breathe, wrenching open my door and reaching for her hand.

"Where are we going?"

"There's a small town just down the road. There's a hotel less than a mile from here. You can stay there for a minute while I figure this out."

It's a good plan–until I realize how little of a chance I have of finding someone to tow the truck out of the ditch at this hour of night–and how full the hotel is when we get there after a twenty minute walk through the snow and ice.

The woman behind the check-in counter slides me a single room key with a wince. I gruffly take the key and steer a sopping wet Sarah toward the elevator. Neither of us speak a word. She's half frozen and wet from the snow, and I'm wondering how the hell I'm going to get her home to her baby, let alone share a room with her tonight.

Matters are made worse when we step inside the room and find a single, full sized bed.

Sarah immediately closes herself into the bathroom with what might have been a sob.

Gutted, I shrug out of my wet tuxedo jacket and hang it on the back of a chair then call Cosette.

"We're stuck on the Hillside," I tell her. "Can you send a warrior to the Alpine Meadows Lodge to pick Sarah up, please?"

"I can't send anyone out in this weather! Are you crazy? You'll just have to stick it out."

Sarah makes a whimpering sound from the bathroom, and I feel like shredding the room to pieces at the anguish in her cries. "Sarah needs to get home. Something's wrong."

"Let me talk to her."

I knock on the bathroom door, and she opens it a crack, quickly taking the phone from me and locking the door behind her.

I use the hotel phone to call for some robes and extra clothes if they have any, which of course, they don't.

The hotel is at full capacity tonight with travelers stuck because of the storm.

So, I wait, sitting on the edge of the bed in the sparse, modern room, while I listen to Sarah being talked down by Cosette, who is apparently promising that Blake will be fine for the night.

Finally, the bathroom door creaks open, and Sarah steps out, holding out my phone.

She sniffles as I take it but refuses to look at me as she says, "I need help getting out of my dress."

"Are you–"

"If you ask if I'm okay, I'm going to lose it," she whispers, then sniffs.

I roll my lower lip between my teeth and take her by the shoulders, turning her around so her back is to me.

The zipper on her dress is low and tight, and I struggle to get it open. The second the zipper gives way, she darts into the bathroom, closing herself inside with one of the robes.

I change out of my wet clothes and put on a matching fluffy, white robe.

This is not how I thought this night would go. I'm not sure I had an ending in mind, honestly, but Sarah whimpering in the bathroom wasn't on my radar at all.

I can't take it anymore, so I go to the door and knock. "Sarah, I'm sorry. I'm sorry we're stuck here. I'm confident Blake is going to be fine. Cosette said she has plenty of milk."

"I know he's going to be okay." She groans as if in pain, and every nerve in my body feels like it's on fire. I try the doorknob, but it's locked.

"What's the matter? Will you open the door?"

"No!"

"Sarah!"

"Sydney, I can't–I didn't bring a–a breast pump and it's–painful–I really need to nurse."

I let out my breath. I honestly don't know what to do to get her to open the door and just talk to me, so I lean my forehead on the door and ask, "Is there anything I can do to help?"

She sniffles. "How could you possibly help me right now?"

"I could…"

The door opens abruptly. She glares up at me, and I feel….

She's in nothing but her robe and her breasts are slightly exposed and I'm… I'm just looking at her, looking into those beautiful eyes that have my whole body tightening as she meets my gaze.

"Let me help you," I tell her. "Please."

"I'm fine," she says in a low growl, and tries to shut the door again, but I hold it open.

"Why won't you let me help–"

"Why do you even care?"

"I hate when you ask me that," I say sharply, meaning every word. And somewhere, deep down, I feel… a flicker. Something I've felt only once in my life with a woman I can't even remember.

Before I can think about what I'm doing and the consequences that will follow, I step into the bathroom, caging her in against the door, and lower my head.

"As your Alpha, I command you to allow me to see to your… welfare."

Her answering snarl sets fire to my blood.

Sarah needs to learn that she can trust me.

It's something I'm going to have to *show* her.

16

PROMISES WE MADE

SARAH

"GET OUT!"

Sydney shakes his head, taking another step, which means I'm either going to hit the door, or move out of his way, forced further into the sterile, brightly lit hotel bathroom.

"You look ridiculous," I spit, snarling the words. In my defense, he does. He's wearing a white, fluffy robe that hits him mid-thigh and not much else from what I can tell.

I'm wearing the same kind of robe.

One would think that would diffuse things a bit, but no.

I'm in pain, and the look he's giving me right now is dizzying. Sydney looks like an *Alpha*, not the kind, slightly nerdy man I've grown to know and like.

His canine teeth are slightly pointed and his eyes... fuck. They glow.

"Are you about to fucking shift?" I dart away, my back hitting the glass exterior wall of the shower.

He grabs my robe and yanks me toward him. I shove him back, my hands slipping beneath his robe and meeting firm, tight muscles.

He's so warm. Feverishly hot. Touching him is unraveling the wall I've put up between us.

I make the mistake of looking up into his eyes, and it's my undoing.

Concern lingers in those wells of stormy blue. Raw, unfiltered worry.

"I'm fine," I try to say, but the words wobble off my tongue at the very moment tears of pain well in my eyes.

My breasts are so swollen and aching to be touched, but I didn't think in this way....

Still, when he raises a hand and slides it between the folds of my robe, I don't flinch away. My eyes flutter closed, and I find myself suddenly leaning against the shower door as his large, warm hand closes around my right breast.

"Take off your robe and get in the shower," he commands in a low, calm voice.

"You don't have to–"

"Please," he says steadily, and I open my eyes, locking my gaze with his.

He'll see me totally naked if I do what he says. A shiver of self-consciousness ripples over my skin, turning his warm touch to ice, so I decide to stay frozen.

"I'll be fine," I try to say, but he shakes his head.

"It'll get worse, and then you could get something called mastitis which will require you to go to a clinic–"

I blink, eying him skeptically. "How do you know all of this?"

"Cosette bought baby books."

"You read those?" I gape up at him. I've been reading them every night–but Sydney?

"Yeah, I did." He slowly massages my breast until I feel all tingling and can barely catch my breath. "You need to relax and work this out. A hot shower will help." He retreats, and the absence of his touch spreads through my body like an icy wave.

"Wait." I grab his wrist.

I'm losing it because I'm drawing him back to me, desperate for his touch again, for anything from him.

His hand lays flat against my chest, his thumb tracing a line down the center of my throat. My eyes close to slits, and in the dim haze of my vision I can see him watching my face, watching the way my lips part as his hand drifts lower to cup my other breast.

More tingles erupt through my breasts and my milk finally lets down in a rush that instantly eases the ache that's been plaguing me since we got into his truck to leave the party.

Maybe I'm imagining it. I have to be because Sydney is resting his arm against the glass wall over my head and leaning down as he continues to work the pain from my body with just his touch.

His lips brush over my hairline, then across my temple, and I feel my body betraying every single thought in my head that screams "NO!" when it comes to Sydney. I wrap my arms around his neck, closing my eyes as I bury my face in the crook of his neck and breathe in that heavy, wooded scent that turns my body molten.

Mine.

I shove the thought away before it can get me into any more trouble than I am now.

"Better?" he whispers into my hair. His voice is low and full of smoke, raspier than usual. Needier and heavy with desire.

I want to tell him not to stop. To keep touching me. To touch me lower. Much lower. But that ache between my thighs sends warning bells ricocheting through my skull.

Sydney pulls his hand from the folds of my robe and reaches into the shower, turning the water on full blast.

"Take a shower," he commands breathlessly then tears himself away.

I watch him, paralyzed and breathless, as he shrugs out of his robe and hangs it on a hook by the door.

In nothing but his boxers, I can see every taut muscle and scar.

More scars than I thought he'd have and they're… awful.

He's gone before I can say anything, and steam fills the bathroom to the point where I can't see my shocked expression in the mirror anymore.

I slip into the shower, dropping my milk soaked robe on the floor and let the hot water run all over me.

When I step out again, towel dried and wearing the robe Sydney left behind, I'm wondering if we can walk away from what just happened.

And if I *want* to walk away from it.

I gather myself before stepping into the main room, which is nothing more than a snug space with a bed, a desk and chair, and a TV that Sydney's watching while flipping through every channel. He lands on the weather channel, where a man dressed in a khaki suit is talking about the storm funneling over Crescent City and the outlying pack territories, telling everyone tonight would be a good time to shift if traveling outside.

I grab a pillow off the bed and an extra blanket off the desk.

"What are you doing?" he asks, straightening up a bit.

I can't even look at him right now. He's beautiful. Strong and fit. But those scars on his legs and ankles have my head spinning and throat closing up.

"Going to bed." I debate dropping the pillow on the floor and curling up in a ball, but the carpet is probably not very clean.

"You're not sleeping on the floor."

"Well, you're obviously in the bed, *Alpha*."

"Don't pull rank with me, Sarah. We're adults. We can sleep in the same bed."

I grip the pillow and lift my eyes to meet his. It's warm in here. Too warm. I feel too hot in my robe as I lay the pillow back down and slide into bed beside him, curling my knees into my belly as he remains seated, the reflection of the TV shining in his eyes as he shuts off the bedside lamp.

I watch for a few minutes then glance down at his bare legs again.

"Do you want to know how I got them?"

My heart rate ticks up, but I silently nod, curling deep into the blankets.

"I went to Eastonia this summer. Moonrise, their capital, was attacked. I was there. I remained as the emissary for my father's kingdom for a few weeks while my aunt was…." He rolls his lower lip between his teeth. "Well, she was off doing something she shouldn't have done, while I aided my uncle's forces."

The wind begins to howl outside, blowing snow against the window. The power flickers, then shuts off completely, sending the room in unnerving silence.

Sydney sighs and gets out of bed, nothing more than a shadow in the near total darkness as he goes to the window and pulls the curtains closed, muffling some of the noise. "My cousin, Kenna, and her mate Evander had their daughter stolen from them by Gabriel's coven. I went with them to find her, and we were attacked. Kenna got away, but Evander and I let ourselves get captured in hopes they'd bring us to where Brie was, and we were right, but it came at a cost."

He walks back over to the bed, shaking out the blanket I'd grabbed earlier and laying it over me before sliding in again. I close my eyes against the visions filling my mind.

His voice is much closer, like he's facing me, as he says, "They tortured us, bound us in silver manacles and chains. I made the mistake of trying to shift, and it nearly tore my legs apart. My powers–those special gifts–were nothing compared to something as simple as silver."

I find it hard to breathe, and the temperature in the room starts to steadily drop, sending a chill through the air.

"But you survived."

"I did."

"Did you find your cousin's baby?"

"Yes. Everyone made it home." I should have been satisfied by this ending, but his voice is so low and pained that it makes every muscle in my body tense.

He'd told me earlier that he wouldn't be finding his mate because of the dangers involved.

I have a feeling something happened that day–to his cousin and her mate–that caused him to decide that.

"You're shivering," he whispers.

I'm not sure if I'm cold or if it's just his story that's sending chills licking up and down my spine, but when he reaches for me, I don't draw away. He rolls me over so I'm facing away from him and pulls me in so my back is flush with his chest.

His warmth penetrates every sense, but instead of drifting off to sleep in his comforting, heavy embrace, my body is thrumming, and that ache between my legs reignites.

Even the rise and fall of his chest is enough to send my body into a spiral of desire and absolute, unending want.

His arm is locked around my waist, clutching me to him. My ass is firmly seated against his groin, and I know, if I move just a little bit, there will be nothing between us but my robe and his boxers.

Desperation clouds my senses. The need to be touched, to be wanted, courses through me like my own blood in my veins to the point I can't catch my breath.

Wetness pools between my thighs, warm and damning.

I want him.

I need him.

He can sense my arousal. I know he can. He's a wolf, after all.

"Sarah," he rasps, dipping his head to brush my name into my hair.

My traitorous body melts into his voice and his touch as he tightens his grip on me, his hand roping around my throat to hold me still.

He nudges the collar of the robe away and grazes his teeth down the side of my neck, drawing out a moan from my lips.

But then he stops, panting a breath, and I go still as stone.

"I'm sorry," I whisper into the darkness.

"Don't say that to me," he replies, but I know he's thinking what I'm thinking. I can feel his heart thundering, sending a sharp vibration into my spine.

We're on a precipice right now, and we both know it. I want this. He wants this. But that voice in my head—that *rational* voice in my head—reminds me why I can't.

Why I *shouldn't* be here, with him, in the first place.

He's thinking of the pact he made with himself, the promise that destined him to a life alone.

It's unfair, really, this hand we've been dealt.

I slowly, timidly, roll over to face him.

Nose to nose in the pitch black, I'm thankful I can't see his face because, for a moment, I can just imagine that this is a dream, and I'm not actually allowing him to stake claim to a piece of my heart.

His hand fumbles for me, finding my cheek. I lay my hand over his, and we lie there in silence, nothing but the beating of our hearts and the roaring wind to fill the air between us.

But I feel him edge closer, shifting an inch or so, and then stop.

"Can I kiss you?" he asks. It's light, innocent. A simple yes or no question with ramifications that could undo both of us in a matter of seconds.

It's all we can have, I realize with heartbreaking clarity. A meaningless act to break apart some of the loneliness we both suffer from.

"Yes," I breathe, and his lips brush mine so tenderly tears prick along my lashes.

He pulls me closer, deepening the kiss, grazing his tongue along my lower lip until I open for him.

He tastes like mint mingled with everything delicious and off-limits, and the kiss awakens something long buried in my soul that I struggle to banish.

Neither of us want to stop, but we have to.

And maybe it's for the best.

I've never been able to have anything for myself before Blake.

Why would that change now?

1 7

——

UNWRITTEN

Sᴀʀᴀʜ

Wᴏʀɴ, weathered hands cup mine in the warmth of a room covered in faded wallpaper. Toys are scattered across a woven carpet of muted greens and yellows, and small voices lift in glee and mischief, blurred and faceless.

The hands around mine are so large compared to my small, child-sized hands. Warm and rough, tender and caring, they curl around my fingers in a mother's touch.

"I know you're young," the woman says, her face a fuzzy, fractured memory, "but you've lived through more than anyone should have to experience in one lifetime."

Rain slams against the windows beside us. The landscape is a tangle of fog and storm clouds with nothing but a turbulent sea beyond.

"Look at me," she whispers softly, gently, her voice so full of love but also pain. Her hands shake as she strokes my fingers. "You know what must be done. I will help you, but you can never go back. Everyone must forget you."

I nod, my mind made up. What else can I do?

The weathered hands fade away, blending into the dreary gray of the storm, and then nothing but unending darkness.

A faint beep pulls me from the dream, and the mattress beneath me shifts.

I blink as the room around me comes into view. White walls. Modern flourishes.

Sydney gets out of bed, sitting on the edge as he answers his phone.

"When?"

I sit up, rubbing sleep from my eyes. When did we fall asleep? My robe is undone, bunched up, and I'm warm all the way to my core.

"I'm on my way."

I look at him, at the back of his head, at his sleep ruffled hair, and reach up to touch my lips.

We kissed last night, nothing else. I remember falling asleep wrapped in his touch.

He doesn't look at me as he rises, grabbing his now-dry clothes from last night. He holds his phone to his ear again, making another call as he walks around the room, gathering his things.

When he finally sees me, noticing that I'm awake, he pauses his conversation.

"One of my warriors is coming to pick you up. He'll bring you a change of clothes, too."

I nod, but Sydney rushes into the bathroom where I hear water running over his voice as he talks to whoever's on the other line.

I get out of bed, tighten the robe around my waist, and walk to the window. It's a clear day, the storm passed, and the entire landscape is blanketed in fresh snow. It's bitter cold, however. I can see the steam lifting from the city in the distance. We're in some pack territory on the edge of Crescent City, and the castle gleams across the ice covered lake at the very edge of my vision.

"I'll call Alpha Pembroke's heir in a few minutes, and we'll sort it out."

I turn back to Sydney as he exits the bathroom, hair brushed back away from his face and now wearing his dress shirt and pants from last night.

"Is something wrong?" I ask.

He slides his phone in his back pocket, looking tired and somewhat stressed. He hesitates before meeting my eyes and replying, "I want to reiterate that you're safe."

"Uhm," I murmur nervously, noticing the unease in his eyes. "Sydney?"

"There was an attack late last night at a club downtown near the lakefront."

My lips part in a gasp. Fights and skirmishes between packs are uncommon, though they do happen. But an attack is totally different, especially one that brings rival Alpha's together.

Based on the look on his face, that's exactly what's going on.

"Rebels?"

"I don't know," he admits. "We thought the rebel threat was long gone–"

"Gabriel," I cut in, my voice going flat, dark, and serious.

He holds my gaze, running his tongue along his lower lip.

"I don't know, Sarah. I'm going to find out. You're going to go back to my manor and stay there until further notice. My father just issued a warning to all packs in his kingdom to close their gates and keep their people inside while we investigate."

This is serious. This hasn't happened since this summer, when the entire kingdom shut down while the Alphas and their warriors hunted the rebels.

Sydney edges toward me, closing the distance between us in three steps.

He leans down and presses an achingly tender kiss to the top of my head, and something snaps in my chest, something heavy.

"You're safe. Blake is safe. My warrior will be here in twenty minutes."

"Your truck?"

He straightens, shrugging. "I won't need it today."

Because he's going to shift and go hunting. My chest tightens at the thought of him getting hurt in any way.

He looks like he wants to say something else, like he wants to reach out and touch me, maybe kiss me again.

I want him to, which is so incredibly selfish.

But he turns and leaves, and I'm alone.

COSETTE SITS across from me in her personal sitting room. Porcelain cats cover a tall shelf in one corner. I've been taking stock of them, noticing the tiny details. I've never seen a cat in real life. Pets are rare, given that we're animals ourselves, deep down.

But Cosette apparently likes them very much, judging by her collection. Counting how many have polka dots versus stripes, or how many are wearing silly hats, is a great distraction from the roiling desperation clouding my senses.

I'm on my third cup of shockingly sweet tea before either of us says a word. The grandfather clock chimes 8:00 PM, and we look at each other.

"He's fine," she tells me—and herself—pouring us another cup of tea.

"I'm sure," I reply, finding it hard to swallow.

"Dahlia, poor thing, is stuck in Windsong for another night, I fear." She stirs her tea with vigor that's totally unnecessary.

Blake yawns in my arms, going slack with sleep.

I tap my foot to the rhythm of the clock.

"I don't think you should move to the cottage. Not right away."

"I agree," I say, nodding.

We stare at each other, our shared stress choking the room. Cosette and I spent two hours pacing the den on the third floor, where a large TV blared the news about the attack. It wasn't just a drunken fight. Several people died when a bomb went off, and three buildings burned down in a matter of hours. An Alpha is dead, too.

The NZ is now being combed for rebels. People there are being forced from their homes and into other pack territories, effectively shutting down the area.

And all day, Sydney has been gone, doing Goddess knows what.

Now we're waiting on pins and needles for his return.

"I could put him to bed, if you'd like."

"It's all right." *Don't leave me here alone.*

It's an unspoken agreement between us right now. She won't leave my side, and I'm sure as hell not leaving hers. We're probably as safe as we can be here in Shadowcrest, tucked away in the Alpha's manor, but still….

Until there's a reason for the explosion, whether it was deliberate violence or something innocent, like a gas leak, we watch every shadow and listen to every noise in the house.

But when the clock strikes midnight, I can't wait any longer. My eyes are heavy, and Blake is too used to sleeping in his crib to get comfortable in either of our arms. Cosette and I reluctantly part ways.

But I lie on the floor in Blake's room, watching the shadows play over the ceiling.

Hours pass. Blake remains asleep, ignorant to the sudden danger in the air.

But I'm aware of it. Grossly aware. I feel it in my bones as a noise nearby catches my attention, and I spring into action.

I grab a lamp off a table, heavy and solid, and yank the cord free of the wall before edging into the darkened hallway.

I'm being insane. This feeling in my chest, this knot, is driving me to act like I am in immediate danger.

I refuse to admit that I've been thinking about Sydney all day long. I've been thinking about his face this morning, when he'd kissed the top of my head and left the hotel. He'd been so withdrawn and tired. Just exhausted. Sick of this game he's forced to play with the rebels who just won't quit.

And I, selfishly, wished he were here with me instead.

I tighten my grip on the lamp like an idiot. This won't save me when the rebels lunge out darkness like something out of my nightmares.

A shadow nears in the dark, heavy footsteps coming in my direction as I flatten myself against the wall and hold my breath.

The shadow reaches for Blake's door, and I swing the lamp, meeting flesh.

Sydney grabs me, pinning me to the wall, breathing rapidly.

He grabs the lamp when I drop it, preventing it from hitting the floor.

My heart beats out of my chest, and his breath comes rapidly as he holds me there, his arm pinned against my chest.

But then he whirls me around and shoves me into my room, closing the door behind him.

He locks it, and the sound of the lock clicking in place sets my blood roiling through my veins.

I don't think. My brain shuts down entirely, and then I'm leaping into his arms and kissing him.

He growls low in his throat in satisfaction as he carries me to the bed. He smells so good. Like perspiration and musk, a more heightened fragrance brought on by being in his wolf form all day, I'm sure. It makes me absolutely feral with desire that I can't shake.

I'm out of control. He's out of control. We're doomed.

Might as well accept it now.

He throws us on the bed, covering me with his body. There's nothing gentle about this whatsoever. He rips my shirt apart in his haste to get it off. My bra is pulled from my body, leaving scraps on my skin where the fabric was yanked free. He presses himself between my legs, and I lock them around his waist as he buries his head between my breasts.

My fingers glide up the back of his neck, tangling in his hair, and I unleash my inhibitions and moan his name like we're the only people in this house, in the entire fucking world, and he's mine.

Right now, I'm his. This moment is brought on by fear, lust, and desperation for touch.

18

EYES WIDE OPEN

SYDNEY'S HAND slides down my side, gripping my ass, tugging me closer to him. My leggings feel impossibly tight and unnecessary right now. I'm desperate to get out of them, and I wiggle my hips for emphasis, which causes Sydney to groan my name and hiss out a breath.

"Get them off," I beg.

He lifts his head, his eyes gleaming with heat and mischief in the soft lamplight coming from my bedside table. His eyes give me pause, a single second to rethink what we're doing. Eyes like a storm brewing over the ocean when the normally crystal blue water turns dark and turbulent.

Eyes that have seen so much beauty in the world and right now, they're full of want for *me*.

No one else has ever wanted me before.

I don't know how to feel.

All I know is that Sydney is kissing lower and lower and every nerve in my body erupts at his touch. I arch against his lips as he kisses past my navel, and then his teeth catch the waistband of my leggings.

He looks up at me with those eyes that are my undoing, but I have a sliver of sense left.

"Don't you dare," I hiss, noticing his sharpened canines. Feral bastard. "These are my favorite leggings."

"I'll buy you new ones," he murmurs, a low rasping tone that sends shivers of heat licking down my spine and settling in my core.

He rises on his knees, hooking his thumbs under the waistbands and pulls my leggings and panties down so swiftly I suck in a breath at the sudden chill of being wholly, utterly, exposed to him.

I close my eyes. I'm sure he's done now. He'll probably get off the bed, laugh, and go find some pretty high-bred lady somewhere who doesn't have stretch marks.

But his hands roam over the swell of my hips, and up to my full breasts, like he's memorizing every inch of my body.

The bed shifts as he climbs over me. I hear his belt hit the floor, and then the sound of fabric follows. His bare thighs graze mine as he settles between my legs again.

But I keep my eyes closed, barely breathing.

I'm afraid that if I open them, he'll be gone, and this will have been a dream. Maybe it's better that way. It'll hurt less in the end.

But I open my eyes, and he's still here, looking down at me, his brow pinched in concern.

"What are we doing, Sydney?" I whisper.

"I don't know," he replies. "We shouldn't, should we?"

"No." The word is barely audible, whisked away by a phantom wind.

But we reach for each other anyway, his lips crashing into mine.

～

Sydney

. . .

FOR REASONS I can't explain, kissing Sarah has me going back in time, back to that night at the club.

Music thunders around us. I've lost Ryan ages ago, and I have no idea where Kenna is. I really don't care, though. For the first time in years–years of training, of school, of shadowing my father in preparation to inherit his throne one day–the only thing I care about is right in front of me.

She's dancing, her face lifted toward the flashing lights in the heavily decorated and exceedingly crowded temple. She's wearing a bright pink dress that hugs her ample curves, and I'm dizzy with a kind of desire I've never felt before.

"Why aren't you dancing?" she laughs, reaching for me. Her hand is slender, but not totally soft, like she's some kind of artist who uses her hands often.

She intertwines her fingers with mine, leading me closer, and I take her in my arms as we sway to the music. I've had a few drinks. We had a drink together. We've talked for what feels like hours about everything that comes to mind.

I don't generally talk with people I don't know, but with her? It's natural. Easy. A dream, if I'm being honest.

When I lead her out of the ball into the warm summer night air, she follows willingly, excitedly. When she continually trips over the hem of her dress, I pull her to a stop against a storefront, kneeling to rip the fabric so it rides above her ankles. She leans down to take off her heels, and somewhere in the middle, we meet, looking into each other's eyes.

I wish I could remember those eyes, that face, that voice that I feel should be burned into my memory.

But it's not. Only pieces remain, torn and fragmented beyond repair.

But I remember picking her up and carrying her into Ryan's house through the sliding glass door off the back patio because the front door was locked. I remember her wrapping her arms around my waist when I pinned her to the wall in the snug hallway off the kitchen and kissed her for the first time.

I remember the sheets beneath me as I lay down, and she straddled me. The way her hair brushed over my chest when she leaned down to kiss me again, moaning my name.

All of that is just a dream now. Part of me wonders if it ever even happened or if this woman from my dreams was just a gift from the Goddess, giving me a glimpse of what was to come.

Because this woman beneath me is real. She's flesh and blood. She's hot to the touch and supple in my hands. The way she kisses me sends fire through my veins, igniting something I feel like I've lost over the past months.

"Sarah," I say, my hand trailing up her neck to cup the back of her head.

She opens her eyes to slits, her full lips parted in that way that makes me dizzy with need.

She wraps her arms around my neck and pulls me in, kissing me deeply, nibbling on my lower lip until that last centimeter of restraint I have left slips.

I came home tonight after a day full of ash and chaos. A day that reminded me why I'd vowed to myself never to find my mate, to have *this*.

But I had to see her. I had to make sure she was still here. Maybe I needed to prove to myself that I could be this for her–the protector. The Alpha. Even after what happened between us last night.

Seeing her in the hallway made those feelings obsolete. I don't give a fuck anymore. If our world is going to hell in a hand basket, I want to experience this with her, even if it's just this one time.

The only thought in my mind is how she'll feel with my cock inside of her and my teeth clamped down on her pretty little neck.

My wolf is begging to be unleashed, and she's egging it on but biting down on my lower lip while grinding her hips against mine, making those little mewling sounds that turn my blood molten.

I nudge her left knee up with my thigh and press my cock inside of her without ceremony. She's soaking wet, and her walls grip me so tightly it steals the breath from my lungs.

Sarah arches off the bed, crying out, her eyes shut, and her lips parted in ecstasy and surprise.

"Fuck," I breathe, pulling out slowly, savoring the feel of her. She's so hot. She fits around me so well. She can take all of me, and does so, arching her perfect hips to the rhythm of my thrusts.

I drag her to the center of the bed and enter her again, hard, my lips crushing her in a heated kiss that's just as feral as the way I'm fucking her.

My mind is totally empty. She is the only thing I can see and hear. The only thing I feel is the way her nails dig into my back and how her pussy grips me so tight I might be on the verge of coming already, but I'm not going over that edge without her.

I rise up, slamming into her repeatedly while reaching between her legs to circle my thumb over her clit.

She's so beautiful right now. Her skin is flushed a soft pink that shines in the lamplight. Her hair fans out around her head like a halo, and those eyes....

They're the brightest violet I've ever seen as she opens them, her lips parting in a silent cry as her muscles tense around my cock.

"You're so close," I rasp, slowing the pace, swirling my hips against her in deliberate, calculated thrusts that make her tremble as she slides her hands down my chest and stomach.

"Sydney," she whimpers, sudden tears in her eyes.

Something heavy snaps in my chest—warm and unnerving, like something is being sewn directly into my heart as each second passes while I'm buried deep inside of her.

I would die for this woman.

The thought hits me directly in the chest at the same moment she arches her back, crying out my name to the ceiling.

Her legs tense, then begin to shake, and then she's spasming around my cock and so impossibly tight I can't possibly hold back any longer.

I crush her to my chest as I come unglued, whispering filthy things in her ear that I hadn't realized were part of my vocabulary.

I'm not thinking straight when I come inside of her. I roll with her so we're lying side by side, both of us short of breath and glazed with sweat as we stare at the ceiling.

It was over too quickly. That's the first thing that comes to mind.

The second thing that comes to mind is, *What have I done?*

But she curls into me, laying her head in the crook of my shoulder. Her eyelashes flutter against my skin, and within moments, she's fast asleep with a death grip on my arm, preventing me from moving.

So I lie there with Sarah in my arms, wondering what to do next. What to say and where to go from here.

Memories of this morning flood back, like waking up next to her in the hotel and thinking I could get used to this. Memories of that first phone call from my dad about the attack and how I'd been jolted back to startling reality that crushed any hope that I might have a choice in what kind of life I get to live.

I remember the strewn bodies, the fire, the blood that coated the ground where that club stood only a day ago and think of that cavernous temple in Eastonia, of Kenna's despair as she watched Gabriel slit Evander's throat.

The distant whine of a baby brings me out of a half slumber.

I untangle myself from Sarah, but she stirs at the sound of Blake's soft cries coming from the baby monitor next to her bed.

"Go back to sleep. I'll settle him," I whisper, gently pressing her back to the bed and covering her with a blanket. She blinks sleepily at me as I edge off the bed and put on my boxers and pants, her eyes glassy in the lamp we left on.

I want to kiss her again, but I know once I do, it will confirm this growing sensation starting to take root in my chest.

I am at serious risk of falling in love with her.

Then what?

I tear myself from the room and slip into the comfortable darkness of the sitting room, Blake's room, shutting the door behind me.

His whimpering tapers off as I pick him up and change his diaper, but he's mouthing my chest, rooting with vigor.

I don't want to disturb Sarah. I peek into her room, and she's fast asleep again, curled around one of the pillows in the exact spot I left her, so I take him downstairs.

In the muted light of the kitchen, I warm up his milk and sit in one of the chairs with him in my arms. He immediately settles, his eyes heavy and cheeks round and rosy.

"I have to go away for a while," I tell him, swallowing the lump in my throat brought on by guilt for a multitude of reasons. "To Moorn, for a meeting with my father and my uncle."

Blake has no idea what I'm talking about, but he stops drinking and looks up at me, his eyes wide, as if he just realized I'm not his mother.

In the light, I can finally see his eye color.

Eyes that I see every time I look in the mirror look back at me.

My eyes.

He got those eyes from *me*.

I tighten my grip on him as a memory flashes through my mind, something lost and dragged forward from the recess of my mind in full, startling color.

Sarah leans down and brushes a kiss over my lips, morning sunlight drifting through the window in the guest room at Ryan's house.

"I'm so sorry," she whispers, her fingertips tracing my cheekbone.

And then it goes black.

19

THIRD TIME'S NOT THE CHARM

I wake to something squirming next to me then sharp fingernails poking at my breasts before Blake latches like the champion he is. I open my eyes, startled to find him next to me, and look down at my son, who's wearing a fresh onesie in sage green and a new diaper, from what I can tell.

I turn my head to look at the clock on my bedside table. It's 7:00 AM.

And there's a piece of printer paper next to the clock with neat scrawl I don't recognize. I flex my fingers, catching the edge of the paper, and drag it toward me while Blake makes soft, blissful cooing sounds as he nurses.

That's when I realize I'm totally naked, and the flavors, textures, and feelings from last night come hurtling back as I clutch the paper and read the text.

I'll be back in two days.

Sydney.

I set the paper down and look up at the ceiling.

What have we done?

My heart starts to race out of rhythm, but Blake pops free of my breast and starts smacking me with his little hand.

I make a silly face at him, letting him ground me, and feel tears prick along my lashes when he gives me a huge, sleepy smile. His first smile.

Soft morning sunlight drifts through the curtains while I play with him, letting him wrap his tiny hands around my fingers and mimicking his coos. It's warmer than usual today. The bitter bite of winter finally let up and allowed some hint of warmth to brush through the air.

The season will change soon. The snow will start to melt. Grass will grow, and flowers will bloom and life will move on.

But how?

How am I supposed to carry on, knowing what I know now?

My heart is heavy as I leave Blake in the center of the bed to kick his little feet against my pillow. I quickly dress, pulling on panties and a matching bra, a pair of black yoga pants, a heather gray crewneck with little embroidered tulips on it, and a pair of fuzzy socks. I watch him from the doorway to the bathroom while I brush my teeth and braid my hair, and then I scoop him up, nuzzling him while making little clicking noises with my tongue that make him beam up at me.

He's so animated lately. He's shedding that newborn slump that makes him more like a baby doll than something real.

Blake squawks as I reach the kitchen, lifting his head from my shoulder and looking around.

The person he wants swoops in on him, excitedly telling us both good morning. But Cosette isn't the only person in the room.

I'm frozen solid as she gracefully takes Blake from my arms and turns with him, mentioning something about, "Making Mommy her morning cup of tea."

I curtsy, my heart hammering.

"Good morning, darling," Queen Madeline says as she approaches me, her voice as sweet as honey. "I wasn't sure I'd see you. It's so early."

"Her Highness likes my special blend of tea, too," Cosette says with a grin as she balances Blake on her shoulder and pours three cups of tea from a kettle with the other.

The queen grins. Goddess, she's gorgeous.

"I'm so sorry, again, for dropping in like this," she says as she walks toward the kitchen table. She's wearing tailored trousers and a soft blue sweater, her hair swept back in a bun at the nape of her neck. Her blue eyes meet mine again, soft and welcoming. "It's rather quiet at the castle, and I never sleep well when Isaac's away."

Isaac, the Alpha King. It's so hard to think of that man as someone's mate and husband, someone's father. He has a reputation for being stern and hard, but the love in the queen's eyes as she says his name reminds me that he's just a man, a man capable of loving someone deeply, like his wife.

"It's always a pleasure to have you here, Maddy," Cosette says softly as she loads the tea service on a tray to bring to the table.

I turn to help her, but she shakes her head, motioning for me to go sit down.

I take Blake from her shoulder instead, noticing the odd look on Cosette's face as she scans me from head to toe, then smiles smugly.

She can't know, can she? That Sydney and I....

"So," the queen says, smiling over the rim of her teacup. "This is your son, then?"

I nod and sit Blake in my lap so he's facing the table. He looks around, wide eyed, toying with the lace tablecloth. Cosette sits between me and the queen. She keeps looking at me, and my cheeks are starting to burn.

"Cosette, do you remember when Hannah had her first baby?"

Cosette chuckles and nods, "How could I forget? Poor Hannah. She was in pieces over how bald Juniper was when she was born."

"And now look at her." The queen smiles, shaking her head. "She looks so much like Cassian with that copper, curly hair. She's so beautiful. She's graduating from Wellington this spring, you know. She wants to be a teacher."

"Since she was a child," Cosette remarks, nodding. "She'll be fantastic."

I watch the two women converse like old friends and start to forget that I'm sitting across from the queen of this kingdom.

But I haven't touched my tea, and Blake is now gnawing on the edge of the table.

The queen watches me, watches him, with a wistful smile on her face. "May I hold him? So you can drink your tea, at least."

My heart nearly stops.

Cosette looks at me expectantly, and I gracefully pass the baby to her, who passes him to Her Highness.

"He's squirmy, Your Majesty. And likes to chew–"

"Oh, please, call me Maddy. Everyone else does."

Maddy.

I watch her as she smiles down at Blake with so much tenderness in her eyes.

She runs her fingers through his dark brown hair, which is starting to thicken up instead of fall out completely, like Cosette warned me might happen sooner rather than later.

"Oh, he reminds me so much of Sydney and Ryan when they were this age." She chuckles softly. "Well, Syd at least. Ryan was the size of a three-month-old within the first two weeks of his life."

I can believe that. Ryan is absolutely massive.

Blake starts to nod off, his eyes growing heavy as he coos with pleasure at her practiced touch, and then promptly slumps to sleep in her arms.

Maddy's eyes meet mine. "He's beautiful, Sarah."

"Thank you… Maddy."

She grins at me, pleased that I used her first name. A nickname, too. Informal and intimate, like I've somehow been allowed into the sacred circle of their family.

We drink our tea in comfortable silence for a few minutes before Maddy says, "Isaac and Sydney are in Moorn."

Cosette sighs, rising to get the kettle off the stovetop. "He didn't even mention this trip to me."

"They left several hours ago," Maddy confirms with a sad nod. "I don't know when they mean to return, but I couldn't take being in that big house by myself. I figured I'd come here and see how everyone was doing."

"Dalia should be home later tonight," Cosette says as she pours more tea.

"I'll miss her, then." Maddy looks down at Blake, her eyes slightly glassy.

Cosette's gaze slides to me again, skeptical, as she sets the kettle down and wipes her hands on her apron. "I have some laundry to finish this morning; you'll have to excuse me."

"I'll catch up with you later, Cosette. Thank you for the tea."

She gives us both a bob of her head in farewell, and suddenly, I'm alone with the queen of Crescent Falls.

Maddy looks toward the windows as she drinks her tea. I sip mine, feeling awkward and slightly uncomfortable. I don't know what to say to her. I don't know how to act or feel.

But she turns to me with a slight smile that brightens her eyes as she says, "I wanted to talk to you alone, which is really why I'm here."

I swallow hard, wondering if I'm in trouble for something. If the flowers really weren't good enough, or–

"I worry about Sydney," she admits, raising Blake to her shoulder and patting his back. "I was afraid I'd never see him smile again after returning from Eastonia this fall but then… you happened."

A weight like a thousand dumbbells settles on my shoulders.

"He told me what happened to you. What you were going through, alone, pregnant, and I… I understand what you must be feeling right now, stuck in this house with this Alpha you barely know. But Sydney is a good man."

"I know," I reply, my mouth going dry. "He really is."

"Yes. I like to think I had a hand in his being like he is, but he's been like this since he was born. Kind, brave, reasonable. Wise beyond his years but he… he tends to shelter himself and draw away from others. When I heard you were staying here with him, I felt like I could breathe again. When I saw how he smiled at you at my party

I… well, Sarah, whatever you've done to my son, I'm grateful. Forever grateful. Sydney has never had an easy time making friends."

She doesn't know the half of it. I nod, doing my best to smile.

I don't deserve this praise, but it settles in my chest, which blooms with warmth.

"My In-Laws are visiting next month when they bring my daughter home. Normally the entire family spends a month in Maatua every year for the Solstice. This was the first winter it hasn't happened since we got married and I wanted to try to bring everyone together here, at least for dinner. Ella and Ryatt have confirmed that they'll come, and I was hoping, if it's not too much trouble, that you'd put together some centerpieces for the dinner."

"Of course, I will."

"I'd love for you to have dinner, too. If you'd like?"

When I don't answer right away, she continues, "I know it's a lot. This family… These royals. Trust me, I was like you once. Maybe I'm still like you." She smiles softly. "I just want you to know that Sydney wouldn't have brought you here had he not meant to keep you in his life somehow, and to me, that means the world. He cares for you, even if he can't say it. Even if he tells him he can't–"

"Why are you telling me this?" The words slip out before I can stop them.

She gently strokes Blake's back, her eyes darkening a shade. "I'm sorry. I've overstepped."

We stare at each other for a moment, and I come to a glaring realization.

I smell like Sydney. I haven't showered since we were together last night. Is that what she's picking up on, or does she know something I don't?

Something I can't know. Not yet.

"I don't know what's gotten into me," she says hastily, her cheeks going crimson, which makes me feel worse than I already do. "Please, do come to our family dinner. You're invited. I'd love to have you there, you and Blake, of course. Sydney is being forced to come."

I nod as she stands abruptly, her blush now creeping down her neck. I rise with her, and she carefully passes Blake to me so he doesn't wake up, but her eyes linger on his face for a moment too long.

Her eyes meet mine.

"You're welcome here, Sarah. Don't let anyone tell you otherwise."

I want to cry. I want to snap and tell her everything, but I can't. I close my eyes as she caresses my cheek, and then she's gone, her light footsteps fading as she turns the corner into the dining room and into the recesses of the house.

I swallow a sob and sink back into my chair. My tea grows tepid as minutes pass.

Eventually, I go upstairs with Blake and tuck him into bed where he sprawls out like a starfish, his tiny hands curled into fists.

I step away from his crib and look down at him. He looks different than he used to. No longer a newborn, his features are beginning to show.

And I'm doomed.

I have little options now. I knew my time with him would be limited, but this is… this is the best place for him. He'd be surrounded by people who love him.

But my mind goes to Sydney, tracing the lines of his face while we fell asleep in each other's arms not once, but twice. Three times, if I'm being totally honest, which I haven't been for a long, long time.

Fate is a cruel bitch, isn't she?

20

CONFRONTATION

Sydney

Snow covers the normally golden plains on the outskirts of Moorn, a small territory far outside of the city center. It took a full day to reach this place, this hovel between two hills where the distant border of Eastonia looms.

I don't want to be here. The distance between Sarah and the damning truth between us is excruciating, damn near tearing me apart.

But I'm still an Alpha. Still a royal. And there are some things I just have to do.

The wind rushes through my fur as I wait beside my father, who's also in his wolf form. We're both large and dark brown with glints of gold throughout.

Night has fallen. I know we're both exhausted. We traveled on foot without stopping for a break. Maybe he needed to run in his wolf as much as I did.

But still, tension makes my muscles lock. My mind is in shambles, and my heart is....

I'm devastated. I don't know what else to say.

Four wolves approach in the darkness, one of them taking up the rear of the group. My uncle Ryatt is hard to spot this time of night. Pitch black, his eyes are his only marker. Silver eyes meet mine in the dark.

Commander Artyom is with them. His silver wolf gleams in the moonlight. Beside Artyom are two golden wolves, father and son.

Granger and Evander.

I lock eyes with Evander, who lowers his head in greeting.

But my dad turns and takes off back up the hill we've just come down, and I'm forced to follow.

We run as a group for over two miles in the endless dark. The moon is full overhead, and the stars are on full display.

But it's frigid. Too cold, even in our full coats, to remain outside for this meeting that could go on until the early hours of the morning.

We reach a small village where Dad has connections and step into an inn where we're the only patrons.

Everyone else has been moved out, and the sign on the door reads no vacancy.

Twenty minutes later, I come down from my room fully dressed and in my human form.

My dad and Uncle Ryatt are talking in low tones with commander Artyom at the bar. Even the bartender has been dismissed, but Ryatt pours himself a glass of whiskey regardless.

Evander sits alone at a table nearby, his golden hair a bright contrast to the dark wood features all around him. A fire burns in a large stone hearth behind him, casting the room in shadows and warmth.

I sit down across from him with a sigh. It's the first time I've been able to stop, to sit, in over twenty-four hours.

He pours me a shot of whiskey from his flask, and I greedily accept.

It burns down my throat, numbing the ache in my heart.

It's not enough, though. My mind drifts back to Sarah.

"Long day?" Evander asks.

I eye him for a moment. He looks like he would rather be anywhere else. I don't blame him.

"Not as long as yours, I assume."

"I don't like having to jump," he says, leaning back in his chair and closing his eyes for a moment. "It's like being a boat for long periods of time. I get rather sick to my stomach."

He slides the flask across the table. I take it, drinking straight from the source. The whiskey is young and bitter, but it will do. "How is Kenna?"

"She's fine," he replies with a shrug. "Pregnancy suits her. I'm sure she'll want another five or more after this."

My mouth ticks into a smile before I can stop myself. Kenna isn't due for another month, at least.

Thinking of Kenna pregnant has my mind reeling back to the moment I met Sarah for the first time–in her shop, when she turned to me and I noticed the swell of her stomach.

But that wasn't the first time I met her, was it?

Guilt floods my system. I take another shot, trying to drown it out.

"What's up with you?" Evander asks in a low tone, taking the flask back and sliding it into his jacket pocket.

I glance over my shoulder at the men at the bar. "Nothing I want to discuss right now."

Dad and Ryatt start walking over before Evander can pry further. I watch commander Artyom disappear through the door leading outside, closing it tight behind him. They've come to some agreement, I realize.

Which means now they want to know about my investigation into Sasha's whereabouts.

Dad sits down across from me, but Ryatt stays standing, both of them looking grave.

"You're sure, Sydney?" Ryatt asks.

I look up at him, at his eyes like liquid silver. Power radiates off him. Even in his human form, he's formidable.

But he's still my uncle.

"Do you doubt me?"

"Sydney," Dad warns, his eyes heavy with exhaustion.

"Sasha is dead. I saw her grave myself," I say with conviction, but I can tell it's not enough.

This meeting was planned shortly after I brought the news to my dad, only hours after the attack in Crescent City. I have no idea what they mean to do with the information I provided.

But I assume that's why I'm here, in the middle of nowhere, for an off-the-books meeting between the allied kings.

"We need to be sure," Ryatt says, crossing his arms over his chest as he leans his thigh against the table across from ours.

"I agree," Dad replies. "Once it's confirmed she's truly dead, we can reopen the borders between our kingdoms. Gabriel will believe we gave up our search for him."

Evander and I exchange looks, but he doesn't speak.

He's thinking what I'm thinking though. I have no doubt about it.

Dread and disgust cloud my senses.

"You're not going to dig up that grave," I say. "We're talking about a child here–"

"If she's still alive, she isn't a child anymore," Ryatt replies hotly. "We can't trust a name etched by hand on a piece of stone–"

"And if there are bones in that dirt," I snap, "what will you do? Have your traitorous mystics pray over them, asking the heavens to tell them who they belong to?"

"That's enough," Dads hisses in warning, but I'm in no mood.

I stand, facing my uncle. Facing the most powerful man in our known universe. "I will not allow it."

"It's not up to you," Dad says as he rises. Only Evander remains seated.

Granger appears out of nowhere, like he was lingering in a shadow. "They're right, Sydney."

"I don't need you to be my voice of reason, Granger." I point at Evander. "None of us wanted to even look for her. You all made it sound like you were doing this to protect her from Gabriel, but you're looking for a way to bait him, aren't you? This was never about protecting a young girl–a young woman–from a madman who intended to torture her for her powers. This was about holding her as a prisoner and letting her take the fall for his crimes because we failed to find him. I'm done."

"That isn't what's happening," Ryatt cuts in sharply, his eyes glowing with power. "If this woman has the power to charge a relic from the time before the veil dropped, then she needs to be found and contained until it's deemed safe. Until she can prove she's not working with him. Do you understand?"

"If you go near that grave," I growl, losing focus, "Ella will find herself ruling alone."

Ryatt's snarl makes the entire building tremble. Dad grabs me by the arm and drags me away from the table, through the door, and into the open night air. He throws me into the snow.

"What the hell is wrong with you, Sydney?"

I leap to my feet. "You can't be serious."

"I'm dead serious," he says in a low, level tone laced with anger. "I don't think you understand how precarious this situation is."

"You have no idea. You weren't in that cave with him—"

"But you were. You know who he is. You know Gabriel better than any of us do, Sydney, and you and Evander are the only ones who understand what he's capable of. We need to know where he is, what kind of relic he's using, and where to find it. We needed Sasha for that. We still do, especially now that Crescent Falls was recently attacked!"

"We don't even know for sure if he was the person behind the attack in Crescent City!"

"Ask yourself who else it would be!"

"You're wrong for this. Sasha is dead and was buried. She was just a child and had nothing to do with her cousin's crimes. Gabriel is acting alone."

"And you may be right, but that doesn't negate the fact that Gabriel is still out there, still capable—"

"I've had enough," I say, my voice cracking over the words.

Dad and I stand in silence for several seconds. His expression softens. "What's wrong?"

"Nothing." I swallow past the lump in my throat.

"Six months ago, you were ready to go through hell to bring Gabriel to justice. We gave a you a choice–"

"I know," I cut in, meeting his eyes. "That hasn't changed."

"Then *what* changed?"

"There're innocent people between us and Gabriel. I can't–I won't–dig up a child's grave to confirm she's dead. I have to draw a line somewhere."

Dad turns from me for a moment, edging toward the door. A sharp, cold wind bites into my exposed skin, turning my cheeks red and numb.

But he says, "Being in power like this changes you, Syd. Things would be different for Ryatt and me if we were just looking out for our families, but we have kingdoms to keep safe. Hundreds of thousands of subjects to protect. We cannot afford a full-fledged war again, not after the destruction Kane caused twenty years ago. If we're dealing with another Kane, another man with stolen power, we need to end this before it begins. If you believe Sasha is dead… if you feel it in your bones that she died as a child and is buried on that island, then I will believe you, and I will make Ryatt believe you. But if there's any doubt in your mind–"

"She is dead. Gabriel needed her. He needed her for the relic, and I believe without her he's powerless. There will be no war, Dad."

I shift, my clothes shredding and falling away, and take off into the night.

My head spins while I run, and run, and run, chasing the sunrise.

I won't be able to think straight until I know one thing for sure– and remedy it.

Eventually, the plains around me give way to forests and narrow roads, and within a few hours, the forest opens up to a gleaming, slumbering city.

The fact that I threatened to kill my own uncle, whom I love, doesn't register until I've reached my home again, having sprinted all the way back to Shadowcrest over the course of seven hours, a new record, I'm sure.

I'll apologize later.

He'll forgive me.

My family drama falls away when I shift back and dress in the darkened garage. It's early morning, the sun has barely risen, and the house is silent as I walk upstairs.

That meeting should have gone differently. It was a secret meeting to plan the next stage of locating Gabriel, whether Ryatt would open his borders again and act like the threat is officially gone, trying to give Gabriel a false sense that the royal families have moved on and are being less cautious, or if we're about to sound the horn of war, officially, after several months of going back and forth.

But I don't care about any of that anymore. I can't.

Sarah isn't in her room.

I wander the house, passing through the library, and see that my office door is open.

Sarah is standing by the window, still as a statue.

I step inside and close the door, locking it.

"He's my son, isn't he?"

THAT'S NOT MY NAME

SYDNEY

SARAH DOESN'T TURN from the window. The sunrise hasn't reached us yet, not fully, but the first inklings of morning creep through the curtains. Frost hugs the glass panes. It will be another frigid day, colder than the last. The faint light ghosts over her skin, illuminating her face in silver.

"Sarah?" I say into the soft light.

She turns her head slightly but doesn't look at me. I notice two pieces of paper on my desk, one of them folded in half with Blake's name written neatly across it.

My heart falls into my stomach as my gaze slides to the second piece, a letter addressed to me.

The truth hits me like a knife to the heart. There's only one reason she'd write her son a letter.

"You're leaving?"

"It's best for both of you that I'm not here." She turns ever so slightly so her face catches the light. Dried tears stain her skin, but her expression is like ice.

"Is he my son?" I firmly repeat, edging a step toward her.

Her eyes are nearly black, drained of all hints of that lavender I dream of. "Will you take care of him?"

"We're not having that conversation. You are not leaving, Sarah."

"You don't understand–"

"I was drunk that night, the night of the ball at the temple. Severely, unapologetically drunk." I close the distance between the door and my desk, laying my hands flat against its surface. I hold her gaze as guilt sweeps through me. "I couldn't remember your name, Sarah. I looked for you, though. For months–"

"I never told you my name." There's no emotion behind her words. They're flat, maybe slightly sad. But she's confirmed what I needed to know. She is the mystery woman I've been looking for. The same woman I vowed I'd never find, not after what I witnessed in Eastonia this summer.

I straighten up at her tone, and she tilts her chin ever so slightly.

"Is he mine?"

"Yes," she whispers.

"Are you sure?"

"I was a virgin," she says, her voice cracking, and I come undone.

I feel like I need to sit down but can't bring myself to back away from her. The desk is the only thing keeping me from grabbing her and asking what the fuck is going on.

"Why didn't you try to tell me you were pregnant?"

"Sydney, I couldn't have–"

"Why not?" Anger rising, I take a step away from the desk. "I would have made it right!"

"You couldn't have done–"

"I would have *married* you. I would have made you my Luna. Instead, you nearly froze to death–both of you!"

"Sydney, you don't understand–"

"Then make me understand! Why didn't you tell me? Did you know I was the father, or is that something you figured out recently?"

I rack my brain for details of that night but come up empty. The memory of her and I together after the ball is so blurry I still can't tell for certain it was her.

But kissing her, and being inside of her once again, it's clear.

There is not a shadow of doubt in my mind that the woman I've been pining for for months is standing right in front of me now but as out of reach as ever.

"You're the only person I've ever–I've ever been with," she says like she's short of breath. Her eyes glaze with tears, but her icy expression doesn't crack. "And I wasn't drunk that night. I remember everything."

"So you knew who I was, yet, you didn't tell me? That day, in your shop, when I came in… you knew then. You were pregnant, Sarah. Pregnant with my son!"

"You're an Alpha," she whispers, pain lacing each word. "I think you forget that differences between us in that regard–"

"Do you think I give a fuck about rank?" I snarl, my heart threatening to beat out of my chest. "Do you know how long I looked for you? I asked around, Sarah. I went back to the temple hoping they had video footage of us together so I could find you again, and it had nothing to do with the chance that I might have produced a child with you. Do you understand? I was desperate to find you because that night–"

"Don't say it," she pleads, tears in her eyes.

Her expression guts me. I try to step around the desk, but she finally moves. She steps away from me, and the act slices through my chest like a heated blade.

"Don't. You need to stay away from me," she says, her voice trembling.

"I don't understand what's going on," I try to tell her. "Why are you crying? Why are you writing notes–" I pick up the letter addressed to me without reading it, waving it between us. "Did I do something to make you believe you're not wanted here?"

"No."

"Did you believe I'd cast you out in the street when I found out that Blake is mine? He has my eyes, Sarah."

"I know he does." Her voice is so small and broken, it makes my heart skip a beat. "I was hoping he would."

I know I should be angry. I should be furious. She lied. She's been living here, in my home, lying to my face every day.

But something is wrong. I can tell by the look in her eyes that she is… afraid.

"You're not leaving," I say, heaving a breath as I shake my head. "I'm not letting you leave. You can think whatever you want of me. You can hate me, but you're not leaving this house. I am going to take care of you both. Blake is my son, therefore my heir, and you are his mother–"

"You don't understand. I have to go. It's better. Trust me. It's better he stays here, and I leave, and you forget me, okay?"

"Forget you?" I step toward her, shaking my head. "I could never–"

"You were supposed to!" Something breaks in her tone. A single fracture in the wall of ice she's hiding behind. "You were supposed to forget everything that happened between us that night. You were supposed to wake up alone, thinking you'd just stumbled home from the ball. I never–" She squeezes her eyes shut while my mind reels over what she's trying to say.

"Did you drug me?"

"No!" she shouts, more tears sliding free. "Of course not!"

"Then what are you saying? You're upset I remembered you? That I wasn't drunk enough to forget you?"

"I need you to promise me that you'll take care of Blake. Please, Sydney. You're all he has now."

"Sarah, this is ridiculous–"

"Promise me," she says with so much despair it gives me pause.

I look her up and down then settle on her eyes again. "I'm not making that promise because I don't need to. You're staying. That is our son. We can be a family. We *are* a family."

"You didn't want any of this. I know how you feel about finding your mate and having a family and I am so, so sorry that I put you in this position–"

"Is that what this is about? Sarah, you have to understand that–

that I–" I trip over my words, trying to form some kind of rationale behind my decision. "I made that decision to try to keep myself safe, to keep my mate safe, but this changes everything–"

"You were right, though," she says timidly. She backs away again when I try to close the distance between us. She holds her hands out in surrender, and she's holding something in the palm of her hand.

The necklace I found at Sasha's grave.

Time stands still for a split second then crashes all around me.

I meet her gaze.

"You were right, Sydney. It's too dangerous. You can't be with me, and I can't keep Blake. It was selfish to believe that I could have *this*. That I could have this with *you* like fate intended, but I was wrong. That night after the ball was selfish. I had to do what I had to do to keep you safe."

"Sarah–"

"My name isn't *Sarah*."

Her eyes hold mine, unblinking. I watch them change color, going from near black to the bright violet.

And then a pain like no other erupts in my left temple. I grip the desk, crying out as my vision goes black and then explodes with color.

It's like I'm watching a movie, seeing scenes play out from a distance. Sarah at a vanity looking at her reflection as she does her makeup while other women laugh and talk in the background about the ball. She's wearing that pink dress I remember, but her eyes are sad as she puts on mascara. Someone comes up to her, their face blurry, and tells her to smile, that they're leaving soon.

Then she's at the ball, and Ryan taps her on the shoulder. He leans in, introducing himself, saying his brother is too shy to ask her to dance, but he wants to. She sees me, and her heart nearly stops when I turn from the conversation I'm having and meet her gaze. I see that moment in crystal clarity. A memory I was robbed of, but is now so clear I can feel the heat in the ballroom and the way my heart was racing when her eyes met mine.

My face says it all. I think she's stunning. She's perfect. I want her more than I've wanted anything in my life.

Her heart is pounding when I come over and ask if she's enjoying the party.

But then the scene cuts out, and she's sitting in a coffee shop scrolling through her phone. It's raining, and the TV in the corner is playing the news. It's a few days after the attack during that same ball. A man in a blue silk mask flashes on the screen with a reward for sightings or information about him.

Gabriel. I feel Sarah's sudden fear. I feel her panic as she rises from her chair and hurries to her apartment, locking herself inside before sliding to the floor and curling into a ball.

Then her memories flash, turning over like pages in a book. Sarah working in her shop, counting her dwindling funds. Sarah pacing in her apartment, peeking through the blinds. A pregnancy test in her hands as she sinks to the ground, wide eyed and scared.

I watch her from a distance as she speaks with the woman who was meant to adopt Blake. She tells Sarah she can't anymore; she changed her mind, and Sarah is desperate now.

I watch the moment I healed her finger through her own eyes. Her grief is immense when I ask if we've met before, and she tells me no. Watching me leave her shop tears her apart, and she sinks to the floor and cries the very moment I shut the door behind me.

The scene flips to another, and another, and then Sarah is screaming in pain, her face blood red and eyes full of tears as she brings Blake into the world, surrounded by strangers.

She can't even look at him when he's placed in her arms. He was born into danger, and she feels horrible about it. She doesn't know what to do. She has no one to ask for help. No one who knows the truth about her situation, at least.

But then I'm standing in a familiar place. I can feel the warm sea air touching my cheeks.

"You can never go back. You can never talk about your past, or where you came from. Do you understand?"

An old woman crouches beside a girl of ten wearing a pink dress, her icy blonde hair braided down her back. Sarah, as a child, standing with Mrs. Havisfield in front of that gnarled tree on Mononoke Island.

"He has to believe you're dead, child. I know you don't understand. You're a very special girl, but no one can know that."

Mrs. Havisfield finishes carving the name Sasha on the flat rock and stands, wiping her hands on her dress.

"You're Sarah now. Sasha is dead, all right? She is dead, and you are free."

They turn, and Sarah drops the necklace in the grass.

The vision fades slowly, turning dark and fragmented, but Sarah's screams echo through my ears. I feel her pain like it's my own. I hear a cackling, child's laugh. I hear metal gears turning and can taste a whisper of magic in the air, filling my mouth with something metallic.

Sarah is pleading for mercy as a knife slices her open, again and again.

"You are mine, Sasha. Your power was destined for me to use. My slave. My bride. You can never leave me."

Sasha screams again as Gabriel bites down on her arm, sucking her powers dry.

Marking her.

I can't breathe as her memories erupt through my head. Memories of a father's love and desperation as he passes her to a total stranger to help her escape across the border of Eastonia. She knows she'll never see him again. She knows Gabriel will likely kill him for this.

But then I'm somewhere… soft. Ryan's guest room fades into view. Sarah is writhing beneath me, her nails digging into my sides as I fuck her into the mattress slowly, tenderly. This is *my* memory. A memory stolen from me, I realize, as I feel the mate bond click into place.

And she feels it too. She opens her eyes, her lips parted, a single tear rolling down her cheek.

I kiss it away.

My mate.

I found her. We found each other.

And I lie next to her until the early hours of the morning stroking her arm with my fingertips while I fall asleep.

But just as I close my eyes, she moves. She kisses me again, slow and tender, her tears falling onto my face as she whispers, "I am so sorry," again, and again, her fingertips tracing the planes of my face like she's memorizing it.

And then it goes black as her powers erupt, stealing any memory of her from my mind.

Reality crashes back to me. I'm nearly bent over my desk in pain, but I look up at Sarah, who's backed against the bookshelf in my office, her cheeks wet with tears and face twisted in despair.

But I feel the bond between us like it's always been there. Her scent is different. She smells like fresh snow in a silent forest. She's changed, becoming even more beautiful than before. Her features are clearer, if that's possible.

It's like she put up a ward around herself, some kind of magical glamor, so I couldn't sense our mate bond.

"Sarah," I plead, tears streaming down my face.

She shakes her head.

"Please," she cries, her voice breaking. "Take care of him." And in a flash of light, she disappears.

22

TRAIL OF BLOOD

SARAH

IT'S FREEZING. The cold air bites into my skin as I roll downward uncontrollably, my body bouncing off rocks and through pockets of ice.

My mind is in shambles alongside my heart. I don't try to stop falling. I don't have the strength, even if I wanted to.

Ten years of hiding my powers… I didn't know what else to do. I can't control them like I used to. I have no idea where I landed, but I know I'm still close enough to Sydney that I feel his gut-wrenching despair, grief, and fury as I continue to roll downhill.

My head smashes against something hard and cold as I come to a rough, jolting stop, half of my body submerged in icy water.

I look up at the clear blue morning, at the frost hugging the trees overhead.

Death is better. Death means Gabriel is useless. Death means he'll never find me, and Blake will be safe.

Sydney and his family are safe at least as I close my eyes and demand the Goddess take me.

~

Sydney

"Sydney!" Cosette screams from the back patio, carefully stepping through knee deep snow as I stalk back toward the house.

Her face is flushed as I brush past her. She grabs my shirt, trying to yank me to a stop.

"You need to tell me what's going on!" she shouts as she clutches my clothes.

She holds on, forcing me to drag her out of the snow and back onto the ice covered cobblestone.

Dalia is pale in the doorway leading into the kitchen where Blake screams in her arms. If I had any room to feel sorry for the poor girl, who just returned an hour ago to madness, I'd apologize.

But I can't even breathe. I can't see or think straight.

I can feel Sarah. She's close, I hope. But that feeling is waning with each passing second.

"Cosette," I growl, shrugging her off as I step into the house and march toward the hallway leading into the garage to fetch a jacket. My fingers are numb, nearly frozen. I've been outside for three hours looking for Sarah to no avail.

"What happened this morning?" Cosette snarls behind me as I pull several coats off the rack, tossing them onto the ground. "Where is she? What did you do?"

"I didn't do anything!" I growl, meeting her eyes.

"I read those letters," she whispers, grabbing my arm. "Those letters you tried to burn in fireplace in the sitting room–"

"Gods dammit, Cosette!"

"Don't raise your voice at me!" she shouts, shoving me hard. "I knew something was wrong with that poor girl. I knew she was in danger–"

"You should have come to me with your concerns–"

"I tried, but you've had your head shoved so far up your ass lately that I couldn't get a word in without you going on about being busy, giving Sarah space, and now look at you!"

I've never heard Cosette cuss before. She shoves her finger in my chest, her fingertip piercing my shirt. "Whatever you did to her, fix it."

"I didn't do anything," I repeat, hissing the words.

"Then find her. Shift, for fuck's sake, and bring her home." She jabs me with her finger again and then rips the coat I'm grasping out of my hands before storming away.

"Call in my warriors. Every single one of them, Cosette. And get them out on the ground to search for her."

Cosette looks at me over her shoulder, shooting daggers as she opens the door back into the house. Blake's cries echo through the garage when she slams the door behind her.

She read the letters. Sarah was smart enough not to mention the truth—that she's not only my mate, but Sasha, the most wanted fugitive in the Allied Kingdoms. The woman my own uncle nearly killed me over when I told him not to dig up her grave.

In the end, my father and Ryatt were right in the suspicions that there wouldn't be bones in that grave.

Sarah's letter to me had been nothing more than a tearful apology, thanking me for my fucking hospitality.

I close my eyes and try to gather myself, but I'm torn to pieces. My wolf has no interest in coming out to aid me in my search, and part of me wonders if I'll be able to find her, even in wolf form.

I go back outside, take off my clothes, shifting before the bite in the air can brush over my skin, and then I'm back in the forest again.

An hour passes then another. Eventually, I cross paths with my warriors. They won't know her scent, though. Not her new scent, the scent she kept masked.

Daylight begins to fade when I come to a stop in a clearing on the outskirts of my territory where the mountains turn to a jagged, cliff-lined expanse of pure nothingness.

The far northern edge of Crescent Falls looms before me.

A couple of warriors have been following me, providing backup on instinct.

One of them steps forward, tilting his tawny ears toward a narrow valley nearly invisible to the naked eye because of the tall, frost covered trees blocking the view down.

I can hear the waterfall. It's been warm enough the past few days with the slow changing of the seasons that some of the ice has broken away again, and the noise is a soft hum through the still, cold winter air.

'Any chance she was making a run for the border? It's across that valley, across the lake at the bottom.'

'It's the only place we haven't looked,' another warrior says.

'Go east. Follow the wolf trail down,' I tell them and turn for the trees where I know a sharp drop off looms.

I disappear over the edge before they can protest.

I navigate the side of the valley with ease despite the rough, rocky terrain. My claws dig into frozen shale that gives way as I leap my way down with the sunsetting above me.

It's been too long. She's been out here far too long in the cold. She was wearing nothing more than leggings and a sweater, her feet bare.

But I come to a stop when the scent of blood hits me.

An ice chute drops straight down to the bottom of the valley, to the ice covered lake fed by the waterfall.

A trail of dark, frozen blood is visible just as the sun sets behind the mountain peaks and casts the entire valley in shadow.

My heart stops, and my mind goes blank as I jump toward the ice. I slide all the way down, unable to stop.

A few large boulders line the lake.

And I see her, half submerged where she broke through the ice.

She's lying flat on her stomach at the lake's shore, her hair splayed out around her and frozen to the ground.

Goddess, no. Not my mate. Please, not her.

This can't happen. It can't. I can't lose her. Blake can't lose her, his mother.

How am I supposed to explain this to him when he's old enough to understand? How do I even go about describing the sacrifice she had to make to keep him safe, the sacrifice she had to make in allowing me back into his life, and into her life, even though she was killing herself trying to keep our bond a secret?

A secret meant to save me.

I can't do this. I can't face the idea of letting her go. I've already lost her once. I can't go through it again.

I pull her free of the water but she's limp. I roll her over, and her eyes are closed, her mouth slightly ajar. Her skin is still pink but tinged with blue, and she's... she *is* breathing.

My howl pierces the night as the first starts come into view.

"GET HER IN THE TUB," Cosette says hurriedly as Dalia cuts through Sarah's sweater in the middle of the foyer. "Now, hurry!"

I lift Sarah and rush upstairs. She's like a rag doll, totally and completely limp in my arms and cold to the touch. Cosette rushes after me, trying to push past me to beat me into the room, but I don't stop at Sarah's door. I run through the second floor, past the narrow library and into my wing of my manor. I kick open my bedroom door, tearing it clean off the hinges.

Cosette is short of breath as she runs up behind me and hurries into my ensuite. I hear water running as I tear off Sarah's leggings, crushing her naked body to my chest.

I had the sense to pull a pair of sweatpants on in the garage when I got home, having carried her for miles on a litter with the help of my warriors knowing we'd move faster in our wolf forms.

Her cold skin bites into my chest, a reminder of how precarious this situation is.

"Sydney, hurry!" Cosette shouts from the bathroom, half choked with tears.

Sarah won't be able to hold herself up in the tub, I already know it. Cosette yelps with surprise as lukewarm water splashes over the edge as I get in and sink into a seated position with Sarah against my chest.

Cosette throws towels on the ground to soak up the water, rasping, "I need to call a healer–"

"Don't," I say, biting down on my lip as the water swirls around me. "No one comes into this house unless I say so."

"She's bleeding, Sydney."

I reach up and cup the back of Sarah's head. A huge gash leaks fresh blood.

"Get the tears."

"You only have one vial. It won't be enough–"

"Get them."

"I'll call your mother–"

"Do not call my mom."

Cosette locks her gaze with mine as she lingers in the doorway. She nods and leaves to get the tears from the safe in my office. She knows the code. She knows just about everything.

And when she returns a few minutes later, she asks me for the full truth about Sarah, and I tell her.

I watch from the doorway of my room an hour later as Dalia and Cosette arrange Sarah in my bed. The tears have had little effect. Her wounds have healed, yes, but she hasn't woken up.

My heart lurches as Cosette tucks her in and turns to Dalia who says there's no milk left for Blake in the freezer.

"Formula, then," Cosette tells her sadly, placing a hand over Sarah's forehead. "It's in the kitchen."

Dalia glances at me as she leaves the room, tears in her eyes.

"No one can know," I remind her, and Cosette nods, sinking onto the edge of the bed with Sarah's hands clasped between her own.

I turn and leave the house.

The stars dance overhead as I pull up to my parents' castle.

I'm ushered inside by a sleepy warrior and met by my mom's lead housekeeper, who was rudely summoned from bed.

Within minutes, my mom is hurrying down the grand stairs in a robe, her eyes wide and worried.

"Is Dad still in Moorn?"

She nods.

I take a step up the stairs. "I need to use the Orrery. I need to talk to Kenna."

2 3

———

MATE'S MARK

SYDNEY

MOM WATCHES me come back downstairs like she hasn't moved from the steps in the grand foyer in the hour I've been in the orrery. The castle is quiet, but several eyes watch my progress in total silence.

Mom's housekeeper whispers something to a maid, who scurries away into the dark recesses of the castle.

My mom grabs my arm as I pass her. I halt mid-step. "What's wrong?" she asks.

I shake my head, unable to find the words I need to convey the situation I'm in, that Sarah's in. When I don't say anything, she asks, "Did something happen?"

"I have it handled."

"Can you tell me–"

"I can't." I meet her eyes. I won't come between my parents. I can't tell her about Sarah and the crushing truth I've learned. I can't tell anyone else.

Because Sarah would be taken from me, separated from Blake, and probably brought to Eastonia, and I won't allow it.

Mom reaches up and cups my cheek. Every emotion roiling in my heart swells at her touch. I want nothing more than to tell her everything, but she'd have to promise that she'd keep this secret from her own mate.

I know she can't. It's too big of an ask.

Her lips part, but I wrench away from her and continue down the stairs, blowing past the confused castle staff and the warriors waiting by the door, waiting for commands in the event I'm here at this odd hour because something serious happened.

I'm not sure where I'm going when I get into my truck, but it's not the road I take home to Shadowcrest. The sun rises over the Neutral Zone, casting the area in streams of gold and pink. The gray, unkempt buildings rise all around me.

Nothing is open yet. Every storefront I pass is empty. The sideways and covered entrances haven't been swept free of snow.

But a bodega on the corner lights up the area with its flashing open sign, so I pull my truck against the curb and step out.

A bell chimes as I walk inside. I keep my head low as I move toward the coffee machine on the far side of the room.

"You know who I am, Rich. Come on."

"Pay your tab, and then we can talk. The boss told me–"

"I don't care what your boss told you," growls a familiar voice that has my head snapping in the direction of the checkout counter. "I'll have the money I owe him after tonight's poker game, okay? I just need in–"

My feet move of their volition, and I've face to face with Mr. Foxglove, the landlord who tortured and swindled Sarah out of so much money it makes my head spin to even think about.

I grab him by the collar of his jacket and slam his head down on the edge of the counter. The clerk stands there, motionless, watching every move I make as I drag Foxglove out of the shop and into the street.

Only then does the clerk follow, watching from a distance as I kick the landlord repeatedly in the stomach.

"Get up," I snarl, kicking him again. "Don't make this so easy for me."

Foxglove sways to his feet, blood pouring down his face from a gash on his forehead, and pulls a knife from his jacket.

I grab his wrist and twist. He drops the knife, and I drive my fist right into the center of his rat-like face.

My knuckles split at the impact, but I'm beyond feeling. Foxglove falls to the ground, motionless, his eyes rolling back in his head.

Panting, I slowly turn to the clerk.

"Do you need him for anything, or can my boss have him?" the clerk asks without an ounce of emotion.

I'm aware of the underground network rife in the NZ, the crime lords who oversee illegal gambling rings and auctions. Dragging Foxglove back to Shadowcrest and having him tried for his crimes against Sarah and his other tenants would be a mercy I'm not willing to give him.

But leaving him to pay for his debts, in blood, to whatever boss he pissed off?

"Take him. I don't want to see this man ever again. I'll repay his debts to your boss if you can make that happen."

"Alpha," the clerk says with a bob of his head.

I get back in my truck, resisting the urge to run Foxglove over, and drive back to Shadowcrest without the coffee.

Cosette sits on the edge of my bed, running a brush through Sarah's hair when I return to the manor.

She looks up at me as I enter the room with dark circles lining her eyes. She's exhausted. She's been up all night.

Sarah's eyes are closed. She looks like she's sleeping, but it's more than that. No touch brings her back. No loud sound. Not even Blake crying for her will rouse her.

Cosette's eyes scan my body, landing on my bleeding hand.

Normally she'd ask what happened and then scold me like I'm a child, but today, she just nods to herself and looks back down at Sarah.

"You should expect guests within the next twenty-four hours. Have a room made up for them, please."

"Kenna, I presume?" She drops all formality. It doesn't matter in a time like this.

"And her mate."

Cosette nods as she rises, her eyes still locked on Sarah. She struggles to swallow before turning to face me, saying, "She has a mark on her arm that wasn't there before."

I close my eyes as the fragmented memory of Sarah being tortured by Gabriel flashes through my mind.

Something heavy roils through our bond. Someone else *marked* my mate. Marked her as a child against her will. She's lived with that mark. She's been hiding it for years using what I presume are her powers.

"I want to cut it out," Cosette says timidly, which is totally uncharacteristic of her. She meets my eyes, taking a shallow breath. "I *need* to cut it out, Alpha. But I can't do it without your explicit permission to… to hurt her, because it will probably hurt, and I need to know that you won't hurt me for touching your mate."

I want to tell her I would never hurt her, especially over something as necessary as this, but Cosette has been around long enough to know that mates are exceedingly territorial and honestly murderous when it comes to their partners.

The idea of anyone hurting Sarah twists in my gut. I see red, unable to stop myself from feeling these emotions.

"You can't be here when I do it. You need to be far away."

"I understand," I choke out.

"I want warriors outside the door."

Warriors to stop me from charging in, shifting, and tearing Cosette apart.

"And you need to talk to someone about this, Sydney," she says with motherly affection, laying a hand on my arm. "Ryan, maybe."

"I can't involve him."

"He would want to be involved."

"Kenna will be here soon. I'll know what we're dealing with then, and then I'll tell Ryan."

"Her friend Hadley called while you were gone. I told her Sarah wasn't feeling well. Does Hadley know the truth?"

"I doubt it." I think Sarah hid this part of herself from everyone. She buried her past and meant to keep it buried on that island for the remainder of her life.

"Can Hadley be trusted?"

"I'll talk to Ryan about it. It doesn't matter now. Sarah just needs to get better."

Cosette nods and starts turning me toward the door. I notice the sharpened knife on the bedside table, a metal jar, and a pair of thick, rubber gloves.

"It's liquid silver," she says in a near whisper. "To eat away the mark if it's deep. It will leave a scar, I'm afraid. But–" She stops in the doorway, turning to face me. "She won't feel it as much, I don't think. It's better to do it now, when she's asleep like this."

"I agree."

"Then you'll let me?"

"I wouldn't trust anyone else with it, Cosette. Please do what you think is best. I trust you." I lean down and press a kiss to her cheek. When I pull away, tears line her lower lashes.

But as I turn, she says, "You need to spend some time with Blake."

"I don't know if I can."

"He's your son, Sydney."

"I'm well aware–"

"He needs you. Sarah needs you to be strong for him right now."

A flash of anger–misplaced and wrong–spirals through my system, leaving me breathless. I shouldn't be angry with Sarah. If anything, I'm beyond devastated for her, for us, and for our son but...

She could have trusted me. She could have told me, the night we met and realized we were mates, who she really was.

I would have protected them both. Instead, she stole my memories. She blocked me out and then nearly died rather than facing this together.

"Where is he?"

"Dalia is with him. She hasn't left him." She gives me a little shove down the hallway. "Take him somewhere today while I take care of the mark."

Cosette disappears back into my room without another word. I find Dalia in the sitting room attached to Sarah's old room. She watches me approach in silence and gently passes Blake to me. "Get some rest, Dalia," I tell her, and she leaves the room, hopefully going upstairs to her own quarters.

I quickly pack a bag for Blake–diapers, wipes, a blanket–and go downstairs for a bottle.

Warriors appear. My warriors. My own packmates. They watch me closely as I maneuver through the house with Blake, analyzing my every move. They don't know why they've been called here today by Cosette, of all people. They likely didn't understand why we were out searching for Sarah, my house guest, all day yesterday.

In time, my pack will learn the truth. They'll regard Sarah as my mate, my Luna. But until then, their only job is to protect her, even from me.

I hate that it has to be this way, but Cosette is right. I can't be here. She needs warriors to protect herself from *me*.

The moment I pull my truck up to the cottage I've been getting ready for Sarah, I feel the first slice of flesh being flayed from my mate through our bond, and I grip the steering wheel to stop myself from screaming in rage.

It's an effort to get Blake out of his car seat and into the warm sanctuary of the nearly empty cottage. My entire body thrums with nervous energy. Sarah might not be able to feel what's being done to her, but I do. Every flicker of pain ignites in my heart, rendering me unstable and blind to everything around me.

Everything except for my son.

I sink to the ground in the living room, my back sliding down the new floral wallpaper. I hold onto Blake for dear life as Cosette, two miles away, cuts Gabriel's mark from Sarah's skin and douses the wound in silver.

I feel every moment like it's happening to me.

She was right to tell me to leave and to take Blake with me. He is the only thing grounding me, the only thing stopping me from shifting and running back to the house.

He looks up at me with eyes that match mine–confused, anxious, and heartbroken.

"It's okay," I tell him, fighting past the physical and emotional pain. I rest him against my chest, my hand covering his back as I lay my cheek against the top of his head. "She's going to be okay."

I watch the light creep through the windows as minutes turn to hours. Blake sleeps against my shoulder, his tiny fists gripping my shirt.

Somewhere in my depths of despair, my voice rings out on its own in a deadly promise.

"Come for us, you fucking bastard. Face me like a man. You told me once that I'd never be able to protect them, and I understand what you meant now. You can't possibly grasp what I'd do to protect what's mine. Come for me, Gabriel. Finish what you started."

The words echo through the cottage.

2 4

HELP FROM ANOTHER REALM

SYDNEY

TWO DAYS HAVE PASSED. I'm not sure how. Every minute feels exactly like the last; achingly slow.

I'm doing what I do best—deflecting. Finding other things to do besides sit at Sarah's bedside and move between begging her on my knees to wake up and being angry at her for putting us in this position.

The wound on her arm is horrendous. Wide, gnarled, and barely healing despite using my healing powers. Gabriel left his mark so deep, it took Cosette over three hours to cut it out.

But now, Sarah's free of him. He will never touch her again. He will never even lay eyes on her, and I'll see to that myself.

Right now, however, I'm sitting on the steps in the foyer with my head in my hands while Cosette paces back and forth, her short foot-steps sending a clacking echo through the room.

I haven't slept in three days, at least. Longer, I think. I've lost all concept of time.

"They should be here by now," Cosette grumbles to herself as she checks her watch.

A soft cry pierces the air upstairs. Blake's awake. I rise to go get him but hear Dalia's soft footsteps somewhere above me, and then Blake's quiet again.

I sit back down, blowing out my breath.

"Where are they?" Cosette breathes, finally coming to a stop. She starts tapping her foot.

"You're driving me crazy, Cosette."

"Dinner is getting cold."

"Well, they're technically not coming here to hangout and enjoy dinner–"

A crackle of energy ghosts through the house. The frames on the walls tremble, and the curtains lift from the windows as if being sucked into a vacuum in the center of the foyer.

Cosette squeaks and leaps back as a flash of dark mist erupts, sending a spray of embers in every direction.

Evander coughs and bends over, resting his hands on his knees, while Kenna dusts soot from her shoulders as if nothing strange just happened.

"You were supposed to be here two hours ago!" I stand, my heart thundering.

"Hello to you too, Sydney," Kenna says, arching a dark brow in my direction.

I scan her face, then her body. She's wearing a dark cape and green dress in the fashion of Eastonia–ethereal, flowing fabrics with jeweled accents. Her hair is spun in several braids inlaid with pearl clips that catch the light of the chandelier as her power simmers and dies away. She's in one piece, though. I worried about her traveling while pregnant, but she's a Firestone witch, after all. They're the most powerful when they're pregnant.

"We were held up in Maatua," Evander says with effort as he straightens. He looks sick to his stomach, and knowing how recently he's had to spirit back and forth between the kingdoms, I understand why.

It's a power I don't have, as far as I know. I prefer to keep my paws on the ground. Looking at Evander, I'm sure he does too. I pity him, not for the first time, for being mated into this family with all of our strange quirks.

Kenna steps forward as Cosette hurries to take her cloak, but her eyes are locked on mine. "You look horrible. You haven't slept since we spoke, have you?"

I run my tongue along my lower lip. She arches her brow again, probably waiting for me to explain why I called her here. I didn't tell her anything when I reached out to her using my dad's orrery. It's tricky, honestly, getting in touch with anyone in Eastonia without the use of the mirrors owned by my father and my uncle. They used to have to use water from the falls in Maatua, too. But Kenna and I have a strong bond and are able to mind-link if I use my powers in the orrery, but it doesn't last long, and I could only tell her that there was an emergency, that I need her help, and she needs to keep quiet about it.

"Where's Brie?" I ask.

"She's in Maatua being spoiled rotten by our grandparents for the next week." She steps toward me, resting her hands on the swell of her stomach. "I told my parents that we were coming here early under the guise of spending a week with you before Aunt Maddy's reunion with the whole family next week. Grandma and Grandpa are traveling here with Brie in a few days."

I nod, slightly overwhelmed. In the background, Cosette is trying to convince Evander to come with her for a cup of tea or glass of whiskey, whichever will settle his stomach, but he's shaking his head.

"What happened, Sydney?" Kenna asks. "You look absolutely wrecked."

I hold Kenna's silver gaze. If I'm going to trust anyone, it's going to have to be her. "I found her."

Evander lifts his head from his conversation with Cosette, but I don't look at him. I step toward Kenna, allowing myself to feel every emotion that's been building since the moment I pulled Sarah out of the freezing water that almost killed her.

"I found my mate."

~

KENNA WALKS AROUND MY BED, her eyes downcast on Sarah as she lies motionless on her back, her eyes closed and chest lifting shallowly with each breath she takes.

Evander closes my bedroom door and keeps his distance as his mate sits on the edge of the bed and takes Sarah's hand in her own, turning it over to trace the lines of her palm.

"I remember her," Kenna whispers. She looks at me over her shoulder, a faint smile touching her lips. "The morning after the ball. I thought she was someone Ryan brought home, remember?"

I do remember that. I remember feeling like I'd been hit by a truck as I wandered out of the guest room with a throbbing headache and wanting to crawl to the coffee maker.

I thought I'd been hungover at the time, but I wasn't. It was Sarah's mysterious powers ripping through my brain and disintegrating my memories of her.

I sit on the other side of the bed with my feet firmly planted on the floor and turn to Kenna and Evander, taking a huge breath.

I tell them everything–about meeting her last fall, then rescuing her from her apartment. I tell them about her talents with flowers, and being trapped in a hotel room with her where I realized how hard I was falling, and that she was falling too.

"Blake is my son," I say in a near whisper. "I figured it out myself. I think she knew I'd learn the truth eventually." I look at Evander, who's still standing near the door with his hands tucked in the pockets of his black pants. "That morning, in Moorn, when we met up… I'd just found out he was mine. I hadn't had a chance to talk to her about it."

Evander nods solemnly. "I knew something was off. Everyone did. Ryatt felt awful about snarling at you–"

"I deserved it," I cut in.

"So you came home and confronted her?" Kenna shifts her weight as she continues to examine Sarah's hands.

I wonder why she's doing that, but reply, "Yeah, I did, and she…"

"She isn't just Sarah, is she?" Kenna's eyes meet mine. "And she's not sick either, is she, Sydney?"

I struggle to swallow and glance in Evander's direction. A light bulb flames to life in his mind as his eyes meet mine. "Sasha?"

I nod. Kenna sighs deeply as she twists a lock of Sarah's hair around her finger. "Well, this complicates things."

"Tell me about it," I reply gruffly, and she glares at me over her shoulder.

"Did you have any inclination–"

"Of course not," I snap, then clear my throat. "And if I had, I wouldn't have cast her out or turned her in to our dads, if that's what you're asking. I brought you here because something is wrong with her. She won't wake up, Kenna. She–she jumped, okay? Spirited away after telling me to take care of Blake, and I found her on the edge of my territory, half dead, freezing–"

"She exhausted her powers, that's all." Evander crosses his arms over his chest.

I shake my head, turning back to Kenna. "She was hurt. She had a gash on the back of her head and several broken bones when I found her–"

"You used Grandma's tears, didn't you?" Kenna trails her fingertips down Sarah's bare arm. "I can sense them. Your powers, too." She pauses at the gauze covering Sarah's upper arm. Kenna makes a low, hissing sound and looks up at me. "Silver? Why?"

"Gabriel marked her when she was a child."

Kenna closes her eyes for a moment as if gathering herself. I feel a shimmer of power settle in the room–Kenna's powers. She's furious at the thought of anyone, let alone Gabriel, harming a child like that.

Evander steps forward, edging toward the bed, but stops a few feet away. "Kenna, what is she?"

Kenna opens her eyes, and they land on her mate, her brow furrowed. "She's a shifter, I can sense that. It's in her scent, actually, which means she'll have the ability to shift but not for a few more months, at least. There's something else–"

"She's a witch then. She'd have to be, being Atticus's daughter." I look between Evander and Kenna. "Right?"

"Well, that's technically true, but she doesn't…." Kenna tilts her head from side to side, perplexed. "She's different. I don't know how else to explain it."

"Try," I tell her, losing my patience. She shoots me a dirty look as I continue, "You have a–a witch medical degree, or whatever. You have to know what's wrong with her."

"Evander's right. She exhausted her powers. But you made it sound like when she jumped, she didn't make it that far. Sasha was rumored to be extremely powerful. Powerful enough to rival me and my parents. But that can't be true if a simple jump left her like this."

Evander's looking at me now, his eyes boring into the side of my face. I glance at him, then close my eyes and tell them the rest of it, the parts I wasn't sure I'd be able to relive, let only vocalize.

Her memories. My memories, stolen from me using powers none of us knew existed.

Kenna listens to every word, rapt and wide-eyed.

When I come to the part where I'm with Sarah after the ball, in bed together, feeling the mate bond ignite between us, Kenna closes her eyes and shakes her head.

"She was trying to keep you safe from Gabriel."

"I know," I reply with great effort.

"I know what she is," Kenna breathes. She looks at Evander, her eyes dark and looming with grief. "She's a mystic."

Evander's brows pinch together at the same moment I shift forward, confused. "No… that can't be right. Mystics aren't just–out here, living normal lives. They're only in Moonrise. They've only ever been in Moonrise."

"You're partly right, Sydney." Kenna rises from the bed and starts to pace, cradling her stomach and the nearly term baby boy within. "We honestly didn't know much about mystics before what happened recently in Moonrise. We didn't think they could deflect. They have a… a hive-mind," she says, her eyes meeting mine briefly before she turns and paces back across the room. "They act together, sharing thoughts and knowledge. I used to be under the assumption that Mystics simply appeared, regenerated somehow, but we now know, after an exceedingly difficult few months cataloging birth records found in the old temples in Moonrise and the Roguelands, that they are born just like we are and come into their powers as children, and those children are highly coveted and protected. Their families don't have much of a choice but to send them away to live with other mystics. They're a one-in a million kind of child, honestly. There's only a dozen mystics in all of Eastonia."

"Gabriel was using mystics to fuel his relic," Evander says hotly, his green eyes glowing with sudden fury. "It makes sense. He needs that kind of power."

"She's different, though," Kenna says. "I think–"

"I just need her to wake up," I cut in, my head spinning. "I don't care about the rest. I just need her to wake up. How do we do that?"

"Mark her." Kenna stops pacing and turns to me. "Claim her as your mate and let your own powers give her strength."

I shake my head slowly. "I can't do that."

"Why not?" Kenna looks confused. She glances at Evander, who shares her sentiments.

"She's already had so much taken from her, so much done to her against her will. I won't contribute to that."

"Then we wait this out," Kenna says. "Those are our only options, Sydney, but when she wakes, and she *will* wake up, she needs to tell us what she can do because these powers…"

"They're dangerous, especially if she were to fall into the wrong hands," Evander finishes.

Blake's cries echo down the hallway. Kenna turns toward the noise, her eyes lighting up. "I have some research to do, but first, I'd like to meet your son, and you need to sleep."

2 5

———

FLASHBACK

Sarah

After the Ball

Alpha Sydney of Shadowcrest pauses during the long trek down the stairs leading out of the temple of the Moon Goddess. He extends a hand to me, and I take it, finding his hands warm but slightly clammy.

I meet his eyes. Goddess, he has radiant eyes. The kind of blue even the best artists can't capture in a painting. Dark blue, like the deepest ocean, and so expressive I can see every thought behind them.

He's nervous. I am too, which is silly. We've been dancing for an hour, singing along to a lesser known local band we both love. He helped me finish the cocktail I didn't end up liking, and somehow we ended up doing... this. Escaping the party together without telling a soul.

He wanted to see my flowers, and I wanted to show him more than anything.

This man is not only an Alpha but the heir to the throne of *Alpha King.*

He's the highest ranking and most powerful Alpha in our lands, other than his father. And right now, he's nervous to be around *me.*

I stoop to take off my heels. "I'm going to break my neck if I fall down these stairs."

He holds me steady as I fumble with the thin straps, my tight pink dress hampering my progress. "I'll carry them for you," he says, taking each shoe and holding them by the straps. His suit jacket is draped over his arm, and his tie is loose. His dark brown hair is ruffled, and he has a twinkle in his eye when I straighten up, run my fingers through my hair, and smile at him.

He looks so at ease right now, nothing like the official portrait in the temple or pictures in the newspaper I've seen. I can't imagine him looking stern.

Not when his smile is the most magnificent thing I've ever seen.

I'm in so much trouble.

"Better?" he asks, his own smile widening.

"So much better," I laugh, and we're off again.

Barefoot, I walk beside him through the summer festival, down cramped alleys where tents and stalls with vendors selling all kinds of food, drinks, and gifts that border on romantically inclined clog the normally busy thoroughfare on the shore of the lake.

I shuffle to keep up with him, cursing myself for being persuaded to wear this dress tonight. It hugs every curve all the way down to my ankles and is impossible to walk in, but I'm doing my best.

"Are you hungry?"

"I could eat," I reply. "Something small, maybe."

"Fries?"

I nod, beaming at him as we stop at a stall and wait in line. Within minutes, we're sitting on a bench overlooking the water where couples and groups have spread out blankets on the grassy lake shore to have midnight picnics and watch the stars bloom to life overhead.

We munch on fries while I point out the floral streamers strung from light pole to light pole and the huge baskets of blooms lining the walking trails down to the water.

"You did all of that?"

"I was on a team, technically, but yeah. I did." I lean into him to snatch another fry. "What do you do?"

"Me?"

"Yeah." I catch his gaze, softening the smile that's been firmly planted on my face since the moment I saw him tonight. He'd been talking in a small group with his brother, Alpha Ryan, the other prince of Crescent Falls, and an unfamiliar woman I believe might have been the Royal Princess of Eastonia. It's rumored she's here for the festival. Everyone has been talking about it.

I spotted him and did a double take, and the moment we locked eyes, I swear time stopped.

But my friends ushered me to the dance floor, and I told myself he's not here for me. I'm definitely not here for him. I'm a nobody. I have no rank and no pack.

But he's sitting so close to me now that our thighs touch as he responds to my earlier question. "I'm an Alpha."

"No way! I had no idea," I laugh, rolling my eyes.

He smirks. "I'm *also* an engineer. Civil, technically. I like to think I do a little of everything. I help my dad on some of his committees when it comes to kingdom infrastructure. My firm is in Shadowcrest."

"That's pretty far away, isn't it?"

"It is. I kind of like it that way. It keeps me out of the city, and it's quiet there."

He offers me another fry. I take it, popping it into my mouth and rubbing the salt between my fingers. "You're good at math then, huh? That's good because I'm not."

"Well, I'm not very artistic, admittedly. It's a good thing I found you."

"Why?" I laugh, beaming up at him as my heart rate spikes.

He shrugs, looking down at me with affection behind his eyes. It's not a look I'm used to. "You seem like the kind of person that can touch something and make it beautiful. I tend to touch things with the ability to break them apart."

I'm not sure what to say, but I feel myself leaning in, chasing more of his touch.

When he asked if I wanted to leave the temple and the sweaty, chaotic ball taking place there, I was all over it. We'd been dancing, touching each other, standing so close I could run my hands up his chest and feel every well-defined muscle beneath.

But that bubble of intimacy burst the second we stepped out into the fresh night air. I expected this feeling of want to simmer, but now it's a quiet feeling. Comfortable, and natural, but the desire for him I felt earlier is there all the same.

He places a hand on my thigh as he points across the lake, clearing his throat. He begins to tell me about his territory tucked in the mountains in the distance while I watch his mouth move. I love the way he talks when he's excited. I love that he seems to talk a lot when he's nervous, especially after flirting with me and realizing what he'd done.

Despite the summer heat, there's a bit of a bite in the air as we walk through the festival together. Maybe it's my own nerves reminding me that these feelings can't be more than excitement and lust. It's better that way. I'm entitled to some freedom, aren't I? This craving to be touched and held has been brewing for a long time.

But it's dangerous. I know better than this.

Right now, I just don't care.

Music thrums to the rhythm of my ever beating heart, and as we maneuver through a particularly crowded street, his hand finds mine again. He guides me through the crowd with his fingers knitted in mine; our hands are a perfect fit.

By the time we reach the edge of the festival and the NZ looms, I start to feel it. That nagging sense that this is going to be over soon.

It's selfish. Selfish of me to think I could spend a night with an Alpha. Goddess, I've never even been with *anyone* before. I've never been kissed.

"Are you okay?" he asks, coming to a stop on the sidewalk in front of a sleepy storefront shuttered against the dwindling crowd.

"Yeah, I'm fine." I shrug, looking down at my bare toes.

He swings my shoes as he scans the crowd moving through the glowing tents and then turns back to me, edging closer–just a step.

I look up as he says, "You probably want to get home now. I could… I could take you back to the temple, if you want–"

"No, it's all right."

He flexes his jaw like unsaid words are on the tip of his tongue. He runs his fingers through his hair. "Look, I… it's late. I realize how long we've been out here and really don't want you walking back to your place alone. I don't even know where you live–"

"I'll be okay," I assure him, but inside I'm dying. "Do you want–"

"I don't really want tonight to end," he says hurriedly, his cheeks going ruddy.

My mouth pops open slightly, and a warmth spreads through my chest that I can't explain. It's new. It's beautiful. It's my undoing if I do anything rash.

"I'm not good at this," he admits, taking another step in my direction and effectively closing the distance between us. "But when I saw you in the crowd I…. You cast some kind of spell on me."

"A spell?" I laugh, a real, almost choking laugh. "You're right, Alpha Sydney. You caught me. It was a *love* spell."

"Oh," he rasps, taking another step. "I knew it. Every second I've spent with you tonight, I've felt like I'm dying. Like the idea of saying goodbye is going to tear me apart."

"We don't have to say goodbye just yet."

"How long does this spell last?"

I smile like an idiot, thinking back on those silly books I used to read as a kid. "Until daybreak. Until the first rays of sun touch the ground. You're mine until then."

"We have a few hours then, don't we?"

My heart races as he closes in on me. I take a step back, tripping over my hem for the hundredth time tonight.

He stoops, crouching, and starts ripping the fabric.

"I loved this dress," I tell him.

"I love it too, but if you're going to come home with me tonight, I'm going to need you to walk, otherwise I'm carrying you over my shoulder."

Another rip and my legs are free. He tosses the fabric to the side and slowly looks up at me. He's so much taller than I am. He towers over me at his full height, but he rises slowly, and we're so close I can smell him—smell that woodsy, early autumn scent that does something to my brain I can't make sense of.

It happens slowly, like time is at a crawl. He cages me in against the brick exterior of the store front, his body shielding mine from a passing group of festival goers. I lay my hand on his chest, over his heart, and feel that it's beating as fast as my own.

We're on dangerous ground. One word, and this doesn't have to happen. I'm smarter than this. I know better. But I've sheltered myself for years now, hiding away, pretending to be someone I'm not to make the world a little safer for me.

But I want this feeling I get from him. This strange connection that locked into place when he introduced himself. I want to live in the moment he put his hand on my waist while we danced in the temple and I felt all tingly and good.

If I can't have this forever, I can have it for a night.

Right?

His mouth brushes mine. I close my eyes, my lips parting as he kisses me. It's slow and tender at first, but he deepens the kiss, his tongue sliding over mine.

It's a rush I've never experienced. The kiss is perfect, too perfect, and before I know it we're passing through the gates to his brother's territory in the cloak of night. He picks me up to help me over the boulders that line the slope of his brother's large log home in Silverhide. We're kissing again in the narrow hallway lined with bedrooms on the second floor, my back pressed to the wall and his hands traveling down the slope of my hips while I unbutton his shirt.

I should tell him I've never done this, but I don't want to stop. I don't want him to stop and reconsider.

He opens a door and carries me inside, laying me in the center of the mattress.

I shimmy out of my dress. He pulls it down off my hips, ripping the fabric off rather than unzipping it.

"Sydney–" I breathe his name, closing my eyes as his hands touch my bare skin. A chill wraps itself around my body as his mouth presses kisses up my left thigh while he crawls onto the bed.

I run my fingers through his thick, soft hair, and he groans with satisfaction.

"Take these off. I can't take it anymore," he rasps against my skin, against my hip bone.

I reach down and start shoving the lacy white thong I'm wearing down, and he helps, sliding it over my knees and down to my ankles.

I kick it off completely, laughing a bit because his stubble is tickling my skin, but then his mouth is…

"Oh, my Goddess," I cry out to the ceiling.

He forces my legs up onto his shoulders and licks me from base to clit, and I melt into his touch, turning molten and heavy. His teeth graze my most sensitive area as he tongue laps at my center until I'm dizzy with need. Need for more. For all of him.

It doesn't take long for the aching desperation blooming to life between my thighs to turn to something bright and white-hot. My nails rake through his hair as I arch my hips, riding his tongue as I come wholly and utterly unglued. My vision fills with stars and my entire body spasms with pleasure, but he's not stopping.

I'm coming down from a high like no other when his mouth is suddenly on mine again, and he's nudging my knees apart.

I didn't even see him take his pants off.

I claw at his dress shirt, which is already hanging off his broad, muscled shoulders, while his cock nudges my entrance. The head slips in, and I lose my breath.

"Look at me," he whispers tenderly, so I do.

He holds my gaze as he thrusts home, past the pain, past the barrier in his way, and I'm… *his*.

There's a word for this dizzying feeling. Some call it love. Some call it destiny.

It's true. All of that is true.

He feels it too. He's just as shocked as I am as he thrusts deeper, his cock dragging in and out of me until we're both panting and clutching each other for dear life, neither willing to let go. His hips grind into mine as another orgasm builds, but my head is spinning.

Those fine, golden threads start weaving through my heart, tugging tight, binding me to him.

My mate. My mate. *My mate.*

2 6

UNLOCKING THE PAST

Sarah

Everything hurts. My head feels like someone took a hammer to it.

I open my eyes to slits and quickly close them again. Pain rushes through me in waves like it has its own tide, and my breath is driving the current.

I know where I am. Sydney's scent is everywhere.

I tried to leave him. I really did try. I thought it was what I was supposed to do to protect him and our son, but the Goddess laughed in my face, didn't She?

I slowly turn my head to the only source of light I can find and carefully open my eyes again.

Sydney's sitting at a desk only a few feet away, his back to me. The soft *click, click, click,* of his keyboard fills my ears as his laptop screen comes into view.

It's a blueprint of some kind. An equation pops up on the screen that takes him a single second to figure out, and then the blueprint shifts, new numbers and letters appearing that make little sense to me.

He turns his head slightly, reaching for the mug of what smells like fresh coffee despite the fact it's fully dark, probably sometime in the middle of the night.

But the light coming from his screen illuminates his face and he's... wearing glasses.

"I didn't know you wore glasses," I whisper, my voice tight and rasping.

Sydney freezes. He slowly turns his head and looks at me.

I blink, keeping my eyes closed for a moment against the headache raging through my temples, and open them again to find him staring at me.

His lips part as he sucks in a breath. He takes off his glasses and rubs the bridge of his nose for a moment, his head bowed, and then puts them on again. "How are you feeling?" His voice sounds like someone took a rake to his vocal cords.

"How long?"

"I asked how you were feeling. That's what matters now." He reaches for the lamp on his bedside table.

"Please, don't," I croak, wincing as I try to sit up. Every joint pops; every muscle strains.

"Don't try to move yet–"

"How long have I been like this?"

"A little over a week."

I have no choice but to lie back down. My body melts into the mattress–his mattress. It's his scent on the soft sheets and his pillow that I rest my head on.

"Blake?" I ask weakly, tears burning to life.

I stare at the ceiling, catching Sydney rising from his chair and moving the foot or so it takes for him to reach the bed.

He sits on the edge, facing me, and lays a hand on my thigh. It's a fight not to flinch away from his touch. I don't deserve it.

"He's fine. He misses you."

I try to swallow past the painful lump forming in my throat, but it's impossible.

"I missed you," he admits. It shatters me.

"I don't deserve your pity or kindness, Alpha–"

"Never call me Alpha again," he rasps.

"Sydney, we can't do this." Desperation clouds my senses. Fear burrows into my heart, twisting hard, tugging on the threads of our bond.

His hand tightens around my thigh. He can feel it now–everything. My fear, my guilt, and absolute sorrow over what fate had in store for us. I showed him my memories. I showed him the truth. I lied to him. I hid a pregnancy from him. His son….

"I can't stand the idea of Gabriel getting his hands on you," I admit tearfully, my vision clearing enough to fully see his face. He's withdrawn, his features hazy with similar grief and uncertainty. "He will never touch you again," he whispers.

"You don't understand what he is–what he can do–"

"I don't care, Sarah. I've witnessed him. I've seen his stolen powers. He's a madman. A demon, something that needs to be banished." His voice suddenly drops, his eyes darkening to a midnight blue edged with fury. "Worst of all, he touched my mate. He marked *my mate*. I am going to find him–"

"No–"

"I'm going to find him," he repeats, cutting me off. "And I will take him apart, piece by piece, just like he did to you. He is not your problem anymore. Gabriel is *mine*."

There's so much vindication in his voice. He's serious. Dead serious. He's going to hunt Gabriel like Gabriel is hunting me, and there's nothing I can do about it.

I lie in silence for a while. My brain is mush, and my powers are nothing more than a whisper under my skin, but Sydney is still touching me, his hand firm and warm on my leg.

He's not leaving. He saved me. He refused to let me die.

"I'm sorry," I whisper, choking on the words. "Sydney, I am so sorry."

His hand moves up my thigh as he scooches closer. "Don't, Sarah–"

"No, I don't deserve this. After what I did to you, what I continued to do to you… you had to forget. I couldn't risk you finding me after we realized we were mates. I had to take that memory from you. I didn't find you after I found out I was pregnant with Blake because I... I couldn't risk you. I couldn't risk Gabriel finding you and hurting you because it would have been my fault–"

"I understand why you did it." He takes my trembling hands. "I don't care anymore. It doesn't matter. What matters now is that you rest and get better."

I try to pull away from him, but a shooting sensation grips my upper arm. I cry out as fresh, tearing pair ignites, causing beads of sweat to prickle over my overhead.

Sydney lunges into action. He scoops me up and lays me in the center of the bed as I start to shake.

His body curls around mine as he holds me to his chest, his hand pressed to the tight bandages on my upper arm. A strange, coursing kind of heat travels through my arm. I close my eyes as soft light fills my vision, and the pain starts to recede.

Sydney's healing powers fill the wound on my arm and make it go numb again.

"How did you keep it hidden?" he asks quietly, whispering the words into my hair as he powers knit through every muscle and wrap around every bone until my body is limp and at peace. "The mark and your scent."

"Our bond?"

"Yeah," he says, swallowing hard.

"It was all in your head. I just didn't let you see or feel those things. They wouldn't have registered."

"So you can control minds?"

"Not... not really. It's not that simple."

He shifts his weight, adjusting both of our positions so my cheek is squished against his arm. He wraps his other arm around my waist and pulls me tight against him, shielding me with his warmth as I shiver uncontrollably. "I'm sorry, Sarah. It's my power in your blood right now. That's why you're shivering."

"I'm fine," I whisper, but my voice is ragged from lack of use. I'm not fine. I know he can sense that. I know because I can feel his concern and feeling of utter lack of control through our bond.

He's silent for a few minutes while my body ebbs with his power. It's putting me to sleep. I'm on the cusp of going under when he murmurs, "We have guests, Sarah. My cousin and her mate are here."

Kenna. It has to be her.

I keep my eyes closed as he continues, "In the morning, if you're well enough, we need you to explain everything to us. How your powers work, why Gabriel needs you, everything."

"Okay," I whisper against his arm, breathing in his scent.

Sydney doesn't move from his place on the bed while I fall asleep in his arms, but I wake up several hours later to the door opening on the far side of the room.

I blink into the warm sunshine–a startling feeling. I peer out the window, noticing the ice hugging the shutters has begun to melt.

I know it's Sydney entering the room without needing to roll over. His footsteps are soft as he rounds the bed and sits down, turning to me.

My heart swells as the familiar scent of my son hits me, and I sit up, ignoring the aches in my back.

Blake squeals, gripping the T-shirt I'm wearing that I believe is Sydney's.

But my breasts are… empty. Even Blakes excited coos and rooting doesn't cause milk to let down.

I meet Sydney's eyes full of guilt and heartbreak.

But he lays a hand on my shoulder and leans down so our foreheads are touching.

"Kenna and Evander are having breakfast with my parents this morning, but they'll be returning soon, and we need to talk before then."

"Okay," I whisper, my eyes downcast on Blake as he toys with my fingers.

Sydney lays his hand over Blake's stomach and closes his eyes. "Are you working with Gabriel?"

My blood runs cold. "Sydney? No, of course not!"

"I had to ask."

I pull away from him and gaze into his eyes. He looks so tired still, like he didn't sleep at all last night.

"Sarah," he says, a bit painfully, "we're in a serious bind, all right? You're Sasha. You showed me that. I've been tasked with tracking you down and turning you into the Allied Kings."

I tighten my grip on Blake. "What's going to happen to me?"

"Nothing," he says sternly, his gaze darkening. "Nothing is going to happen to you, I promise. No one is going to know that you're Sasha."

"But I am." There's no way around it.

But Sydney shakes his head. "Not anymore. You haven't been Sasha since you were a child. You're Sarah. Sarah, my mate. Sarah, the mother of my child. My Luna." I shake my head, but he continues, "Even if it's not what you want, it has to be done. I am the only person who can stand between you and the Kings. We have to marry. You will be Luna of Shadowcrest."

"You didn't want this–"

"I want you," he says, his eyes a heartbreaking shade of blue. "I wanted you even when I thought my mate was still out there. I wanted you before I realized you and her were one and the same. I thought I was the one protecting you by vowing to never find my mate, never having children…" He looks at Blake with so much love in his eyes that it nearly breaks me. "I didn't know you were doing the same thing, and how much it was killing you. That's all I've thought about all week while you lay in this bed, out of reach. How did you do it? How could you stand to even be around me knowing what I was to you, yet I couldn't remember?"

"I did it for him. I had to do something right for him, even if it meant I couldn't have you but you… it happened anyway, didn't it?" I know we're both thinking of the hotel room, of lying side by side after the kiss when we wanted so much more from each other but couldn't bring ourselves to act on those feelings, knowing the consequences.

"Sarah," he breathes, looking suddenly boyish and shy, "I have one request."

I nod, knowing at this point I owe him the world. I can't say no, no matter what it is.

"I want to remember that night. All of it. From the moment I laid eyes on you for the first time to the second you took that memory from me. You only showed me pieces. I want it back."

"I can show you," I tell him and reach up to cup his cheek.

My powers tremble, tired and aching, then flow freely, unlocking the wards I'd spun around those memories when I locked them away in the furthest reaches of his mind.

Sydney's eyes soften before he closes them, leaning into my touch. I watch his mouth tick into a smile as he sees the images I robbed him of and feels those feelings like they're fresh and new.

A tear glides down my cheek at the same moment the door to his bedroom opens, and Cosette steps inside, looking immensely relieved to see me sitting upright and alert.

She's holding a tray, and I know without a shadow of doubt that my favorite tea is in that teapot.

"Welcome home, sweetheart. You have no idea how long I've been waiting for you to come back," she smiles tearfully, and crosses the room.

UNBURYING SASHA

Kenna

I KNEW something was up with Sydney several months ago when he sat in my sitting room looking so stern and withdrawn after our battle with Gabriel.

Now, I see why he was acting that way. Now, I finally understand.

He's standing next to Sarah's bedside holding his son. I almost can't believe it, but I always knew the Goddess was going to bless Sydney with all the riches he tried to avoid.

A radiantly beautiful mate. A perfect, golden child. A boy. His heir. Healthy and strong.

The image of them together as I walk into the room is flawless. But there's a crack in the perfect picture. I can see it in Sarah's violet eyes–such a strange color. I can see it written all over Sydney's face as he places a protective hand on Sarah's shoulders.

They're afraid of what comes next.

Sasha. I remind myself her name is Sasha. This woman is Atticus's daughter. The niece of Petra. The cousin of Gabriel.

She's the granddaughter of *Kane*.

My heart sinks as I come to a stop in the center of the room. Evander slides a chair in my direction, and I sit down, throwing a grateful smile at my mate. He knows I'm sore and tired, but I'm nearing the end of my pregnancy. Just another month or so to go, but I have a feeling our son is going to be late.

Sarah watches me with a predatory gleam in her eyes. I can almost taste her unusual power now that she's awake. At first, when she was completely subdued by her lack of power, it was just a glimmer of magic on her skin. It was something I could feel but couldn't make sense of.

Now, I can taste it. Her power radiates off her like nothing I've experienced before.

"You are not a witch," I say by way of greeting.

To my surprise, one corner of her mouth ticks into what could be a smile. "No, I am not."

I run my hands down the curve of my belly and rest them in what's left of my lap. I've been an Alpha for several months now. Watching my parents go from feral, ill-mannered renegades to powerful, respected rulers over the course of my life has taught me a thing or two about how to negotiate and break bad news.

But this is family. I'm not talking to some random pack member. I'm talking to the woman Sydney is falling in love with. His mate.

"Do you want to be called Sarah or Sasha?" I ask.

Sydney heaves a breath. She glances up at him, and he squeezes her shoulder. I wonder if they've discussed this, but based on their expression, I doubt it.

"Sarah."

I nod, smiling softly at her. "Do you remember your father at all?"

"I have pieces of memories of him. We were separated long before he helped me leave Eastonia."

Evander, standing at my side with his hand resting on the chair's backrest, nods. "As was common in the Draven Coven. Children being separated from parents–"

"Yes." Sarah cuts in but tilts her head to the side, "The girls, mostly. He wanted the boys strong and healthy, so they stayed with their mothers longer–to nurse. Girls were taken right away in most cases, to keep them small, easy to break."

Codependent, submissive, scared. I can see the unsaid words on her tongue.

"My father hid us, but when I was five, Gabriel's overseer, Morticus, found my mother and killed her. He took me back to Gabriel, and my father was forced to rejoin his ranks to keep me safe."

"Is that what you know or what you were told?" Evander holds her gaze.

"It was what I was told," she says, almost shyly.

I watch Sydney's fingers tighten on her shoulder in support.

We can't push her too far, not today. Coming out of a power induced coma is a serious thing. It could be days, maybe even weeks, before she's at her full strength again, both mentally and physically.

I look at Sydney. He knows this. I told him to take things slow with her, to be gentle with not only his touch but his words. But he has to be holding some of the anger I know he has buried deep, deep down. Anger at Sarah, anger at the situation his mate is in, anger at how she was treated as a child, left alone in the world.

It's a lot. I feel it as if it's my own burden weighing heavy on my shoulders.

"You don't have powers like Petra or Atticus," I say after what feels like several minutes of silence, each of us lost in our own thoughts.

"No, I don't."

I meet her eyes, watching as they shift from a bright violet to a dark amethyst. Interesting.

"Do you know what you are?" I ask, and to my shock, she nods.

Even Sydney stiffens, taken by surprise.

"Are you a mystic?"

"Yes," she whispers, and silence eats away at the room around us while I ponder what exactly this means. But she continues, "But there's something about me that's different. I've never understood it, and I've never had the chance to learn what my powers can do outside of what I deem necessary." She winces; so does Sydney.

She wiped his memory of her. How is that possible?

I chew my lip and look at Evander, his green eyes fixed on Sarah as she slowly reaches up and finds Sydney's fingers, covering his hand with her own.

"Gabriel has plans for me, plans he can't enact until I turn twenty-one and come into my full powers as both a wolf and a mystic."

"I didn't know anyone could be both–"

"They can't," she says, and her eyes shift back to pale violet. "Like I said, I'm different. I knew about the mystics from when I was young because Gabriel's cronies, his overlords who were preparing him to overthrow your parents when he came of age, were trying to trap one, but it was impossible. They share a mind, you know."

"I'm aware." I'm feeling suddenly nervous. I try not to fidget while Sarah straightens up a bit, and Sydney lowers Blake into her waiting arms.

"Do you know what he wants you for?"

I shouldn't have asked. I can sense it the moment the words leave my lips. Sarah pales, her eyes going glossy as she clutches her sleeping son to her chest.

Sydney's expression twists into something cold and dangerous. "That's enough. We're done for now."

"I have nothing else I can tell you," Sarah says tearfully. "I'm sorry. I was ten when I was brought here."

Evander helps me rise. "I understand. We're just trying to help, to figure out a way to… to make this possible." I wave a hand between Sydney and Sarah.

Cosette enters the room in a hurry, huffing as she says, "Alpha Sydney, Alpha Ryan called again. His packmate is desperate for news about Sarah."

I turn to Sydney, confused. "Did you tell Ryan yet?"

"No," Sydney says as he ushers us out of the room, leaving Cosette with Sarah and the baby. He shuts the door to the bedroom, and I follow him and Evander downstairs, to the formal sitting room.

"Ryan doesn't know, but I told him she's been sick, and it might be contagious because I've also been ill. It's a lie, but it was all I could say until I knew for sure what we're dealing with. But her friend, Hadley, has been calling the house incessantly."

Evander sits in one of the armchairs near the hearth while I take the couch. Sydney, however, paces back and forth, his hands tucked behind his back. "What does this mean?"

"Sarah being a mystic? Nothing, likely. We won't know until we know what kind of relic Gabriel has, and it's obvious to me she was young enough when she escaped him that the details are lost on her."

"Then none of this matters," Sydney says with finality. "Her powers don't matter."

"As long as she stays out of Gabriel's hands." Evander leans his head back against the chair. "The Ghosts are still operational and looking for Gabriel. It's only a matter of time until he's found."

"And then what? He'll be held accountable for his crimes against the Allied Kingdoms?"

"Of course," I tell Sydney, but he looks angry. Exhausted. Worn thin.

"What about my mate?" he growls. "What justice does she get?"

I understand now.

I rise, my back cracking. I wince, blowing out my breath, but fix Sydney with a look. "I'm going to give you a piece of advice, and you're going to hate it, but I need you to listen to me carefully. Tell our family about Sarah. The whole truth."

"I can't do that."

He's going to hate what I'm going to say next even worse, but I press on. "She belongs in Eastonia, Sydney. She doesn't know her powers. She had no one to train her. She's lucky she didn't scramble your brain–"

"I'm not separating her from Blake."

"Blake can come, and it wouldn't have to be forever–"

"Your father will treat her like a prisoner–"

"You don't know that. You can't know for sure how our parents will react. Sarah was a child. She's not involved in his schemes. She's just a piece of the puzzle, Sydney. But she deserves to understand what she is. She needs to be with the other mystics."

"No," Sydney says flatly and attempts to leave the room, but Evander stands.

"I agree with Sydney," he tells me quietly.

I frown at him. "What? Why?"

"She can't go back to Eastonia. Her life is here. She should remain Sarah, not Sasha. She seems to have enough control over her powers to keep them at bay unless she needs them. Training them would only make her more useful to Gabriel if he were to get his hands on her."

Okay, that is a good point. But–

"Do you know this Hadley woman you mentioned?" he asks Sydney.

"Barely. She's part of Ryan's pack. I've wondered if he….Never mind."

"Well, I recommend Sarah stays here for the time being. No guests. No visitors. No friends. Not until we know more about Gabriel's plans."

Sydney nods, but I'm seeing red. "You want her to stay locked up here?"

Evander meets my gaze, loving and gentle, but his words ring through the air to remind me how dangerous of a position Sarah is in. "The Draven Coven was highly skilled in the art of manipulation and espionage. I don't believe the coven is totally disbanded. I believe they're still here, in Crescent Falls, and I'm not convinced someone as valuable to them as Sarah could slip through the cracks."

"What are you saying?" Sydney asks, narrowing his eyes at Evander.

My mate steps forward. "Don't trust anyone right now, Sydney."

He watches us leave the sitting room. We've recently started staying at the castle because Brie is on her way from Maatua with Grandma Isla for Aunt Maddy's upcoming dinner.

I get in the car, Evander sliding into the driver's seat.

The manor fades into the distance as the sun begins to set. I send a prayer to the Goddess to watch over them and to give Sydney the guidance he needs to move forward.

"Do you think Gabriel knows where she is right now?" I ask my mate.

I catch his eyes in the reflection of the rear view mirror.

"Yes. I think he knows exactly where she is."

2 8

QUEEN OF WISHFUL THINKING

SARAH

TIME IS AN ILLUSION. I've never slept so much in my entire life.

My body feels weak and heavy as I linger on the edge of sleep, refusing to let myself succumb to the inky, black, depthless slumber I've been experiencing for days even though my body is begging for it.

I know it's the tea. It has to be. It's the only thing I've been able to keep down since spiraling back to reality, and Cosette has a habit of hiding her nasty herbal concoctions behind copious amounts of honey and cream.

A burst of pain launches me back into alertness. I sneeze loudly, ripping my eyes open to find myself face to face with Blake, who's gripping my nose with an iron fist.

He beams at me, his eyes going all squinty with delight.

"Did you just stick your finger all the way up my nose?" I ask, arching my brow at him.

He sucks in his breath and does his best impression of laughing, which comes out as a broken coo, then smacks me smartly on the cheek. I'm under the impression Cosette or Dalia drops him off during his naps, letting him sleep beside me.

"Do not go in there and bug her!" Cosette's voice rips through the air, muffled by the closed door on the far side of Sydney's room. "She is fine, Alpha Sydney. And you know it, too. Pestering her won't speed up her healing."

"I'm not pestering her. You know I have to get the full story here eventually-"

"And eventually you will," Cosette snaps, her tone icy and dripping with maternal annoyance. "But not today. In fact, I've seen far too much of you over the last ten days. I'm sick of you, Alpha Sydney. You need to leave."

I hear Sydney scoff, the suck in his breath with a wince like Cosette just jabbed him with her finger.

"Get out of the house. Go to the firm; there's an idea. Or better yet, go shift and burn off some of this nervous energy you're drowning the house in. I want you out, Alpha."

"This is my house."

"Is it?"

I watch the door while Blake, totally oblivious to the match of wits taking place just beyond the threshold of the room, plays with my fingers. Cosette has no qualms about putting Sydney in his place. I imagine her looking up at him, her hands planted firmly on her hips, while waiting for his answer about who really owns this house.

Sydney does, of course. But he's not the boss here, despite the fact that he's the Alpha.

I bite my lip to stop from chuckling as Sydney says, "Would you like to tell me how to run my pack too, Alpha Cosette?"

"Get. Out. Do not darken the doorway until sun down, at least. Leave Sarah alone. She's fine. She has to be out of bed today, anyway."

"Why?"

"Your mother called-"

"I said no-"

"She's in pieces, Sydney. I told her Sarah was horrifically sick, you know, so we could take a few vials from her of your grandmother's tears without raising suspicions. She's been calling for updates and is absolutely heartbroken you didn't allow her to check in on the two of you."

"What was she going to do? Bring us some soup?"

"This is why I've had enough of you!"

Sydney draws in his breath in another wince. Cosette must be pinching him now.

"What does my mother have to do with Sarah?"

"Now that Sarah is feeling better, your mother wants to see her and has invited her over for tea today–at the castle. It's perfectly safe–"

"No!"

"Kenna is there, remember? Kenna wouldn't risk Sarah's secret. I think it would be good for Sarah, honestly, to spend some time with the women in your family. If anyone knows the trials and tribulations of being mated into this clan, it's them."

Sydney's quiet for a moment. I sit a little straighter as the door-knob begins to turn then stops.

"Fine, but I'm sending her with an escort."

"I'm her escort, and I already have a warrior lined up to drive us with a second one following behind. It'll be a little convoy, okay? Gabriel isn't going to jump out of the bushes and kidnap her during the half hour drive to the castle."

"Don't let anything happen to her."

Sydney's words settle in my chest, suffocatingly heavy. We've barely spoken since I woke up two days ago. I've been asleep for most of that time, moving in and out of consciousness to find him sitting at his desk, on his computer, or lying next to me but just out of reach as he stares at the ceiling, or scrolls on his phone.

Blake, however, seems to just appear beside me anytime I'm on the verge of going under again. The difference is he's always happy to see him. Sydney just looks at me like I'm going to disappear again.

It hurts, but I deserve it. There's nothing I can do, or say, to make this up to him. I'm not sure I can.

When the door opens, it's not Sydney. Cosette bustles in with her usual breakfast tray and shuts the door behind her with her hip. She smiles at me, looking smug as hell as she motions me to sit and places the tray over my lap.

"I'm sure you heard all of that," she says with a bit of a lift in her voice. She swoops Blake up, balancing him on her hip. "Sydney is going to work today, *finally*. He hasn't been to his firm in over a week."

I turn the tea cup in front of me in a circle, wondering if she's spiked it with some sleeping draft again, but if I'm going to see the queen today, I highly doubt it. I take a cautious sip.

"Sydney is going to be fine, you know. He's just worked up."

I don't want to talk about Sydney. I feel like I don't even deserve to say his name.

Cosette watches me as she bounces Blake on her hip, her eyes narrowing as she watches me drink the tea and ignore everything else she piled on the tray. "Sydney isn't normally like this. He can be very funny and exciting to be around–"

"I know," I cut in, my chest achingly tight.

She narrows her eyes even further. "I hope you know," she begins, adjusting Blake's weight as she shifts him to her other hip, "that no one blames you."

"I don't deserve this, Cosette. We both know it. This kindness, this care... Sydney will never trust me again. I've accepted that, but I can't–" I grip the tea cup so tight I'm suddenly worried it might shatter. I loosen my grip, closing my eyes as I try to untangle the mess of emotions rolling through my mind. "I can't do this to him."

"Him being a brooding, bothersome nightmare isn't because of anything you did!" She laughs, shaking her head.

"I lied to him and wiped his memory! Then I straight up left."

"I told you once that Sydney is protective. He's a good, solid Alpha. This is in his blood."

"It doesn't mean this is right."

"You are his mate, Sarah. The knowledge that you've been hunted half your life, and were brutally abused in the past, is what's driving him insane. Gabriel tortured him in Eastonia. He has a vendetta against him already. It's nothing you did."

I pale, my eyes downcast on the tea cup.

"The best thing we can do now is go back to normal. Everything is fine. You're fine. He's fine. He just needs to get out of the house, and so do you. So, eat something. Drink your tea and get dressed. We're leaving for the castle in thirty minutes."

"Has he left yet? I want to talk to him."

"Neither of you are talking to each other until you've gotten out of bed and had a day to just be Sarah again."

I gape at her as she walks away, Blake gnawing on her shoulder, and disappears through the door, which shuts behind her.

There's no arguing with Cosette, so I don't bother. I nibble on the food, brush my hair until it gleams, and walk on wobbly legs to my room on the other side of the second floor, using the wall for support. Over a week in bed, barely lucid, makes my muscles feel like jelly, but I manage to fight my useless body into a smart white cashmere sweater and the burgundy trousers Cosette ordered for me some time ago that always felt too formal to wear around the house.

I haven't put makeup on in ages, but a few swipes of mascara and some blush make me look a little more human and less like I've been rotting away in bed for days on end.

Without a minute to spare, Cosette ushers me and Blake outside to a waiting black car, and then we're off.

The cool morning air is a welcome feeling. I haven't been outside in so long.

But the closer we get to the castle, the more I'm spiraling back into despair.

"I do like her head housekeeper, but I can never remember her name," Cosette says to the warrior driving the car, the two of them having been lost in conversation as we drove out of Shadowcrest and into the city center.

My chest is in knots when we pull through the gates, and the castle looms ahead, towering over the trees lining a private road.

It hits me then.

I'm about to go into the castle. The *castle*. Where the queen and king live.

I clam up immediately and bow my head to hide the crimson red color flooding my cheeks.

I'm not sure how to feel. Being wanted, accepted, and being worried over are new feelings I'm not sure how to process.

I've never had a family. I've lived my entire life being a tool, something to wield and let run dry, and then hidden away to gather dust, forgotten.

But then I look at Blake, who is fast asleep with his cheeks squished against his car seat straps. He looks like his father. His dark brown hair gleams with copper as the sun pours through the windows. He's safe, warm, and happy.

He has a shot at the life I never had.

My mind hurtles back to Sydney, and that familiar ache ignites. I don't have a moment to ponder the logistics of our mate bond–the very thing I tried to bury deep down to protect him in the event Gabriel found me, found traces of Sydney in my soul that led him to Blake.

But I didn't know Sydney had met Gabriel until the night we spent in the hotel.

I run my knuckle over Blake's cheek and wonder, just for a second, if things will ever be easy between me and Sydney.

Because I want something easy. I want something normal.

I just don't know what normal is supposed to feel like.

I also want… I want Sydney. I want him so badly it hurts.

I close my eyes the moment the car jerks to a stop. Cosette murmurs something to the warrior about his lack of skill behind the wheel and tells him to pick us up in a few hours.

I get out, keeping my head down, and lift Blake out of his car seat. He whines, having been so rudely awakened from a blissful, somewhat bouncy ride in a warm car.

But two people appear on the wide front veranda.

Maddy smiles widely at us, her eyes glimmering with true, unadulterated joy to see us; to see me.

But my eyes slide to Kenna, and I'm reminded of the fragility of my situation.

Maddy can't know. Not about me, and worst of all, not about Blake.

Not until we've all figured this out somehow.

It's also not my secret to tell.

This is Sydney's family, after all.

"Oh, Goddess, I am so happy you're feeling better. I was so worried," Maddy rushes out, planting a kiss on my right, then left, cheek.

"Where's that baby, Alpha Kenna? I've been dying to meet her," Cosette says behind me as she lugs Blake's diaper bag up the stairs to the massive front door.

"She's inside with my grandparents." Kenna smiles, her expression as sweet as sugar. But as she shows Cosette into the house, her eyes catch mine again, and those wells of liquid silver silently tell me everything is going to be okay.

But I'm about to come face to face with the woman who started it all.

Maddy shows us into a formal sitting room where the smell of tea spices the air. Bright yellow wallpaper sets a sunny, uplifting atmosphere despite the nervous, irregular thundering of my heart.

Pale golden hair catches the light raining down through several stained glass windows depicting the Moon Goddess in her various forms, illuminating the slight, beautiful woman seated in a high-backed armchair.

She turns her head, the corners of her eyes creasing as she bounces a dark-haired toddler on her knee.

"You must be Sarah," Isla says, grinning.

2 9

———

IT'S OBVIOUS

Sarah

I LOOK at the women in the sitting room, wondering if I should pinch myself to make sure this is real, and I'm not cooking this vision up in my muddled brain.

I have no idea where Cosette went, but Isla remains in her wing-back chair, her legs crossed as she balances a steaming cup of coffee on her knee. Her head is slightly bowed as she speaks in low tones to Maddy, who is fluttering around a low lying coffee table, arranging cookies and pastries on a little tray.

Two queens. A mother and daughter by love and marriage with a bond forged by hard times.

My stomach does a little flip as I sink to the white carpeted floor with Blake babbling incoherently in my arms as he reaches for the hazel eyed babysitter only a few feet away.

"Careful, she's crawling now," Kenna says with some effort as she sinks to her knees, then stretches her legs out with her back resting against the couch. Brie's curly brown hair sticks up at all angles as she hones in on Blake, her pudgy fingers gripping the carpet for support.

"How old is she?" I ask, and Kenna's eyes light up with so much love it could illuminate the room.

"She turns one this summer. She's a little over nine months old now," she smiles, catching Brie by the back of her pants and dragging her backward. "She loves babies and kittens. Anything smaller than her is fair game."

I can't help but smile as I lay Blake on his stomach. He lifts his head, squawks with displeasure, but settles when Brie squeals with delight and claps her hands at them.

This is rather cute, honestly. They're cousins. Blake has a cousin, a born friend. Just like Sydney and Kenna.

Isla suddenly rises from her chair, and Maddy leads her out of the room, the two of them still talking in hushed murmurs and quiet laughs.

Kenna and I watch them go, and when we're alone, she turns to me. "How are you feeling?"

I run my fingers through my hair and sigh. "I'm all right."

Kenna arches her brow. I eye her, searching that strange silver gaze. I've often wondered why my power manifests in my eyes, why my eyes change color based on my moods or how much power is roiling in my blood, but Kenna is the same. I see hints of her powers swirling in her irises like the promise of an epic storm.

"I'm not okay," I say without thinking. I'm tired of thinking. I'm tired of worrying and breaking my own heart over and over.

"I wouldn't be either," she whispers, her smile fading into something much softer and empathetic. She licks her lips, allowing Brie to gain a few more inches on Blake before pulling her back again. "I would have done the same thing to Evander, you know."

I shake my head. "No. What I did was inexcusable."

"What you did was necessary. Sydney might not get it, but I know he would have done the same thing to you if it meant keeping you safe."

I chew my lower lip. Kenna scooches closer, wincing a bit as she adjusts her position next to me. Brie makes little grunting noises as she tries to claw her way toward Blake while Kenna keeps a finger hooked in her pants, keeping her in place.

Kenna is very pregnant. I was that pregnant recently; I remember vividly how uncomfortable it was.

"Look," she says lightly, glancing at the archway leading to the foyer to confirm we're still alone. "I understand, okay? Having powers like this–confusing, deadly powers with the ability to maim someone beyond repair–it's hard enough. I was also hunted by Gabriel. I thought that attack on the ball was because of me, but you were there too. He got close enough to you to scare you, didn't he?"

I close my eyes for a moment. "Yeah, I... I didn't know until a few days later what had happened at that ball, and I saw him on TV and just.... I'd already wiped Sydney's memories. I'd hoped it would be enough, but I saw Sydney again a few months later, this past fall. He came to my shop, and it was obvious he'd remembered me, somehow, just enough to ask if we'd met before."

"Have you ever done this to anyone else?"

I nod, looking down at my lap as Brie gives up on her progress toward Blake and resorts to picking at the hem of my trousers instead. "The family I used to live with. It was my house mother's idea. She knew bits and pieces about my powers from the people who snuck me over the border, but I was just a kid then. I couldn't use them. She had no way to train me. But when I was a teenager, I returned to the island to visit. I was older and had been experimenting with my powers for a few years at that point. I was worried Gabriel, if he ever found me, would find her and punish her for what she did. He'd torture the truth out of her, so I gave her the option of taking those memories of me away, and she agreed."

"Did it work?"

"Yes. It was flawless."

I also did this to Ryan, in the atrium. He'd remembered me. He'd almost said so, but I wiped those memories clean off the map woven in his mind.

I lift Brie into my lap on impulse, needing something to ground me. Kenna watches us with a smile on her face. "But it didn't work on Sydney, not totally?"

"It's because we're mates. I can wrap my powers around his memories and shield them, dissolving them, but I couldn't erase our bond. Only the Goddess has that power, you know." I clear my throat. I might as well just spill it all, laying everything out in the open. "He felt our bond. It's why he came back the night he rescued me. He was drawn to me. I knew he'd come back one day, and I dreaded it, because I'd have to dive into his mind again and pick out any trace of me when the time came for me to leave, but I couldn't do it." I meet her eyes. "When he learned the truth about Blake, when I found the necklace in his office…." I can't describe my heartbreak. "I wanted him. I didn't want to leave him again, but I had to. I just couldn't stand the idea of ripping myself out of his head again. I wanted my memory to stay there so somewhere, someone would remember me. Someone would remember my name. I left knowing the time we spent together was still in his mind, clear and whole, because I couldn't stomach the idea of having to live a life where my own mate couldn't remember my face, and it was the most selfish thing I could have done."

"It's not selfish," she whispers, clutching my arm. "I can't imagine having to do what you did. Evander and I had a rough go of it at first, of course. Being mates isn't an easy thing to come to terms with. It's not all rainbows and butterflies, even though I often dreamed it would be. Evander didn't want me to be his mate because he swore to keep me safe and didn't think he could do so if distracted by our bond. I was able to talk him out of that, though." She winks at me, patting her belly.

I chuckle, and the ice around my heart cracks a bit, letting in some warmth.

"What I'm trying to say is that no one blames you for what you had to do. You were protecting Sydney. He was tortured this summer in Eastonia. I know someone must have dug around in his mind. If they'd found you, you wouldn't be here. Blake wouldn't be here. And Sydney would likely be dead. You did the right thing."

I did the right thing.

The words echo through my head, shattering that ice once and for all.

"It doesn't negate the fact he won't ever trust me again."

"Oh, please," she laughs, waving her hand in dismissal. "Sydney is goo-goo eyed around you. This isn't about trust at all. He loves you. He won't admit it, but he does. He's just being an Alpha male and obsessing over protecting you, not wanting anyone to even look in your direction. This will pass, and one day you'll back on all of this and laugh."

"Do you look back on what you went through with Evander and laugh?"

I have no idea what happened to her, but a darkness fills her eyes. She shakes her head, giving me a timid smile. "Not yet, but I'm confident I will. If my parents can joke about the terrible things they went through, then one day, so can we."

Brie tumbles out of my lap, grunting. Kenna chuckles at her daughter as she rolls toward Blake, expertly coming to a stop in front of him on all fours.

Brie cautiously extends her tiny pointer finger toward him. Blake goes nearly crossed eyed as he watches her finger coming closer, and closer.

"Boop," Brie says, flashing Blake a two-toothed grin as she pokes him on the nose.

Blake squeals with delight, and then Kenna and I are laughing, tears in our eyes.

"What's going on in here?" Maddy asks with a smile as she returns to the sitting room with Isla.

"Brie is trying desperately to eat this other baby," Kenna says with a laugh.

As if on cue, Brie leans down like she's going to give Blake a kiss, but tries to close her mouth around his fist instead.

"No biting," Kenna says in a deep, growling voice that Brie obviously adores because she belly laughs.

"Blake is such a handsome baby, Sarah," Isla says as she sits on the armrest of the couch holding another cup of coffee. "All that hair, and blue eyes, too."

"It's a shame he didn't get your eyes," Kenna says teasingly, but I feel a little pang in my chest. It's a reminder to tread lightly, to keep my big, fat mouth shut if possible.

"I love your eye color," Maddy gushes. "It's the same color as my office. I spent weeks trying to find the right mix of colors to achieve it." She plants her hands on her hips, tapping her foot. "You know what, I want to show you. Come on, I haven't given you a tour yet."

I'm not given a choice. I look over my shoulder as Isla kneels on the ground with Kenna and the babies. Maddy hustles me up the grand staircase, which is sweeping and opulent, and soon I find myself in a maze of hallways where art lines the walls and portraits of King Isaac's ancestors stare back at me, unblinking, the ghosts of which are likely reading my thoughts.

I step into Maddy's office and find that she was right. Her lavender wallpaper is, in fact, a perfect match to my eyes. She's pleased with herself, grinning like mad as she rounds her wide, pale wood desk, and sits down.

"I suppose we should talk about the flowers now."

"What flowers?" she asks, opening a drawer. "Oh, for the dinner party. No, no. I'm not putting you to work so soon after you've recovered. But I do hope you'll come as a guest, of course." She pulls out an old notebook and flips through it.

I sit down in a large, warm chair the color of cream and wonder what exactly I'm doing right now.

"Cosette wanted a recipe," she murmurs, flipping a page.

"Oh," I reply, clearing my throat, but then Maddy sighs deeply and runs her hands over her face. "Are you–are you all right?"

"I don't want to pry," she says hurriedly, tucking her hands in her lap. She's fidgeting, which doesn't quite register in my head because, to me, this woman is the queen, and not a regular person with feelings and little quirks. Her eyes meet mine, the same shade and shape as Sydney's... and Blake's. She sighs again and makes up her mind about something.

"Sydney was in pieces when you got sick. I've never seen him so worried before. It broke my heart."

"He's been taking very good care of me."

"I know he has, and that–" She licks her lips, gazing up at the ceiling. "Oh, Sarah. Sydney is head over heels for you. I know I shouldn't say anything because it's not my business to get involved, but I worry about my son so much that it drives me insane. He's so much like his father, you know. Hard headed. Both of them, Isaac and Ella, are like that. I just want Sydney to let himself be happy."

"He's happy," I say, but I have no idea if it's the truth.

"When I saw him last, he had Blake with him. It's so kind of you to trust him with that boy. When Brie was taken this summer… Goddess, Sydney has never been the same."

"He's so good with Blake," I say as tears begin to well in my eyes. "They're so alike." I choke on the words, trying to take them back, but Maddy's gaze meets mine.

She's a mother. She understands wanting, and needing, the best, safest options for her children. She, other than Kenna, might be the only person who understands what it's like to have a child in grave danger.

"They are so alike," she says in a whisper, and I see the realization dawn in that clear, dark blue gaze.

I cover my face with my hands at the very moment she stands, sucking in a breath.

"You're *her*. You're the one he's been looking for–"

"I can explain–"

"Blake is his?" her words crack with so much happiness, so much relief, if I'm being honest.

"Please don't tell anyone. We haven't talked about–" I feel her wrapping her arms around me. It's a warm, soft embrace dripping with motherly affection.

It's everything I've ever needed.

"I knew it," she whispers into my hair. "Oh, Sarah, I knew from the moment I met you at my party. I won't tell anyone, not until you're ready, but welcome." She takes me by the chin, forcing my face up so I have to look into her teary eyes. "Welcome to the family."

30

THE AIR I BREATHE

I STAYED OUT ALL DAY. I didn't come home until the sun faded and the sky turned an inky, endless black dotted with stars.

Admittedly, I stayed at my office until nearly 10:00 PM just to piss Cosette off, thinking she'd be waiting by the door to cuff my ears even though she was the one who bullied me out of my own home this morning.

Being alone, thrust into a somewhat normal routine again, felt right. It felt good. I feel somewhat like myself again after a day working and several hours spent shifting and running through the woods.

But I also didn't stop thinking about Sarah all day long. I replayed those memories she returned to me over and over again until the night we spent together after the ball was so clear I could taste the vanilla ChapStick she was wearing and smell the floral perfume scenting her skin.

Now I'm home, walking through the garage door, and the house is quiet and dark.

But the light to the sitting room off the foyer is on.

I drop my gym bag and turn into the room, expecting to find Cosette waiting for me, but it's Sarah.

She's sitting on the ground in front of the fireplace, wearing a silly pair of fuzzy socks and her favorite leggings. My faded Wellington University crew-neck sweatshirt hangs to her knees as she watches the fire crackle in the hearth, the reflection of the flames blazing in her eyes.

"Hey," I say, edging into the room with my hands stuffed into the pockets of my sweatpants.

She turns to look at me over her shoulder, giving me a tight smile. "Hey."

"Are you okay?"

She sighs heavily and looks back at the fire. It's a stupid question. Of course, she's not okay. Hell, I'm not okay. We're in one of the shittiest positions I can think of.

There's so much left unsaid between us right now. So much we need to work through so we know where we stand–together–as mates and as parents to our son.

"I fucked up," she says quietly, her eyes meeting mine again.

I arch my brow. "What do you mean?"

"Your mom." She stretches out her legs, wiggling her toes. "She knows."

"Tell me again," I say, stepping out of the shower twenty minutes later.

Sarah paces back and forth in my room, her footsteps leaving indents in the carpet. "She just knew. I slipped up, but not that bad, I don't think. I mentioned how alike you and Blake are, and she ran with it, like she brought me up to her office, alone, because she already knew something was up. I started to cry and that sealed the deal."

I tie a towel around my waist and grab a fresh one off the rack next to the shower, running it over the top of my head. "But she doesn't know you're Sasha?"

"No, of course not! But she knows I'm the one you were looking for after the ball."

I shrug, hanging the towel up and leaning on the doorway, the door open a crack so we could talk while I was in the shower. I watch her turn on her heel and pace back in the direction she came, following the trail she's laid for the entirety of my shower. Her hair is pulled back in a ponytail that falls down her back in a sheet of pure, pale golden silk. Her face is flushed a rosy pink, lightly dusted with makeup. She looks pretty. Young, and vibrant. It's a nice change, honestly. Seeing some light in her eyes has some of the tension leaving my shoulders.

"Why are you looking at me like that?" she snaps.

"Smiling at you?"

"This is serious. You told me–you told all of us who know–that this needs to remain a secret, and I messed it up already."

"They were going to find out sooner or later that Blake is mine. He looks just like me."

"I understand that, but we haven't talked about what happens now, Sydney. This!" She motions between us. "We haven't talked about this."

"We're mates, Sarah."

"I know that, but we've–Sydney, I don't even know where to begin. I don't know what to do or how to act...." She finally stops pacing and wraps her arms around herself in a tight embrace.

There's two ways to do this. We could sit down and hash out the details in a businesslike manner. Who are we to each other? Do we want to be with each other or simply play the roles I know will keep Sarah as safe as possible while giving her the rank she deserves as my mate and mother of my child?

Or I can be stupid and act on the desperation that's been clouding my better judgment since the moment I found her in her old apartment.

I'm being reckless. I can feel it in my blood as I step forward, in nothing but a towel to top things off, and say, "Say it."

She shakes her head.

"Say it," I repeat, my heart thundering. "Do you want to leave?"

"No, that's not–"

"Would you be more comfortable living in your cottage in the village rather than here, with me?" I ask.

She looks confused, shaking her head.

"Then say it," I push, but she narrows her eyes at me.

"What do you want me to say?"

"Reject me."

Her eyes go wide. "Sydney, what the fuck are you talking about?"

"Reject me, Sarah. If you don't want this–"

"I never said I didn't want this!"

"Then talk to me," I urge, taking a step toward her. Sarah is finicky. Like a doe being hunted, she freezes, but I can almost hear her heart beginning to thunder against her ribs. "I've been wondering why you didn't reject me to begin with, all those months ago. You kept our bond intact. Why?"

"Because I–I wanted to."

"Why, Sarah?"

She turns pinker than before, her eyes flaming that deep amethyst color that sets my skin prickling with both unease and heavy desire.

Reckless. Dumb, and rash. I'm egging her on despite the fact we have things to shell out, to explain, to decide.

Those things go beyond how we feel about each other.

They don't matter right now. Seeing her awake, lucid, and… happy. It's doing something to my body that I can't ignore. I can feel her emotions through our bond. That despair that's been lingering there, plucking at the fine, golden threads between us, has waned, replaced by hope.

That's enough for me. That's all I need.

"Why didn't you shatter our bond?" I step toward her. "You stole my memories of you but left the bond intact. I need to know why."

"Because I love you," she says rapidly then covers her face with her hands.

When she peeks through her fingers again, I'm closer, within a foot of her.

She turns on her heel and tries to beeline for the door, but I grab her arm, holding her in place. "Sydney, please, let me go."

"Do you think I don't feel the same way?"

She doesn't move. She's holding her breath, her body rattling with the effort. "You can never trust me again after what I did to you. Everyone is telling me how protective you are, how good you are, and I am grossly aware of how little affection I deserve from you, Sydney. We're mates, but that doesn't mean we have to be together."

"Sarah, this goes beyond the mate bond for me." I gently pull her toward me. "Did you look through my memories?" I ask. "Do you have the ability to peer inside each moment, to feel what I felt, to think what I thought?"

She shakes her head, silent, refusing to look at me and keeping her gaze toward the door.

I lick my lips and pull her closer, reaching up to move her hair away from her neck. I run my fingertips down to the base of her throat where her shoulders converge. "Do you want to know what was going through my head that night I spent with you? Not when we slept together but before? When we were in the temple?"

She lets out her breath in a hesitant moan like she's trying to hold it back. I lean down, my lips brushing over the back of her neck in a featherlight kiss as I wrap my around her waist.

I shouldn't be doing this. My need to touch her, to feel her warm and supple in my hands, is making everything else hazy. All the threats to our lives, all the uncertainty, the vow I made to her, my mate, at arm's length… it doesn't matter anymore. Not now. Maybe not ever.

"I saw you," I whisper against her skin, "and I told myself I'd marry you, the mate bond be damned. I didn't care if you were my mate or not. You were made for me. You were mine, from that moment on, and that hasn't changed."

She relaxes–melts into my touch. I unwind my arms from around her waist and pull the sweatshirt up and over her shoulders. She's not wearing anything underneath, thank the Goddess.

I reach for her breasts, my lips pressed against her shoulder. I can feel her heart racing as my teeth drag over her skin.

"I was too shy to tell you how badly I wanted you that night," I tell her. "I shouldn't have been. I should have carried you over my shoulder back to my house, my pack, the moment we left the temple."

She leans her head back against the crook of my shoulder, her eyes closed as my hands slide down her belly to the waistband of her leggings.

"I loved you then," I whisper against her temple. "I love you now. That's why this is so fucking hard, Sarah, because if you leave me again… Gabriel wouldn't be the only man tearing the world apart to find you."

My hands travel upward, ghosting over her arms. The bandage on her arm from where Gabriel marked her draws me out the haze of desire in an instant, and then I'm spiraling into rage I can't contain.

Someone else marked my mate.

She turns to me, pressing her hand against my cheek and drawing my head down to meet hers.

"Don't think about it."

"I can't–" It's not me funneling into rage, not entirely. It's my wolf. That feral, instinct driven side of me that wants nothing more than to pin her down and leave marks on her skin so that everyone who sees her knows who she belongs to.

She can feel these things through our bond.

"Do you understand why I made that vow last summer?" I ask.

She wraps her arms around my neck, one of her hands cupping the back of my head while her fingers tangle through my damp hair. "For the same reasons I took your memories of me. We're in this together."

"Then let's be in this together."

"How, Sydney?"

I don't know the answer. Memories of being in Gabriel's dungeon flash in my mind. He'll find her one day. He'll come here to take her, but he'll have to face me first.

We have to have a life somehow, a life that's not weighed down but fear, grief, and despair.

I want to be able to take her on a date–a real date, with dinner and a movie and walks along the lake–without feeling like I have to continually look over my shoulder.

I want to walk with her into the village while we drop Blake off at school without a worry in our minds about his safety.

I want to live.

Beside her.

My mouth crashes into hers. Her lips are warm, wet, and coaxing as she grips the back of my head and slides her tongue along my lower lip. I open for her, biting her lip, my tongue swirling over hers in a frantic, dizzying dance.

She jumps into my arms, her legs wrapped around my waist.

Nothing else matters. Not Gabriel, not the threat of us being separated.

Just this.

I fall onto the bed with Sarah in my arms. I pull her hair loose from the scrunchie holding it in place and let it fall over me as I roll so she's straddling me.

Her breasts are soft and heavy, pressed against my chest. She's all around me–the only thing I can sense and taste. She's the very air I breathe.

I'm going to mark her.

Then, I'm going to hunt Gabriel down and make him beg for mercy.

31

THE ANCIENT ART OF MARKING ONE'S MATE

Sarah

This feels like the very first time. There's nothing frantic about this. Each touch, every stroke of his fingers, is calculated and meticulous, honed to my pleasure.

Sydney's hands graze up my back as I continue to straddle him, my thighs locked against his hips. I grind against him, growing desperate with need.

His fingertips drag down my spine in a touch that sends chills cascading over my body, like he's hitting every nerve and setting them aflame.

There's nothing in my head. My mind is blissfully quiet as every ounce of my energy focuses on the way he's touching me and how he tastes when I kiss him again and again.

"Sarah." He growls low in his throat when I bite down on his lip. I grind against his cock, nothing but my leggings and the towel he's wearing around his waist to separate us.

"Please," I whimper. "Please, Sydney. I need this. I need you inside of me. I'm desperate." I don't even recognize my own voice. Whoever's speaking sounds like a siren, her voice low and sultry.

He gasps when I pull away and lean down to brush a kiss over his neck, raking my teeth over his skin in the same way he did to me only moments ago. I have the sudden urge to bite him. To clamp down on his shoulder and sink my teeth into his skin until I taste blood.

My wolf is dormant, too young to emerge, but she trembles inside of me.

He grips the back of my neck to hold me there, my teeth leaving small indents on his shoulder. His other hand fumbles with my leggings, pulling them down over my hips.

"Don't stop doing that," he rasps as he runs his hand over the slope of my bare hip. He jerks beneath me when I bite down again, sucking a bruise into his skin.

This is insane. What we're doing right now–to each other–feels so wrong but also so right. Maybe I feel this way because he's the only person I've ever been with before, but something about this feels… instinctual. Natural. Like it's a part of who I am.

My senses are going haywire. He smells divine. His touch warms me through and through.

He pulls my leggings down farther, taking my panties with them, but in this position there's no way to get them off completely without me having to get off his lap, and I'm not budging.

I kiss my way back up his neck. My lips are swollen when I kiss his mouth again, and his hand tightens on the back of my neck, his fingers tangled in my hair.

"Please," I beg, panting.

Sydney opens his eyes to slits as I pull away to look down at him fully. I rest my hands on his chest. I can feel his heart racing beneath my palm. Bruises dot his right shoulder surrounded by small bite marks, nothing that broke the skin.

Yet.

I meet his gaze and feel the mate bond sweep through me and snap in place like it's the first time all over again.

He feels it too. His gaze is heavy and dark with need, and his grip on my hips tightens to the point of pain before he rolls me over so I'm beneath him, on my belly.

He rips my leggings off in one swift motion.

"Sarah," he says in a tone I've never heard before. It's like he's holding back a growl, like he's about to shift, letting his wolf side free. "Do not move."

My breath catches in my throat as he lowers himself to cover me with his body.

A memory flutters forward from the recesses of my mind. An obscure detail about shifters I'd long forgotten, having buried it away with the rest of my schooling.

Sydney traces a line up my spine with his tongue. My eyes nearly roll back in my head.

Synapsis fire. My nerve endings erupt with a new kind of pleasure, something ancient and deeply ingrained in the part of me that's shifter.

Shifters have special nerves in their back, spine, and shoulders. Once, long ago, when we were more wolf than man, mates used to scent each other, marking each other with their tongues, not just their teeth. Little bites would accrue all the way down the spine, the base of the neck, the wrists. This occurred back in the times of knotting, when shifters were scarce, and they had to do what needed to be done to produce more children.

It was a ritual. An event between mates to make their bond official. It's primal and feral, and he's doing it to *me*.

But we're modern wolves; such practices are a thing of the past.

"Ohhh," I moan when he bites down on the place where my shoulder meets my neck. He sucks the skin there, peppering it with a bruise. His cock rests against the globes of my ass, rigid and hot, but he isn't in a hurry.

I flood with desire, though. I wiggle my hips, chasing any kind of friction I can find. It's not enough.

"I told you not to move," he rasps, breathless. He bites down on my shoulder blade, his teeth sinking ever so slightly into my skin but not hard enough to leave a mark.

I grip the sheets, crying out as he kisses another bruise onto my skin and moves on, his tongue gliding down my shoulder.

He presses one of his hands to the mattress while the other snakes between me and the bed, his fingers wrapping around my throat. He starts grinding his hips, his cock, against my ass, and his breathing picks up as he so carefully, so thoughtfully, searches for the perfect place to leave his mark.

His knee slides between my legs, nudging them apart.

"Mate," he rasps against my spine. His breath is heavy and uneven, and I sense him losing himself in the feel of me as he slides his cock into my pussy. He hisses a breath, and I squirm beneath him, arching my hips up to meet him, to take him deeper.

Goddess, I'm losing it. I grip the sheets and cry out his name as he thrusts as deep as I can allow.

"Goddess, Sarah," he pants, groaning with satisfaction.

I'm beyond words. Every stroke of his cock has me coming unglued, my mind in shambles, and my body thrumming with heat.

I bite down on my lip and turn my heated moans to hums as pressure builds in my lower belly. He kisses my nape–sucking and gently biting–and it feels so intimate, so excruciatingly sweet compared to the way he's absolutely ravishing me everywhere else.

"Grab the headboard," he says, brushing the words over the top of my ear.

Oh, Goddess. What now? I'm not sure how much more I can take as I reach up, wrapping my fingers around the slates in his headboard.

"I'm not going to hurt you," he whispers against my shoulder blade, but I sense an edge in his voice. "Do you trust me?"

"Yes," I moan as his thrusts slow and drags himself out of me fully, the head of his cock teasing my entrance.

He pants a breath, running his fingers down my side as I strain to keep my sweaty hands locked on the headboard.

"You're beautiful," he whispers, his touch turning more rough, more exploratory. He slaps my ass, and I whine with pleasure, biting down on my lip so hard I taste blood. "You're mine."

There's something about being this wanted that makes me turn molten. His possession is fire to my blood, and I'd do anything to hear him say it again. *Mine*. I belong to him. I am his mate. I am his.

He enters me again, slowly. It's so gentle I could cry. He puffs out a breath, ragged and strained, as he holds himself still and drinks in the feel of me clamped around him. He adjusts my hips so I'm resting on my knees. My hands slip down the slats in the headboard, but I keep holding on.

He curves his body over mine and pumps into me, one hand holding my hair back, the other resting on the mattress beside us, propping him up.

A moan slips out before I can bite it back. Tension coils as tight as a bow string in my thighs and belly.

"I'm so close," I whimper.

"Quiet," he orders, his voice low and full of smoke.

This is different. This is a ritual. I am being worshiped like my body is an altar, and he is laying out his offering, and my blessing is blood.

He bites me on the little knob at the base of my neck, where my shoulders meet. I feel pain shimmer down my back, down my spine, and settle in the pit of my stomach. I cry out, and he lets go of my hair to clamp his hand over my mouth.

He holds me there, his teeth sinking into my skin, and thrusts into me once, then twice, and I come undone.

My orgasm floods my mind before exploding through my body. The tension snaps—sharp and hot—and then I'm shaking, my pussy spasming around his cock while he edges closer to his own release.

He holds on with his teeth like he's trying to keep me in place, causing the mark to sink deeper into my skin.

There's no doubt it'll leave a scar.

And the results are… stupefying.

He lets me go with a pop, panting, and drags me away from the headboard, roughly flipping me onto my back. The mark stings with pain, but I ignore it. His face is washed with longing as his mouth meets mine in a feral kiss. He enters me again roughly, groaning without restraint, and I meet him thrust for thrust until we're both crying out, and I'm totally, completely, dizzy with pleasure.

He cups the back of my head and presses my face into the crook of his neck.

"Mark me, Sarah," he says through gritted teeth as my body locks up again, another orgasm drowning me in ecstasy I don't have the words to describe.

"Oh, Goddess!" I scream, blind with pleasure, and squeeze my eyes shut against the torrent of tension snapping loose and flooding me completely.

I taste him, his blood, unaware that I've bitten down at the base of his neck. He grunts, hissing out a breath, and comes inside of me, filling me with warmth.

I only let go when my body starts to feel hazy with the need to take a breath.

I open my eyes, panting, my head knocked back in exhaustion, and meet his gaze.

He looks… happy. Utterly, wholly, and completely happy.

He lowers his head to kiss me.

"I love you," I whisper, my voice barely audible.

"I waited so long for you," he replies in the same breathless, exhausted tone.

I STARE at the headboard as I sit naked on the edge of the bed. Sydney is beside me, turning me to face the wall while dabbing at the mark between my shoulder blades.

"How did you learn how to do that?" I ask, my eyes finding shapes in the texture in the paint on his wall.

"Do what?" His voice is scratchy as he gently runs a damp rag over the mark. I wince, and he grimaces, murmuring, "I'm sorry."

I was right about it being deep. It hasn't stopped bleeding yet, but I already refused, twice, when he wanted to use his healing powers on it.

I lick my lips. "You were… scenting me, in the old way."

He chuckles softly. "I don't know why people don't do it anymore."

I do smell like him. It's an almost overwhelming feeling. Like he's everywhere, like my entire body is now bound to him in this way.

"I don't think our kind was ever meant to stray so far from what we are intrinsically," he continues.

"Will you do that to me every time?" The words slip out before I can stop them.

He rests the rag against the mark. "I don't think I could stop myself from doing it again."

Now I'm the one chuckling. I look at him over my shoulder, smiling. His eyes crease with pleasure.

Knotting, though… the thought of that makes me bite my lip with sudden apprehension. He knows exactly what I'm thinking about, and his cheeks go a bit red as he clears his throat.

"We should sleep," he says.

"Are you tired?" I'm not. Energy like I've never felt before runs wild through my veins. I have a sudden sense–a sudden desire, really– to shift, even though I'm still too young.

At least, I think.

"I'm not." His eyes suddenly narrow on mine. He grabs my chin. "Open your mouth."

"Why?" I laugh, but my lips part on their own accord. His finger jabs into my mouth. I wrench away. "Hey!"

"Hold still," he says. He brushes his finger over my lower lip, looking suddenly lost in thought, but shakes himself out of whatever he was thinking of, and runs his thumb over the edges of my top teeth. "Sarah."

"What?" I ask when he removes his finger and fixes with me an astonished look.

"Can you shift?"

"I've never tried."

"Because you're too young. When's your birthday?"

"I honestly have no idea," I admit with a shrug.

He looks momentarily confused, mouthing, "You don't know your own birthday?" but blinks, taking me by the hand.

"We have two hours until Cosette wakes up. I want to see if you can do it. Are you okay with that?"

3 2

———

HUNTED BY A WOLF

"This is humiliating!" I whisper, trying to cover my naked body with my hands. The cold night air bites into my skin, numbing the pain of the fresh mark, yes, but stinging everywhere else.

Sydney, in his wolf form several feet away, paces back across the patio and says into my mind, 'If you shift, you'll be warm.'

He did this on purpose. He didn't so much as offer me a robe, probably to enjoy the sight of me in just my skin, shivering and at his mercy.

"I know," I bite out, annoyed. "I don't know how!"

'You'll feel it. Just tell your body what you want it to do.' He comes to a stop, and in a glimmer of movement and faint light, shifts back into his human form. "See?"

I frown at him before squeezing my eyes shut. *All right, body. Shift. Turn my hands into paws, or whatever.*

Nothing.

I run my tongue over my canine teeth, testing. He'd noticed they'd sharpened after I marked him, but they feel normal to me.

243

"Sydney, I can't do it."

He shifts back into a wolf like it's nothing for him, and I groan, my teeth chattering.

'Try,' he orders.

"I am!" I say out loud. I'd throw my hands in the air for emphasis but one arm is clutched to my breasts, keeping them somewhat out of view. He doesn't deserve a show after making me stand naked in the cold like this.

'Tell your body what to do. I can feel it in you. Your wolf is there.'

'I'm not just a wolf, remember?' I tell him through the mind-link, which is suddenly clear and open between us. Benefits of being mates, I presume.

He huffs a wolfish breath, flattening his ears to the top of his head. His stance is menacing, and a flicker of fear licks up my spine. "Syd?"

'Try, or I'll… chase you, and scare it out of you.'

'You wouldn't.'

'Do you want to test that theory?'

I back toward the house. He bares his teeth at me as he takes a step in my direction, his ruff standing on end.

"Sydney! Stop it!"

'One,' he says, taking another step.

"Absolutely not," I bite out, my teeth clashing as a bitter breeze ghosts over my skin.

'Two.'

"This is-is asinine, Sydney! Do not ch-chase me. I am *naked*–"

'Three.' He lunges, and I take off at a full sprint, resisting the urge to scream.

I run around the side of the house toward the door leading to the garage, but he's hot on my trail. I can't wrench it open fast enough before he's close enough to take me by the ankle in his powerful, lupine jaws if he wanted to.

I keep running, naked as the day I was born, and cross the boundary of the wolf trail leading toward the cottage I didn't end up needing.

My bare feet slip over ice as I descend the trail, huffing and puffing. This is crazy. What is he going to do? Jump on me? Bite me?

I know he's holding back, which makes this worse. He's probably incredibly fast in his wolf form. I wouldn't normally stand a chance.

Coming to my senses, I skid to a stop in the dark, empty woods and whirl around.

But he's not there.

"Sydney?"

A rustling of branches behind me has me whirling back in the direction I was running.

"Where are you?"

He's hunting me. Stalking me like prey. Real fear creeps through me despite the knowledge that this man would never, ever hurt me. He's my mate. That's in his blood.

A crack echoes through the forest. My skin pebbles as I slowly turn toward the sound. "Sydney?"

What if it's not Sydney?

That idea spins its way through my body in a rush of fear so great I find myself suddenly dizzy with adrenaline.

Another crack, and a shadow ghosts through my peripheral vision, and there's no way in hell I'm staying here.

I start running again, frantically jumping over rocks and piles of half melted snow. My heart starts to race so fast I find it hard to breathe, and then a snapping sensation ripples up my spine, vertebrae by vertebrae.

I choke out a breath before I fall forward, my legs unable to hold me upright. My face slams into the cold, icy ground with a crunch.

I'm rolling, head over heels.

Paws over paws.

Oh, my Goddess. I did it.

'Stay on your feet!' Sydney bellows into my head.

I try to find my footing, but my legs feel like jelly as I wobble back to all fours. I look up at a nearby ridge, only a few feet above my head.

Sydney stands there, his wolf illuminated by the clear, crescent moon behind him. His eyes glow with power.

But then he takes off, disappearing into the night.

I follow, slowly, trying to figure out this new body and the new, unusual powers propelling me forward. I feel stronger and somehow lighter as I maneuver off the well beaten trail, following my senses of sight, sound, and scent. Those senses are so much stronger now. I can sense him nearby as I cut into a snow covered clearing illuminated by the moon.

'Try to run,' he says into my mind, so I do.

It's tricky work. I trip over my own paws several times before my front legs and back legs start moving in tandem.

'Now jump,' he says.

I have no idea where he is, but he must be nearby, watching me. His voice in my head has lost that teasing, boyish gleam and is now serious and laced with heat. It propels me forward, and I find myself suddenly desperate to find him.

I've never felt this way before. It's too good of a feeling to ignore. Why did we ever start living our lives mostly on two feet when we could have *this*?

I reach the street leading into downtown Shadowcrest. It's silent, early morning, too early for others to be awake, but Sydney isn't here.

I pad across the street, panting, and take off at a sprint again once I reach the woods on the other side.

I follow his scent as the desperation to locate my mate reaches new heights.

Soon I find myself in front of the cottage, the pink door beckoning me inside.

'Sydney?' I say through the mind-link.

I walk up the stairs and nudge open the door. It was already slightly askew, and he's here, I can feel it.

My heightened senses burn with the thrill and desire to find him, to claim him again–over and over.

What's wrong with me? Is this normal?

I gasp as the snapping sensation happens again. My breath is forced from my body as I shift, unable to stop it from happening.

But Sydney is there, holding me upright. I look up into his eyes. They shine with pride.

I grab him and kiss him, hard, our teeth and tongues clashing in a delicious dance. He backs me against the wall and groans, his cock rigid against my bare leg. Goddess, we're still naked. There's nothing between us as he reaches between my legs and curses under his breath when he finds out how wet I am.

"Fuck, Sarah," he growls, stabbing two fingers inside of me. His thumb presses on my clit, moving in slow, teasing circles. He buries his head in the crock of my neck where the bruises he left earlier thrum to life with fresh pain, accentuating my desire.

This is definitely a mate thing. This feeling like I'll die if I can't him right here, right now.

He drags me to the ground and enters me without ceremony. I scream his name to the ceiling. There's no one around to hear us now.

He's rough with me. I like it. I claw his back with my nails as he grinds his hips against mine and fucks me like an animal.

When we're through—spent, and heavy with exhaustion—the sun is just breaching the horizon and sending sprays of soft, pink light through the frosted windows.

Sydney is fast asleep, his cheek pressed against my breasts, his arm wrapped protectively around my waist.

I look up at the ceiling of the cottage and watch the light play across it, tears welling in the corners of my eyes.

Happy. Safe. Warm. Whole.

Things I've never allowed myself to feel before.

I will do anything to remain this way.

Cosette pulls a twig out of my hair without a word, but her expression says everything I need to know about her sentiments.

She's doing her best to look displeased that Sydney and I stole away in the middle of the night and shifted together, but she can't stop the way the corners of her mouth are twitching into a smile as she brushes through my tangled hair.

Blake bounces in my lap, gnawing on the edge of the vanity.

The door to my old room opens, and Sydney appears, dressed with his hair combed back away from his face.

His eyes meet mine in the reflection of the mirror. He arches a brow. Cocky bastard.

"I'm leaving," he says, more chipper than usual.

"Where to?" Cosette asks, whirling to face him.

"I have a meeting with Ryan. I'll be back in a few hours."

Cosette huffs as Sydney closes the door, but he pauses to wink at me before shutting it completely.

I blush deeply. Cosette smirks.

"Would you be interested in a contraceptive draft, by chance?"

The blush deepens to pure crimson as it creeps down my neck. "Uhm, no, I don't think so."

"Good," she says, chuckling to herself. "Blake could use a sister."

I roll my eyes to the ceiling and laugh, unable to stop myself.

Cosette sets the brush down on the vanity and starts braiding my hair, but her expression turns serious. "Sarah, the dinner at the castle is tomorrow night, and you're going."

"Yeah." A crack forms in the bubble of delusion I'm holding onto for dear life. "I don't think I have a choice."

"Queen Ella arrived in Crescent Falls this morning," she says, swallowing hard.

Another crack, this one threatening to shatter the bright, happy mood I'm in completely.

"Is it possible she can sense what you are?"

"I don't know," I answer honestly.

Cosette nods at our reflection in the mirror as she ties my hair off and winds it into a bun at the nape of my neck.

"I fear the truth might come out before either of you are ready."

"I know," I whisper.

I don't want to think about that. I want to go back to last night, when all that mattered was Sydney's touch.

But she's right.

This is serious.

Maddy already knows Blake is Sydney's son, and now Sydney's mark is on my body. We can't go back to the way things were before.

"I think you should tell them the truth," Cosette murmurs. "I don't think we have much of a choice anymore."

"I know," I repeat, and that bubble shatters, crashing down around me.

TELLING RYAN

SYDNEY

I PULL my truck through the gates of Silverhide thirty minutes after leaving my own territory. Tall pines rise up all around me as the road leading out of the city center, and the NZ, narrows, and turns to finely packed gravel dusted with snow.

Ryan's house is the first building visible in the dense forest. It rises above the trees, stately and modern despite being a log home. The windows reflect the snow as I drive past his private driveway and dip down into the village.

Silverhide is a small, exclusive pack. After the war twenty-two years ago, several of the rogue villages along the base of the mountains that border Eastonia moved inward, trying to integrate into the packs in Crescent Falls. When Ryan and I came of age and started our own packs, he chose this old, undeveloped territory and opened his gates to whoever wanted to follow his lead then promptly shut them again.

His numbers are small even compared to mine. A hundred or so pack members, mostly young adults and a scattering of young children, live and work here.

I pass through the village square. It's quiet and mostly empty save for the diner connected to the bar, which is busy with people stopping in to grab breakfast and coffee before heading to work.

No one even looks in my direction, not until I roll onto another narrow road and turn into a wide, gravel parking lot where a huge warehouse rises before me, two of its five bay doors open.

Sports cars are being lifted. A few men walk inside, carrying toolboxes. A third bay door cracks open to reveal several more fine, exotic vehicles.

And then there's Ryan, sitting in a worn out swivel chair drinking from a huge thermos.

He cocks a brow as I bring my truck to a stop and step out.

"Well, well, well," he says, swiveling in my direction. He's wearing thick work pants, gray and splattered with oil and grease, and a Henley shirt in cobalt blue. His hair–longer than mine–touches his shoulders. I walk up to him, nodding in hello to his employees.

"Ryan," I say in greeting.

"I thought you were dead. It's been almost two weeks since I saw you last."

I smirk, but Ryan narrows his eyes at me. At my neck. I reach up to adjust the color of my jacket, but the damage is done.

"You filthy dog," he grins. "I guess congratulations are in order. Who's the lucky lady?"

"Is there somewhere we can talk privately?" I ask, tilting my head toward the metal stairs leading to his office on the second floor.

He sips low and slow from his thermos while keeping his eyes on mine. "Sure."

I sigh as he makes a show of moving as slowly as possible, standing up to stretch, to dig something out of his pocket, giving some of his employees claps on the shoulders and asking what their mates packed them for lunch.

Finally, I'm following him up the stairs into the loft that overlooks the massive garage. Two-way windows give a full view of the events happening below as Ryan shuts the door behind us and saunters over to his desk, which is untidy and covered in folders and oil smeared work orders.

"Sarah is your mate, I'm guessing," he says, sitting down. I notice his busted knuckles, mostly healed, but still dusted with green and yellow bruises.

"Yeah, she is."

"Well, can't say I'm all that surprised. I wouldn't expect you to take someone in like you did if she wasn't someone special."

I sit on a worn leather couch across from him, glancing at the magazines lining the surface. Cars, trucks, catalogs. The usual mechanic fare. "Her son is mine."

"Yeah, of course." He reaches behind him to turn on a coffee pot. "I'm sure Dad'll allow Blake some territory of his own when he comes of age. I don't know about succession, though, given that he's your stepson–"

"He's my son, Ryan. By blood."

Ryan stares at me for a moment, unblinking.

I lick my lips and continue, "Sarah and I met at the ball last summer. She's the woman I brought back to your house and had a one-night-stand with."

"Okay…" He slowly pours fresh coffee into his thermos. "You're sure?"

"Yes."

He drums his fingers on the desk. I can feel his gaze boring into my face as my eyes drop to my lap, to my hands.

"Why do I feel like there's more to this? You're acting weird."

"I'm not sure how to begin, honestly," I say with a laugh.

"What's going on, Sydney? I called you several times, you know. Hadley's been up my ass about seeing Sarah, and Cosette said she was sick, that you were both sick, but you've never been sick a day in your life–"

"Sarah is Sasha, Ryan."

He exhales long and slow. "Fuck, man."

"I know."

"How'd you find out?"

I knew Ryan wouldn't question me on this. He wouldn't cast doubt. If I'm sure of something, he's along for the ride–always.

"I found out about Blake first. He looks like me–like us." I meet his eyes again, motioning to his face. "He has the eyes we share with Mom, a little bit of red in his hair like we do. But his eyes gave it away. When I confronted her about it, the truth came out."

I tell him everything. I paint him a mental picture of that night, how Sarah begged me to take care of Blake before sending her fractured childhood memories spiraling into my mind. I tell him about my newly restored memories of the night after the ball, though not in detail, when I slept with her for the first time, and we realized we were mates, and how she took those memories away to remain a faceless figment of my imagination.

Ryan listens with rapt attention, barely blinking. When I tell him that Kenna and Evander know the truth, and that Mom found out about Blake's true parentage, he raises his brows.

"Well, shit. This family dinner is about to be way more fun than I thought it would be."

"Is that what you took from this? That this will cause some drama and excitement when our entire family gathers in one place? You forget that I was tasked with finding Sasha and turning her in to our dad and our uncle."

"Well, you can't do that now, obviously." He pours me a cup of strong, bitter black coffee, sliding it to the edge of his desk. "I knew she looked familiar, man."

"You introduced us," I tell him, then I realize it's likely Sasha wiped his memories that day they saw each other in that atrium.

He frowns, scratching his head as I lean forward and grab the coffee mug with a nod in thanks. "So, what exactly is the plan?"

I close my eyes for a moment, taking a drink. Caffeine blooms through my system, but it's not enough to totally clear my mind.

I didn't sleep much last night. I finally had a good reason to stay up at odd hours, and I don't regret spending a night exploring every inch of Sarah, getting to know her as my mate.

Marking her.

Her mark on my neck still stings with pain, but it's fresh, and bright, and fills me with a kind of peace I'm not familiar with.

"Sarah hasn't lived a normal life, not at all. I want that for her."

Ryan leans back in his chair and stares blankly out the windows behind me in thought.

I continue, "She can shift. She's a strong, agile wolf. A fucking beautiful one, if I'm being honest. All white with some silver mixed in. No issues there. Her other abilities… she never had training. She's a mystic, but she's the only one in Crescent Falls."

"Beside you and Dad," he cuts in.

"It's never been confirmed whether Dad is a mystic."

"But you both read the stars in the orrery, or whatever. Can Sarah?"

I haven't asked her that. I actually haven't given the orrery a single thought since I used it to call Kenna. "I don't know, but I'll take her to see when we're at the castle tomorrow for dinner."

He nods, pursing his lips. "So you're not telling anyone who she really is?"

"No, and it's going to stay that way."

"Dad might not react the way you think he will."

"I can't take that risk. He's Dad, yeah, but he's the Alpha King first. Same with Uncle Ryatt. They have a duty to their kingdoms, to their people." I wave my hand in dismissal as a tightness winds its way through my chest. "I understand why they need her now. They can't get to Gabriel without her. They'd put her on trial, too, letting their elder councils decide her fate, whether she's an enemy to the kingdoms or an innocent bystander." The words tumble out. I haven't pondered any of this out loud yet.

"I guess I agree, but the truth will come out eventually. Hell, Aunt Ella can sniff this shit out with their powers, just like Kenna."

"I know," I grumble over the rim of my mug before taking another sip. Horrible coffee. The kind that comes in a can, pre-ground. "I'm just not taking any risks now. She has a shot at having a normal life, a safe one, for both her and Blake. I'm going to marry her."

Ryan grins.

"Soon too, no fancy wedding."

"You really want Mom to cry?"

I close my eyes. "She'll forgive us eventually. She already has a secret grandchild. That should be enough for now."

"You're not giving our family enough credit. Hell, Dad and Uncle Ryatt forgave each other, and they went to war against each other once, technically."

"I'm not going to give Sarah up. I refuse to separate her from Blake to go stand trial in Eastonia for what could be months, even years. This remains a secret."

"All right, if you say so."

I roll my eyes to the ceiling.

Ryan shifts his weight and rises, walking to one of the windows behind me. "Hadley wants to see her. She asks me about her every single day, you know. You gotta let her go up to your house."

I turn on the couch to face him. "That would be fine. Has Hadley given you any inclination that she knows the truth about Sarah?" I honestly don't know Hadley well enough to know the answer myself. All I know is that Hadley is Sarah's best friend, her only friend, and the only person who stuck around when everyone else in Sarah's life faded into the past when she got pregnant.

"No, I don't think so." Ryan is suddenly gruff, his tone dropping to something more serious. I watch him flex his injured hand.

"What happened to your hand?"

"A little tiff with the Alpha of Raven Hall, nothing major." He slides his hand in his pocket and turns to look at me over his shoulder. "I'll tell Hadley she can go see Sarah this afternoon. That okay?"

"That's fine, I have some work to do anyway."

There's a look in his eyes as he turns back to the window that has unease rippling over my skin. "Is there something going on between you and Hadley?"

He chuckles. "Goddess, no. There's just a little drama between her and James."

"What's going on?"

He turns around and leans his leg against the back of the couch. With a shrug, he says, "He wants to send Hadley back to Eastonia, to their familial pack, where their parents are from. He said it was because Hadley has been hanging out with some people he's worried about, a bad group, but he won't elaborate."

"Hadley's an adult. That shouldn't be his decision."

"Barely," he says with a sigh. "She just turned twenty. I don't really have much room to talk given we stood with our parents when they chose to send Misty to Maatua instead of letting her go to Wellington."

"Misty was in danger, that's the difference."

"Yeah, well–" He sits down with a soft groan. "Doesn't really matter, does it? James is her brother. He's my Beta. I have no say."

"But you're her Alpha."

His eyes go slightly glossy for a moment before he shakes his head with a soft smile. "Anyway, I have an idea to help launch Sarah into her new, normal life."

"And what is that?"

His eyes light up again, banishing whatever emotion he was fighting to hide. "Does she know how to drive?"

3 4

DON'T TRUST HER

SARAH

BLAKE LIFTS his head from the carpet in the sitting room off the foyer, his chubby fingers gripping the carpet fibers as he whines, his mouth pulled in a frown.

"This is supposed to be good for you, honey," I urge when he starts to fuss. Dalia, on her knees beside me, nods in silent agreement. "See? You're learning how to push up with your arms. Soon you'll be rolling over onto your back if you want it bad enough."

In response, Blake turns purple with rage and lets out a howl that I'm sure can be heard in the village.

Dalia and I exchange looks, but she chuckles softly and promptly scoops him into her arms. "Bath time, then bed, I think," she says, meeting my eyes for confirmation.

I nod, shrugging. I watch them walk away and feel a pang of guilt ghost through my chest. My milk dried up. It was my fault for being so stupid and reckless. Blake doesn't need me for that anymore, but I've been spending all my days with him. Dalia is a massive help, though. I often don't feel like I know what I'm doing, but Dalia has so many siblings, she's a professional baby wrangler, and I'll take all the help I can get.

But my free time is just that... free. I have nothing else to do. My flowers and plants in the atrium are fine, needing very little pruning this time of year. Outside, the snow is still thick and the warm late spring weather hasn't made a dent in the silver-white landscape. It'll be a few weeks until I see anything green again.

Cosette appears in the foyer carrying a basket of laundry. I walk toward her. "Can I help?"

"Get away," she says sharply, but her smile is teasing. "As the lady of this house, you're meant to sit around, rest your feet. Let your hands grow soft."

"Cosette, please," I beg, padding over to her. I'm wearing one of Sydney's sweatshirts from college and a pair of jeans, my hair tied back. I don't feel like the lady of his house in this outfit. Shouldn't I be wearing a fancy robe that flows out behind me while I stalk his hallowed halls, counting our gems? "I'm bored. I don't know when Sydney's supposed to get home. And honestly, with the lady of the house thing, we haven't confirmed anything of that nature—"

A sharp knock on the front door makes us both jump. Cosette mumbles a curse as she sets the basket down on the stairs. "Who could that be at this hour?"

"It's only eight," I reply, following right behind her as she flutters to the door and throws it open.

"Thank the Goddess," Hadley says. She looks between me and Cosette. "Aren't you going to let me in?"

"Of course," I say, stepping forward, but I notice the odd look on Cosette's face. She opens the door all the way for Hadley despite looking suddenly... suspicious. Weird. Cosette can be really odd sometimes.

"Alpha Ryan kept telling me you were sick, and I shouldn't bother you. She did, too." She jabs a thumb at Cosette.

To my surprise, Cosette has nothing sharp nor witty to say. She closes the door with a snap, turns to me, and says, "I'll be upstairs for a few minutes," and walks away.

"Do you like her?" Hadley asks, watching Cosette disappear out of sight.

"I love Cosette. Why?"

"I dunno, I guess she kind of rubs me the wrong way." Hadley takes a minute to look around the foyer before tucking her hands in the pockets of her jacket. "So, what the hell happened?"

"It's a long story."

"Those are the only kinds of stories you have," she laughs.

I lead her into the sitting room. She shrugs out of her coat and lays it over the back of the couch before plopping down. I sit on the other side of the couch, thankful she's here, but also curious about Cosette's odd look earlier. I shove it aside for now and turn to my friend.

"Sydney and I are mates," I begin.

Hadley looks shocked but smiles wickedly. "So that's the real reason why you're here, huh?"

I chew my lip, unsure how far to take this. Do I tell her the whole truth?

"So he's gonna be like, Blake's stepdad, right?"

"Blake is his son, Hadley."

Hadley listens as I tell her about the night after the ball. She hadn't been there that night for whatever reason, so I was on my own, hanging out with a group of friends from our old high school. I tell her about the one-night-stand without going into too much detail, but when it comes time to elaborate on my reasons for not telling him sooner, and for not telling her who the father of my son was, I find that I can't bring myself to do it.

I can't tell Hadley that my name is actually Sasha. She knows I came from a group home somewhere rural, that I don't have parents or family looking out for me, but we met as teenagers in the city, and that hadn't mattered back then.

But those secrets, secrets I should be able to tell her, my best friend, stick to the tip of my tongue.

"I didn't think he'd believe me," I tell her instead, a bold lie. "But he found me and Blake, and we've grown close since then. The mate bond clicked into place and… yeah."

Discomfort travels up my spine. I shift my weight, trying to banish it. I don't like keeping secrets from her, but I feel like I have to. It's for her safety, honestly, not mine.

If Gabriel does come for me, he'll tear a path through the people I love most, and I don't want Hadley stuck in the crosshairs.

"Wow," Hadley laughs. "You're going to be Queen of Crescent Falls one day. You realize that, right?"

"When I'm old and gray," I amend, shaking my head. "Sydney's parents are still so young. I don't even want to think about it. I'm just happy–" I'm just happy being happy. I'm happy being with Sydney.

That's all that matters.

Hadley leans forward and squeezes my knee. "I'm happy for you, Sarah. If anyone deserves what's coming, it's you."

I smile. "Thanks, Hads."

I tell her about the family dinner tomorrow and how Maddy found out about Blake before the rest of the family. She sits quietly, listening as I spill my nerves and doubts.

"We just did things so unconventionally. Sydney doesn't think it's that big of a deal, but he should be with a princess or something."

"Well his mom's not a princess, per se, but I heard a rumor she's actually an Alpha's daughter."

"Exactly. I'm not."

"Well I'm sure whatever you guys do will be fine because Alpha Ryan is still up to his fiendish ways," she jokes.

"Really? What do you mean?" I'm reminded of how weird Ryan was around Hadley when they visited me in the atrium a few weeks ago. Ryan, who looked at Hadley like she has the ability to light up his world, and Hadley, totally oblivious.

"James is always telling me to leave him alone," Hadley admits with a sly smile. "I've been texting Ryan–about you, mostly–but sometimes I flirt with him a little, and he likes to flirt back. It's cute."

"Just cute?" I ask.

"I think he's cute," she laughs. "But James hates it. He threatened to send me away if I kept it up."

"Send you away?" I move a little closer to her.

"Back to Eastonia." She yawns, rolling her eyes. "I told him good luck with that. I'm not going anywhere anytime soon."

"He'd send you packing for–for flirting back and forth with your Alpha?"

"We've done more than flirt."

I open my mouth, but I can't find the words I'm searching for.

She leans in, smiling from ear to ear, "I kissed him. The night we left here, when I saw you last. He drove me back to Silverhide, and I leaned over when he was at a stoplight and kissed him, and he kissed me back. I wanted him to take me to his place, but didn't. He said we couldn't."

"But you said he was being fiendish?"

"I assume that's why he didn't want to take me home. Maybe he had someone waiting there for him already."

I scan Hadley's face and see an expression I've never noticed before. She's normally so bright, light as air, and slightly oblivious.

Right now, her gaze is cool and calculated, though.

"Are you okay? You seem… worked up–"

She stands, grabbing her coat. "I'm super late," she says, ignoring my question completely. "James is going to be livid. So, you won't be here tomorrow night, right?"

I shake my head.

"I'll come back over this weekend, then. You can tell me all about your dinner with his family."

I rise, reaching for her so I can give her a hug goodbye, but she whirls and walks out of reach.

"I'll see you later," she calls out from the foyer then walks right through the front door.

I race after her, but her little blue car is already turning around in the driveway. Slowly, I close the door against the cool night air.

"I don't want her coming by the house anymore," Cosette says.

"Goddess, Cosette, you scared me to death!" I turn to her with my hand pressed against my racing heart. "Why? She's my friend."

"Did you tell her the truth, Sarah?"

I eye Cosette, who's standing on the bottom step looking more serious than I've ever seen her before. "About Sasha?"

She nods, a bit of panic flashing behind her eyes.

"No, of course not."

She lets out the breath she must have been holding and nods, running her fingers through her hair. "Good. That's good."

"Is something wrong?" I'm beginning to think I'm growing crazy. Maybe it's just that I've been cooped up in the house all day, but Cosette isn't normally like this, and neither is Hadley.

"Just be wary of who you trust right now, that's all."

"I can trust Hadley," I laugh, trying to shake away the heavy feeling of her stone-cold gaze. "I trust her with my life."

"All right," Cosette says, nodding, but she doesn't look any less tense.

I'm missing something. Something happened here tonight that I didn't catch.

"Cosette–"

We both turn to headlights flashing through the windows on either side of the front door, and then the sound of the garage door rolling up thrums through the house.

"I have a lot to do before dinner tomorrow night. Goodnight, Sarah." Cosette turns on her heel and walks upstairs, disappearing into the darkened recesses of the second floor like a ghost.

A few seconds later, Sydney appears carrying a briefcase, his hair slightly disheveled and eyes lined with fatigue. He kisses me on the top of the head, but pauses there. "Why are you just standing in the foyer?"

"I was talking to Cosette," I tell him.

"Okay..." He glances around, looking for her. "Did Hadley come by?"

"Yeah," I try to say as brightly as possible, but it comes out totally flat.

Sydney pulls away and looks down at me. "Are you okay?"

"I don't know," I admit, rubbing my temples. "Just tired, I think."

"Well, we didn't sleep last night. We should probably do that."

"Yeah." I look at the place where Cosette disappeared, a sinking sensation blooming to life in my belly.

I should definitely get some sleep.

Tomorrow might be the best, or worst, day of my life so far, and I can't face his entire family with my brain as rotten as it feels right now.

I follow my mate upstairs and turn into my room instinctively, but he takes my arm. "You're with me from now on, remember?"

35

A DIFFERENT KIND OF BOND

SARAH

"YOU LOOK FINE," Sydney assures me, resting his hand on my thigh as he drives us toward the castle the next afternoon. Rain patters against the windshield, and the frigid landscape is suddenly changed—the silver glow replaced by deeper shades of brown, black, and red.

Spring is nearly here.

A few months ago, I was pacing in my apartment wondering how'd I'd survive alone, with an infant, with an empty refrigerator and barely any money left.

Now I'm sitting beside my mate on our way to break the news to his family.

I squeeze Sydney's hand and look over at him. His blue eyes soften, but his brows are still pinched with a glimmer of anxiety.

Last night, lying in bed together, we talked about what tonight needed to look like. Sydney is going to take the lead, making an announcement sometime during the dinner proceedings that we're mates. He was excited as he talked about it, and I realized that this—

me—was all he ever wanted—and all he told himself he could never have.

I didn't really give him the choice in the end, did I?

Blake whines in his car seat, which is surrounded on either side by several dishes Cosette insisted she prepare for the dinner party despite choosing not to come. I found that odd, given that she's so close with Sydney's family and the staff at the castle. Today, while she helped me blow dry my hair until it gleamed, and chose the navy blue trousers and white blouse I'm wearing, she barely said a word to me. Her eyes were heavy and sad, and she looked... worried.

I've never seen her worried before.

"We're almost there, bud," Sydney says as his hand slips from my thigh. He reaches back, his eyes still fixed on the road, and strokes Blake on the top of the head. Blake grunts with annoyance but eventually gives in, his whines turning to soft coos. "He really hates that car seat, doesn't he?"

"Loathes it." I reach into my purse and open the makeup compact Cosette gave me, checking my reflection in the tiny mirror. We left my hair down and perfectly straight, fastening it away from my face with little silver pins depicting the phases of the moon. Soft brown eyeshadow makes my violet eyes pop, and a smudge of pink lipstick finishes off Cosette's masterpiece.

But I feel like an imposter—because I am one. Really, honestly. Tonight, Sydney will introduce me to his family as his mate. His future wife. His Luna, and one day, his queen.

Sasha has no room here. Sasha isn't part of this equation. Looking back, the tiny little girl who didn't truly understand what was happening when she saw her name being etched on a gravestone never stood a chance.

Sydney drives through the gates of the castle but doesn't pull along the circular driveway leading to the grand front entrance. He pulls around back where several archways lead into the garage. He parks the truck right outside the garage doors and starts gathering his things—keys, wallet, phone—tucking them into his pockets while I try to stop my heart from racing out of my chest.

"There's going to be a lot of people here, Sarah. We'll be lost in the fray until the dinner begins, so don't worry about anything now. I'll take the lead. You won't have to explain anything if you don't want to."

I nod, holding his gaze. I watch him walk around the front of the truck. He opens my door, but steps up to me instead of letting me exit. He leans in, caging me against the seat, and kisses me soundly.

It's the kind of kiss that has warmth ghosting down my spine, giving me a glimpse of what's to come later tonight, I hope.

He pulls away, a bit breathless, murmuring something about how maybe, just maybe, we could locate a supply closet and find the relief we both desperately need, but Blake lets out a growl that sounds like it coming from a much larger creature than a tiny shifter baby.

I chuckle a bit, wiping my smeared lipstick off Sydney's lower lip. "I'm ready. Are you?"

"I am," he whispers, giving me one more gentle kiss.

He lifts Blake out of the car seat, and I follow him through the castle's back entrance. Kitchen sounds fill the air, and a flurry of excited maids dart from doorway to doorway as we make our way down a long hallway that's obviously meant for the staff. Sydney stops one of the maids to let them know about the food in his truck, and then the hallway widens, and we've reached the foyer.

It's empty.

Sydney adjusts Blake on his shoulder and looks around.

"Where is everyone?" I ask, but then a flash of golden blonde hair appears.

At first, I think it's Isla. A much younger version of Isla, down to the slight build and delicate facial features. Blue eyes that don't match Sydney's narrow on him in a slightly annoyed look. "Wow, you're super early. How embarrassing. You're supposed to be fashionably late like the rest of the family." She crosses her arms beneath her chest and tilts her head, her golden hair falling in soft curls over her shoulder.

"Misty," Sydney grumbles. "It's always so nice to see you."

She shrugs, flipping her hair over her shoulder before her eyes slide to mine. She grins at me with a cat-like stare, and I feel my stomach do a little flip. I've heard about Misty, of course. Everyone seems to grumble when they mention her name. Beautiful, popular, seventeen-year-old Misty who had to be shipped away to Maatua for her own safety instead of going to the prestigious Wellington University with her friends.

She's a bit much, according to her brothers.

"*Holy shit*, you're gorgeous. What the hell are you doing with him?" she giggles.

My mouth pops open in a laugh at Sydney's expense.

"Go bother someone else," he growls, but her eyes light up.

"There's nobody here yet, dumb-dumb." She plants her freshly manicured fingers on her hips and frowns at Sydney. Her dress–bubble gum pink–matches her nails. "I've been so bored."

"Where're our parents?" he asks, taking a few steps toward her.

"Having a meeting or something upstairs in Dad's office with Aunt Ella and Uncle Ryatt. Kenna kicked me out of the library because I was 'bugging' them with questions about Evander's Ghosts." She twirls her hair around her fingers and pouts. "They're all the rage, you know," she says to me. "The Ghosts are so handsome and *manly*."

Sydney groans, and her smile widens.

I've always wondered what it would be like to have siblings. This exchange is, apparently, a very accurate glimpse of what that could have been like for me.

"What are they meeting about?"

"I *was* eavesdropping but I heard a car pull around back. You interrupted me, so it's your fault I have nothing juicy to tell you. I'm sure it's more about what they're doing with the Gabriel situation or whatever."

"I'll give you twenty dollars to go back upstairs and find out what they're talking about."

"I want eighty."

"Fifty," Sydney says with an arch of his brow.

"Fine," she says, flipping her hair over her shoulder. She extends her hand, and he digs for his wallet, slipping her a crisp fifty dollar bill. She turns for the stairs but pauses, looking at me over her narrow shoulder. "I'm going to sit next to you at dinner tonight."

"Oh, okay–"

She floats away, Sydney watching her with an annoyed expression. His eyes soften as he turns back to me. "Sorry about that. Misty is… Misty. I don't know how else to explain it. My grandfather, Maddox, told my dad this is what he deserves after the whole 'wife competition' stunt he pulled during his early years on the throne. She'll be impossible to marry off, and I pity whoever ends up mated to her."

I choke on a laugh, and Sydney seems to relax a bit.

"I guess we can go up to the library then and see Kenna–"

"Why are you so early?" Ryan says as he comes around a corner holding a can of beer.

Sydney sighs. "I didn't think we were that early. This is the time Mom told us to show up."

"Well, we've got another hour until dinner," he groans. "Sarah, nice to see you."

I smile at him, and he smiles back, but seeing Ryan has my mind reeling back to my strange interaction with Hadley last night. It is possible they're mates?

I definitely think they might be. That would be perfect, honestly. My best friend and my future brother-in-law.

"We were going to go upstairs for a while. Misty said Kenna and Evander are in the library–"

"Yeah they are, I was just up there. Come on, I'll go too."

"Do you know what the meeting is about in Dads office?"

"Yeah, Ryatt thinks he knows where Gabriel is. A few Draven stragglers were found near the border of Eastonia and confessed when Ryatt took over the interrogation. Misty told me. She heard the whole thing. Other than that, it's just family gossip. Apparently, Ryatt owes dad some money for an old bet they had going about Kenna and Evander and whether they were mates."

My head turns back and forth as I watch the brothers talk.

"I just gave Misty fifty dollars to go back and listen in!"

"Are you surprised?" he turns to look down at me as I follow them up the stairs. "A little word of advice; never play cards with our sister. She's a filthy cheat."

"She counts cards," Sydney adds with a laugh. "If she wasn't a princess with a ridiculously lavish inheritance coming her way in a few short years, she'd carve her own path as a criminal mastermind, I'm sure."

"Oh, definitely," Ryan agrees, but Sydney gives him a slightly secretive look, and I realize they're using the mind-link, having a totally different conversation out loud than they are in their heads.

I follow them up and over the grand staircase and into the depths of the second floor, which is full of twisting hallways that branch off into new corridors, new rooms I haven't had a chance to explore.

One day, Sydney and I will live in this castle. That doesn't feel real.

I continue to follow them in silence as they have a conversation between their two minds. I'm honestly not bothered by it at all. I know they're talking about Gabriel. I know Sydney wants all of the information he can get about this update.

But I'm also incredibly relieved he's keeping me out of it. I don't want anything to do with Gabriel. I'd wipe my own mind of his memory if I could.

Sydney stops walking. I nearly run into him as he says to Ryan, "I need to talk to them. I should be a part of this conversation and whatever they're planning."

"I agree. I'll keep Sarah company, don't worry. Take Blake with you as a buffer."

Sydney smirks but looks down at me apologetically. "I'll be right back."

"It's okay," I assure him.

When Sydney walks out of sight, I slowly turn my attention to Ryan, who's standing beside me with his hands tucked in his pockets.

He clicks his tongue. "Sydney told me everything."

I chew my lower lip. "Everything?"

"I like the name Sarah better, anyway. It suits you." He nudges me with his elbow.

Some of the tension in my shoulders unwinds.

"Do you want to go to the library or do you need a minute? There's a little sitting room nearby. It's rarely used. Cozy, you know." He shrugs.

I take a deep breath. "Honestly, yeah. I could use a minute to just… prepare."

"I get it, totally." We start walking again, side by side. He opens the door to the sitting room in question, and I find myself standing in the embrace of emerald green walls with dark trim, and a crackling fire.

Ryan stands in the doorway. I turn to him, tilting my head toward the twin armchairs. "Do you need a minute, too?"

"Sure, fine," he smiles and closes the door behind him before sauntering over to one of the chairs and plopping down, spreading his legs in a very manly fashion.

Sydney is very tall. He's also built like an athlete, firm and lean. Ryan, however, looks like an absolute giant in the chair. He's a little taller than my mate and built like he has to eat a million calories a day to retain his muscle mass.

But he's soft hearted, I can tell. In fact, there's something strange about Ryan that I can't figure out. Like I'm drawn to him, but not in a sexual way, of course.

I'd just really like to be his friend.

There's something else about it though, and he seems to pick up on my confusion as we both shift our weight in our respective chairs.

"You feel it too, right?" he asks.

"Feel…what?"

"I figured it out after Sydney told me the truth," he breathes, arching his brow at me. "You looked so familiar, but I couldn't place you, even before you wiped my memories in the atrium that day. But there was still a piece of you in my mind, nagging at me." I flush, but he continues, "Sydney and I are twins."

"I know–"

"You and I… well, your mate bond with my twin brother connects me to you in some weird way."

I squirm a bit, frowning.

He notices and laughs softly. "We're not mates, Sarah. Sorry to break your heart."

"Are you saying we have a bond?"

"Familial, yes." He meets my gaze, and into my mind, he says, *'We can mind-link, and you're not part of my pack, and haven't yet said your vows before the Goddess to join our family. Weird, right?'*

'This is weird.'

'Tell me about it.'

We smile at each other.

'I'm glad you're here, Sarah. Sydney needed you.'

'I needed him.'

Somewhere in the bond between us, which now that he's mentioned it, I can almost see the single thread binding us, something he also shares with Sydney, I get a sense of… someone else.

His mate. Her imprint lingers there, so faint I can barely feel it, but she's there. He found her. He definitely knows who she is.

I meet his eyes and realize he knows exactly what I'm thinking right now.

"Is Hadley your mate, Ryan?"

His eyes darken. "Sarah–"

'Where are you?' Sydney asks through the mind-link, and the moment between Ryan and I shatters.

"Time to meet the rest of the family," he says gruffly, extending his hand to me.

3 6

CAN'T KEEP A SECRET

Guests are arriving—extended family I haven't seen in years—when I meet back up with Ryan and Sarah on the second floor landing. I wave down to my great uncle Ben and his mate, Emery, the long-standing Alpha of Obsidian temple. Some of my grandma's other siblings are here, too, bringing their mates, children, and grandchildren along. I realize why Mom insisted on setting up several long tables in the ballroom. There's at least fifty people here.

This isn't going to be a typical family gathering. Not at all. And now, looking at my mate, who has gone so pale I'm wondering if she's about to faint and fall down the stairs, I'm rethinking our means of sharing our news.

I hold her steady as we linger at the top of the steps with Ryan.

I missed whatever meeting Dad and Ryatt were having. I walked in right as they were preparing to go down to dinner. I formally pulled myself off the Sasha investigation, obviously, so I'm technically no longer included in these talks.

Still, as an Alpha, I feel like I have the right to know what's going on.

Especially since this affects me and my family–Sarah and Blake–directly.

There is one thing I have to do before this night moves forward, and it can't wait.

I pass Blake to Sarah. "I need to talk to my dad for a minute. I'll meet you downstairs."

She nods, looking nervous, but Kenna and Evander appear in the hallway leading to the landing, and some of those nerves disappear from Sarah's eyes.

Kenna ropes her arm around Sarah's, beaming, and leads her downstairs while I hang back with Ryan and Evander for a moment.

My brother looks withdrawn, and Evander looks exhausted.

"I need another drink," Ryan says heavily and starts down the stairs.

"You look like you could use one, too. Whiskey?" Evander asks me, but I shake my head.

Mom passes us, smiling down at the arriving guests. I see Ella out of the corner of my eye. She and Ryatt must have taken one of the servants' staircases, probably out of the need for a moment to confer privately. Ella looks radiant in an emerald green gown in the ethereal style of Eastonia, her long, dark brown hair falling down to her waist as her hand rests in the crook of Ryatt's elbow.

Ryatt looks up at me and nods. I nod back. I should probably apologize to him.

Later, I think.

My eyes slide back to Ella when she turns her head toward the entrance of the ballroom. Sarah is standing with Kenna, talking to my mom. Mom reaches for Blake, and Sarah smiles as she places him in her arms.

Ella is watching Sarah, her back suddenly rigid. I watch Kenna slowly meet her mother's gaze and discreetly shake her head.

"Fuck," I whisper, mostly to myself, but Evander is watching it play out as well.

"Go talk to your father. I'll handle this." He walks down the stairs in a flash of dark blond hair. The black fabric of his suit seems to absorb the light raining down from the chandelier.

A slight pang of pain echoes through my left temple as I turn from the railing and make my way toward my dad's office for a second time this evening, finding him still seated at his desk.

I close the door behind me. He looks up, his eyes lined with fatigue. "Good. I needed to speak to you before dinner tonight. I promised not to ruin your mom's evening."

I lean against the door. "This is about Gabriel, I'm guessing, since I wasn't privy to the meeting that took place just before we were told to arrive?"

"We have evidence that Sasha is alive. You were wrong about the grave."

My blood starts to pound through my ears. "You dug it up?"

"No," he says steadily. I sit on the couch across from his desk. Red leather. It's been here since before I was born. I used to sit here doing homework while he worked. Now, I feel like the room is caving in on me as he pushes a folder across his desk. I open it, finding pictures of devastation.

"How could something like that have happened?" I ask, flipping through pictures of what once was the temple on Mononoke Island. It's gone now, reduced to ashes. The house Sarah lived in as a child is nothing but smoldering embers. Several graves, those of her house mother and the woman's mate, have been dug up with their coffins shattered.

Sasha's grave. The headstone is cracked like someone took a pickaxe to it, and a wide area has been dug up, the shadow of the hole left behind stretching several feet down.

I flip to the last picture. The bartender, the man who'd directed me and Ryan to the temple, lays face down in the middle of the street, dead. I narrow my eyes as I look closer and see what looks like a brand on his back, burned through his shirt. A snake in the shape of an eight.

That symbol floods my head, and the pain in my temple skyrockets. A vague, fractured memory splits my mind in two as I grip the folder.

I'd lost consciousness several times when Evander and I were being tortured by Gabriel. I remember being dragged, half lucid, from our cell into another room that was blazingly hot. On the ceiling, that symbol had been painted in red. That's the room where I tried to shift and shattered my legs, which were in chains.

It took all of the strength I had left to heal my bones with my own powers in the hours before Kenna arrived.

I close my eyes and put the folder on the desk.

"I know she's not dead." I meet my dad's gaze. "But she's as good as dead, Dad."

He eyes me, scanning my face. Behind the mask of icy emotions he wears, I can see glimmers of concern behind his eyes.

"She needs to remain missing. Presumed dead. Please."

"What are you not telling me?" His eyes roil with mingled confusion, concern, and maybe a bit of heartbreak.

He fucking knows.

"I found my mate. She's downstairs, with my son. *Our son*." I rise from the couch. "I wanted to talk to you privately about it first, of course, to go over the logistics of Sarah moving into this new role in not only our family, but this kingdom, as a princess and heir to Mom's position, but none of that matters right now." I meet his eyes.

He slowly stands. Dad's not stupid. He can read behind the lines etched in every word that leaves my lips.

"My only prerogative is keeping my family safe. I will do whatever needs to be done in order to ensure my mate and son is safe and by my side."

Dad rounds his desk and comes to a stop near the door. "This changes everything about this mission."

"This mission ended the day I found her and my son starving and nearly frozen to death," I rasp. "You can't stand here and tell me this woman is capable of the crimes the Allied Kingdoms want her tried against. She was a child, Dad."

"Who knows?" he asks, his voice dropping, softening, as he stares at his shoes in thought. "Who knows that you're mated to Sasha." His eyes rise to meet mine, but to my surprise, there's no ice in his expression.

"Kenna, Evander, and Ryan. As well as my staff at the manor. That's it. And Ella. I have a feeling she'd find out just by looking in Sarah's direction."

"This isn't just about me, you know. Ella and Ryatt have the right to interrogate her–"

"She is my mate, and I will not allow it."

"Spoken like a true mate. If your mother was in a similar position, I'd feel the same way. I'd be making the same choices. But you didn't have to keep this from me."

"What's going to happen to her?"

Dad crosses his arms over his chest and leans against the wall. "We need her to get to Gabriel. If he's putting together another coven somehow, we need to stop it before it grows out of proportion. Ryatt and Ella can't have another war on their hands after what happened last summer. Things in Eastonia are already precarious enough after the attack in Moonrise."

"You're saying you want to use her as bait?"

"It shouldn't have to come to that."

"Whatever this comes to," I say, edging a step toward him, "I need you to promise me something. Gabriel is mine. I decide what happens to him if he's caught, but when we know where he is, it'll be me going in and ending this fucking nightmare. I have a score to settle with him. He is mine."

"You have my word," he says quietly, his eyes meeting mine.

Silence settles between us, thick and uncomfortable. I wouldn't say there's a rift between my dad and me, but the moment I became an Alpha, our relationship changed. I am his heir. I'll be standing in this office one day calling it my own.

He's always been harder on me because of it.

"Your mother told me about Blake already. I'm sure most of the family knows."

I blow out my breath, fighting the dull ache still hammering away at my skull. "I had a feeling she wouldn't be able to keep it a secret."

Dad straightens a bit, his mouth ticking into the ghost of a smile. I don't flinch when he steps forward and places a hand on my shoulder.

"Congratulations," he says, squeezing my shoulder. Pride shines behind his eyes, which confuses me a bit.

But I can't question him about what's going through his head right now because the door to his office opens, and Mom steps inside holding Blake, who is fast asleep on her shoulder, his cheeks smudged with several different shades of lipstick.

"What are you two still doing up here? Dinner is on the table!" she hisses, patting Blake's back as he drools on her dress. Dad turns to her and smiles like I've never seen him smile before. It's so loving–and so private.

It's the same kind of smile I have on my face when I watch Sarah rocking our son to sleep. It's a smile shared solely between mates.

Mom looks between us, her eyes going glassy.

I promptly tear myself from the room, leaving them with their grandson.

I hear their soft voices down the hallway. Dad's surprise, mom's relief and excitement, a sweet, tender moment they're sharing as parents, now grandparents.

Ryan was right about Blake being a perfect buffer.

I jog down the stairs and turn into the ballroom, sweeping my gaze over the tables full of my family members.

Ryan catches my eye first. He's sitting with Evander and Kenna, and Sarah is smooshed between Kenna and Misty. Misty leans into her, showing Sarah something on her phone.

Misty always wanted a sister. She got stuck with us instead. At least I can give her Sarah.

I start walking through the ballroom, saying hello to extended family. When I finally reach Sarah's side, Mom and Dad have entered the ballroom, and Mom shows no signs of giving Blake back. She shows him off, and I've never seen her look so happy.

Ryan and I exchange a glance.

I place my hand on Sarah's shoulder and squeeze.

"Can I have your attention, please. I need to make an announcement," I say, my voice booming over the mingled conversations sending a buzz throughout the room.

3 7

IT ALL COMES OUT

SARAH

MY HEART POUNDS over Sydney's voice, his words clear and steady.

"My mate," he says proudly, and the rest of his words are drowned out by the thrum in the room. Some people stand in shock, but everyone is smiling, everyone is turning from us to Sydney's parents, who are beaming with pride and I'm…

In a dream. This has to be a dream because, suddenly, I'm on my feet and people I don't know are hugging me, shaking my hand, raining blessings upon blessing on us.

I look through a part in the fray and find Ella turning ever so slightly to Maddy, her dark brows arched as Maddy mouths something that can only be, "I told you so."

They disappear as more people come up to us, the dinner forgotten entirely.

This goes on for at least another twenty minutes. Eventually, Sydney sits me back down at our snug table, shoulder to shoulder with Kenna and Misty, and piles my plate high before walking off and dipping into conversations with excited family members whose names I still don't know.

Misty giggles beside me, leaning over her plate to tell Kenna she expects to be a bridesmaid and asks Kenna to invite all of Evander's friends from the Ghosts.

Kenna just rolls her eyes and tells Misty to butt out.

I smile like I've never smiled before and find it impossible to get a bite in as an hour passes, and our table is visited by family coming to introduce themselves.

But the festivities wane as dessert is brought and served buffet style. The younger family's–distant cousins on Isla's side–funnel out of the castle to put their young to bed on time. Soon, it's just the immediate family. Even Ben and his family have taken their leave, meaning to visit some friends in Moorn in the morning and needing to start the hours long drive now to make it in time.

The ballroom is suddenly ten times bigger than before without so many people crowding the tables.

"Goddess, I can't sit in this chair any longer," Kenna groans, shaking a bit as she tries to rise.

"We'll help," I tell her, motioning to Misty to take Kenna's other arm.

Misty groans enthusiastically, giving Kenna a teasing grin. Kenna huffs a breath. "Misty, one day you'll be pregnant, and I'll give you endless shit for it."

"I'll probably deserve it," she laughs. "Let's go to the sitting room upstairs before the guys take it over talking about politics and whatnot. Boring!"

But as we're leading Kenna out of the room, Sydney comes up to me followed by Evander, who gives his mate a critical once over before taking her by the waist. "You're going to bed," he says dryly.

"I'm fine, I swear."

"Your wrists and ankles are swollen, Kenna. This was too much." Evander tries leading her away, but she digs in her heels, turning to me.

"I have to leave tomorrow with my parents. I'd like to stay longer, but I'm due two weeks from now, so I should really be home preparing."

"We'll come visit soon," Sydney says. "Go get some sleep." His eyes slide to Evander's and he gives him a quick nod. I wonder what's passing between them through the mind-link, but Sydney whisks me and Misty toward the formal sitting room on the first floor while Kenna is led upstairs and out of sight.

"Where's Blake?" I ask, looking back toward the ballroom.

Misty plops onto the fine, antique couch with her heels propped up, whipping out her phone faster than lightning.

"With Mom. How do you feel about staying the night here? I've had a bit to drink after all of the toasts made in our honor. Mom won't let Blake go." He smiles softly. "He's pretty tired, and I think he'll sleep fine in the nursery upstairs with Brie."

"Oh, that's fine," I smile back. To be honest, the idea of stuffing ourselves in his truck and driving all the way back to Shadowcrest sounds awful, and the quiet solitude of the sitting room beckons to me as I sit on the couch next to Misty and lean my head back on the headrest.

Sydney tucks his hands in his pockets and looks like he's about to say something when two shadows ghost through the room.

I immediately straighten. I can taste the power around us. It feels… familiar. Like a walking, talking reminder of a home I once knew and lost before I had a chance to figure out who, and what, I was.

Alpha King Ryatt of Eastonia, Shadowking of the Roguelands and Veiled Valley, stands in the doorway beside his wife.

They were the only people who didn't come congratulate us, and based on the looks on their faces right now, they're not here to do that now, either.

"Misty, honey, we need the room," Ella says softly to her niece.

"I don't want to listen to boring kingdom business anyway," she says, rolling gracefully off the couch and practically floating to the doorway.

I watch her go and wish fervently that she'd stay, put up more a fuss about it, especially as King Isaac walks behind her and shuts the giant doors to seal the room closed.

Sydney stiffens and steps to stand beside me. He places a hand on my shoulder, preventing me from rising.

"Your mother is upstairs putting her grandchild to bed," Isaac says with a bit of a smile he can't hide touching his lips.

Goddess, Sydney looks like him. I feel like I'm staring at a future version of my mate as his face comes into the muted chandelier light. Having met Maddox, however, I can say Isaac and Sydney closely resemble Isla's side of the family. They have her delicate beauty and Maddox's sharp, masculinity.

Ella… she looks nothing like her brother. She is all fire and brimstone as she gracefully sits in one of the armchairs across from me, folding her hands in her lap. Sea-green eyes the color of tropical waters meet mine, but there's nothing harsh or cold about her expression. Curiosity blooms behind those wells of blue-green, and I suck in a breath as my gaze sweep upward to her hairline where tiny symbols dot her forehead, silver scars in the shape of an ancient language long lost to time.

I don't remember my shifter mother. Her face is blurred in my memory. Her voice is a soft whisper lifted in a song. A lullaby about the return of the Firestone witches to lead our kind to the promised land. She is a reminder of all I've lost.

I swallow hard, breaking from Ella's gaze.

"So this is why you threatened to duel with your own uncle when we mentioned needing to dig up that grave on Mononoke Island," Ryatt says dryly, casually, his voice smoky and deep. It rattles through me in a wave of power that nearly chokes the air from my lungs.

Sydney shifts his weight from foot to foot. "Are you at all surprised at the lengths I would go to protect what's mine?"

"Not at all," Ryatt replies, sitting on the armrest of Ella's chair. "You forget our trials and those of your parents when it comes to our own mates. I wouldn't expect anything less. I'd be disappointed, actually, if you hadn't threatened to kill me to protect her. You were raised to be like this. Obviously, we did something right, wouldn't you say?" Ryatt looks at Isaac, who nods.

I realize with a start they know exactly who I am. I want to turn inward, to shrivel into nothing and disappear in a puff of mist, but I can't.

"You were fooled, Sydney," Ella says, and a hush whispers through the room.

Sydney's grip on my shoulder tightens. "What?"

"You were told we needed Sasha, that she was a criminal, and dangerous, someone who needed to be brought to justice. I knew different, but we couldn't find her without our allied kingdoms believing she was something terrifying and dangerous, so I spun a story."

Her eyes meet mine, soft and apologetic. "Your father was the only person who showed me an ounce of comfort during a horrific time in my life. I returned the favor recently. You are alive because he made an incredible sacrifice to keep you safe, and when Ryatt and I called for you to be hunted, we had to do so delicately to ensure you'd be found by the right people."

"By the right person," Isaac says, and Sydney looks like someone has just smacked him across the face.

"You sent me because you knew I didn't agree with bringing Sasha back to be tried for Gabriel's crimes?"

"We knew you'd protect her, protect what you knew about her, even from us. It was a difficult decision to make–"

"You lied," he says, looking around the room.

"We had to do what needed to be done to ensure her safety. With a call from both kingdoms for her capture, which meant manpower on the ground, we believed Gabriel would be less likely to continue his hunt for you. We had other's out looking, giving them false leads to follow in the event Gabriel was watching. It worked. You found Sasha first, saved her, protected her."

"Did you know we were mates?" I ask Ella before I stop myself.

Ella shakes her head. "No, honey. I didn't." She looks at Sydney then, saying, "But I can't believe I missed it. You told me that Gabriel told you that you wouldn't be able to protect them. He meant Sarah and Blake, didn't he?"

"I didn't know at the time," Sydney says, a bit choked up. He's in actual shock right now.

I reach up and lay my hand over his.

Ella nods, her eyes a bit glassy. "This is a serious situation, but I think you know that." She turns her attention back to me. "You are as safe as you can possibly be now."

Isaac nods, but there's a grim shadow hanging in the room. "The other thing, Ella," Ryatt nudges softly. He grimaces as he meets Isaac's eye, as if neither of them agree with what Ella's about to say.

"Do you remember your father?"

"Barely," I admit. A pang resounds in my chest, and Sydney, feeling it through the bond, steps closer so the top my head brushes against his belt, his hand continuing to rest on my shoulder, grounding me.

"He wouldn't tell me what he had to do in order to get you out of Eastonia, but it must have been a very complicated task because you were able to skirt the border. You weren't listed on any immigration paperwork."

"Gabriel…" I lick my lips. I haven't told anyone this. Not even Sydney. I showed him bits of those memories, yes, but that's it. "When it was sensed that I wasn't just a shifter, and that whatever powers I possessed would be useful to him, I was taken away from my father and placed in the care of Gabriel's old regent, Morticus. His handler, really. Gabriel was maybe twelve, I'm not sure, but he held me down one day and cut me with a knife that… It sang to me. Like it was drawn to me somehow, and he used it to drown out my powers. I could feel that happening. He did it over and over again, and he was so excited at the result. Then he marked me so that everyone would know who I belonged to. He told me I was the one he was waiting for. I don't know why."

"The knife is a relic," Ryatt says, standing. "Can you describe it?"

I shake my head. "I kept my eyes closed."

Sydney thrums with rage. I can feel it echoing through our bond.

"That's enough for tonight," Ella says, rising. "We should get some sleep." She turns with Ryatt for the door but turns back, saying, "When this settles, there is someone who desperately wants to see you again."

"Who?"

"Your father, of course," she says with a soft, melancholy smile.

I hadn't realized he was still alive.

"Your old room is made up," Isaac says to Sydney. "I'm going to go drag your mother out of the nursery. Goodnight and congratulations."

The three royals leave.

Sydney runs his fingers through his hair. "There's something I want to show you before we go to bed."

"What is it?"

3 8

———

WHISPERS IN THE STARS

SARAH

SYDNEY PULLS a large book from a shelf in the massive, stately library. I leap back, muffling a shocked yelp with my hands covering my mouth as a trap door swings open, revealing a spiral staircase.

"Come on," he says jovially, excitement blooming behind his eyes.

"Where are you taking me?" I let him take my hand and tug me into the cramped secret stairwell. He pulls a lever on the wall, and the door swings shut again in near silence.

"My mom had this built for my dad when I was nine, for their wedding anniversary. It took nearly a decade to complete."

I follow him up the stairs. Up so high, my thighs are burning and my breath comes in rapid puffs. "Is this one of the towers?"

"It is," he says like this is nothing but a walk in the park. At the top of the stairs, he pushes open an old, wooden door, something I'm sure is original to the castle, and we're met by total darkness.

I follow his echoing footsteps, but I can't see a damn thing in here. "Sydney?"

A loud cranking sound like gears whirling breaks through the

291

dark silence. I stand totally still as the ceiling splits, and the clear night sky appears overhead, stars shimmering and the moon at half power, still rising.

My mouth pops open. "What is this?" I whisper.

The glint of brass catches my eye as moonlight spills over the room.

A knot forms in my stomach, though.

"What do you think?" Sydney says as he reappears, motioning to the tangle of metal sprawled out before me.

A large, rounded table sits in the very center of the room. On its surface, the planets of our solar system slowly dance around our moon. I step toward it, gazing down at the stars etched onto the surface of the table.

"Sydney, why didn't you tell me your family had something like this?"

"Can you use it?"

Can he not hear the voices? That strange song that seems to start in the darkest of shadows and bleed into the moonlight? Words sung in an ancient, terrifying song?

"I use it to connect with Kenna," he says, shrugging. "She has one in Veiled Valley that's modeled after this one, as well as the larger orrery used by the mystics in Moonrise." He swallows, watching me closely. "I know you're not familiar with your powers and didn't have any training when it comes to the art of being a mystic, but… I can read the stars this way. They tell me nothing of substance because I don't know what it means, but I'm willing to learn. With you."

"Are you sure you want to?"

"I think you need to know who you are."

My mate steps toward me, moonlight reflecting in his eyes.

"What if I don't want to know?"

He stops with only a few feet of distance between us. "Sarah—"

"I don't care about what I am or why I was given these powers." Tears start to prickle along my lashes, hot and stinging. "I buried that part of me a decade ago on that island. I walked away from it. My feelings haven't changed."

"You're powerful–"

"I don't want it. I want this. I want a family who loves me. I want to wake up next to you every morning. I don't want to know that something in the universe is calling out to me, trying to lure me into a greater purpose. I don't want that. I just want you."

He takes a breath and looks momentarily hurt. "I didn't–I'm sorry, I should have asked before I brought you here."

I step toward him and take his hands, knitting our fingers together. "I want to be normal. I want to be Sarah. Sarah doesn't read the stars and weave prophecies together. Sarah is a mate, a mother, and someone who is capable of living without feeling like she has to look over her shoulder all the time. Let me be that–"

He kisses me tenderly, smoothing my tears away with his thumbs. "I'm sorry. I know. You don't have to worry about any of this anymore. I can carry it for you."

"I don't want you to have to do that–"

"We're close to finding Gabriel, and soon, this will all be over, and we can move on. I promise."

Another kiss has my knees growing weak. I just want to be in bed with him. That's all I've been thinking about all night.

He pulls a lever, and the moonlight fades away, casting the orrery in darkness that drowns out the voices whispering throughout the room. I don't think he heard them at all, but I did.

They echo through my mind as he leads me through the quiet castle, through the dim corridors and shadowed alcoves, until we reach a wing of the castle unfamiliar to me.

He opens the door and slips me inside. The only sound I hear is my rapid heartbeat as his arms come around me again, and he lifts me up. I wrap my legs around his waist while he carries me to bed.

He drops me onto a firm mattress less than half the size of his bed back at the manner. I squeak in surprise, nearly rolling off the edge. "Sydney!"

"Hold on," he laughs, grabbing my leg to hold me steady. He crawls over me and reaches for the lamp on the bedside table. The warm glow illuminates the room. I crane my neck to look over his shoulder at the posters on the navy-blue walls. A stately dresser that could be several decades old is the finest piece of furniture in the room. Everything else is… boyish. Trophies, posters, and old school books scatter the room.

I sit up a bit, forcing Sydney back.

"I'm sure we can find a guest room, but my feet carried me here on impulse. It's been several years since I spent the night at the castle, and Dad mentioned this room was ready." He shrugs, sitting back on his legs.

I scan the room, taking in the pictures on a bookshelf situated between two of the ceiling height windows.

Sydney, as a young boy, standing in the middle of a gaggle of kids roughly his age on a beach. Ryan is easy to spot with his chestnut brown hair and ruddy cheeks, his eyes the same shade of blue as Sydney's. Kenna is also in the picture, missing her two front teeth, her dark hair braided away from her face. She has her arms wrapped around a young Evander's neck as she rides on his back, and Evander, tanned from the sun with his coppery blond hair gleaming in the sun, is wearing the same scowl I've often seen on his face as an adult.

Misty, no more than five, fights her way into the picture, pinching Ryan on the hip.

"You all had each other," I whisper, my heart lurching. Kenna and Evander are the most striking of the group. They loved each other then. It's obvious. A childlike, innocent kind of love that blossomed into matehood, but still….

I don't have a single picture of me as a child.

More pictures, more memories. Sydney as a teenager holding a trophy after a 'Wolfball' tournament. Sydney and Ryan standing in front of the gates to Silverhide, which looks like nothing more than a densely wooded, massive acreage of land. Sydney and Kenna at her graduation from whatever constitutes a high school graduation to royalty.

I blink back tears and turn to Sydney, who's watching me closely as I take in the little pieces of his life.

He caresses my cheek, leaning his forehead against mine. "Blake will have this."

"I know," I reply, trying to swallow past the painful lump in my throat. "I just don't know how I'm supposed to feel right now."

"Are you happy?"

"Yes," I breathe, choking on the word. "I really am. I'm not–this is just a little overwhelming, I think. You have such a big family."

"I know." He pulls me into his chest and lays us down on his twin-sized mattress. We barely fit, but I relax into his warmth as his fingers drift up and down the length of my spine. "It went better than I thought it would."

"What did you think was going to happen? Everyone throwing their silverware, me being tackled by your dad's warriors?"

"Something like that," he laughs, obviously teasing. "I think, in reality, my parents didn't think I'd find my mate. I was against it, you know. Then you came along, and things just feel… good. They feel right. I feel like I'm exactly where I need to be."

"Lying with your mate in your childhood bed?"

"It's not exactly ideal, but I honestly have no idea which room we should move to" he laughs, rolling over to look down at me. He bends down to brush his mouth over the curve of my jaw. The touch sends shimmers of desire rippling down my spine, settling low and spiraling into want I can't ignore. "I've never even kissed anyone in this bed."

"I find that hard to believe."

"I'm being serious." He kisses me tenderly, drawing it out. He parts my lips, and I open to him, softly moaning as his tongue sweeps over mine. "I've never brought a girl to the castle before."

He lowers himself on top of me. The bed squeaks painfully, rattling a bit. "We're going to break the bed," I gasp as his lips travel down my neck, sucking little bruises down to the bodice of my blouse. "We can't be too loud. Your whole family is here–"

"They won't hear anything. The walls are made of stone–"

"Sydney," I whine as he reaches behind me to loosen the little pearl buttons along my back keeping my blouse in place. He tugs my shirt free, slipping it over my head, and tosses it on the ground.

"I like this bra," he says with sincere admiration. "I think I'll keep this one intact."

I let out my breath as he unclasps my bra and gently takes it off, but his body tightens as my breasts bounce free.

He looks into my eyes for a split second before leaning down to suck one of my nipples between his hot lips.

I cover my traitorous mouth with my hand to muffle a deep moan and cup the back of his head with my other, my eyes nearly rolling back in my head.

"I wish I'd met you earlier," he says against my skin. "I would have taken you to formals at Wellington and shown you off to everyone."

"How do you know I would have said yes?"

"You haven't been able to resist me yet," he rasps, kissing down my stomach.

I squirm when he starts pulling my slacks down, his kisses tickling my hip bones.

"I went to a public high school, Sydney. You wouldn't have hung out with someone like me."

He trails a kiss all the way down my naked thigh and pauses at my knee, his eyes meeting mine in the lamplight. "I would have been drawn to you, no matter what, Sarah. You're–" He drags his tongue over my thigh, "perfect."

I lose myself in his heated touch. He hooks his arms under my legs and drags me down to the edge of the bed so my legs are resting over his shoulders, then lowers his head to the apex of my thighs.

One lick, and I'm quaking.

He laps slow, delicious circles around my clit, taking his sweet time as he works me into a drawn-out frenzy. I tangle my fingers in his hair and pull, biting down on my lower lip to keep quiet, humming my pleasure.

He stabs two fingers inside of me, hooking them, dragging them in and out until I tense and come undone around them. Only then does he take off his pants and sink his cock inside of me, groaning with relief.

The bed squeals repeatedly, but Sydney is trying his best to keep quiet. It's thrilling, honestly, and soon I find myself riding the wave of another exquisite release. He kisses me fully, his tongue dancing with mine as he thrusts into me hard enough the headboard of his rickety old bed claps against the wall.

"I'm going to come," I bite out, pulling his face down to mine. "Please, Sydney–"

He bites down on my neck and jerks, coming undone at the very same moment I do.

"Sarah, I love you," he says against my lips.

I wrap my arms around him, holding him close as he spills himself inside of me. Warmth trickles through my body, and somewhere deep down, I feel a little spark.

Something new. Something exciting and driven by our bond.

"I love you too."

The bed creaks, leans to one side, then Sydney is clutching me to his chest and rolling to the ground as his childhood bed collapses with us still on top.

I yelp in surprise, but Sydney laughs with tears in his eyes.

"We should go find a quest room now," he says.

I pull him back down for another kiss. That can wait.

I've never been more comfortable in my life.

39

WHAT'S UP WITH HADLEY?

SARAH

WE'VE FALLEN into a normal routine at the manor. It's been almost a week since the family reunion where Sydney announced our bond. While no formal announcement was made about Blake, it's obvious who his father is.

I run my knuckles over Blake's chubby cheek, smiling down at him as he naps peacefully in my arms. His hair has grown thick and lightened up since our time in the manor, turning a soft chestnut brown. And his eyes?

They're just as rich and blue as Sydney's. I often wonder what our next child will look like. Will they have eyes like mine? Like Sydney's? A strange combination of both?

I shouldn't even be thinking about that right now. We're still finding our footing, deciding the best course of action. Sydney is at his office right now, and to be honest, I'm starting to grow antsy about doing... something. Something outside of the house. Something useful to his pack—our pack.

Because I'm his Luna.

I look up at the ceiling in Blake's nursery and watch the late afternoon sunlight play through the crystals in the dainty chandelier and let my mind wander over everything we've been talking about lately, and it's… a lot.

Maddy and Isaac want us to have a real wedding, to stand before the High Priestess in the temple and exchange vows to not only each other, but the Goddess. It makes sense. I will stand in Maddy's shoes one day as the Queen of Crescent Falls, and the people of this kingdom have expectations of the royals, which includes being allowed to witness and mark these occasions in our lives. Blake needs to be baptized by the priestess as well, and I know for a fact Maddy is already planning that event in length. I'm lucky to have her, honestly. She is a doting grandmother and a really good ally to have while navigating this new, slightly complicated, life beside Sydney.

I have become, in all actuality, a princess.

Which means Cosette is busy training me to act and think like one.

I lay Blake down in his crib and creep out of the room, gently closing the door behind me. The manor is quiet today. No guests dropping in. Sydney isn't here loudly taking phone calls or meeting with pack members in his office down the hall. Cosette and I sent Dalia down to the village this morning to do some shopping and to see one of her friends for lunch, but I'm sure she'll be home soon.

I find Cosette in the kitchen where she's kneading dough on the long kitchen island, her curly brown hair pulled away from her face as music trickles softly from a speaker on the far side of the counter.

"Can I help with anything?" I ask, tucking my hands in the pockets of my jeans.

Cosette's eyes meet mine and crease as she gives me a slightly exhausted smile. "I could use a cup of tea, but you're my boss, remember?"

"Have you ever admitted to not being the boss before?" I laugh, turning toward the stove top. The gas range flames to life as I fill up the kettle and start pulling out the herbs she uses in her special blend.

"I can readily admit it's nice to not be the only one responsible for the welfare of our Alpha anymore." She sighs, her slight frame flexing as she slaps the dough on the counter and continues kneading. "And you need far less care than he ever did. You sleep, and eat regularly, which is a nice change of pace. I'm no longer hounding anyone to take care of themselves."

"I think you could use a nice, long vacation, Cosette."

She chuckles, shaking her head, "To where, exactly?"

"I've heard Maatua is very nice this time of year."

"It's hurricane season in the spring, darling."

"Well, it's better than spring snowstorms." I glance out the windows beyond the kitchen table at the light, fluffy snow falling in dizzying spirals. It's nearly April, and it's still snowing almost daily, although it doesn't stick to the ground. The forest around the manor is every shade of brown and red, the trees only a week or two away from budding.

I pour the tea exactly how we like it, adding copious amounts of cream and sugar. Cosette continues kneading the bread, her knuckles turning white, as I sink into a chair by the window and close my eyes.

I crack an eye open and watch her, noticing her pitched brow. We haven't spoken about her weird behavior regarding Hadley last week. Hadley didn't visit over the weekend like she said she would, and I've just been too busy to think about it.

This is honestly the first time I've had a few minutes alone with Cosette since Maddy's dinner party. I sip my tea and adjust my weight in the chair, watching her closely.

"I can feel your eyes burning into my face," Cosette murmurs. "Is there something you'd like to talk to me about?"

"You have an uncanny ability to read minds."

"It's not mind reading, Sarah. I'm an old mother. One day, you'll be able to look at your children and see exactly what's going on behind their thick skulls, trust me."

"Are you saying you consider me a daughter?"

She cracks a smile but doesn't meet my eyes as she starts to roll out the dough. "Well, I'm all you have in that regard, so yes. Call me Mom if you wish."

Now I'm smiling, but her eyes meet mine briefly before she turns to fetch her pastry knives. "Cosette… I've been wondering why you were acting so weird around Hadley last week. You seemed really cold around her."

She sighs as she cuts the dough into long, thin strips. "There's something about her that I don't like. That's all."

"But what is it, exactly?"

"I'm not going to lie and say I didn't overhear your conversation about Alpha Ryan, first of all. I've known Ryan since he was a boy, and I know for a fact that while he's a prolific playboy, he wouldn't kiss his Beta's sister if it didn't mean something more. He's very professional. He has a good set of morals, that one. He doesn't sleep around within his pack."

My cheeks color a bit. I'm tempted to bring up the strange conversation I had with him at the castle, but I'm still trying to understand the weak bond I share with him that ties us to Sydney. It's a twin thing, apparently. At least I'm telling myself that.

"I was honestly shocked when Hadley told me she'd kissed him. She initiated it."

"And do you think that's normal behavior? You've known the girl for years."

"We were teenagers when we met, you know. We lived in the same boarding house while her brother was off at warrior training, and we attended the same high school. She's different all of a sudden."

Cosette starts dropping what I hope are those sweet, honey and cream filled pastries I love onto a baking dish. "Different, how?"

"I guess I never knew her to be so reckless. Her brother basically keeps her in chains–"

"Beta James?" Cosette laughs, holding my gaze. "What gives you that impression?"

"She was never allowed to go out. She got in trouble often for visiting me in the NZ."

"I've known James for several years now, Sarah. I can tell you with confidence that the picture she's painting is far from the truth."

A heavy feeling settles in my chest. I sip my tea to try to banish it, but it spreads, my shoulders going painfully tight. "Hadley has been my only friend for a while now. I just feel like maybe I didn't know her as well as I thought, or maybe I'm the only one who is changing."

"Well, you're mated and a mother now. That does change relationships."

I tilt my head. "Can I tell you something in confidence?"

"Of course."

"I think Hadley and Ryan are mates. I can feel it. Does that make sense?"

She sighs and shakes her head in defeat, turning for the oven with her tray of raw pastries. "Ryan has known who his mate is for years now, Sarah."

"What? Really?"

"Kenna asked me last summer if I knew who she was. I guess Ryan mentioned something about it. I figured if that's the case, it had to be someone younger, still unable to feel the mate bond. Has Hadley given you any inclination that she's felt that, or her wolf powers, yet?"

"We've never talked about it. She's only twenty, though. Her birthday isn't until next winter."

"Then she very well could be Ryan's mate. Time will tell. I would just... tread lightly with her."

"Do you not like her?"

"I don't trust her, Sarah. But I might be... well, after everything that's happened and continues to happen, I don't really trust most people right now."

I decide that I'm going to talk to Hadley about it, whatever it is. If anything, I'll tell her how I feel like there's a weird rift between us. Maybe I'm the problem. I went from party girl to poor girl to a mother to a Goddess-damned princess in the space of a year.

Hadley might be the same as she always was, but our friendship is changing.

Blake wakes up two hours later, and I go about our usual early evening routine. I'm just getting him out of the bath when Sydney gets home. I meet him at the top of the stairs. He gives us both a kiss and says something about a shower before disappearing into the recesses of the house. I hear his phone begin to ring as his footsteps fade out of hearing range.

Blake and I settle in the sitting room downstairs while Cosette finishes up with her dinner preparations. He likes being on his belly now and can almost roll over.

But just as Sydney walks down the stairs to join us, a knock sounds through the foyer, and Sydney walks to the front door, checking his watch.

"I hope I'm not interrupting," Hadley says as Sydney opens the door wide enough to allow her to enter. She stomps her boots on the floor mat and shrugs out of her coat as I walk out into the foyer with Blake in my arms.

"We were just about to have dinner," I tell her but catch Sydney's eyes.

"Actually, I have to go to Silverhide tonight. I just got a call from Ryan."

Hadley looks between us then at Blake. I fight the disappointment brewing in my chest as I look up at my mate, but then I notice the nerves playing behind his eyes. "Is everything okay?"

"I'm sure it is. He just needs my opinion on something. I'll take Blake with me so you two can have some time alone, if you want."

I nod, handing Blake to him.

"Are you sure? He could stay here, with us," Hadley cuts in.

Sydney gives her a soft shrug. "It's fine. I'll enjoy it, and I'm sure Ryan wants to see him." He steps around Hadley and brushes a kiss over my forehead, whispering, "I'll be home in an hour or two. Apologize to Cosette for me about missing dinner."

"I will," I sigh, and with that, he's gone, carrying a very happy Blake with him. I turn back to Hadley, noticing the shadows under her eyes. "Are you okay?"

"A little tired." She shrugs but reaches into her coat pocket before hanging it on the hooks beside the door. "I got you something, though."

"What is it?"

"Do you remember that chocolate shop that opened up in the NZ for, like, a month?" She steps toward me and extends her hand. A small, glossy piece of something wrapped in gold paper falls into my waiting palm. "It's the turtle kind, with pecans. Remember how much you liked them?"

I dig through my memory for any mention of this chocolate shop and my preference for this specific kind of candy but come up short.

"I–"

"You probably don't even remember, seeing as you were so busy setting up your shop at the time," she laughs, wrapping her arm around mine. "Come on, try it."

I unwrap the chocolate and pop it in my mouth, chewing slowly to see if it will jog my memory. If anything, it reminds me of sitting at the kitchen table eating Cosette's famous chocolate cake after starving for several months, finally feeling warm and whole again.

"Now, about that dinner," Hadley beams, tugging me across the foyer. "I'm starving, and we have a lot to talk about."

40

HUNTING HIM DOWN

SYDNEY

BLAKE BABBLES the entire late evening drive to Silverhide. He likes rock music, especially when it's loud enough to send a tremor through the truck, and squeals with delight every time I go over a bump or a corner too sharply.

Sarah would kill me if she knew how loud the music was or how reckless I'm driving, but Blake notoriously hates his car seat, and he's having the time of his life right now.

I can't lie. I really enjoy having a kid, especially a son. Lately, when my thoughts aren't on his mother, I imagine what kind of life we'll have together. What kind of sports he'll want to play, whether he'll go to Wellington to pursue academics or warrior training. I wonder whether he'll continue to look like me or grow to resemble his mom. I wonder what our next baby will be like, especially since we're not trying to stop that from happening.

The idea of Sarah pregnant again sends heat coursing through my body. I remember how beautiful she was when I stopped at her shop for the first time.

This time around, I'll get to be there for all of it.

And the next, and the next, because I honestly can't keep my hands off her, and I'm sure Blake will have more siblings than I have when it's all said and done.

But my light as air mood shatters the second I pull up to Ryan's house and notice the two cars in the driveway.

I bang on the front door, carrying Blake's car seat around one arm, and find myself face to face with James.

He's a handsome man and roughly my age with curly, black hair he keeps brushed away from his angular face. Dark eyes meet mine as he bobs his head in greeting. Normally, whenever I have the displeasure of running into him, he greets me with silence and a heavy dose of skepticism. I've never liked him, but admittedly, I never took the chance to get to know him.

Ryan, apparently, adores him enough to justify making him his Beta.

Right now, however, James looks withdrawn and exhausted. He holds the door open for me. "We're all in the kitchen."

"You and who else?" I set Blake's car seat down for a moment to slip off my boots.

"Alpha Ryan and Evander."

"Evander?" I look up at the Beta. "Why is he here?"

Suddenly, this doesn't feel like a casual hangout with my twin brother under the guise of picking up my soon-to-be-wife's car, which she doesn't know how to drive.

I scoop Blake up. He gives James the biggest smile I've ever seen in my life–all gums–and to my surprise, James gives him a smile back.

I've never seen James smile.

I follow him to the kitchen and find Ryan and Evander cloistered around the kitchen island in front of the ancient laptop Ryan used at Wellington that somehow still runs. "What's going on here? I thought you left for Eastonia several days ago?"

"I'm back on Ghost business for Commander Artyom," Evander says dryly. "It was not my decision."

I narrow my eyes at him. "What's going on?"

"Remember those rogues I mentioned?" Ryan sighs, rolling his neck.

Vaguely. The memory drifts back to the forefront of my mind while Blake reaches for James, babbling incoherently. "The wolves spotted skirting the far edge of your territory?"

"Yeah," Ryan practically growls. "James sent scouts to pick up their scents so we could follow them, find out what they wanted and what pack they belonged to. I've been having some issues with our neighbors to the west, Raven Hall, as you remember." He flexes his hand, the one that was busted and peppered with healing bruises when I went to his shop. "I thought it might have been some of their pack members, maybe kids just old enough to shift goofing off in their wolf forms, but our scouts found evidence of them coming and going from Silverhide into the NZ and followed their scents to a known underground rogue den."

He turns the laptop toward me. Blake squeals, and I look over my shoulder to find James making faces at him. James catches me and immediately goes rigid and serious again, much to Blake's dismay.

I catch Evander's eyes. "What do you have to do with this?"

"The Ghosts are still looking for Gabriel and whatever sympathizers he has here in Crescent Falls since he's been run out Eastonia with his tail between his legs. I might be ruling beside my mate in Veiled Valley, but King Ryatt has me heading this mission now. I assume you understand why."

Because this is about family. One of our own is at risk again. My mate.

My son.

Speaking of my son, he damn near launches himself out of my arms to get to James, who is standing a few feet away. "Will you hold him for a second?" I ask gruffly. James nods, and accepts Blake into his arms. Blake immediately settles and starts playing with the hood of James's sweatshirt.

I give them both a skeptical once over before turning back to the computer. "You think these wolves you tracked have something to do with Gabriel?"

"That's what we're trying to figure out. My pack doesn't do business with anyone in the NZ," Ryan says sharply, bitterly. "We already have enough issues with our neighbors on either side. I need to know what exactly these wolves want and why they're involving my territory."

"The Ghosts have surveillance set up in that den from back when I came here this summer, and they did a bust on an illegal breeder auction," Evander says without an ounce of emotion. "We're going through the footage right now."

I glance at James and Blake before rounding the counter to watch the somewhat grainy CCTV footage. "Is this live?"

"No, it was taken early this morning." Evander clicks a few keys, zooming in on the video. It's a wide room with an untidy bar set up in one corner. Two unassuming men are seated at a table talking, a third pouring drinks.

James walks up beside us. "We picked up Hadley's scent in the NZ, mingling with whoever had been running along the boundary of the Silverhide territory."

"Hadley?" I glance at Ryan and James. Ryan's eyes darken as he dips his head back to the footage, but James sighs deeply, adjusting his grip on an especially squirmy Blake.

"She's been acting suspicious for a while now. Making trips into the NZ, lying about it."

"My mate–Sarah–is her friend. Sarah lived in the NZ for a while."

"I'm aware, but she wasn't going there to just meet up with Sarah. I had no problem with that, in fact, I begged her on several occasions to bring Sarah back to Silverhide. I made sure Hadley was bringing food and vitamins to Sarah, but she kept telling me Sarah wouldn't leave."

Something ugly and dark twists its way through my gut, spreading like a disease. I think back on every conversation I've ever had with Sarah, every moment she mentioned that Hadley was the only one helping her, but Hadley had to do it in secret because her brother was controlling and abusive.

But the man standing next to me holding my son doesn't fit that description. An asshole? Sure, that's a personality trait common in most men with power.

My head starts to pound with a sudden sharp ache as I slowly turn back to the computer.

Another man enters the room, wearing a hood. The seated men stand, and the three start conversing rapidly before the hooded man slowly turns his head, half of his face illuminated by the grainy fluorescent lighting.

"Gods," Evander rasps. "We got him."

"That's Gabriel," I growl, my blood boiling as Gabriel's face comes into view as clear as day. "How long ago was this?"

"This was at six A.M." Ryan speeds up the video. Gabriel moves in and out of the frame for the next two hours of footage, but then two more people arrive. "Ten hours ago, give or take."

One man, and one woman.

James thrusts Blake into Ryan's arms and crowds the laptop as Hadley steps into the room. Ryan shoves back in front of the laptop, and the look on his face as I swiftly take Blake back into my arms is….

Heartbreak. Pure, and unforgiving.

James and Ryan watch the screen without blinking as Hadley talks to Gabriel. We're all thinking the same thing right now as the impossible plays out before us—but she has to be there against her will. There's no way Sarah's best-friend is working against her.

But when Hadley smiles and throws her head back in a laugh, that idea shatters.

Then I remember where Hadley is right now.

"Oh fuck," I say, feeling like I'm going to lose my balance. "Hadley—she's with Sarah at the manor."

"We're going," James says without an ounce of emotion as he tugs on Ryan's arm, but Ryan's eyes are still glued to the screen like he's trying to make sense of it. He shakes his head repeatedly. "Alpha, come on. We need to go get her."

"Why is your sister working with Gabriel?" I snap. If Blake wasn't in my arms, I'd pin this man to the wall and choke the answer out of him.

"I didn't know," James growls. "I knew something was up which is why I got Alpha Ryan involved–"

"We don't have time for this," Evander says, and I look over to find him staring back at the computer screen with Ryan.

Time moves to a crawl as Evander pulls up the live footage.

Gabriel is back at the den, lounging in a chair while sharpening a knife.

My mind goes blank as my senses go haywire. A sharp pang of pain radiates through my left temple, waking me back up.

"Hadley's at the manor? You're sure?" Ryan asks somewhere in the distance. I feel like I have tunnel vision. Gabriel is right here, just a few miles away, and Sarah….

"Oh, my Goddess." I pull out my phone. Blake starts to whine, upset by the sudden shift and onset of tension in the room. Sarah doesn't answer her phone, a new replacement for the one she had to sell several months ago. I try Cosette instead. Nothing.

I have to go up there. I have to go home to my mate, but…

Gabriel looks directly into the camera and smiles.

"We need to move, now," Evander says, shutting the laptop. "Ryan, James, go get Hadley. Bring her to the castle." He pulls a phone out of his pocket, pressing it to his ear.

"Stop," I growl. Evander looks at me as I shake my head. "He's mine. Call off your Ghosts."

"You need to go get Sarah," Ryan says sharply.

He's right, but this won't end until Gabriel is dead with his blood staining my hands. I slowly hand Blake to Evander. "Take him to my parents," I say slowly.

"Sydney," Ryan growls in warning.

I turn to my brother, looking between him and James. "Go get Sarah."

I'm gone before anyone can protest. Shouts follow me to the door, followed by Blake's high-pitched wail at my absence.

Sarah can protect herself. She knows how to shift. She can jump, just like the day she tried to run away from us, from me. She can spirit away somewhere safe. I have to believe that she will and that Ryan can get to her in time.

I only have a few minutes to get to Gabriel before that tricky bastard disappears again.

I leave Ryan's house at a sprint. I don't even bother shifting, not yet. I'll need all of the power I can get when I'm standing in front of him.

The NZ comes into view before me, covered in thick, rolling fog. Spring air ripe with the scent of garbage and burning rubber hits me like a shockwave, blurring my senses for only a moment as I turn toward the entrance of the alleyway leading to the den from the videos. I recognize the side entrance to the five story apartment building with a small grocer on the first floor. I see the exterior steps Hadley had to journey down to get to the basement, but it doesn't matter.

All I know is that the pain in my head is getting worse the closer I get to Gabriel.

I thought it was Sarah's doing. She broke something inside my head, something that shimmers to life with fresh pain whenever Gabriel is mentioned, but I was wrong.

It's my powers telling me where to find him. I've had this ability all along.

I rip open the door to the basement and step inside, but it's empty.

I look up at the camera, at the smoke detector now hanging from the wall, the wires torn and sparking.

Slowly, I turn back toward the stairs and hike up them, sniffing deeply for his acrid, rotting scent.

The fog rolls in so thick I can't see below my knees, but the pain is still there, growing stronger and hotter with each step I take.

People mill along the street. Restaurants and shops are still open for the night. It's busy, too crowded, as I pass through a group loitering in front of a small pub.

A man darts between two buildings, his dark cloak giving him away.

I follow, and he knows I'm right behind him.

Gabriel thinks he can run.

I'm still faster, even after he shattered my legs.

I don't turn down the alley. I keep walking, waiting for him to cut back down between the tall, narrow buildings.

And then there he is, running like he's being chased just a few feet in front of me. He whips around at the very moment I leap toward him, tackling him to the ground.

But the cold pavement disappears into the fog. I fall into… nothingness.

The bastard spirited away, *but I'm going with him.*

SOMEONE HAS TO DIE

Sarah

"It really wasn't that bad," I explain, seated next to Hadley at the kitchen table. For the past half hour, I've been telling her about the dinner party and how Sydney announced our mate bond. Hadley's been listening while picking at her food, nodding along and smiling when I explain the juicer bits.

"Well, look at you, getting to explore the castle. One day, I want to see it."

"It sounds like we're going to have a big wedding after all. I suppose the reception will be held there."

Hadley smiles and pushes her plate away. "How are you feeling?"

"In general? A little overwhelmed, honestly–"

"No, right now."

I look down at my plate. I've barely touched my food. In fact, my head hurts a little bit, and my stomach is in knots. "It's been a busy week. I think I'm just tired."

I glance at the kitchen where Cosette would normally be fluttering around cleaning up from dinner, but she excused herself to do the laundry ten minutes ago, giving me the privacy I needed to talk to Hadley about Ryan.

I share Cosette's sentiments. Not because I don't think Hadley deserves Ryan, but because it seems like, to her, this is a game. Like she's holding the fact she kissed the Alpha above her head like a beckon, a prize.

She has no idea he's her mate, and it's not my place to tell her, but she'll be the Luna of Silverhide one day, as well as part of the same family that has welcomed me with open arms.

I don't want her to hurt Ryan, though. It's a weird feeling. I trust Hadley. I know her. And her suddenly sly smile and propensity toward gossip is new behavior.

"Hadley, I have something I need to talk to you about," I say, twisting to face her. I go to grip my fork, but my fingers feel numb. I flex them, trying to stretch the prickling sensation away, but it seems to spread instead.

"About what?"

"Ryan–"

"Sarah, you look exhausted. Are you feeling okay?"

"Honestly, no," I admit. Can I really be this exhausted? "I shifted with Sydney last night. We were out pretty late, and I guess I didn't get enough sleep." I lift my hands and cup my face, resting my elbows on the table.

"I'll go find Cosette. We'll help you get to bed." She stands.

I follow her with my eyes, unable to do much else as the numbness spreads through my arms and into my chest. My heartbeat wanes, slowing significantly, as the room around me starts to fade. But a nagging voice inside my head screams, "Wake up!"

I lift my head from the table and gasp as darkness swarms around me. The lights are off, and lifted female voices echo from what must be the foyer as I slide out of the chair and onto the ground, struggling to find my footing. The house feels cold and stale as I grip the chair and pull myself upright. It's like the heat has been turned off, the power cut.

My head pounds as I look around, noticing my plate still on the table, the food untouched and cold. "Cosette?" I croak, trying to blink away the darkness still swelling in my vision.

Something crashes to the ground, shattering, the sound of glass breaking echoing down the hallway leading to the foyer. I push myself from the floor and throw my body against the kitchen doorway, clutching the wall to steady my weak legs.

Dalia screams, and my body reacts without my mind needing to catch up. I stumble down the hallway, leaning my shoulder against the wall as darkness threatens to pull me under again.

In the light of the nearly full moon, three figures tussle in the foyer. One of Cosette's precious porcelain vases lies shattered in the center of the carpet.

Dalia screams again as one of the figures grabs the other. "Stop!"

"Dalia?" I whisper.

A low, crackling laugh echoes through the darkness. One of the two figures falls to the ground, her face coming into the light as she scrambles back to where Dalia is crouching surrounded by porcelain shards. Cosette, her face bloody and hair as wild as her eyes, doesn't flinch as the shards cut through her hands.

The figure still standing turns, the moonlight touching her profile, and my heart sinks deep into my stomach.

"What are you doing, Hadley?" My weak legs nearly give out, my knees trembling violently as I drag myself forward, gripping the railing of the staircase.

Hadley looks murderous as she turns to face me fully. I barely recognize her.

"Hadley?!" I shout, and it takes a great effort to do so. My voice sounds like I've been punched repeatedly in the throat. "What did you do?"

"How are you feeling, Sarah? A little weak? A bit dizzy?"

"She poisoned you," Cosette growls.

I let go of the railing in an attempt to walk to Cosette and Dalia, but my legs give out. I clutch the railing again at the last moment, saving myself from another fall. "What did you do?" I rasp.

"It's just a bit of wolfsbane," Hadley clucks, snickering. "Oh, but the ground silver isn't doing you any favors. It's slowly working through your system. You'll succumb to it soon, I'm sure."

I shake my head. "You didn't–why would you hurt me?"

"When you mentioned you'd shifted, I knew I'd have to do something more extreme than just the wolfsbane laced chocolate. I could have given you anything, you know. You've always trusted me so blindly, especially when it came to food. You're still so used to having to scrounge for anything you could get. And look at you now." She laughs bitterly, reaching behind her to pull something free from her belt loop. "Mated to the heir of Crescent Falls, the son of the Beast."

I shake my head, sure this is some kind of sick dream. "Hadley–"

"You thought you could forsake your own destiny, didn't you, Sasha?"

My real name rings through the air like the steady beat of a drum. Hadley twists a blade over her fingers, the moonlight catching on its surface. I can barely catch my breath as I glance at Cosette, who is holding a sobbing Dalia in her arms.

Hadley follows my gaze and smirks, casually pointing her blade at Dalia. "That little bitch caught me cutting the power to the house after I left the table. I had to drag her by her hair into the foyer."

"Why are you doing this?" I beg.

"Gabriel is the true king. All of this should be his. He can make it so."

"You don't know what you're talking about, girl–"

"Shut up!" Hadley sneers, jabbing her knife at Cosette.

"Hadley, please, put down your knife and talk to me."

"Like you'd listen." She slowly turns back in my direction. "Our kind has been held back by the Goddess for far too long, and now the true king is rising to take back our power."

"You are deranged," Cosette hisses.

Hadley moves swift as lightning, chucking a shattered piece of porcelain at her. It grazes Cosette's arm, but her howl of pain is enough to jog me into total awareness.

"You knew who I was this entire time, didn't you?"

Hadley turns back to me and nods, her smile widening. "My brother and my parents were always so grateful for our lives here. They left Eastonia with nothing after their pack fell to Kane's armies, leaving them packless. Here, they thought we'd have more opportunities. But when they died, James left me alone in that fucking boarding house so he could become a warrior. He abandoned me."

"You were never abandoned, Hadley. You had family still–"

"I was born here. I was never meant for this place, just like you. I wanted to know why my parents hated Kane so much when he could have given them anything had he prevailed. We are mere wolves. Do you know what we used to be, Sasha? We used to have powers like the ones your precious royal family guards within their bloodline. Now, we're reduced to workhorses, to beasts with claws and teeth, not the immortal gods we could have remained."

"Sarah, get out of here, now," Cosette growls, but Hadley laughs bitterly.

"It's too late for that. The wheels are already in motion for the new era. My Lord Gabriel has seen to it. All he needs now is you, Sasha. The born-again queen of the mystics. The angel of the other realms. The decider."

"What are you talking about?" I choke out, tears blurring my vision.

"SARAH, GO!"

Hadley growls, "I'm sick of your interruptions, bitch," and launches herself toward Cosette, her blade sinking into Cosette's side.

I leap forward, but my legs give out, my knees crunching against the floor as I scream Cosette's name.

Dalia sobs, begging for their lives as Hadley pulls the blade from Cosette's side.

"Don't touch her!" I scream, reaching a weak hand toward Hadley. "Take me. Don't hurt them anymore."

I scream down the bond for Sydney, but it's radio silence. I can't feel him. The wolfsbane and silver echoing through my blood must be choking out our bond somehow. "HADLEY!"

Hadley raises her blade toward Dalia. Dalia's tear-filled eyes shine in the moonlight before she closes them in anticipation for Hadley's killing blow.

But then the door to the foyer bursts open off its hinges, and two wolves rush inside.

The first wolf is black as night with eyes that match Hadley's. He rushes toward me, blocking the view of Hadley as she ignores the wolves completely and slashes her blade toward Dalia.

But instead of the song of metal meeting flesh, a deep, guttural growl echoes through the room before the other wolf reaches Hadley, and she screams, her voice full of blood and pain.

I clutch James's fur to pull myself upright so I can see over his back and then I'm…

I'm frozen.

Hadley's blood coats the wall. She's lying lifeless at the feet of the wolf before her, her eyes open but unseeing.

"Cosette? Cosette?" Dalia sobs, shaking our friend. Shattered porcelain squeaking beneath them is the only answering sound.

But my attention is on the wolf who just killed the woman I thought was my friend—my closest, dearest friend. I'll never know why Hadley did this, if she's been spying on me for years, or how she got swept up in Gabriel's games.

My mind goes blank, and my heart lurches as the other wolf slowly turns to face me, his deep, stormy blue eyes shining with pain I can't find the words to describe.

"Ryan?" I sob, clutching James for dear life. "Ryan!"

Ryan walks a few paces away from Hadley's body before collapsing in a heap of fur, his groan of anguish echoing throughout the foyer.

Cosette moans, and over the sound of James's rapid breathes I can hear Dalia murmuring desperate prayers to the Goddess.

How can this be real?

I let go of James and crawl to Ryan, porcelain scraping the palms of my hands. I grab his head, pulling his fur so I can look into his eyes. They're dim with pain. "Ryan? Ryan, where is Sydney? Where's Blake?"

'She was my mate,' Ryan says into my mind, his tone broken in a way I didn't think possible. *'I killed my own mate.'*

4 2

TIME FOR ACTION

SARAH

"WHERE IS HE?" I pace around the kitchen table toward where James is sewing Cosette back together while Dalia sits at her side, her face colorless and eyes wide with shock. "Ryan, where is Sydney?"

"I don't know," Ryan growls. He's wearing one of Sydney's T-shirts which is too small for him. It's already ripping at the seams as Ryan takes a swig from the bottle of fine scotch I dug out of the bar in the dining room. Ryan is as drunk as a wolf shifter can be right now. His eyes are unfocused as he blankly watches James put another perfect stitch in Cosette's side.

She doesn't even flinch as she stares at the ceiling. Her eyes are dry, and her expression is vengeful.

"You told me he went after Gabriel. You need to take me to that den, right now!"

"You're not going anywhere, not until Evander–"

"Where is my mate?" I grab his arm, shaking him violently. It's been over an hour since... since Hadley died. My poison-addled brain

323

is still trying to wrap itself around the cold, hard truth of what just happened.

Now, I know what happened to Sydney and Blake tonight. I know about the den, the CCTV footage, the fact that James has had suspicions about Hadley for months but wasn't able to confirm what she was doing and who she was doing it with.

James hasn't said a word. He just started helping where he could in total silence. I know he has to be in shock like the rest of us.

Ryan is worrying me though. His cheeks are dry, but I can see the silver streaks of tears. I know he put a hole through the wall in the hallway upstairs when I'd sent him up there for clothes for him and James.

I don't know what this means for him. I've heard getting rejected by a mate is so painful that some people wish for death. What does it feel like to kill your mate, though?

"You have to take me to my son," I tell him, falling to my knees. "Please, Ryan. We have to do something."

"Evander is going to meet us here."

"We don't have time to sit here and wait for him," I grind out as Ryan takes another long, drawn out drink from the nearly empty bottle.

Ryan's phone buzzes on the table. James looks at his Alpha, his eyes heavy with grief and guilt. Ryan slowly reaches for it, but I beat him to it and slide my finger across the screen.

"Hello?"

"Sarah?" Evander's voice floods my ears.

"Where is Sydney? Do you have any idea where he is?"

"Where's Ryan?"

James called Evander half an hour ago after we got Cosette into a somewhat stable position. Ryan wasn't in the state of mind, and it's obvious looking into his blank, depthless eyes that he may not be in the position to do much right now, either. "Tell me what you know. Have you found Sydney? Is Blake with Maddy and Isaac?"

"You need to come to the castle. Royal guards are being dispatched all over the kingdom. I can't get to you now. I'm looking for him, Sarah, but I don't think he's here anymore."

"What do you mean he's not here?"

Evander sighs heavily. Ryan's eyes slide to mine.

"I had a few Ghosts comb the NZ before the guards were dispatched. We have a group of witnesses who saw two men fighting on the street. They disappeared."

My stomach hollows out. "You think–"

"I think Sydney either jumped with Gabriel to prevent a public scene, or Gabriel spirited away, and Sydney grabbed him, one of the two. Either way, Sydney is not here, and you need to be at the castle where it's safe."

I nod, tears filling my eyes. Ryan, to my surprise, reaches out and lays a hand over mine, squeezing. The act causes tears to spill down my cheeks as pure, white-hot despair tightens my throat to the point of pain. "Okay. We'll come."

"Is James there?"

"Yes."

"Tell him he needs to stay at the manor. Guards will arrive soon to clear out the… the body."

I squeeze my eyes shut as memories of me and Hadley rush to the surface, cutting through my heart like a knife.

I want to be mad at her, but I can't find the fury yet. I'm sure it'll come, but right now, I'm grieving my friend just like Ryan is grieving his mate, and James is grieving his sister.

Grieving what could have been if only–if only Gabriel hadn't been involved.

That rage ignites at the thought of Gabriel, and my tears vanish.

"Get to the castle immediately." Evander hangs up, and I slowly set the phone face down on the table and turn to Ryan.

"We have to move now, Ryan. We have to go to the castle."

He shakes his head once, reaching for the bottle, but I take it from him. "What happened is over. We can't think about it right now. You have to take me to my son. We have to find Sydney. You know we have to stop Gabriel. We can't lose both Sydney and Hadley tonight. Please? Our mates–" I choke on the words. "Please, Ryan?"

"I can't drive," he says with guilt lining each word.

I look at James over my shoulder.

I've never driven before. Evander told me to keep James here. I can tell by the look on his face that he knows he's likely going to be interrogated soon. He was Hadley's brother. I trust that he didn't know what she was up to and was telling the truth, but this is serious.

Then I look at Cosette. She's so pale. We don't have any of Isla's tears here right now. I need to get her to a healer.

"I can drive us. You, me, Cosette, and Dalia."

"I'll stay with James," Dalia pipes up. She rarely speaks, so I glance at her, noticing the way she's looking up at James like he's her knight in shining armor.

For a moment, I almost crack a smile. "Okay. That's fine. Ryan, I can drive us. You just need to tell me what to do. I can't shift right now. My powers are gone."

"You still have poison in your system making you weak. We can't risk it."

"I can't risk something happening to my mate," I tell him. "I need to go there, to your parents, and make sure Blake is safe before going after them."

I can feel everyone looking at me, but I hold Ryan's gaze. Ryan slowly stands. He doesn't sway like I thought he would. "Get your coat." He fishes in his pocket and tosses me a key. "It's your car, anyway. Might as well learn to drive it."

I glance over my shoulder at Cosette, whose head is resting against the window in the backseat, her eyes fluttering as she tries to keep them open.

The sleek, silver SUV has a cream-colored interior and an engine that roars when I turn the ignition. Driving can't be that hard. All I have to do is steer and put my foot on the gas pedal, right?

"Put it in reverse and back out at an angle, then put it in drive and steer toward the road," Ryan says gruffly, motioning to a stick-like object between us. When I stare blankly at him, he curses under his breath and slides the stick toward the letter R. "Give it some gas."

I slam my foot on the pedal, and we jerk backward. Cosette yelps in surprise, and Ryan hisses, his eyes meeting mine.

"Gently," he says.

I continue backing up until he tells me to stop. I shift into drive, and suddenly we're bounding down the narrow, curving driveway and down the mountain side road that leads into Shadowcrest. The car jerks forward and backward as I try to get used to the brakes, but my legs are still weak from the poison, and I'm starting to doubt myself.

Ryan reaches for a button on the visor when we reach the main gate, waving for me to stop.

'It's Ryan. We're on our way to the castle. Silver SUV with RWT-L89 plates,' he says to the guards through the mind-link. He motions for me to go again, and the automatic gates swing open, revealing a thick layer of fog choking the dimly lit road leading into Crescent City.

By the time we reach the city center, I've gotten the hang of driving to the point I feel comfortable enough to really give the car some gas as we speed through the fog, ignoring stoplights and the occasional group of warriors canvasing the neighborhoods and shopping centers.

Other than the warriors, it's totally empty out here.

"Ryan," I say as the lake comes into the view, the castle just visible over the tree line, "I'm sorry–"

"Don't say it," he whispers, turning his head toward the window.

I swallow back my grief, resisting the urge to touch him. I am just beginning to feel that strange bond between us again now that poison is filtering out of my body. The single thread is coated in despair, and it's killing me.

I maneuver onto the private road leading to the castle. The gates swing open, heavily guarded by wolves and men alike, and pull up to the front of the castle. It's a rough stop. I park halfway up onto the

curb that wraps around the circular driveway where a dormant fountain rests in the grassy area in the middle.

Guards file out of the front door before I even put the car in park.
Ryan groans as he gets out, slamming the door shut behind him
before fetching Cosette, barely lucid and still bleeding despite her
stitches, from the backseat.

Three shadows appear on the porch. Maddy runs down to me, her
eyes wide and hollow with concern. I fall apart the moment she
clutches my face, turning my head from side to side to look for
damage before taking me into her arms. "Blake's asleep. He's all right,
I promise."

The sob I've been holding back erupts. I come undone at the
seams. Just yesterday, everything felt perfect. I had everything I
wouldn't allow myself to even dream of, and now it's been taken away
by the one person who's been hunting me for a decade.

"She needs a healer," Ryan booms over the gathering crowd of
guards. He carries Cosette up the front sets where King Isaac and an
unfamiliar man stand side by side.

"Take her into the sitting room. We have everything set up there,"
Isaac says, but his eyes slide to mine, searching my face.

The other man, maybe a few years older than Isaac, looks me up
and down. His hair is a deep, dark silver that's pulled away from his
strong face in small braids that are gathered on the top of his head.
His skin is dark, but his eyes are a strange pale blue that seem to glow
in the light of the full moon still hanging overhead.

I feel a sense of power when Maddy leads me past him, and I catch
his name when Isaac says, "Artyom, find out where Evander is. I need
to speak to him."

Maddy rushes me into the sitting room where I witness Cosette
being laid out on one of the couches. Ryan stuffs a pillow under her
neck before turning on his heel and tearing away from the room.
Maddy watches him, confused, as he steps between a trio of maids
carrying medical supplies who squeak and have to jump out of
his way.

Maddy tries to sit me down on the opposite couch, but I clutch her hand. "Maddy, Ryan–Ryan killed Hadley."

She stares blankly at me, shaking her head.

"Hadley, my friend–she was working for Gabriel this whole time. He killed her to save Dalia, our maid. He–Hadley was his mate."

Maddy lets out her breath in a strangled gasp. She turns to the doorway where Isaac has just entered, having heard every word I just said.

"I'll talk to him," Isaac says with heartbreaking calm. His eyes betray his feelings, though. There's so much hurt and confusion behind them.

"This is all my fault," I whisper, fresh tears stinging my eyes. "I am so sorry for the pain I've caused your family."

"Don't say that," Maddy begs, shaking her head. "Blake is in the nursery upstairs. Go to him. Just look at him for a moment, Sarah, then we'll talk. He's safe. You're safe."

"I have to find Sydney."

"I know," she rushes out but shakes her head again, her eyes going glassy. "We will find him, but we can't lose you both. Blake can't lose you both."

She turns me toward the stairs, and I'm lost in a sea of maids and guards as I side-step through the foyer. I pass Artyom again, noticing the way he's looking into the sitting room as several pcoplc, likely healers, start tending to Cosette.

I look out over the second floor landing, my heart hammering.

The nursery is to the right, down a short hallway filled with moonlight. Eight steps and Blake will be in my arms again, safe, and whole.

But if I turn left, the library will come into view, and from there, I'll have access to the stars meant to guide me to my destiny.

Can they guide me to my mate?

I turn left.

43

———

SILVER AND GOLD

I ROLL ONTO MY BACK, unsure how much time has passed. One second, I was tackling Gabriel into the fog-soaked pavement, and the next, I'm here, in a lightless room that seems to stretch for miles.

I'm not alone. Gabriel coughs nearby, followed by the sound of his leg dragging over what feels like tile.

My eyes eventually adjust to the darkness, and the ceiling comes into view several hundred feet above my head, domed and intricate, with sweeping murals from an age long lost to time.

"Where did you take us?" I ask, turning my head toward the slightly blurry figure resting his back against a shadowed wall.

Gabriel looks at me, his light brown hair brushing over his shoulders, much longer than the last time I saw him. His eyes narrow, and his mouth parts in a firm scowl. "I didn't take you anywhere. You shouldn't be here. You're not the one I needed, and I'm running out of time." He groans softly, physically dragging his leg up so it's bent at the knee. I watch his leg begin to tremble before he lets it slump to the ground again with a wet splat.

It's broken in several places. Good, he deserves it. "Running out of time for what?"

"Wouldn't you like to know?"

I roll onto my knees and stand, flexing my body to test my strength. I'm slightly sick to my stomach from the journey to wherever the hell we are, but also from the dank, moldy smell in this place. I walk toward him cautiously, crouching a few feet away. Gabriel rolls his head to the side, opening one eye to look at me.

"I knew you'd be a problem the moment I met you. We met at the ball, you know. You probably don't remember. I was another faceless patron of the festival in a mask. I watched you leave your precious cousin behind and decided to formally introduce myself to Kenna to see if I could use her like I needed to use Sasha, but her powers weren't compatible."

"Compatible with what, Gabriel?"

"Kane's orrery, of course. That's where we are, a whole mile under Rifthold, where his fortress once stood. It was his most powerful possession." He waves a hand into the darkness. "It's how he knew the Beasts would return to try to topple his throne. My father was a believer of the old gods, you know. Kael, the god of night, the supposed mate of the Goddess, and their son, Annwyn, the god of the underworld. But the shifters only cared about the Moon Goddess because of Her gifts. She rebelled against Her mate and son in favor of Her people, who they kept enslaved, and for good reasons. We'd grown so powerful we could have toppled their empire and banished the lesser gods who made us in their image."

"You're talking about fairy tales."

"Am I?" he laughs painfully. "Tell me, princeling, do you never question why your family possesses their special gifts and others do not? Kane wanted to prevent that stain from spreading, to keep the powers intended for the gods for the gods."

"He considered himself a god, didn't he?"

"He was one."

"No. He stole power from others. Leeched them dry—"

"And those useless slaves deserved every second of it. Your aunt deserved it when he cut those powers from her with the same knife I cut powers out of Sasha to fuel my inheritance. Eastonia is mine. I am the rightful king."

"You're an inbred piece of shit who can't even shift–"

He snarls, "You're lucky my leg is broken, princeling. Otherwise it would be your blood spilled on the orrery."

I smile down at him. I could kill him right now. I could squeeze the life out of him, but that doesn't seem like enough, not after what he's done to my mate and my family.

"You still can't grasp what your mate is capable of, can you?"

"Enlighten me, Gabriel. You only have a few moments of life left. You might as well get it off your chest."

"I was going to turn back the clock," he breathes, his voice jagged with pain. "To a time when Kane still sat on his iron throne and ruled with his Firestone mask. I was going to turn back time to the day your father failed to kill Ryatt on that battlefield, when Kane's forces failed to see the deception that was Ryatt, the false son of Kane. I was going to turn back time to the moment your grandmother was born and wipe her off the map so none of you would have happened, and the Alphas of Crescent Falls would have rioted against your grandfather and strung him up to the gates of the kingdom he was failing."

"Had you done that, you wouldn't be sitting here bleeding out from a compound fracture."

He smiles darkly, his teeth stained with blood. "And you, Prince, would be a speck floating in the heavens, and your mate would be in the underworld where those of her kind belong, but we don't always get what we want, do we?"

He reaches into his pocket and draws out a knife. The blade is pure silver, and the hilt is cast in iron with a startling rare moonstone of perfect clarity at the hilt.

"Kane's blade was all I could salvage when I grew old enough to take over my coven. I was ten, you know. Just a boy. The boy, you see, who was destined to be king. There were even loyalists left to see to my care, and when Sasha showed her promise, I made sure to take what I could from her. But she was too young. There wasn't enough power in her blood to activate the orrery. I couldn't enact my plan until she came of age. I planned to keep her as my slave, my breeder if her powers could carry through our bloodline, but she was stolen from me. I learned only recently that it was Atticus, my uncle, who betrayed me."

I close my eyes as fury I can't contain rips through my body.

"He had her hidden well, I'll admit. I made the moves I had to make, hiding in secret, but my coven grew larger, and I finally had the numbers I needed to find her, but I needed more power. I had some mystics kidnapped to drain them, to fuel my blade, and it worked, but not enough to fuel the orrery. I needed even more, and then your generation started making waves. Kenna, the Firestone and Shadowsynger hybrid. I could have kept her as a breeder, too, but I needed… someone like your sister, if I had lost Sasha forever."

"My sister?" The words leave my lips in a snarl that makes the corners of his mouth curve into a smile.

"Oh, Misty is going to be exceedingly powerful. I've seen it, you know, in the stars. In what brief moments the orrery activities for me. Curse breaker. Kingdom toppler. She will part the southern sea and bring war to lands we've yet to explore all in the name of love."

"You're lying."

"I guess we'll never know." His eyes flutter as he begins to pale. "You and I could have been so powerful together, you know. Your powers are pretty useless to me, but your manners are… sadistic, deep down. Feral, savage. You hide those parts of you well behind your tailored clothing."

I lunge at him, dodging the knife, and grabbing him by the neck.

It's a mistake. He's stronger than I thought.

Pain blooms as I rear back. His silver blade hangs from my stomach before clattering to the ground at my feet.

Silver. I can feel it creeping through me, weakening me, eating away at the healing powers trying to knit the festering wound back together.

"Now neither of us can have her."

"You sick fucking bastard."

"Kill me now, princeling, before your body gives out."

"I owe you nothing, especially not a merciful death."

His eyes glimmer with pain. "How did she taste, Sydney? I thought Sasha's blood was the sweetest thing to ever touch my tongue. I dream about it often."

I clench my fists and fight the urge to give into his taunting. He wants me to kill him. He knows he's in a bad spot, that he's lost, but I can't give him the satisfaction of a swift death.

"A son, I hear. Congratulations are in order, are they? I wonder if Blake will be like his mother. Maybe one day he'll grown to know the truth of our kind and follow the path I so graciously laid out for him—"

"He will never even know your name."

"As so. He won't, will he? Because Sasha's precious friend is up at your gilded manor gutting her from chin to navel to collect her blood right as we speak. Tell me, can you feel your bond with her right now?"

It strikes that I can't. "Hadley wouldn't do that."

"Hadley was one of the more… excited of my followers. She loved breaking rules, and what easier target is there than someone young, alone, and angry at her brother for leaving her behind to serve Crescent Falls as a lowly warrior? She melted like butter in my hands, Sydney. She will kill Sasha because I commanded it of her. She's been waiting for this moment for years."

"You're a monster. You've ruined so many lives."

"I am a god," he rasps. "Like my father and his father—"

"You are a liar." I step toward him. "A worthless, powerless liar."

Snarling suddenly cuts through the darkness, echoing off the walls.

Gabriel grins madly. "You should have killed me when you had the chance. Now, I might get my way after all."

Four sets of enormous eyes sprint toward me, long, jagged teeth coming into view. Rogue wolves—tall and thin, gray and mangled. Their eyes glowing a deep crimson.

I grab the knife and throw it at him with all the strength I have left before using the last of my dwindling powers to shift.

Gabriel chokes out a cry and then slumps over the knife, where it pierces him through the heart before lodging itself in the stone wall at his back.

In my wolf form, I can see everything clearly. The darkness blooms with muted color, and several hundred feet away, I see *it*.

A massive orrery, three times, if not bigger, than the one at my parents' castle. Above it, the night sky comes into view from a gaping hole in the ceiling.

One of the rogues launches itself at me but I duck, turning to grab it by its hind leg with my teeth. It's surprisingly light as I swing it as hard as I can into the wall, where its half-rotted body splits and shatters into flesh and bone.

I can feel my powers dwindling. Blood stains my fur crimson as I snarl at two of the approaching rogues. I grab the first one by the neck and slam it down onto the ground as the other locks its jaws on my back, yanking me backward.

The fourth rogue approaches slowly. Larger than the last, it's waiting, I realize, judging every movement I make, deciding its best course of action.

Quite suddenly, it dawns on me that this is a losing battle.

I'm ready to die. What's a life in the heavens when I have that every time I see my mate holding our son?

The third rogue picks me up and tosses me at the feet of the fourth.

I can barely move. I'm stuck in my wolf form with no power left to shift and go for the knife that is currently sticking out Gabriel's chest. Silver eats its way through my veins like acid, rendering me useless.

'I'm sorry, Sarah,' I cast through the bond, yanking tight on those golden threads, and struggle to my feet to face death like a man.

But a blur of golden movement darts past my periphery, and the rogue screeches in pain. Behind me, the third rogue darts in a circle, chasing something… white.

My heart beats once, twice, but gives up on the third, and everything goes black.

44

TURN BACK TIME

Sarah

I PULL the crank that opens the ceiling in the tower, watching as the night sky comes into startling clarity. The stars are faint overhead, shielded by a layer of thin mist that moves across the sky like wisps of smoke. The moon, however, is full and painted a pale blue. It's stunning, and even through the haze of poison still in my system, I can feel its pull.

The voices that usually come from the orrery are silent as I move toward it, taking note of its gears and spiraling tangles of sleek steel and brass. The planets in our solar system circle around the moon in this version of the heavens instead of the sun like a direct line to the Goddess, and as I approach, my heart in my throat, the moonlight reaches the flat surface at the base of the orrery and sets the entire alight in dancing shadows.

My heart rate quickens as the voices start up, whispering through the room like the mist hanging below the stars.

"I don't understand you," I whisper back, swallowing past the lump in my throat. "Please, I just need to know where my mate is. That's all I want to know." I reach for the lever at the base of the atrium, twisting it in a rough, clunky circle. The gears shift, and the orrery begins to move. I let go when the voices reach a fever pitch and ring through my ears. I stumble back, watching the swirling metal.

The moonlight drifts over each planet and reflects off the moon at the center of the orrery. The room erupts in light so bright I have to shield my eyes.

"Our lost sister returns at last. Welcome, Guardian of the Gates of the Other Realm." The voices scream through my ears in conflicting tones and accents, converging into pure noise. I cover my ears as the voices continue, *"Call on us, Guardian. Tell us what you wish to see."*

"My mate!" I bellow, tears stinging my eyes.

The light explodes into nothing but pure white, then slowly fades. I open my eyes to silts and peer into the sudden darkness all around me. I can see… scorched earth. A once great city reduced to rubble, overtaken by nature. Twisting roots from new growth trees claw into the scorched soil down into what appears to be an empty abyss.

But it's not empty.

At its base, another orrery lies.

"This is in Eastonia," I whisper to myself, my mouth growing dry.

"Yes, sister. Tell us what you wish to know."

"Can I see him? Is he still alive?"

But the image explodes in color, and suddenly, I'm standing in a brightly lit room, sunlight pouring through ceiling height windows I find incredibly familiar.

I watch myself–slightly older, with my hair falling down to my lower back, wearing a gown of pale gold–cross the room to lift a baby from a crib drenched in warm sunlight. I cradle the baby in my arms as I turn to the other figure in the room, my lips moving but my words totally muffled.

A boy, no more than ten, runs up to me, dragging another little boy with him, while a little girl follows behind clutching a teddy bear in her arms.

Sydney kisses me on the forehead, his voice echoing through my ears, *"Are you ready?"*

The vision of my future breaks and is replaced by darkness again, by growls and echoes of pain. Sydney watches a knife fall from his belly and clatter on the ground as he slowly looks right at me… but I'm not *me*.

"Now neither of us can have her," I say to him, my voice replaced by Gabriel's.

I stumble backward, clapping my hands over my mouth and closing my eyes. *No, no, no!*

Someone grabs me from behind and yanks me out of the moonlight.

"Sarah?" King Isaac takes my face in his hands. "Sarah!"

"Gabriel stabbed him. I can't–I think I know where he is!"

Isaac looks over the top of my head, his eyes reflecting the moonlight drenched orrery. "You hear it too, don't you?"

"It showed me a vision of the future."

"Don't trust it," he tells me, dropping his hands and taking my arm. "Every step we take affects the future in some way." He turns me to face him. "Listen to me closely, Sarah. I'm going to go get him, but you have to help me get there."

"How?"

He takes my hand and squeezes. "Think of where he is. That's all you have to do."

I imagine the vision of Eastonia at the same moment Isaac sends us whirling through space and time. I feel like I'm being pulled apart and put together again in the space of a breath, and before my heart can beat again, my feet meet solid ground.

It smells like blood and rot. My eyes open, and I'm met with bone and sinew of some creature from my worst nightmares.

But a golden wolf stands beside me, his blue eyes locked on the rolling, seemingly endless darkness.

A wolfish whimper bleeds out of the darkness, followed by an answering snarl. My heart leaps out of my chest, and I shift without meaning too, my clothes ripping away as I hurtle into the darkness.

I have to find *my mate.*

'Two Rogues, Sarah!' Isaac says into my mind as he runs ahead of me. The orrery comes into view, leaking power I can't even describe. Every fiber of my being tells me to run, that this place is evil, that it's calling to me, and I have to escape.

I'm momentarily blinded by the orrery, by the dozens of planets and stars I'm not familiar with, but something crashes into my side and sends me flying through the air like I'm as light as a feather.

I hit the ground and roll to a stop on my back just as two glowing red eyes creep out of the darkness. The biggest, ugliest teeth I've ever seen in my life clack and drip with saliva as the rogue, those mythical–*I fucking thought*–beasts formed by wolves who give up their souls to remain in their wolf forms forever, closes in on me.

Blood stains his jowls. My mate's blood.

Anger propels me to my feet just as the rogue lunges, but I'm smaller and faster, and I dart between its legs, my back brushing its hairless belly. I clamp my jaws around its boney ankle and thrash. The beast roars in pain, trying to twist toward me, but I yank hard on its ankle and send it skidding on its side.

Its back crashes against the wall of what I believe must be an old temple, or a castle of some kind, lost and buried deep underground. A crack echoes through the space over the roars and clacking teeth of the rogue Isaac is battling.

I watch the light behind the rogue's red eyes dim then flicker out.

But Isaac is still fighting with what I believe is the last rogue left. I charge toward him, rounding the orrery as moonlight begins to drift over its surface, illuminating the strange network of gears and rusted metal. Thrumming voices chant to the beat of ancient drums, calling out my name. *Sasha, Sasha, Sasha.*

I'm not Sasha anymore.

Sasha is dead. Buried. Forgotten.

The chanting follows me as I turn from the orrery and use every ounce of my powerful legs to propel myself into the air, coasting over the bodies of two more rogues, and catch the rogue fighting with

Isaac by the rough of its naked neck. I sink my teeth into its flesh as I fly through the air, begging my body to become dead weight, and bring the rogue with me as I crash into the ground once more.

It shrieks in pain before I'm crushed beneath it.

'Sarah!' Isaac's voice calls through my mind.

I'm totally squashed beneath the rogue, but I kick my legs, trying to claw my way out. Its skin is oily and thin, and my claws leave trails of its blackish-green blood as I pull myself free of its weight and breath in the comparably fresh air.

Isaac runs toward me, favoring his right front leg, his golden fur blotched with both red and green-tinged blood.

But the rogue lifts its head, its powerful jaws widening, just as Isaac attempts to leap over it to get to my side. It catches Isaac around the belly and tosses him against the orrery.

'NO!' My howl rips through the air as Isaac falls limp to the ground, his head bouncing on the cracked, slimy stone tiles.

I'm stuck in place, frozen in horror, as the moonlight illuminates the two wolves lying only a few feet from each other. Isaac, with his golden pelt, and... and Sydney, who is so still I can't tell if he's still breathing.

This can't be happening.

The rogue sways to its feet, taking a few uneven steps in my direction. My eyes are still on Sydney and Isaac. I can't lose them. I can't. I can't go back to a world without my mate. My mind floods with Maddy's image. I imagine breaking the news to her that her mate is gone, and my heart shatters in my chest.

A prickling sensation ghosts through my fur, making the silver-white tufts stand on end.

Sasha, Sasha, Sasha.

I watch as the moonlight hits the center of the orrery. Gears begin to turn on their own accord, casting a crackling, whirring sound throughout the space. The rogue is closing in on me with slow, calculated steps.

The powers I refused to acknowledge, powers I refused to train, ignite. I don't hold them back like before. I let them flow, twisting into something new, deadly, and *beautiful.*

I take several slow steps forward to meet the rogue before speeding up and bouncing off the tips of my claws, sailing over its head, shifting in mid-flight and stretching my human fingers toward the moon at the center of the orrery. The rogue snarls, its jaws nearly snapping closed around my ankle, but it misses. I scream in determination, stretching my fingers, hurtling through the air so swiftly that the ground beneath me blurs. The second my fingers brush the decaying, chipping surface of the moon, light erupts in sprays of silver and violet, and I'm swept away.

Time spins. All around me, the rogues stand once again. I'm watching this scene play out like I'm rewinding a movie on the ancient VCR at my home on Mononoke Island. I watch as Isaac and I in our wolf forms battle in reverse, then I watch us shift, then arrive in a burst of light. It goes dark again, and I watch in horror as Sydney lowers his head to the ground in defeat only seconds before Isaac and I could get here. Then he's fighting the rogues, killing two of them.

Then, he's crouching in front of Gabriel.

I raise my hands and time stops, my powers falling away in wisps of violet mist.

"You and I could have been so powerful together, you know. Your powers are pretty useless to me, but your manners are… sadistic, deep down. Feral, savage. You hide those parts of you well behind your tailored clothing."

I grab Sydney's arm at the moment he lunges toward Gabriel, and Gabriel raises his blade. Sydney jerks back, turning to me in shock.

I wonder what I look like right now. I can feel my hair flowing out around me. I'm casting a pale silver glow over both men. I move slowly, and my voice is… distant, and ethereal, as I look into my mate's eyes and say, "*Kill him.*"

Sydney stumbles away but blinks, shaking his head in shock.

"*Kill him,*" I repeat.

Sydney yanks the blade out of Gabriel's hand and stabs him in the heart. I watch the light in Gabriel's eyes dim as the first sounds of the rogues appear, their claws scraping over the ancient tiles.

"Sarah?" Sydney breathes. "Are you really here?"

"I'll be here soon," I tell him, breathless, as I snap my fingers, and I'm sucked through time again.

4 5

———

WHAT SHE CAN DO

I JOLT UPRIGHT, blinking into near total darkness. Moonlight sweeps over a cavernous space, illuminating darkened corridors and intricate carvings along the green-gray stone of the wall I'm facing. Condensation drips down the stones, gathering in pockets of moss.

Cool night air touches my skin as I scan the perimeter, catching sight of four gray, wolflike bodies bleeding green onto the tiles.

Reality sweeps over me like a tidal wave that washes me back into my body. I clutch my stomach, finding myself clothed somehow. I pull my shirt up and run my hand over my muscles. There's no stab wound where Gabriel's knife pierced my stomach.

"Syd?"

"Dad?"

A groan echoes off the walls as I rise to my knees and look around, spotting Dad on his side only a few feet away.

"Dad, *Goddess fuck*, what happened? How are you here?" I crawl to him, my pants soaking with the blood of all four rogues, and clutch Dad's shirt. "Are you injured?"

345   ·

"Surprisingly, no. What happened? I was tossed by one of the rogues and then–" He draws in a breath, his icy blue eyes going wide. "Sarah, where is she?"

My stomach hollows out as the memory of her standing beside me, gripping my arm with a phantom touch, hurtles back to the forefront of my mind. She appeared a moment before I'd nearly ended my life falling on Gabriel's blade. She'd been dressed in... light. Appearing like an angel, like she's walked out of the heavens to stop me from making a critical, life altering mistake.

My heart is beating out of rhythm as I help Dad to his feet. "SARAH?!"

"SARAH!" Dad shouts, our voices bouncing down the empty corridor at the base of the room that houses the orrery, echoing on and on.

I take off at a sprint down the corridor, my boots splashing through what could be water or blood, I don't bother to check, and skid to a halt when a flash of silver catches the moonlight still stretching along the far wall.

My breath catches in my throat as I look down at Gabriel's body, his blade still lodged in his heart. I hear Dad call out to Sarah again as I crouch and roughly pull the blade free, tucking it in my belt loop. "SARAH!"

A weak whisper drifts through the air. "I'm here."

I hear Dad switch directions and start sprinting over the blood soaked tiles. I whirl, running back down the corridor to the open air of the orrery just as Sarah lifts her head.

She's lying on the orrery, her body twisted around the pieces of metal holding up the renditions of the planets. Her long, pale blonde hair is caught in one of the stars. She winces as she tries to tug herself free.

"Sarah, hold still," Dad commands as he grips the edge of the flat, round surface and pulls himself up. He pulls a pocket knife from his pocket and slices through her hair. "Wrap your arms around my neck."

"Pass her down to me," I call up to him, stretching my arms out.

The surface of the orrery is well over a foot above my head, but within seconds Sarah is lowered into my waiting arms, and I crush my mate to my chest.

Her cry of relief resounds through our bond, plucking those tight, golden threads. "Thank the Goddess," I breathe, cupping the back of her head and pressing her face against my neck as I fall to my knees.

The room around us trembles, disturbing the puddles of bloody water I'm kneeling in. Dad, standing on the edge of the orrery, grips the base of one of the planets and looks toward the sky where the moon is starting to fade from view with the incoming light of the morning sun.

Sarah, dressed in a sweater and jeans, the same outfit I'd left her in back at the manor, lifts her head to look up, her eyes burning the brightest violet I've ever seen. She looks pale and exhausted.

"About damn time," Dad growls as a thick, heavy blanket of dark, whirling power settles over us and disperses in a matter of seconds.

I can only hear the sound of someone's splashing footsteps before the wet blanket of magic fades enough to see again. Uncle Ryatt, looking absolutely, unapologetically murderous, steps out of his fog of shadows holding his Shadowsword, the gems gleaming in the night air.

"What the fuck are you doing?" he growls, sweeping the perimeter of the room before his eyes land on Dad.

Dad decides it might be better to stay where he is based on the look on Ryatt's face. But then Ryatt's eyes slide to mine and soften.

"Gabriel's body is down that hallway," I tell him, my voice scratchy and somewhat pained.

"We encountered rogues. Four of them." Dad jumps down, landing with agile precision to splash Ryatt with the foul, bloody water.

My uncle scowls as he sheaths his sword down his back and lowers his hood. "Is everyone all right?"

I clutch Sarah closer, feeling how her heart is beating out of rhythm. She clutches my shirt so tight her hand is trembling, but she's whole. She's whole, and she's here.

And we're safe.

"We're fine," Dad sighs, running his hands through his hair. "I have more questions than answers right now, so don't bother."

"You're in Rifthold, you know," Ryatt says, turning toward the void of darkness where Gabriel's body lies. "We have to leave, now."

"Are there more of these creatures?" Dad asks.

Ryatt shakes his head. "No, but I can't stay. This place makes my powers want to shrivel and die. I need to get back to Moonrise immediately. You're lucky I even came to your aid—"

"What's going on?" I ask, noticing the slight hitch in Ryatt's voice, which is totally unlike him. I imagine the worst—war. More attacks, more death. More people like Gabriel coming out of the woodwork to try to hurt my family and take my mate.

Ryatt sighs, his shoulders slumping. Even Dad catches the odd behavior and arches his brow at his brother-in-law. "Ryatt?"

"Kenna's in labor," he chokes. "Evander is in Crescent Falls cleaning up this mess on your side of the mountains, I assume. I can't reach him, and she's—she's struggling. It's been several days. I sensed something off and came to investigate, thinking Artyom and Evander accidentally spirited here, but found this instead." He sweeps his arm around the orrery, his gaze landing on Sarah. "Is she all right?"

I try to nudge her a bit, but Sarah's eyes are closed. "I think she's asleep."

"Drained her powers, most likely," Dad says, and I can tell by the look in his eyes as he stares at my mate that I missed something incredible. They battled together. Dad must have brought her here to find me. And this?

I look at what remains of the rogues and shudder, instinctively running my hand over Sarah's arm and side to check for injuries.

"We're going to Moonrise, now," Ryatt says, stomping toward us. Dad follows, putting a hand on my shoulder as I close my eyes in anticipation for the snapping sensation that comes with jumping from one place to another.

I hear Ryatt unsheathe his sword, the metal singing an ancient song as the tip meets the stone tiles at my knees, and then the world twists into a depthless kind of darkness, taking my breath with it.

"GET HEALERS INTO THEIR ROOM, IMMEDIATELY," Ella shouts behind me as I race with Sarah in my arms down a hallway of pure gold with archways overlooking a stunning sunrise. The lake is bathed in golden hues as the city soaks up every color cast by the incoming sun. It's a sharp contrast to the dark gloom of the hell we encountered only hours ago.

I'm right in assuming Ella is sending me to my usual rooms in the family's personal wing in her castle in Moonrise. I skid around a sharp corner, following a maid who throws open the double doors leading into my old apartment so I can dash inside.

Hurried footsteps follow me in.

"She's filthy! Do not lay her on those sheets yet!" Ella cries out, so I lay my mate on the floor instead, pushed and shoved back by several maids, a few healers in their gray robes, and to my great surprise and unease, a trio of mystics.

I eye them with skepticism as their crystal masks reflect the sunlight through the tall, open air windows. One of them lifts her head to look right at me, her milky, swirling eyes locking with mine.

I tear my gaze away as Ella grabs me by the arm and pulls me out of the small foyer at the entrance of the apartment. "You need to shower and report to Ryatt's office."

"I understand." She lets go, but I turn to her, noticing the lines of concern creasing her eyes. "Is Kenna okay?"

"She'll be fine. She's a midwife." She closes her eyes and shakes her head. "She's waiting for Evander."

"Is there anything I can do?"

"Get that foul stench of rogue off, first of all." Her slight smile unravels some of the angst tightening my chest. "Other than that, Ryatt will be waiting for you in his office once you've cleaned up. Sarah will be fine. Trust me. She just needs to rest. So do you."

I watch her whirl, her crimson cloak flowing out behind her as she's followed out of the foyer by two of her lead maids.

I turn to the group gathered around Sarah. Part of me wants to push through them, to stop them from poking and prodding her, but this is the safest place she could be. I do give the mystics another cautionary glance, finding the third one still watching me closely. I turn from them, and it takes all of my strength to do so.

I unravel completely in the shower. The nearly scalding water isn't enough to stop my body from trembling. I press my hands to the tiled wall and my head, watching blood and other unmentionable grime swirl into the drain until my skin is red and raw, and the entire gilded bathroom is washed in hot steam.

When I leave the bathroom, dressed in a pale blue T-shirt and very basic dark pants in the Eastonian style, Sarah has been laid out in the center of the four poster bed I've spent many a night in while visiting Kenna and her family.

Someone braided her hair. She's clean, her cheeks a rosy pink instead of splotched with dirt and blood. A healer stands on the far side of the bed holding a small glass obelisk in the palm of her hand. A sphere of pale yellow light swirls above it. Smaller ribbons of multi-colored light dance within the sphere in the rhythm of a heartbeat.

I don't bother asking what it is. Eastonia doesn't need EKG machines, do they? Not when they have magic.

I edge toward the bed. The healer–a pretty, dark haired woman in her thirties–turns her head and meets my gaze. "She's all right. You needn't worry yourself."

"She's my mate–"

"As so," she cuts in tartly, but gives me a gentle smile, "let us do our jobs, Your Grace. There's food and drink laid out for you in King Ryatt's office. Your father is there, waiting for you."

A maid comes through the double doors leading to the foyer of the private apartment carrying a tray of dried herbs and several vials of swirling liquid.

My first thought is to physically remove these women from the room and lock them out. I have healing powers. I can tend to my own mate.

But I look down at my hands. I'm exhausted, and my powers are a muted hum through my veins. I'd barely be able to heal any scrapes Sarah has right now.

A tickle in my skull forces me to turn toward the door and push through it. I'm being summoned.

A few minutes later, I'm walking into Ryatt's office. The air is rich with coffee and a hint of bourbon as I sink into an armchair and rest my face in my hands.

"Drink this," Dad says, nudging my shoulder with a coffee mug.

"Wait," Ryatt says with effort, like his mouth is full. I hear a quick pop and then liquid pours. I look up at Ryatt, who has a cork between his teeth as he pours a copious amount of whiskey into the steaming mug of coffee.

"Goddess, Ryatt, are you trying to kill him or take the edge off?" Dad narrows his eyes playfully but hands me the coffee mug.

I nod my thanks but can't bring myself to drink it just yet. Everything that happened last night feels like a blur. I don't know if I just don't understand it, or if Sarah messed with my memories again.

"So," Ryatt says, leaning on his desk and crossing his arms over his chest, "your mate can turn back time."

I look up at my uncle, shaking my head.

Fuck, this is a lot to take in.

I take a sip of the coffee, then drain the mug, extending it to my dad. "Another, please."

46

IT'S A BOY

Warm, golden sunlight beats down on my skin. I blink into it, squinting against the onslaught of differing colors and the sense that I'm somewhere totally and completely unfamiliar. I'm in a bed, that's obvious. The sheets beneath me are soft as butter and smell like roses with a faint hint of pine. A delicate lace canopy hangs from the posters of the bed, drifting in a warm spring breeze. The light–golden with hues of magenta and violet–drifts over a domed ceiling and reflects rainbows on the intricate floral wallpaper hugging the room, which is….

I sit bolt upright and hug a thick, satin duvet to my chest. Where the fuck am I?

Several windows line the far wall, the view on the other side of the glass obstructed by multicolored stained glass. I turn my head slowly toward a strange object on the bedside table. It's no bigger than my forearm, and a pale circle of light floats over its pointed tip. Slowly, I reach out and touch the light with my finger where it disperses in a pale puff of mist before swirling back together again.

353

Chills like I've never felt before lick up and back down my spine before I throw myself out of the bed. The drop is longer than I expected. I cry out as my ankle twists to the side.

But no one runs to my aid, or better yet, barges through the wide, heavy looking wooden doors on the opposite wall from the windows. In fact, it's totally quiet.

I vaguely remember Isaac cutting my hair free from the orrery and handing me down to Sydney. I remember being swept into sleep when Ryatt appeared, their voices mingling into a strange lullaby.

But now I'm alone.

I run my hands down my stomach, over the silken fabric of a plain, light blue night dress that brushes my ankles. A cream colored robe hangs on a hook near the door. I pad across thick, bouncy carpet that feels like heaven on my bare feet. I shrug into the robe, expecting the doors to be locked, but I slowly turn one of the knobs and silently pull it open with ease.

A small sitting room appears, washed in light that must be the sunset. A tray rests on a low coffee table between two couches, a tea kettle sending wisps of steam into the air. Vases of fresh flowers decorate the otherwise simple room. A few bookshelves hug the walls. A fireplace lies dormant, nothing decorating its hearth.

But an archway leads into another room–a foyer. Two more rooms branch off of it on either side–an office of some kind with a single desk, some empty bookshelves, and a large bathroom with a shower and clawfoot bathtub.

My heart races as I slowly edge toward what I believe are the doors leading outside of whatever this place is. Surely, these are locked.

I pull the door open and swallow back a gasp.

Gold. Gold everywhere. Alabaster columns stretch to the sky where the ceiling is covered in sweeping murals like something out of a history book. The ground is all golden tile–an intricate mural. And the corridor stretches on for what seems like forever.

Long, desperately expensive looking carpet runners stretch the length of the corridor. I stand at the center of the hallway, unsure which direction to turn. Everything looks the same. I pinch my arm as I choose to walk to the right.

Did I die? Am I in the Goddess's palace right now, somewhere high in the heavens?

I nearly jump out of my skin when a pair of maids in pretty, starched white uniforms exit through a doorway, both of them giving me radiant smiles and slight bobs of their heads as they pass me.

I whirl to watch them walk away.

No one is stopping me from leaving the room I woke up in. No one is chasing me, yelling at me to come back, to halt.

In fact, there's a warm feeling to this place. It's huge, yes, wherever I am, but I feel… safe.

I shiver nonetheless, tucking my robe tight around my waist. I'm not wearing a bra. I pause in the middle of the hallway and close my eyes, wincing as I run my hands down over my hips. I'm wearing underwear, at least, but someone definitely put them on for me while I was asleep, or knocked out cold, whichever it was.

A low, guttural groan drifts down the hallway, setting all of the fine, downy hair on my body on edge. Soft whispers of encouragement follow, all female.

"I don't give a shit. Where is he? Why isn't he here?" Kenna's voice is broken by exhaustion and pain.

I recognize that tone. My own cries of pain and echoes of feeling utterly, completely alone during Blake's birth come rushing back to the forefront of my memory.

I take off at a sprint before my brain has a chance to catch up with my body, sliding to a stop in front of a door that's slightly ajar.

Before I can push it open, another maid steps out carrying a tray full of untouched food and drinks. Her eyes are downcast and disappointed as she steps past me without a word.

Kenna's pinched silhouette is hugged by a halo of sunlight as I slide through the door and close it with a soft click behind me. She turns her head to look at me. Her dark, wavy brown hair falling over her back and shoulders is damp with sweat. "Sarah?"

"You're in labor," I say stupidly. It's painfully obvious what's happening right now. Kenna is stooped, gripping the back of an armchair as she rides out an absolutely crushing contraction but does so with so much grace that the only telling sign is the way her belly tightens through her thin, knee-length dress.

"Grab that vase," she says weakly, motioning to the side table next to the door.

I pick it up, confused. "Why?"

"I want you," she breathes, her brow furrowed as pain radiates behind her glassy silver eyes, "to hit me over the head with it and put me out of my misery."

I huff a breath and set the vase back down. "Kenna, how long–"

"Three days," she grits out.

"Where's your midwife?"

"Back in Veiled Valley." She slowly straightens and clutches her back, trying to pace on unsteady feet. "Evander was called away, and I decided to come here. I went into early labor during the jump and have been suffering slowly ever since."

"Are we in Moonrise?"

She gives me an odd look. "Did you just wake up? You arrived over a day ago." She tries to sit down but decides against it, pacing instead. "Yes, you're in Moonrise. Sydney is here too, somewhere. Last I heard my father and Isaac were returning to Crescent Falls to try to fetch Evander, but that was yesterday."

My stomach hollows out. Did something happen to Evander? Is that why he's not here right now?

"He's fine," she grunts, using the wall to keep steady as she paces from one side of the room to the other. "Brie is with my mom."

"Why are you alone? I'm sure they're midwives here."

"I told everyone to get out and leave me alone."

"Oh." I start backing toward the door. "I understand." I do, honestly. The last thing I wanted when I was this far into labor was being touched and fussed over.

I also did this on my own, though.

It was the worst feeling.

Kenna's eyes are wet with frustrated tears as she turns to look at me and shakes her head. "Stay."

"Okay," I say quickly and sink into one of the armchairs.

"Evander will get here in time," she says confidently.

I nod. "Yes, he will."

"If not, I'm going to kill him."

"I'll help hide the body."

Her eyes meet mine and her forehead creases, but she doesn't laugh. She sucks in a breath and clutches the footboard of the huge bed in the corner of the room, rocking her hips before straining. "I think I have another day or so."

"That's a very long time–"

"No for a shifter. That's my problem." She rests her forehead against the headboard. "The women in my family always have a horrible time in labor. My grandma died and was resurrected, you know. So was my mom when I came four months early. Oh, and Mom had to stop time to give Aunt Maddy a rest before she somehow managed to deliver a nearly ten pound Ryan into the world with a head the size of a bowling ball–OUCH!" Her howl of pain echoes through my bones.

I sit absolutely still, not even daring to breathe as she rocks through the contraction.

But then a snapping sound bursts through the room. I'm out of my seat and rushing toward her at the same moment her water breaks.

"Goddess, finally," she breathes, relieved.

"Kenna, I need to go get help."

"Don't bother. This is happening right now, Sarah."

I look at her in disbelief. "You're going to deliver this baby by yourself?"

"Well, you're here."

"Kenna, I'm a botanist, not a midwife!"

She looks pale as she straightens up and waddles toward one of the armchairs, cradling her stomach. "All you have to do is make sure I don't die or bleed out. I'll do the rest."

This is insane. I gape at her as she rides through another contraction, then another, each coming within seconds of each other. Kenna is nearly silent, which is worrying me greatly. When she finally bellows with pain, I launch toward the door.

"Do not leave!" she begs, but I shake my head.

"I don't know how to deliver a baby, Kenna!"

"Just hold my hand. I already sent the alert through the mind-link." She sinks to the ground on her knees and pitches forward, thrusting a hand between her thighs. "I'm fine. It just hurts. And Evander–" she chokes on his name. It's a desperate, painful sound. "He should be here. I wanted to wait for him. I can't."

Hurried voices and thundering footsteps echo from beyond the door. Kenna looks up at me, her eyes heavy and wet with tears. "Please stay, Sarah."

"I won't leave," I mouth as the door opens wide and several maids rush in, followed by what I believe are healers.

But Kenna isn't happy about this at all. "GET OUT!" she screeches at the healers in their gray robes. They whirl on their heels and dart back out of the room. "The rest of you–I need blankets, hot water, my kit from the infirmary downstairs. You, get me some tea with blood-bane and hyacinth. Go. Go now!"

Everyone funnels out and my relief wanes.

"You're really doing this on your own, aren't you?" I ask as I kneel by her side.

"His head is out," she pants. I help her lay down on her back. "Get a few towels from the bathroom."

I'm honestly impressed by this. Kenna isn't afraid at all right now.

I come back to her side with all of the towels I can hold. I help her lay them out where she needs them. She tilts her head and screams through another contraction, her anguish bouncing off every wall.

"Where is your mom?" I ask breathlessly as she guides my hand between her legs. Sure enough, there's a baby there.

"With Brie," she pants, wincing. "His shoulders are stuck, Sarah. I need you to turn him."

"Kenna, please," I beg. "I don't know what I'm doing."

"You won't hurt me for very long," she assures me with what I can only describe as her best attempt at a smile. "I'd do it myself but I can't reach. I'm going to press down on my belly while you turn him, ever so–so slightly–" She screams again and I jump into action, but then the door bursts open, slamming against the wall.

Kenna sits up, her eyes flaring. "Where have you BEEN?!"

I whip my head around. Evander stands pale in the doorway beside Sydney.

"SYDNEY GET OUT!" Kenna screeches.

Sydney's mouth pops open in a delirious smile. He claps Evander on the shoulder, who looks dirty and significantly worse for wear, and then shoves him into the room.

Sydney meets my eyes for a flicker of a second before he shuts the door behind Evander.

"Sarah, do it now," Kenna grunts as Evander rushes toward us.

"What are you–" Evander tries to ask, but Kenna's scream as I carefully, oh so carefully, turn her son's shoulder just a touch.

I gasp, choking on an elated scream, as the baby slides free into my waiting hands.

"Kenna? Kenna–" Evander cries, climbing over his mate and clutching her face between his hands. "Sweetheart–"

"It's a boy," I say weakly, wrapping the perfectly pink baby in a towel. I pat him down vigorously while Kenna mumbles something to Evander, who relaxes, sinking back on his knees.

"You asshole," she laughs, heaving several breaths. "I knew you'd get here in time. You just had to do it at the last second."

Tears run down Evander's cheeks, the biggest smile on his face as he caresses his mate's damp, red face.

I jerk back to awareness when the baby in my arms screeches. "Uhm, what do I do now?"

Kenna remains on her back when the door opens again and a maid returns, pale and nervous, with a large medical bag in her arms. She sets it down, does a quick scan of the room, and retreats with a squeak, murmuring something about Queen Ella coming shortly.

"Cut the cord, Evander, please," Kenna whispers as I continue to clutch the squirming baby in my arms, wrapped protectively in a towel. Evander digs through her midwifery kit and gets the tools he needs, everything shiny and exotic to my numb brain, and cuts his son free.

I promptly hand Evander the baby and scoot backward until my back bumps into the side of the long, antique-looking couch, and watch the happy couple meet their newborn son for the first time.

I barely notice Ella arriving with two healers, who quietly begin to examine Kenna, and the maids who follow with food and tea.

I jump when Ella places a hand on my shoulder. She looks remarkably casual right now in a soft dark green sweater and khaki pants, her long dark hair swept into a bun on the top of her head.

"Hi, there."

"Can I leave now?"

She laughs, nodding. "I'm sure this was quite a surprise after coming out of a power reduction coma."

She helps me to my feet. My legs shake like I'm the one who just had a baby. "There's someone waiting for you outside."

4 7

HELD IN CHAINS

Sarah

I'm not sure I've totally come back to reality when I leave Kenna's room and fall directly into Sydney's waiting arms.

"Did you just deliver a baby?"

"I think so?" I rest my head in the crook of his shoulder as he wraps his strong arms around me, holding me tight. "Am I awake right now?"

"You've been out for over a day, Sarah. I don't think you should even be up and walking around yet." He scoops me up and carries me back to the room where I woke up, telling me in a quiet whisper that this is his personal apartment whenever he visits this side of his family. My back hits the mattress, but I'm not alone.

Sydney curls his body around mine, and the quiet solitude of the room settles over us like a wet, cold blanket.

We're silent for a long time. I watch the light of day fade through the windows, casting silver beams of moonlight across the carpet.

"Is Blake safe?"

"He is. He's fine, Sarah."

I nod, my eyes filling with tears I can't blink back. "Gabriel is dead."

"Yes. His body was brought here and burned. I saw to it myself." He turns away for a moment, and I hear a drawer open, then close. I close my eyes as a sense of magic settles around me. "This is yours now."

He curls my fingers around the hilt of Gabriel's knife. I smooth my thumb over the moonstone. It thrums to life beneath my touch, lighting up a small spot on the bed. "Destroy it."

"Are you sure?"

I turn and curl against his chest, leaving the knife behind. He holds me close, cupping the back of my head as I let two decades of trauma ebb through my body and flow outward.

"It's over, Sarah. We can go home. We don't have to worry about this anymore. Evander spent the last few days hunting down Gabriel's co-conspirators. They're dead. It's done."

I feel him reach over me to grab the knife. He puts it back in the drawer, returning his touch to my body, smoothing my hair away so he can run his hand down my spine.

I fall asleep somehow. He might have, as well, because I wake to him still lying beside me, my cheek resting on his arm as he absently strokes his knuckles over the curve of my waist. Dim light spreads across the carpet. Early morning.

"She needs to eat something soon," says an unfamiliar voice, alerting me to another person in the room.

"I'll make sure of it."

Weathered hands grasp the strange obelisk on the bedside table. The glowing orbs burn out, and the hands retreat.

I only sit up when I'm sure I'm alone here with Sydney.

"We're going to go home tonight." He sighs as if preparing to say something he knows I won't like. "There's something you might consider doing first."

I sit up, resting on my elbow. "What?"

He sits up too, tucking my hair behind my ear. "Just… breakfast is out in the sitting room. You should shower and eat something, then we need to meet with Ella and Ryatt."

It sounds serious. He starts to get out of bed, but I grab his hand. "Kenna and the baby?"

"They're fine," he smiles, leaning down to kiss me but stops. His hesitation guts me.

"I'm okay, Sydney."

"I just–" He leans his forehead against mine. "You manipulated time, Sarah. You changed the outcome of that battle. I was dead, I'm pretty sure. My dad was mortally injured. We all would have died but you… you went back."

"I had to–"

"I love you," he says, kissing me tenderly. "Sarah, I love you. But never do that again. Never put yourself through that again. Your powers are… extraordinary, but they're immense. You've been out for an entire day, and there were a few moments when I wasn't sure you were going to wake up again." He lowers his head, kissing my hands. "I don't know what else to say. Even my aunt and uncle don't understand the scope of what you can do."

"I don't care," I tell him, chuckling a bit. "I feel fine."

He shakes his head, "I just can't wrap my head around what happened yet."

"I promise you, I have no plans of having to go back in time to rescue anyone again… unless you need it."

"I think we're done with danger for a while," he says, meeting my eyes.

"I hope so," I reply. I pull him toward me and kiss him slowly, tenderly, savoring the feel of his mouth on mine.

"You need to eat something. I'm going to take a shower and then we'll go."

"Go where?"

He pushes off the bed and runs his hands through his hair. "Ella distracted herself during Kenna's labor by arranging the arrival of someone I think you might want to see. If not, you don't have to."

"Who?"

"Your father."

~

I FOLLOW Sydney down another long, gilded hallway. This castle is massive. I've never been anywhere quite like this, and I immediately lose track of where we are as we take another set of spiraling stairs down into another level of the fortress that overlooks an equally golden city.

It strikes me quite suddenly that this is my homeland. My grandmother on my father's side came from this place–Moonrise.

But I don't feel at home in the winding hallways or amongst the witches who flutter around us, going about their duties as maids, healers, and scholars who work in the incredibly gargantuan library Sydney briefly showed me.

During our walk I got the run-down on how Kenna's doing and confirmed that I had, in fact, delivered a baby in the last twelve hours, and that hadn't just been a weird dream. The baby boy's name is Aris, and Sydney said he is about as bald as they come, with the faintest hint of blond hair like Evander.

Finally, when my thighs are burning like fire after our sixth set of unending stairs, we come to a very simple, very old wooden door.

"We're eight stories underground," Sydney says lightly, as if that's supposed to calm some of the nerves ricocheting through my skull. He opens the door inward, ushering me inside a small, empty room with dark stone walls. I rub my arms, chilled by the stale air. I'm wearing another flowy dress, similar to the gowns I've seen Kenna and Ella wear from time to time. Simple, one color, but vibrant and silken, the dress and matching robe of deep red flow out behind me as I look at the second door on the far side of the room.

It's heavier than the last, and the metallic taste of magic hangs thick in the air as the door opens a touch, and Ella pokes her head out. "Oh, good. I was starting to think you weren't coming. Are you ready?"

Am I? I haven't seen this man since I was a child, and even then, my memories of him are fragmented and blurred by time. I nod nonetheless, and she holds the door open for me and Sydney. He's not going to leave my side. He promised, and I squeeze his hand in confirmation as Ella leads us down another long, narrow hallway toward an archway that spills amber light across ancient stone tiles that line the floor in jagged, hooked squares.

Ryatt's voice, low and rough, thrums into earshot as I edge toward the archway.

But another voice follows, and my body tenses with sudden excitement that my mind hasn't allowed. It's more lifted, more sophisticated, with a slight accent.

"She's here," my father says before he comes into view. Chains drag on the floor. A shuffling of feet as someone turns around....

It's like looking at an older, much more masculine version of myself. Atticus–his long blond hair, the same icy shade and texture as mine, meets my eyes. His eyes are different–a different shape and shade.

I got my eyes from my mother.

"I understand that you go by Sarah now," he says softly, carefully.

I look down at his wrists, which are bound by thick chains of silver, but cuffed by iron. He's a prisoner. Gabriel's henchman but for the sole reason of protecting me.

It's enough to cause my chest to tighten painfully. "Yes, I do."

"Your mother hated the name Sasha, but her pack held the tradition of the elders choosing a newborn's name during their first full moon," he says. "Sarah was her first choice, but they considered it too modern. Sapphira. That was your name between her and I. Sarah for short, in her lullabies."

My heart wrenches at the quiet, dull pain in his voice. I spot Ryatt in the corner of my eye, his arms crossed and his silver eyes glowing with unnatural power as he watches the exchange, his expression unreadable.

Sydney steps up beside me. Atticus's eyes slide to him, looking him up and down. "I owe you my gratitude, Prince, for finding her and ensuring her safety."

Sydney simply nods, and the room falls quiet.

I suppose I should say something. "Do you know why I am the way I am?"

"Your powers?" When I nod, he smiles sadly, shaking his head, "Your mother is to blame for that, I believe. You were conceived during a rare full moon which held significance in her pack. She told me you'd have the powers of the Goddess. I prayed that you wouldn't, that you'd take after her shifter side, but you are half-witch regardless."

Ella shifts her weight somewhere behind me. "Atticus, we're on borrowed time–"

"I understand," he says sadly, his eyes downcast for a moment before his gaze rises to meet mine. "You're safe now. I know you've been through hell, Sarah. I am sorry I wasn't able to protect you from the beginning. I tried–"

"I know you tried to protect me," I blurt out, my eyes going glassy. "I remember–I do remember–"

His eyes water as he looks away. "She would have been so proud of you."

Even Ryatt, normally stoic with an eternal scowl, flexes his jaw and seems to be trying to gather himself.

"Gabriel is dead," I tell Atticus, choking on the words. "I'm free."

"It's all I've ever wanted for you."

"What do these powers mean?" I ask, my voice straining. "What am I supposed to do?"

"She will be offered the same ritual we offer mystics who chose to leave the order," Ella cuts in, and Atticus nods, swallowing hard.

"You can give them up, give them back to the Goddess," he says quietly, "but you'll fit right into this family if you keep them."

Something inside my heart snaps, sending a torrent of emotion hurtling uncontrollably to the surface. Sydney, sensing this, steps closer and places his hand on my lower back.

Atticus catches his movements and smiles softly. "I am a prisoner of Eastonia, Sarah, for good reason. I'd do it all again if it meant you'd have this outcome. A mate, and a son, I hear, already born."

"Blake," I whisper, choking back a sob.

"Blake," he repeats, smiling around the word. But something shifts in the room. Magic. I can feel it seeping in, coating the room in something inky and dark. Atticus notices and sighs, turning his eyes to Ryatt, who nods. "One day, I'll meet him. Until then–" he looks at Sydney, "guard them with your life. That's all I ask of you."

"I will." Sydney's voice is sharp and clear, echoing over a haze of magic that settles over the room and snaps.

My father disappears, chains and all.

"Where did he go?" I gasp.

Ella and Ryatt exchange glances. Ryatt replies, "Back to the prison in Tarsian where he'll remain until his trial next year. It's out of our hands, even as king and queen."

"He's the son of Kane, Sarah," Ella says sadly. "We didn't have a choice, even knowing the truth."

"I know," I swallow, aching to be back in bed, to hide my tears.

Ella approaches me, her face twisted in grief. "I'm sorry for everything you've been through. We do have a ritual we could perform to give your powers back to the Goddess. It's exclusive to the mystics, used when their own kind wishes to leave their order and sisterhood. It would work for you."

Sydney stiffens beside me. Give up my powers?

Powers I just learned came from the mother I'll never remember?

"No," I whisper.

Ryatt and Ella nod, but Sydney gently tugs on my arm. "Let's go. We need to prepare to go home."

"We'll leave at dusk, when the sun sets," Ryatt says.

4 8

———

STARTING OVER AGAIN

Sarah

I spend an hour submerged in the bathtub up to my chin. Sydney isn't in the bedroom when I finally emerge, wrapped in nothing but a robe. I curl up in bed on top of the duvet and stare at the sunlight raining down through the glistening windows, my mind in shambles.

I have to knit myself back together somehow. I was taken from this place as a child, given a new home, a new shot at life. I have that now. I have a son, a mate, and a family that loves me and wants to see me whole.

I can't go back to Crescent Falls carrying any burdens.

I hear the door open and close softly. Sydney's familiar footsteps brush across the carpet. He touches my hip, likely just to see if I'm asleep, but I turn to him.

He looks exhausted. Broken and worn thin.

I open my arms to him, and he falls onto the bed on top of me.

"I think we're going to be okay," I whisper after a few moments of heavy silence.

He lifts his head, managing a smile. "I think we will be."

"Is it over now? All of it?"

He nods. "It's over."

"Now what?"

It's a heavy question. He crawls over me, propping himself up on his elbows to look down at my face. "When I woke up in that orrery and couldn't find you, I thought–I thought I'd lost you. I realized then, maybe for the first time, how little I cared if the world was burning down, if I couldn't keep you safe, if every evil known to our kind was coming for us... I realized none of it fucking mattered if you weren't here anymore, Sarah. Safe, happy, and normal wouldn't matter. I love you. I've loved you since the moment I saw you, and I'd walk through a thousand fucked up lifetimes just to be by your side again."

I cup his face and draw him down to me, kissing him deeply. He melts into the kiss, covering me with his body, his knee drawing up between my thighs.

Maybe it's just the need to feel each other, to feel alive and whole. I don't understand it, and I don't care to, I just know that nothing has ever felt as right as being in his arms.

He slides his hand beneath the robe and clutches my breasts, kneading and plucking at my nipples until they rise and harden. I arch my hips against his as I moan against his lips, desperate to have him inside of me.

I just need to know he's here. That we have that golden future I saw.

Sydney rips my robe off and throws it away from the bed. His mouth leaves a trail of heat over my neck and collarbone as I reach between us and pull his belt free in haste. My fingers slip over his zipper. I'm panting, struggling to catch my breath. I feel like time is ticking by too fast as he shoves his pants down and thrusts his cock deep inside of me without preamble.

"Sydney!" I moan, rocking my hips against his, trying to adjust to his side. He steals the moan with another rough kiss, crushing my mouth, his tongue sweeping over mine in a desperate dance.

I place my hands on his chest, finally meeting his eyes. "Slow," I beg, a single tear falling across my cheek. "Slower."

He slows down, locking his gaze with mine. Every thrust is honed exactly where I need it the most. He lowers his head, brushing his nose over mine before burying his face in the crook of my neck, buried in my hair.

The eruption of hot need gives way to pleasure that floods my body, blurring every sense. His mark on my back ignites, the threads binding us together tugging tight.

"I love you," he groans, over and over. The words make those threads sing, creating a beautiful song just for us.

An earth shattering orgasm tightens through my thighs and lower belly. Stars fill my vision as I pant his name, gritting my teeth as my pussy clamps down and spasms around his cock. He pumps into me again, hard, and spills himself inside of me with my name on his lips.

Then his eyes are on mine. The bluest of blue. The most beautiful color I've ever seen.

So much for pink.

"Let's go home," he says, and his smile is my undoing.

Two hours later, after a light dinner in Kenna's bedroom with her, Evander, and their precious new baby, Sydney and I walk hand in hand to a wide, sweeping terrace overlooking the glorious, ancient city of Moonrise. I'm wearing the sweater and jeans I came here in, everything freshly washed, free of the blood of the rogues and the stain from Gabriel's death.

I turn to look at Kenna and Evander, who stand side by side. She's holding their son, and Brie is asleep on Evander's shoulder.

Safe. We're all finally safe.

"I'll see you soon," Kenna says, smiling like she smiled that morning I ran into her at Ryan's house, when I snuck out on the verge of falling to pieces.

"Soon," I tell her and reluctantly turn back to where Ryatt is waiting for us, his sword already unsheathed.

There's so much up in the air right now. I haven't given myself a single moment to properly grieve Hadley or to understand why she did what she did. I haven't been able to wrap my head around Ryan and his loss and what he sacrificed so that I could be standing here beside his brother preparing to go home to our child.

My heart is heavy as Sydney walks us toward Ryatt. I don't know what to expect when our feet touch the ground in Crescent Falls, but I know one thing for certain.

I'm not doing this alone anymore.

"Your father will be waiting for you to debrief about the situation in Crescent Falls, Sydney. As far as I know, there's no longer a threat." Ryatt's eyes slide to mine. "And you… if you ever decide to give up these powers, we can do it. You just have to say the word, and it will be done."

"I understand," I tell him, squeezing Sydney's hand.

"Take us home," Sydney says, and within seconds, my body is being pulled apart and knitted back together again. Light and sound blur into one before exploding with new color, then familiar sounds and scents wrap themselves around me in a warm embrace.

The castle in Crescent Falls is bathed in early morning sunlight when we arrive. Ryatt spirited us right into the center of the back garden before disappearing in a blur of dark magic. My legs feel like jelly but propel me forward at the speed of light, only one thing on my mind.

"Is he in the nursery?" I hear Sydney ask Maddy, but I'm already sprinting toward the foyer, toward the staircase.

The last time I stood on this landing I made a choice that eventually determined whether my mate lived or died. I turned left.

Today, I turn right.

It takes two seconds to reach the crib where Blake is clutching the railing, his eyes wide and teary. "Baby," I gush, bursting into tears as I scoop him into my arms and sink to my knees. Sydney is close behind me, his arms wrapping around the two of us as he falls to the ground, too.

Home. *I'm home.*

～

MADDY

THE CASTLE IS QUIET, everyone who lives within the secure, sacred walls long asleep.

Isaac never came to bed, however. He returned a day ago when Ryatt came looking for Evander, who had been deep in the underground looking for the last of the rebels. I can't say it's been easy the past few days. We've had so many years of peace that I've forgotten what this feels like and what it does to my mate.

Isaac's office is cozy and warm when I lightly knock on the door and slide inside. "It's almost three, Isaac."

He turns from the window overlooking the back garden. "I know. I'm sorry."

"Don't be sorry." I close the door behind me and walk to him, taking his hands in mine. They're cold to the touch, so I curl my fingers around them and squeeze. "Sydney and Sarah are back at the manor and settled in. They're going to be all right."

"I'm not worried about those two," he laughs softly, sadly.

I nod, feeling another incredible weight settle on my already sore shoulders. "Have you spoken to Ryan today?"

"I went to Silverhide after Syd took his family home." He looks down at our joined hands, shaking his head. "He wasn't at his house. I found James in the pack house talking to their elder tribunal liaison about Hadley and his interview with my warriors. He told me Ryan shifted and left, so I came back here."

What are we going to do about Ryan?

I let go of his hands and walk to the couch in front of his desk, sinking down. He follows, and we sit in silence for a moment, both of us lost in thought.

"Can he have another mate at this point?"

"We'll need to talk to the High Priestess," he replies.

"It's a delicate situation. No one should know—"

"He did what he felt needed to be done. He's a trained warrior, Maddy. He was protecting an innocent—"

"This woman was his mate, and he killed her."

Another beat of silence settles heavily. I fight the tears welling to life in my eyes, wiping them away with the back of my hands.

Isaac reaches over and lays his hand on my thigh. "I'll talk to the priestess tomorrow. We'll figure out what needs to be done."

"I look at Sydney and see him finally happy and now–Ryan was always our happy one, Isaac. The jokester. The one who made us smile and laugh. I worry this is going to change him."

"It will." Isaac shifts his weight, sighing. "I spoke to Ryatt. He's finally opening up part of his territory, the Deadlands, to settlers. It's mostly barren, but the few tribes who've lived there for the past several decades have luck farming and hunting, and their leaders have agreed to join their kingdom."

"What does this have to do with our son?"

"I'm considering sending Ryan and his pack to Eastonia."

I blink, unsure I've heard him correctly.

Isaac continues, "Ryan has been having issues with his neighbor, the Alpha of Raven Hall. Silverhide is a small pack. Ryan keeps his numbers low. Raven Hall sees that as a weakness, and I think Ryan would be better suited to more space."

"You can't send him away."

"It would be his decision. Ryatt is considering it as well, whether this is an appropriate move, whether Ryan could handle the Deadlands."

"It doesn't change the fact he killed his mate, Isaac."

He hangs his head, his hand finding mine.

"Ryan will find his way out of this, Maddy. But he has to want it. He has to overcome this grief. I don't know how else to help him."

"What should I do?" My voice is broken as I turn to my mate, my husband, the father of my children, and the love of my life.

For the first time in the two decades we've been together, Isaac looks at me, and I can tell he has no clue how to fix this.

Isaac can fix anything.

But he can't fix the void in Ryan's heart.

4 9

SECOND CHANCE MATE?

SYDNEY

A Few Days Later

I POUR another ladle full of chicken noodle soup into the bowl on the tray I've been putting together for the last thirty minutes. The kitchen all around me is a complete disaster, but the tray looks nice. I smile at the little yellow flower I plucked from Sarah's collection in the atrium. She's been spending most of her days there this week, taking inventory in preparation for the spring planting season. She has huge plans for not only the historic gardens surrounding our manor, but down in the village as well where I've carved out a few new parks for pack use.

The kettle squeals, and I pour a cup of tea–the kind from a box. I have no idea what Cosette puts in the tea she's always drinking with my mate.

I carefully pick up the tray and turn my back on the mess I left behind in the kitchen and make my way down the hallway toward the sitting room at the front of the manor where a TV now blares some odd reality dating show Sarah has Cosette hooked on.

Cosette, propped up on the couch, eyes me with heavy skepticism as I set the tray down in front of her.

"I'm not even going to ask what the kitchen looks like right now," she grumbles then gives me her best attempt at a smile.

"I could heal you, you know. Hell, I could give you a dose of my grandma's tears—"

"No, thank you. Save that for emergencies."

"You got stabbed in the ribs, Cosette. That constitutes an emergency."

"Well I survived, didn't I?" She picks up the remote and turns the volume up.

I tuck my hands in my pockets and frown at her. This is only temporary, of course. The first day we returned from Eastonia, Cosette was still at the castle being mended by the healers, refusing the tears and any attempts of divine intervention. She was never going to die, not after James's quick thinking and surprisingly advanced first-aid skills. But Cosette is healing slowly, and I know it has to do with the stress of Sarah and I suddenly being whisked away.

"You're going to be back on your feet sooner if you eat regularly."

Cosette sighs, her eyes flicking to mine. "Thank you for the soup."

"Of course." I turn on my heel and head back to the kitchen to deal with the destruction there, but a knock sounds on the front door. I'm not expecting anyone, and Sarah is out in the village with Blake, but she wouldn't knock on the door and wait to come inside.

Cosette doesn't even notice me changing directions. I pull the door open and pause, my heart sinking into my stomach for a fraction of a second.

Commander Artyom in his black Ghost commander's uniform stands on my porch.

"Commander?"

"I'm sorry to intrude," he says, and I brace myself for the worst. What criminal mastermind is at it now? What war is on my doorstep? I wait for my phone to start ringing with a call from my dad, but then

I notice the wildflower bouquet in his hand. "I'm checking on Cosette."

"Oh." That's all I can manage. I open the door wide for him and move out of his way, motioning for him to come inside. He looks around, and the casualness of his stance and expression is slightly unnerving, honestly.

I've known Commander Artyom my entire life in a professional sense. He's one of my uncle's longest serving commanders, having held his position for close to two decades. He's the leader of the highly trained, covert Ghost forces.

He's a shadow. A true ghost. He also has strange powers similar to Ryatt's, but no one has ever been able to tell me definitively what they are.

But now he just looks like a… man. A man, I realize, in love.

I stand in the foyer as he turns into the sitting room. Cosette gasps, and I wonder for a moment if I need to intervene. But then I hear a sound I haven't heard in a very long time.

Cosette laughs as she turns off the TV, asking what Artyom is doing here.

His reply is cut off by the gentle hum of the garage door rolling up, alerting me to my mate returning from her errands.

I tear myself from the foyer and meet Sarah in the hallway as she pushes into the house with Blake, asleep in his car seat, in one hand and a few grocery bags in the other.

"Commander Artyom is in our sitting room," I whisper, taking Blake from her.

"What? Why?" Sarah furrows her brow and hurries after me as I walk into the kitchen to carefully transfer Blake into his swing, which is the only place he'll nap the past few days.

She dumps the groceries on the counter and turns to me, whispering, "Why is he here? What happened?"

"I don't think anything happened," I whisper back as I edge away from the swing like there's a live bomb inside of it instead of a sleepy, very grumpy baby. "He brought flowers."

"Flowers?!"

I nod vigorously, motioning to the widow. "Wild flowers. Like he walked up here and picked them on his way."

"Flowers for who? Not for us."

"No, not for us. For Cosette."

"Cosette?!" Sarah's eyes light up. I grab her arm as she whirls toward the kitchen door.

"She's happy, Sarah. Finally. We need to leave them alone."

Sarah pouts, but by some miracle, Dalia runs into the kitchen, her cheeks flushed with excretion. "You'll never believe what I just saw!"

I run my hand over my face, but Sarah whispers, "What? What did you see?"

"Cosette and that weird Eastonia commander guy are sitting next to each other on the couch. He's making her laugh. She's smiling like a schoolgirl!"

"What else did you hear?" Sarah begs.

"Both of you–"

"He complimented her on the soup."

I feel a little smug about that, smirking. "I made–"

"And he asked her if she wanted to go get dinner together–tonight. To get her out of the house for a bit."

"Dinner? Like a date?"

The kitchen door swings open, revealing Cosette, who doesn't look the least bit injured all of a sudden. She looks around at the mess and the three of us huddled in a whisper conversation.

"I'm not even going to ask what's going on," she sniffs, glaring. "I'm going out. You're on your own for dinner."

Sarah beams at her, and Cosette rolls her eyes before smiling slyly and turning on her heel.

"Do you think they're mates?" Sarah asks from the ensuite bathroom several hours later.

I swivel in my desk chair to face her as she steps out of the steamy bathroom in nothing but a towel, her hair wet and falling over her shoulder. "Cosette had a mate, you know."

"You can have more than one if you lose the first, right?"

"So I've heard."

I watch her walk to the dresser, rifling through my selection of old shirts she prefers to sleep in. The image of her dressed in a pair of my pajamas after her first night here springs to the forefront of my mind. She'd been so thin then, so pale. So terrified, honestly.

Sarah's at home now, though. Everything she does makes this place warmer. Everything she touches is better for it. "Come here."

She peers at me, trying to hold up her towel as she yanks a particularly ratty shirt I've kept since high school free from the drawer. "Why?"

"I just want to look at you."

She walks over, smiling at me as she stops between my legs. "Are you working tonight?"

"I just needed a distraction for a minute." I reach over and turn off my computer, the design I was working on fading to black.

"I asked you a question, remember?" She slides onto my lap, hiking up the towel over her thighs. She's been shifting almost every night, going on long runs through the fresh, spring forests blooming all around us. Her legs are solid muscle now as I run my hands up her thighs and between the seams of the towel.

"Do I think they're mates? Well, I don't think Cosette would give him the time of day if she didn't think he was special." Her skin is still damp from her shower, and she smells different. There's a little shop in the village that sells soaps and other potions for the skin and hair, and it's been her favorite to explore so far.

"The night you left with Gabriel, I saw him looking at her after we brought her to the castle for help. He had an odd look on his face, like he was seeing something."

"Something that finally made sense?"

She smiles softly, nodding. "That's a perfect way to describe how this feels." She wraps her arms around my neck, resting her forehead against mine. "I hope they're mates."

"Me too," I answer honestly, savoring her warmth.

She pulls away and slides off my lap, walking back into the bathroom.

"Where are you going?"

"I got something in the village today," she says over the sound of her towel hitting the floor. I can just see her reflection in the foggy mirror as she pulls the navy blue shirt over her head and smooths it down her sides before reaching for something on the counter.

She lingers in the doorway. The nervous look on her face makes my spine straighten. "Are you okay?"

"I'm fine," she says weakly.

I rise from my chair and walk to her, smoothing my hand up her forearm. But then she uncurls her fingers, and my life flashes before my eyes in a way I hadn't expected.

Everything good I ever did–every trial and tribulation–comes to this. This moment.

With her.

"You're pregnant?"

"Yeah," she says, tears welling in the corners of her eyes. "I am."

My lips meet hers in a rough kiss. The pregnancy test falls to the ground between us as I back her against the doorframe and kiss her like my life depends on it. My hands tangle in her hair as I cup the back of her head. "Sarah."

"Are you happy?" she cries, choking on the words.

I nuzzle her neck, pressing my weight against her. "Of course, I'm happy. I've never been happier."

"We weren't…. It's so soon."

"We weren't doing anything to prevent it," I remind her, nose to nose. Then, I'm laughing, delirious with joy.

A baby. Another baby.

And I get to be here for every minute of it this time.

We're safe.

I pick her up and carry my mate to our bed, laying her down on sheets that smell like us, in a home we'll raise our family in. Our growing family.

I fall asleep that night with Sarah nestled close, her hair falling over my chest in long tendrils of pale gold, and cast a prayer to the moon.

I don't know why the Goddess felt I deserved this, but I'm glad She didn't listen to me, maybe even laughed, when I swore I'd never allow myself to fall in love.

50

A SUMMER WEDDING

Sarah

3 months later

I clutch the steering wheel as I turn my car toward the private driveway leading to the castle. Blake claps his hands to the music humming through the speakers while Sydney, seated beside me, digs through his briefcase, mumbling under his breath.

"What are you looking for?" I ask, glancing at him briefly.

Summer is in full swing all around us, shading the road beneath the thick, deep green canopy of trees.

"I had something drawn up for Cosette," he murmurs. "From our estate. I think I might have left it at home." He runs his fingers through his hair then down his face, murmuring a curse. "We might have to turn around."

"I'm sure you have it, whatever you're looking for," I laugh, and Blake squeals with delight as we drive over a bump then turn through the main gate.

The front garden has been totally transformed. Roses in every shade are in full bloom. White tables and chairs have been arranged all over the garden, and in one corner the wedding arch I've been working on for weeks is propped up, covered in roses and twisting vines, with baby's breath and lavender sprigs adding some pops of white and green.

A warrior waves us toward the garage where several other cars are already parked. I jerk to a stop and throw my SUV in park while Sydney continues rifling through his briefcase. "We're going to be late. I'm sure the ceremony is about to begin. Come on!"

I give Sydney a look before shutting my door and fishing Blake out of his car seat. He's dressed in a silly baby tuxedo, already damp with drool. He uses my hair like reins as I walk him toward the back entrance of the castle, but whirl around to face Sydney, who now has his briefcase laid out on the hood of the car. "Sydney!"

"I found it," he breathes, holding up an envelope.

I roll my eyes and turn into the castle where we're immediately met by Dalia, who has been here since early this morning–tending to a very peeved Cosette.

"Is she dressed?" I ask, balancing Blake on my hip.

"She's causing a huge fuss upstairs. I've never seen anyone so uptight. Lady Hannah is with her, trying to get her ready. Queen Ella, too."

"Should I–"

"Sarah! There you are," Maddy's voice echoes down the hallway. She rushes toward us, beaming, her arms outstretched to whisk her grandson away to be spoiled and doted on by her and the friends who have gathered in, I assume, the sitting room on the first floor. "Where is Sydney?"

"He was right behind me." I turn, finding the back entrance empty, the door still open.

"No bother. Isaac and Ryatt are out back talking to Ryan. He probably saw them and went there instead. I don't blame them. The castle is exceedingly feminine right now."

"I think they're trying to convince Commander Artyom that

Cosette isn't going to throw herself from the third-story balcony." Dalia snorts, and we all laugh.

"Wasn't this wedding Cosette's idea?" I follow Maddy and Dalia toward the foyer.

"Hannah's and Ella's, actually, but I did end up being the one who convinced Cosette to do this," Maddy replies with a snug smile. "Cosette designed my wedding dress when I married Isaac, you know. That's how we met."

"I had no idea!" I turn into the sitting room and find a small gathering—some familiar, and some unfamiliar faces—who smile at me in greeting. Brie crawls at the speed of light toward us, screeching with delight at the sight of Blake, who is trying to bounce out of Maddy's arms to get to his cousin. He's not crawling yet, but at almost five months old, he's getting close.

Maddy kneels with Blake to greet Brie. I step past them, walking to the chaise lounge where Kenna, wearing a pretty pale purple dress, is nursing Aris. "Look at him." I grin, sitting beside her. "He's going to be blond like Evander!"

"I know. He honestly looks so much like my father-in-law that it shocks me sometimes," Kenna laughs. Aris opens one eye to look up at us, then promptly closes it again, nuzzling deeper into her touch. Kenna's eyes hold mine though. She reaches out and lays a hand on my thigh, warm and comforting. "How are you?"

The question is loaded. "I'm doing well. We both are." Sydney and I found out I was pregnant shortly after returning from Eastonia three months ago. Kenna is the only person I've told so far that I'm pregnant. Because I used so much magic while I was pregnant, I didn't want to take a chance at losing the baby. "I've been taking the herbs you sent."

She arches a brow. "...And?"

My slight, mischievous smile is answer enough. They've helped, and I'm still pregnant. She grips my thigh, her hand shaking. "I'm so glad to hear that."

"Shh! We haven't told anyone yet. We were going to tell Cosette after the ceremony as a little surprise."

She presses a finger to her mouth, smiling around it, but her eyes dance with excitement.

Ella sweeps into the room, her cheeks pink from excretion, "Everyone outside! The ceremony is about to begin!"

I help Kenna up and hold Aris while she fixes her dress. Maddy and Ella disappear with Blake and Brie, and we follow the crowd out into the foyer. But I don't see Sydney anywhere when I step outside onto the front steps. "Where are all the men?" I ask Kenna, who shrugs.

I chew my lip and walk back through the castle, down the hallways I've come to learn and turned to memory. I silently open the door leading onto the wide back deck and see Sydney and Evander talking in low tones with Flynn, Kenna, Evander's Beta, and a man named Connor, who I've been introduced to before. Friends and colleagues of the groom.

"It's starting," I tell them quietly then notice the two men standing further away in the back garden, their backs to us.

I haven't seen Ryan in several weeks. He keeps to himself lately but did come up to the manor a few times to visit after everything was said and done..

But he hasn't been the same since that night. I don't think any of us have. Sometimes, when I walk through the manor at night, I can still hear Hadley's scream when Ryan... when he killed her to save Dalia, Cosette, and me.

To save *me*.

"What are they talking about?" I ask Sydney as he rests his hand on my lower back to guide me back into the castle.

I glance over my shoulder again just in time to catch Ryatt gripping Ryan's shoulder.

"Ryatt offered Ryan a substantial territory in Eastonia."

"What?" I pull Sydney to a stop while the rest of his friends walk ahead.

Sydney rolls his lower lip between his teeth. "I've known about it for a few days. I wasn't sure what was going to come of it after Dad told me he gave Ryatt his blessing to even offer it to him. He'd be moving his entire pack there, to the Deadlands. Apparently, it's the one place in Eastonia where packs under Ryatt and Ella's rule haven't been established. Only a few small tribes reside there. Ryatt offered him the whole thing."

I gape at my mate. "Is he going to do it?"

"I don't know." He takes my hand. "Let's not worry about it now."

"I'm not worried," I admit. "It might be good for him, actually, to get away from everything that happened."

"I hate that I agree." There's grief laced between each word. Sydney doesn't know how to help Ryan. None of us do.

He doesn't want our help.

All I know is that Ryan isn't the goofy, boisterous, teasing guy he used to be, and it's killing all of us.

We walk out into the front garden and find seats. It's entirely casual, and we tuck ourselves right behind Kenna and Evander, who turn to talk to us as we wait for the ceremony to begin. Ella flutters around, nervous, glancing back at the entrance of the castle.

When Commander Artyom appears, walking up to the arch side by side with Ryatt, Ella relaxes a bit.

"Why is Cosette so nervous?" I ask Sydney. "They're mates, after all."

"Cosette never had a wedding when she was mated for the first time, remember?" Sydney whispers. "My mom and aunt practically forced her to do this."

"She deserves to be pampered like this," I whisper as music starts to play.

Sydney and I didn't have a wedding. We took our vows before a priestess in the temple with a few family members involved and enjoyed a cozy dinner back at the manor. It was all we could manage, considering everything we'd been through.

But looking back on the past three months, I feel a sense of peace. We've finally had time to just be a family, to love each other, to look forward to the future instead of wondering if we'd have one.

That's a blessing, and I count them every day.

Cosette is walked down the aisle by her daughter, who is a

younger, happier version of everyone's favorite lead housekeeper. Cosette looks like she wants to be anywhere but here, but after two decades of pampering others, today is an opportunity to return the favor.

She looks beautiful in a soft, cream gown of satin and lace. Her thick, curly brown hair has been woven into a crown dusted with orange blossoms. She looks like a young woman as she turns the corner and finally has a view of her mate–her second chance at love.

Sure, it's only been a few months that she's known, but the look of relief and excitement in her eyes as Artyom smiles at her melts any doubts I had in my heart.

But my eyes catch on the man standing toward the back of the seated crowd. Ryan is dressed in a tux with his hair swept back. He's grown his beard out, which makes him look older and harder. His blue eyes watch the precession with skepticism that cuts me to the core.

I hope he goes to Eastonia. I hope he finds himself again there. I hope one day he can return to us whole and healed.

If Cosette can find her second chance–if Maddox could, and everyone who lost a mate before and after them–so can Ryan.

But there's still that nagging truth that often festers in my chest. He didn't lose his mate. He wasn't rejected. He killed her.

Not even the High Priestess could give us an answer when asked what this meant for him.

Sydney nudges me as Cosette and Artyom begin to exchange vows. I knit my fingers between his, leaning against him.

It's a quick ceremony with no frills. I wouldn't expect anything less from Cosette and Artyom, the fearsome commander of Ryatt's Ghost army. But his Ghosts, and several others in the crowd, shout and holler as the happy couple run away from the priestess at the finish of the ceremony and sprint toward the castle for a moment alone before the real party begins.

Sometime later, Kenna says, "So?" The two of us are tucked in one of the second floor sitting rooms with our mates and friends while the older generation drinks champagne and carries on downstairs in the ballroom, "I heard Cosette and Artyom plan to remain in Shadowcrest."

"Well, she's technically spending a few months in Eastonia, doing a little tour there with Artyom, before coming back," I correct.

"I never thought Artyom would retire," Kenna smiles, resting her back against the couch. "Evander is going to take over as Commander of that branch of the army now."

"He wears a lot of different hats," I laugh, and she nods.

"He likes to stay busy."

I look over her shoulder at Maddy, Ella, and Cosette, who've apparently come to check on the young folk seeking refuge from the cheek-pinching aunties downstairs.

Kenna gives me a little nudge. "I think you should tell them now."

My hand rests against my lower belly where that new flicker of hope resides. I catch Sydney's eyes. He's been watching me, and the soft, knowing smile on his face sends pure love and ease coasting between our bond.

"I think you're right."

THE END

5 1

OUTRUNNING THE PAST

James scribbles on a piece of paper as people file into the pack house out of the rain. The two-story community building I had built three years ago, when I established Silverhide, is built in a traditional style I forced Sydney to help me plan out. The walls are made of thick logs burnt a deep black. The first story is just a giant room with several long tables and enough chairs for everyone–all hundred or so members, including a few babies born this summer–to fit comfortably with room to spare.

A fire roars in the massive stone hearth at the very center of the room, sending heat licking down my back as I pace back and forth behind the main table.

James, my Beta, looks up as another group filters inside, writing their names down. Andrew, my head warrior, the commander of my meager forces, technically, sits on James's other side, his hands folded neatly on the table's surface.

I'm not sure what to expect. I've spent the last two days debating our next moves with James and Andrew. It's nearly winter now, and if we're going to go through with this, my pack needs time to prepare.

Because, if my people agree, we're leaving Crescent Falls.

The door shuts with a snap as the last pack members arrive. The echo of rain fades into the thrum of excited conversation over the sound of the fire crackling at my back. Approximately one hundred faces turn to me as I come to a stop. I glance down at James, who checks his list, then nods up at me.

"That's everyone."

I lick my lips, nodding, and round the head table to stand at the center of the room. I don't have a throne. I don't even have a raised platform to separate me from my pack. I face them like an equal even though the burden of this community weighs heavily on my shoulders.

I know every name. I recognize every face. I've made a habit of visiting each family weekly, checking in on the workers who keep my pack running strong, on the newly mated couples, on the mothers and children. We have no elders to act as a tribunal. I only have James and Andrew to confer with about pack matters.

So, when I was offered a substantial territory to settle in Eastonia, they were my listening ears, playing both sides of support and devil's advocate.

We decided to put it up to a vote. It has to be a unanimous one. If a single member decides they don't want to go, the deal is off.

"Good evening, everyone," I say, my voice booming through the room. A few children giggle in a corner where a few baskets of toys have been arranged to keep them busy, but otherwise, a hush falls over the gathered crowd. A few men stand along the far wall with their arms crossed over their chests, looking grim.

Word spread after Hadley's death, of course. It's no secret who struck the blow that ended her life. I've lived with the fallout, the questioning, the rumors.

No one here, including her own brother, knows she was my mate.

I buried that like I buried every other feeling that's ever crossed through my heart, turning it to stone.

"Some of you are aware that there's been talk about moving Silverhide to a new territory. I've been in talks for several months trying to decide our best course of action in the best interest of the pack, especially the young families." A rush of murmurs bleeds through the air, mostly excited, but a whisper of nerves follows as I continue, "I've decided leaving our current territory for a fresh start is in the best interest of everyone."

There's more murmuring, louder this time.

"Where?" someone shouts.

"It's no secret that we've been struggling with our neighbors in Raven Hall and the NZ," I say loudly over the chatter. "We don't have their numbers. We live simply. We don't involve ourselves in the conflicts that plague the united Alphas of Crescent Falls. In essence, we do not belong here." I tuck my hands in my pockets and scan the room. "I've been offered a substantial territory in Eastonia."

The murmurs turn to actual gasps and shouts of surprise. I anticipated this. Most of my pack are first generation, either born here in Crescent Falls or came over with their parents from war-torn Eastonia during the final battles against Kane two decades ago.

"Eastonia?" someone bellows. "Are you saying we're going to the Roguelands?"

"Eastonia, yes. The Roguelands—" I roll the word over my tongue, smirking. "No, not the Roguelands. Alpha King Ryatt has offered me the Deadlands. The entirety of the Deadlands. We'd have over five-hundred square miles of territory."

Several people stand. Others start shouting. I expected this. Everyone, even those who grew up in Crescent Falls and have never once stepped foot in Eastonia, has heard of the Deadlands. Miles and miles of nothing. Barren, rolling hills. Creatures who plague our wildest nightmares. Rogues, hellhounds, other horrors that are rumored to be unseen by the naked eye.

I raise a hand, and the voices die out. "We have a chance to start over. The past year, we've been restricted by our neighbors. Our people have been bullied and ostracized. You've come to me wanting more for yourselves and your children. Now I have a solution."

Everyone watches me as I go into the details. We'd have all winter to pack, to prepare for the move. We'd leave Silverhide with everything we can carry, forming a caravan that would take us to the border just past Moorn. The journey to the Deadlands could take up to six months, mostly on foot because of the lack of roads and vehicles that can make it over the tough terrain, and once there, we'd have only a few weeks to set up a new pack house and smaller cabins and huts to live in until winter passes again, and we can start constructing our new home, our way.

Unlimited hunting. Unlimited land to farm and raise cattle. No neighbors. No rival Alphas.

"The Deadlands are home to tribes, Alpha," one man says as the others start conferring in small groups. "They don't have Alphas, but they have elders and have been known to be violent."

"Alpha King Ryatt has assured me that the tribes in question now fall under his leadership. They are aware of us coming, and one of their leaders is actually hoping that we do. The Deadlands have changed over the past two decades. The land isn't as barren. The creatures that once haunted its forests are disappearing." I look every single member in the eye when I say, "We won't have an opportunity like this again."

James stands, holding up a few sheets of paper. "We're putting it to a vote. If every member over the age of fifteen votes yes, we prepare to move. If a single member votes no, the move is tabled indefinitely."

I hear more nervous whispering. I scan the far edge of the room where a few of the men are standing, men I work with, men with children and mates who'd be uprooted from their lives here to start anew.

They stare back at me in silent deliberation.

"Would you be an Alpha King?" a young woman asks, rocking a sleeping infant in her arms.

My eyes slide to meet hers.

"I'd be Alpha King of the Deadlands, yes."

The murmur that follows is full of awe. I wasn't going to even bring it up. The Deadlands are so far removed from the Roguelands, situated between Ryatt's old stomping ground and the wide, raging rivers separating the western edge of Eastonia with what was once Rifthold, with Tarsian beyond.

James and Andrew toss blank paper down on the tables, directing everyone to write their votes. Pens scribble as I walk back to the head table, leaning my leg against it. After a few minutes, the first man, Jacob, who helps run our mechanic shop, approaches the head table. He holds my gaze as he drops his vote in a large metal bowl, then nods.

One by one, my pack files up to the head table. It's quiet as the votes are cast. Even the children who'd been playing in the corner have gone silent, watching their parents, aunts, uncles, and older siblings decide something they can't possibly understand.

James and Andrew read the votes slowly, three times, while food and drink are laid out on the table. A feast, in actuality. A feast to celebrate either outcome.

I already know we're not going. There is no way not a single person voted no.

But James motions me over, both men looking slightly uneasy.

"It's fine," I tell them. "I figured–"

"Everyone voted yes."

Shock. That's the only word to describe my feelings as I turn toward the crowd and clear my throat.

"We'll do it in two waves," I say to a group of men a week later, everyone gathered around a plastic work table in the commercial garage on the far side of the territory. "A group of men will go ahead of the rest in late winter to set up camps and start construction on the pack house and outlying huts for the families, and the women and children will follow in late summer escorted by our warriors. Alpha King Ryatt will intercept us at the border with his own forces who will stay to help get us prepared for our first winter in the Deadlands."

The men nod as I continue. "I'll be leading the first wave and will stay in the Deadlands to oversee construction then return to Crescent Falls to escort the rest of the pack. I need you all to gather and decide who will be traveling with the first group."

I leave the men to talk and walk out of the garage. It's raining again, the sky is dark gray against the naked trees. Winter is impending. It could start snowing any day now. We only have a few months to start preparing, and it doesn't feel real yet.

My dad is aware and has been supportive. The chances of me being Alpha King of Crescent Falls are incredibly low. Sydney and Blake are the next two in line, and if Sarah's next baby, due this spring, is another boy... well, there's no future for me here.

My phone buzzes. Sydney, of course. He calls me every day.

"Yeah?"

"Still coming up for dinner? Sarah is insisting."

"I'll be there." James pulls up in his truck and steps out, looking slightly grim. "I have to go."

Sydney starts to say something but I hang up as James stands, walking over to me, his head bent against the rain.

"What's going on?"

"I need to talk to you about something," he says, tilting his head toward the garage.

I lead him up to my office, closing the door behind us as I anticipate some bad news about our plans, the move, or the current climate surrounding our pack territory here, but he says, "Dalia is coming with us."

"Dalia? Why?"

James purses his lips. "We're going to get married."

"Oh." I tap my knuckles on my desk. "Have you spoken to her Alpha about it?"

"Your brother?"

I shoot him a look. "She's part of Shadowcrest. She's also only twenty."

"She's my mate. I can feel it. She says she can too."

"You'd be taking her from her family. The chances of her returning to even visit within the next several years are low."

"She wants to travel with the first wave. We could use someone like her."

"To what? Build houses?"

"To cook for the men," he says. He holds my gaze. "I know it complicates things with Sydney. She's part of his household."

"I'll handle my brother. Do what you have to. I don't have a problem with it."

I leave my office without another word, fighting the onslaught of emotion that starts to form cracks in the stone replacing my heart.

Sometimes it's hard to look at James. I see Hadley every time. We haven't ever talked about her. Her death was like closing a book and tossing it in an attic to rot and be forgotten.

I've been told my actions were justified.

But I killed her.

I've known we were mates for years and never once told her.

Would that have changed things?

It doesn't matter now. A year from now, I'll be in Eastonia, facing new challenges and distractions.

That's why I agreed to go. To outrun my past.

To outrun Hadley.

Thank you for reading! Preorder Spare of the Alpha: The Alpha King's Breeder Book 10 here

ALSO BY BELLA MOONDRAGON

The Alpha King's Breeder series:

Bought by the Alpha: The Alpha King's Breeder Book 1

Loved by the Alpha: The Alpha King's Breeder Book 2

Lost by the Alpha: The Alpha King's Breeder Book 3

Luna of the Alpha: The Alpha King's Breeder Book 4

Legacy of the Alpha: The Alpha Kings's Breeder Book 5

Daughter of the Alpha: The Alpha King's Breeder Book 6

Descendants of the Alpha: The Alpha King's Breeder Book 7

Shadow of the Alpha: The Alpha King's Breeder Book 8

Son of the Alpha: The Alpha King's Breeder Book 9

The Luna's Vampire Prince series:

The Culling

The Kingdom

The Conquered

Pregnant With Four Alphas' Babies

Chosen As the Breeder

Mated to Four Alphas

Threats Against the Breeder

At War for the Breeder

The Stolen Breeder

Four Alphas, Four Babies

Becoming the Luna Queen

Descendants of the Breeder

Desired by the Devil series

Whispers of the Devil

Banter of the Devil

The Mafia Kings series

Indebted to the Mafia King

<u>Loved by the Mafia King</u>

Claimed by the Mafia King (releases 11/15/2024)

Sign up for Bella's newsletter here.

Follow Bella on Facebook here.

www.ingramcontent.com/pod-product-compliance
Lightning Source LLC
Chambersburg PA
CBHW070403310726
48977CB00003B/543